SILENT MISTRESSES

Copyright © 2025 by John Rigoli and Diane Cummings and Lisa Cerasoli

All rights reserved.

No part of this book may be reproduced in any form or by any electronic or mechanical means, including information storage and retrieval systems, without written permission from the author, except for the use of brief quotations in a book review.

    ISBN (Paperback): 978-1-7368118-3-2
    ISBN (eBook): 978-1-7368118-4-9
    ISBN (Large Print): 978-1-7368118-5-6

Cover Design by JD Smith

Title Production by The BookWhisperer

PRAISE FOR THE VATICAN CHRONICLES

"An inventive—and highly believable— biblical revisionist tale. The authors go right to the heart of one of the great unknowns of Christian history: the role of women in the early church. The journey is ultimately more thoughtful and satisfying than a mere holy grail."

— KIRKUS REVIEWS

"The narrative is well written, intriguing, and inspiring... This story blends an ancient conflict with present day debate in a fictional yet eye-opening manner... Just when you think all has been unearthed and exposed, you realize there is much more to this story. The Mystery of Julia Episcopa is a great beginning to a promising conspiracy series."

— READERS' FAVORITE (5 STAR REVIEW)

"This was an unexpectedly moving mystery. I hope to hear more of The Vatican Chronicles! I cannot recommend this audio book enough—truly an awesome listen. Not a dull moment!"

— AUDIO BOOK REVIEWERS - ABR REVIEWER CHOICE AWARD WINNER

THE VATICAN CHRONICLES BOOK 3

SILENT MISTRESSES

JOHN I RIGOLI
DIANE CUMMINGS
LISA CERASOLI

In loving memory of my wife, Delphine

For my father, Ray–my guiding light

In remembrance of my sweet mom, Sheri

CHAPTER ONE

Palermo, Sicily
1998

MARIA SAT ON THE EDGE OF THE BED, SHIVERING IN HER NEW room, a spartan cell in the old abbey. She wept ceaselessly in the cold, silent space as if catching a breath was no matter. Only yesterday, she had stood with her father at the wide-planked monastery doors of Abbazia di Santa Lucia, their hearts splintering as he stepped away into the rain.

Now, the one she loved more than anything was dead. In a heartbeat, her world had capsized.

A soft knock caused her to turn sharply, drying away tears with the backs of her hands.

A smiling, rosy-cheeked vision in white appeared. "May I come in?"

"Uh-huh," she hiccupped.

The door opened wide, and an angel—it had to be—whisked inside. Her simple, white habit was slightly wrinkled, and her veil revealed escaping strands of curly, blonde hair.

"I'm Sister Delfina." The nun sat beside the girl. "And I

know that you're Maria. Maria Caruso." *Heaven's gift,* she thought. *She's so frail a gust of wind may well sweep her away.* Delfina noted the colorful cane with silver stars standing in the corner.

"I'm eight and a half. In case you didn't know," Maria said solemnly. She stared at the rumpled nun and deadpanned, "You look very messy."

"Do I?" Sister Delfina considered her attire and laughed lightly. "So, I do. Well, I'm a, uh, *student* nun, and I've been working in the kitchen. It's steamy in there." Sister Delfina Bouvier had been a novitiate for almost two years and was due soon to take her final vows.

"Oh, okay." Maria then threw herself at Delfina, let go with a full-throated sob. Through sustained gasps, she cried, "My father is dead, and my mother doesn't want me."

When she calmed, Delfina dropped to her knees, taking the young girl's cheeks in both hands. "Small as a mite, but aren't you a pretty one," she said with a smile. Her hands dropped to Maria's shoulders, giving them a squeeze. "Do you always wear pigtails?" She gently, playfully tugged at her thick locks, shining in the warm hue of spiced cider.

Maria managed a giggle. "No, these are braids. Sometimes I have pigtails. I can do them myself."

"I'll bet you can," Delfina said. "I would like to watch some time. Okay?"

Thinking it over, Maria said, "*Sì.* I can show you."

She drew the girl's eyes to her own, took hold of her wrists, and gently rubbed them with her thumbs. "Maria, this change is hard. I know it is. But you will get used to us, and I'll look after you. I promise. You'll always have a home here."

Yet, with no weekly visits from her father, Delfina wondered what this already unconventional arrangement would look like. It was unfathomable that her mother had come, delivered the devastating news, and left. Delfina said nothing. She was too wise to impart silly platitudes. She knew that children gave themselves entirely to the moment but were also resilient. And she was undoubtedly no fortune teller.

"Maria, everyone's excited to meet you." Everyone didn't include Sister Eunice, who'd been assigned to see to her needs, but with an aversion to children—well, all things capricious—Delfina had convinced the convent head that Eunice was not the wisest choice.

There was a knock on the door.

"Mother Superior sent me," Salvatore Savelli said on entering. "The bunny is back in the garden. She said if Maria wants to help me catch him, she can keep him."

Maria looked up and down at her new visitor. "You're a man. Why are you here?"

"This is Salvatore. He's our gardener, and our plumber, and our painter, and our bunny catcher. Of course, nuns can't catch bunnies. We'd trip on our habits chasing them about."

A vision of nuns scrambling in the grass caused another giggle to sneak past the gates of Maria's grief.

"After we catch him," Salvatore said, "I'll show you and the bunny all the secret hiding places around here. It's like a magic castle."

A hard knock on the open door interrupted the chat.

"Busy place," Salvatore noted.

The door opened, and a plain-faced nun with a hook nose entered with a tray. Saying not so much as a hello, she set the tray on the desk. With a side-eye to Salvatore, she remarked, "You're not to be in the cells." And then Sister Eunice was gone.

Salvatore stepped outside Maria's room. "The sun's out now, and I'll be in the garden if you want to help." Looking backward at Maria, he said, "And you can call me Tori."

"Would you like to spend some time outside after you eat?" Delfina asked.

"Yes. I'm so cold in here."

"It is cold." It seemed as if the stone walls were spitting icicles. "I'll get a heater for you. Now, while you eat, I'll unpack your things."

It didn't take Maria but a moment to uncover the tray. She found a bowl of steaming broth, slices of lamb, hunks of delicious-looking dense bread, a plate of fresh fruit, and hot tea. Wrapped in cellophane were two marzipan candies shaped like little bears. Maria wasted no time tucking in and demolishing the meal.

As promised, Tori later gave Maria a tour, quite unlike the rules-oriented run-through of Mother Superior early that morning. Then, given time alone, she returned to the basement stairs, lost in wonder about one secret place.

Reaching the bottom step, Maria shuffled toward the old bookshelf propped under a cracked window. She pressed a tiny shoulder into its side and slid it across the wall. She then pushed the hidden door behind it and stepped inside with the little speckled bunny swaddled in a sheet wrapped crossbody like a newborn babe.

She shoved the shelf back in place as best she could—and into the tunnel she went. "Now, don't be afraid, Pippi. It's dark in here, but it's very safe. Don't you worry."

To soothe both her new companion and herself in the murky space, she began singing her favorite nursery rhyme. *"'Batti batti le manine ... Che son belle e piccoline ... Son piccoline come te un, due, tre!'* When the song is over, we'll be at the end. You'll see."

"... Son picoline come te un, due, tre!"

Sure enough, just as she finished the last line in the refrain, they reached the wall with the wooden ladder. Maria climbed up, pushed on what looked like a small cellar door, and—voilà! The golden glow of the late-day sun greeted her.

They had to be a hundred meters out, on the other side of the fence bordering the property. It was a great trick. And the convent was no longer the drab, musty, plain-walled, stone prison she'd thought it to be.

It was a magical castle, indeed.

But then she remembered—this was the worst day of her life. And the memories came flooding back. Never again would she hear her *papà's* footsteps climbing the rickety stairs to their apartment after work. Never again would she read a book he had picked out for her at the library. Never again would they sit side by side in front of a computer

As her tears flowed once more, she carved out a spot between the tall blades of grass, sat down, and stroked Pippi.

It wasn't but a moment later that Tori appeared carrying a rake—his prop. He had no thought of gardening today, only keeping tabs on Maria, ensuring she was getting on well, or at least getting on, given the circumstances.

He sat down beside her. "Shall we watch the sunset? Maybe you'd like to tell me your favorite story about your *papà*."

"Oh, I could never pick just one."

"Then, please, tell me all of them."

CHAPTER TWO

Vatican City
Present Day

CARDINAL ANGELICO CACCIATORE COULDN'T TELL WHETHER HE was suffering from heartburn or heart failure. Such was the level of his distress. It didn't matter, in any case. Given his schedule of meetings on the current crisis, he had no time for infirmities.

This time, the bank's VP had been dragged out in handcuffs, charged with embezzlement and money laundering to the tune of €30 million. The press had turned the steps of the bank into its playground, and Vatican watchers in Rome and around the world had trained their eyes and ears on the new scandal—and just when the Vatican was still bleeding from other self-induced blows.

First, it was that female bishop Julia Lucinia, who'd been drudged up from the first century and paraded around for all to see the lies his two least favorite scientists had been promulgating. *"There have never been female Church leaders!"* But no— Valentina Vella and Erika Simone had to prove them all wrong.

And even a gag order couldn't keep the body of the mysterious Julia Lucinia in the grave.

Then came the *Secret Temple Scroll*. Vella's cohort in all things anti-Church—ex-Mossad Yigael Dorian—went and discovered the very first writing on Yeshua's life, from when he was alive. It predated the gospels by twenty years. Was it hand-delivered to the Vatican, its rightful owners? No. The script was verified by Vella and Simone...and then snatched up by the paws of the Church's premier religious rival—the nation of Israel.

To make matters worse, more than a hundred perfectly preserved scrolls rained down from Herculaneum, the ancient city that was rewriting history, all penned by the same Anonymous Scribe. These documents were famous now, the collection referred to simply as the Diary.

Shortly after that, Cardinal Carlo Lavoti was handcuffed just outside the pope's library on suspicion of conspiracy to murder the previous pope, Augustine. Things had finally quieted down.

Now, this!

The Institute for the Works of Religion (IOR), often called the Vatican Bank, had never known how much money was coming in, going out, or allocated. *"It's no easy task, given the massive influx of cash, not to mention investments including gold, art, and real estate owned across the globe ... to calculate the worth of the Church ...."* Pope Lucius said back in the early nineties, rationalizing the fast and loose behavior of the Church's financial institution. No one inside the organization had ever tried to balance the books for those reasons, among others.

In the face of the decades-long mishandling of Church funds and hoping to stay ahead of future trouble, the pope had established the Commission of Cardinals to report to him on matters of the bank. The Commission, in turn, had appointed a seven-member Board of Superintendence to sort out the complicated glitches and get the IOR running as it should. Cacciatore had wormed his way into both groups over a decade back. It was important for his purposes to keep tabs on every bit of tumult.

And so it was that he found himself in the death zone of the latest Vatican tornado.

The cardinal tucked a finger inside his dog collar and pulled, thinking that was the reason he couldn't get enough air.

What now?

That was the multimillion-dollar question. Finding a replacement to hop into the position of VP to serve as his puppet—neither of his two remaining members had the street smarts for the job—seemed about as likely as Cardinal Lavoti walking away a free man. More urgent than that, the media quagmire needed diffusing. But, above all, stood an undisclosed matter that only he could sort out.

Seated alone at a conference table in a soulless, windowless office space in the heart of the IOR, the cardinal waited for three of his underground collaborators, along with his secretary of sorts.

Drumming his fingers on the table, the cardinal's impatience was unmistakable.

Bishop Archibald Burbidge, the first to arrive, slunk into the room, his presence almost as unremarkable as his appearance. With his fading brown hair, average build, and quiet demeanor, save for the unfortunate mole anchoring the middle of his right cheek, he was a study in ordinariness. Burbidge was a textbook yes-man, unwavering in his loyalty to anyone above him. That's why the cardinal had rolled him into the committee. He'd comply with the cardinal's will, questioning nothing, doing only what was instructed. He took a seat opposite his boss.

Finally, his executive assistant, Massimo Pugia, hurried in, a beefy, hulking man whose stony expression and faint scar tracking along his left brow rendered him a menacing presence.

The cardinal acknowledged him but with a glance and turned to the door as Massimo's cousin, Pepper Pugia, entered, whipping her long, blonde hair about like a scythe in the Grim Reaper's clutches. Pepper, all six feet of her, wore skinny everything on her scrawny frame—a double *frappé* would not go amiss.

The strange pair stood out at the IOR like peacocks in a dove aviary. Cacciatore had hired them five years back to ensure any trouble would not—*could not*—happen in his world. *So much for that.*

Massimo gave the cardinal a sort of half-bow salute. "Angelico," nodded to Burbidge and then sat, slouching in his seat, mind blank.

Pepper gave no greeting at all as she pulled out a chair.

Once they were both seated, the cardinal, with a trace of a quiver in his right hand, let out a huff, darting a look from one cousin to the other as the room fell into inelegant silence.

Enlisting all seven extraocular muscles to keep her eyes from doing a dramatic pirouette, Pepper cleared her throat and said plainly, "The Software Sister."

After another long minute, waiting for further explanation, the cardinal threw up his hands. "What?"

"The Software Sister. She's the answer to your problems."

"Who?"

"She's a nun down in Sicily."

"We don't need a housekeeper. We need an accountant," Cacciatore said in his trademark hushed tone.

"She created the software program *Convent Counting* and keeps an immaculate set of books."

He closed his mouth and frowned. "A woman to run the IOR?"

"A woman?" Massimo Pugia commented in a different tone, eyebrows raised in intrigue.

She gave her cousin a death stare.

"No, Pepper, I mean that'd be good, a distraction *per certo*."

"Angelico, she's not just a woman. She's a nun, and she's lived with cloistered nuns her whole life. She'll grab the headlines and steer everyone away from this scandal."

"But she's a woman," the cardinal rebuked.

"Yes, and she's young too. The Church will be viewed as progressive."

"Young? No, no, no." The cardinal felt his neck flush with anger. "We need someone older, with one foot in the grave. That would be ideal until we find a permanent replacement more aligned with our vision."

"Your vision. What ... to protect the sacred laws of the Church?" A chuckle, or maybe a scoff, escaped the raw-boned woman's mouth.

"What's that about, cousin?" Massimo asked.

She ignored him. "This sister has a rare, life-threatening blood disease, Thalassemia."

They grabbed their phones in concert and googled the term.

The thought of her dying before long perked them both up.

Feeling satisfied by the dismal outlook Wiki stats offered on Thalassemia, Cacciatore set down his phone and relaxed his shoulders. Massimo, conversely, sat straighter in his chair.

"How'd you find her, Pepper?" the cardinal asked.

"Given what I bring to the table, I'm surprised you'd ask," she retorted.

Massimo gave her another look. While he knew only too well how to toe the line, his female counterpart did not.

The cardinal raised a bushy eyebrow. "The Software Sister. Certainly," he concluded. "This will clear with the pope." *I'll bypass the Commission, go straight to His Holiness.* "The media will love it, and so will the people."

"Exactly," Massimo chimed in. "This might be our best move yet. A nun as VP."

"No," she said with an exhaustive sigh. "You can't move a young girl into a VP position held by old men for the last millennium. It wouldn't be credible. We hire her as head of forensic accounting. Her job will be to right the books, *so this never happens again.* And it'll buy you some time."

"Right. Exactly." Then, the cardinal considered, "But what if this woman, this nun, is too good?"

Pepper snickered. "She invented an accounting program, Angelico, not the dark web."

The cardinal nodded his approval. "His Holiness will hail our brilliance." He picked up his phone. "A sick nun," he mused as he called Pope Julius.

"Good." She took his cue, pushed her chair out, stood, and headed for the exit without a *ciao,* Massimo in tow.

"Wait. Her name?"

But they were gone.

Lingering at the table, the cardinal mused that a frail, disabled nun tucked away in a distant nunnery might be just the ticket. *I can mold her into my loyal confidante. That shouldn't be a problem.* He would have to tread carefully, though—the stakes were high.

CHAPTER THREE

Palermo, Sicily

IN A FLUSH OF ANXIETY, SISTER MARIA CARUSO FIDDLED WITH AN old USB drive as the train departing *Palermo Centrale* whistled its imminent departure. The relic, a gift from her late father before his untimely death, was her lucky charm and rarely left her pocket.

She caught sight once more of Mother Delfina and Tori on the platform outside. They raised their hands, and she waved back. Though not of the same blood, they were family, the older nun and the convent's groundskeeper, and she missed them already.

Moments before, Mother Delfina had given Maria the once-over and, when she passed inspection, enveloped her in a brief but hearty hug. *"Andare con Dio,"* the abbess had said before whispering some words into Maria's ear.

Salvatore had removed his hat and pulled it to his chest, his glistening tears speaking words he could not. Tori had become her closest comrade since they'd met when she was eight.

After two decades of convent life, Maria had begun to feel

restless. Some days, the confines of the cloister wore so heavy that she became hot with panic as if a scream were brewing from deep inside. She struggled to hide her feelings from the others. After all, her fellow devotees lived the life she did—though they seemed to do it with such ease by comparison.

Mother Delfina recognized the disquiet in Maria and set about finding a way to respond. Since her order was not governed by the Holy See but by its own constitution, she held the power to grant leave when circumstances called for it, and Maria's certainly did. Just as the Reverend Mother was deciding where best to serve Maria's healing, a most unexpected call came in from a cardinal at the Vatican. The abbess's enthusiasm cracked wide open as she called Maria to her office.

That was six weeks back, but with time accelerating to one big blur after Mother Delfina's announcement, it felt like but a few moments.

Maria shivered. She was not used to the chaos of travel, as busy families and preoccupied tourists filled the railway car, all vying for luggage racks and the best seats.

A muscle-popping, thirtyish American hoisted his rucksack onto the overhead rack, thumping Maria's shoulder.

"Ouch," she protested. "Please, watch what you're doing."

"Sorry, ma'am." He took a seat across from her and grinned.

The train whistled again and clackety-clacked forward, quickly picking up speed. Maria took a deep breath and straightened.

Hours later, her fears intensified when the train's horn blared mournfully, and its brakes hissed to a stop in Messina. No one else seemed alarmed, though, and certainly not the young American man across from her, who'd slept through the whole ordeal.

Next to Maria sat a plump, middle-aged woman wearing a dress so tight-fitting that the buttons on the bodice threatened to pop open.

Noticing Maria's unease, she said, "You don't travel much." Then, scanning her outfit top to toe, she added, "You come from that little place, the cloister, in Palermo?"

"Yes." Her traveling clothes, a white button-down blouse, black, pleated, calf-length skirt, and cable knit cardigan, even without a headpiece, were a dead giveaway to her vocation, at least to locals of southern Italy.

Maria locked a hand on the arm of her seat. "This is the first time I've traveled anywhere."

The train rolled onto a barge headed for Villa San Giovanni Port in Reggio Calabria.

"Don't worry, dear," the woman said as Maria stared with fright at the scene below. "You're quite safe. I'm Besina Bruzzini, by the way. My friends call me ZZ or just Z."

"Really? Mind if I call you Besina? I'm Maria. *Suor Maria*."

"I would love for someone to call me by my name."

"Okay. So, I never learned to swim, Besina."

"Well, you won't have to learn tonight." Her seatmate hooted.

Maria knew it was silly to worry that the train would jump the rails and descend to the sea. Still, she hadn't bargained for a trip over water.

But, before she knew it, they touched land again and chugged off, and Besina joined the rest of the travelers and went to sleep.

Maria had called Abbazia di Santa Lucia home since childhood. She had cut a habitual course through life at the convent, praying with her sisters, running the convent office, tending the garden with Tori, and trekking back and forth to the clinic for the blood transfusions that managed her life-threatening infirmity.

Though thin and bony, a physical characteristic she could hardly overcome, Maria had blossomed in other ways. Her complexion, once translucent like that of fine porcelain dolls, had turned sun-kissed from hours spent outside, and her features, a turned-up nose with freckles atop cherry-tinted lips, had become alluring by her teen years. Her eyes had always sparkled with a ready smile. Her childhood bangs were a thing of the past. Now, she wore her shiny, sable-brown locks pulled back from her face and fastened with a clasp at the crown. This brought out her honey-gold highlights. Maria's countenance was of strength, despite her life's difficulties.

While her condition would always be her nemesis, Maria's illness had significantly improved. She would always need blood transfusions, but new oral medications had transformed her care. For most who knew her, Maria seemed healthier. If anyone wondered about the limp, they didn't ask.

As the train sped by a changing landscape, she watched the greens, blues, and purples of summer shimmer by. But the night was closing in, and before long, those colorful scenes disappeared.

Maria never imagined that her path would encompass such a significant transfer to a destination so imposing. As she sat back and closed her eyes to the hum of the train, she prayed the uneasy roiling inside was just the fava bean soup talking.

CHAPTER FOUR

Rome

FATHER ORIO RINALDI WASN'T UNHAPPY ABOUT LEAVING HIS JOB at the Holy Office as secretary to the disgraced Cardinal Carlo Lavoti. While the man hadn't exactly made him feel at home, Orio never could've imagined him capable of murder. But now, in the office of the late Cardinal Antonio Ricci, his boss before Lavoti, he wondered what would be next after he finished the demeaning task of clearing out the office. With two jobs gone in just over a year, the ground under the priest felt wobbly.

He chucked a box of office supplies into a corner. With sweat trailing from his forehead, laboring far beyond what he was used to, Orio looked around. His eyes came to rest on Cardinal Ricci's massive desk. He decided to clear the drawers next, a task he could perform while seated.

Orio lumbered over and hoisted himself into the oversized leather chair, preening for a moment at his perceived self-importance in this place of authority. He opened the middle drawer and thrust a paw inside to sweep the contents forward.

That's when his fingers curled around a little wooden box. He pulled it out.

The box was ornate, with a small latch and tiny lock attached. *Odd*, he thought, but then remembered Cardinal Ricci's obsession with secrecy. Oh, how he had tried and failed to pry information from his old boss. Orio picked up the box and jiggled it. He heard a rattle. Wild with curiosity, as secrets were as tasty as salted almond Swiss Toblerone to this lonely guy, he slid the box across the desk and rummaged through the remaining drawers. Failing to find anything resembling a key, he returned his attention to the desktop, accidentally sweeping a pencil case to the floor. Orio sighed, swiveled the chair, and bent to pick it up. And there, taped to the bottom, was a tiny key.

Orio peeled back the tape, readjusted in his seat, and studied the little box on the desktop. The key and the lock seemed to match up. Surreptitiously, he looked around to see if he was being watched, then, flushing with embarrassment, he muttered, "He's dead, for pity's sake." Orio drew the box close and inserted the key.

It fit.

Inside, he found another key, brass, attached to a metal ring. He pocketed that one, surmising it belonged to something in the cardinal's bed chamber, perhaps a file box containing personal papers or family mementos. Orio shuffled the remaining desk contents into a box, then continued his work.

Pivoting to the wall of shelves behind him, he hooked his hands around a collection of books and heaved them into another cardboard carton. Behind the row of thick tomes labeled *Biblical Archaeology* lay quite the surprise—a safe.

Two keys and a safe?

The resentment the priest had always felt at being treated as a servant rose in him again. He flushed with anger at the imagined insults of not being valued, always kept in the dark, not trusted even by the man into whose service he had found himself for over a decade. He shook off his dark mood as best he could.

The safe had a bronze-toned slot for a key. Orio reached into his pocket and then stopped, his conscience and duty to the late Cardinal Antonio Ricci and the Church getting the best of him.

But temptation won, and he pushed the bronze key into the lock.

Bingo.

The door swung open to reveal a manila envelope. He placed it on the cardinal's desk.

Orio felt his heart pounding. But this time, no shame about checking for possible detractors encircled his conscience. He sped to the door, opened it, and peeked into the hallway. Seeing no one, he ducked back inside and turned the lock. Returning to the desk, he unwound the string tie and tilted the envelope. A file folder and a couple of photographs slid out.

The photographs—two of them—were sharp though faded. They had to have been taken with an old-school, high-powered lens, pre-camera-phone days for certain. The first showed a man and a woman at a distance, engaged in conversation. The woman was attractive by anyone's standards. A child playing at the seaside in the background appeared to collect shells. A candid shot. The second photo invited Orio's curiosity.

Clear as day, lit by the afternoon sun, was a close-up shot of the man's face: Cardinal Justin Parina, head of the Vatican Library. The cardinal was younger in the photo, thirties, but the wavy hair and startling, light-blue eyes told Orio it was Justin without a doubt.

"What on earth?" he said out loud.

He set them aside and opened the folder. In it were bank statements from a private account at the IOR in Justin's name. A monthly auto debit from his account to a ... *Katarina Silva* was highlighted. As he leafed through the pages, he saw that the records went back years and started at a time that likely coincided with those photographs.

As the curious priest contemplated the payee, this Katarina Silva person—likely the woman in the pictures—he heard a click, then a key jiggle in the lock, and then another click. He looked up as the door swung open.

"Oh, it's you." Orio breathed a sigh of relief. "What are you doing here?"

Monsignor Francesco Ricci ignored the question. "Why is the door locked?"

"Oh, is it?" the priest feigned ignorance.

"You know it is, Orio. Luckily, Uncle Antonio gave me a key. I'm picking up his personal belongings." Francesco looked around. "You need a hand? I thought everything would be packed up by now."

The monsignor had recently moved to Rome from Ostia after a promotion and reassignment. He now headed Chiesa di Sant'Agata, a parish a few blocks from the gates of Saint Peter.

"Sure. Nice to have some company." Orio stared down at the file he'd discovered, unsure what to say or do.

The two priests went back to their seminary days. Francesco's road to the priesthood had been smooth. He was bright and quick-witted, and his fellow seminarians liked him. For Orio, it was a different story. He'd proved himself to be a hapless student of uncertain enthusiasm for his priestly vocation. But Francesco's generous nature and empathy for all underlings made taking Orio under his wing as natural as breathing. It was due to his perseverance in tutoring and mentoring that Orio escaped expulsion.

Edging toward forty now, Francesco Ricci and Orio Rinaldi both looked older. Francesco's weather-beaten complexion put five years on him, while Orio's girth, making him slow and awkward, added ten.

"Orio, I'm sorry about, uh, Lavoti," Francesco said, "I mean, I'm truly shocked, but for you, it's a tough break. Can I help?"

"This time, you don't have to, Fran. What's next has been decided for me. I've been assigned to the carpool."

"Hey, great. This will keep you busy, and you'll meet some interesting, important people." He thought this might be good for Orio—not too challenging—maybe just right, he hoped.

Orio perked up. "You think so?"

"Of course. And with your, uh, animated personality, you'll get visitors off to a good start."

"Well, okay." Then, eager to share his news, Orio changed the subject. "Look what I've found, reason I locked the door." The priest beckoned him over to the desk.

"What?"

"Something odd."

"What do you mean?" The monsignor looked at the desk with loose pages scattered around it.

Orio assembled the pages in order and handed them over.

Francesco read the first page and flipped through the rest. "This was in my uncle's belongings?" He set down the withdrawal sheets and picked up the photos. "Justin. This is who that is, no?"

"Sure, that's Justin."

Orio pointed to the shelves behind him. "You know anything about that safe? That's where I found this."

"How odd that something about him shows up here."

"Why?"

"Because those two didn't get along."

"Really? Why?" Orio hoped for a clue.

"Uncle Antonio never said, but I thought things came to a head when Justin got the job at the library. I think my uncle wanted it. You know what a history buff he was ... two PhDs in the subject, for goodness' sake. And Justin was so much younger. I'm guessing that Uncle Antonio felt insulted when he lost out to him. And let's not forget how charismatic Justin is."

"Oh boy, *sì*, and downright pulchritudinous," Orio shot back.

"Pulchri ... what? Where'd you pick up that word?"

"Pulchritudinous? Everyone knows that word. Means great beauty and appeal."

"I can't argue with that," Francesco said. "He's always been a man on the rise, and everything has come easily to him."

"Not so for your uncle. Sorry to say so, Fran, but it's the truth."

The monsignor gazed down at the photos again. "That's Justin, all right. But the woman, the child, could be his sister, maybe a cousin. He might be the child's godfather."

"I don't know, Fran. Why would pictures of a sister or cousin be locked up in his office safe? It seems suspicious to me. It seems more than suspicious."

"What are you suggesting?"

"I don't know. But looking at these pictures and where they were kept, hidden along with private bank records, I'm thinking blackmail."

"Then, you must think that Justin is ... well, doing something wrong with this woman."

"It's possible. And if he is, even though he's our friend, especially yours, we need to tell someone about it."

"No."

"No?"

"No. We're not getting involved. We have no reason to. We don't know a thing, and these could be perfectly innocent. My uncle wasn't always the nicest guy, but I never knew him to be malicious. Orio, we must just let this be."

"Well, what are we going to do with this stuff?"

"I'll take everything with me. Don't worry about it."

Orio scooped up the paperwork and the photos, put them

in the folder, then the envelope, and placed it in the monsignor's hands.

Francesco headed for the door. He looked back. "Dinner tonight?"

"Definitely," came Orio's enthusiastic reply. "Right after I see Human Resources to sign some papers because I start driving in the morning."

Francesco smiled and slipped out.

"Fran," Orio beckoned, but it was too late. *I thought you were going to help me finish packing.*

CHAPTER FIVE

Porsel, Switzerland
1998

A SOFT RAIN SPILLED FROM THE HEAVENS ON A WARMER-THAN-usual spring day as Katarina Silva stepped toward the rectory over a thick, grassy carpet shaded by droopy weeping willow trees. She wore a flowery sundress and carried a blue-and-white striped umbrella. Arriving ten minutes before her appointment time, she set her umbrella down outside and took a seat in the outer office, feeling calm and optimistic.

Mass had been hit or miss for Katarina since her son, Peter, was born, but the old priest was kind and did not seem to judge her for it. She'd known Father René Favre for a while, since moving to the town for work after college.

"Katarina." Father Favre's head popped out from behind his office door, and he flashed a warm smile. "Come in. It's been so long that I barely recognize you."

"I know, Father," she said simply.

The priest moved two chairs in front of his desk to face each other and gestured for Katarina to take one of them. He sat in the other.

"Your child?" the old priest inquired.

"Peter's almost three now. He's growing like a beanstalk and healthy as this May morning. He's at Petite Étoile daycare, or I'd have brought him along."

"Ah, this is what I like to hear." Father Favre's smile grew wider. "How can I help?" He folded his hands in his lap with a mild expression of inquiry.

"Father, I would like to have my son christened."

Peter's father had baptized his son immediately after birth in Katarina's kitchen. He wanted to ensure his son was made a beloved child of God right from the start. But now, Katarina wanted her son's christening to be documented and for him to be made a member of the Church.

"Yes, of course, my dear. Your husband ... is he still away? Will he be here for the service?" Father Favre knew as well as any member of his congregation that the elusive "husband" of the woman before him was not an international businessman but more likely a world-class criminal. Still, he was bound to an oath to love and respect each member of his flock. And he prided himself on that.

"No, he won't."

The priest's eyebrows upped a notch. He waited for further comment.

Katarina was not forthcoming.

"Certainly, it's not required for both parents to attend the ceremony," he said, "but it is in accord with the Church's foundational family principles that all share in the sacred rite. Perhaps, we can wait until he returns from work."

"Father ... well, that's the thing." Katarina would finally confide the truth to someone. And who better than her priest? He would keep her secret and advise her. Unafraid, she looked straight into Father Favre's eyes.

"Peter's father is not traveling for work," she said. Katarina had done her best to keep that story alive. "He never has been. Peter's father is a priest. He sees us when he can get away. Certainly, in his position, he cannot come. So, I am on my own in this."

"I see," Father Favre said levelly. Adjusting slightly in his chair, he asked in a low voice, "Who else knows about this?"

"Only my mother," Katarina said, "but that isn't why—"

"What makes you say a priest is the father of this child?" Father Favre's voice was amiable enough, but his manner had shifted, and he couldn't control it. He'd rather the man was a mobster. What he was hearing infuriated him.

Katarina stared at the priest, but she was not intimidated, and she said with heat, "Because I know." Then she wondered how the subject had turned so. "That's not why I'm here," she repeated.

Father Favre rose and moved to the oversized chair behind his desk, his position of authority. "It is not, ah, comely that you've had relations with a man who's not your husband," the priest said, his voice turning stone cold.

Katarina sat in stunned silence. "But—"

"No more talk of baptism." The woman before him was educated and older, not some doe-eyed teenage girl. It wasn't just a matter of decency. What story would he have to spin if word got out that he baptized *this* child?

Father Favre had a flawless record. He'd followed his oaths to the letter. A smooth and peaceful retirement was five years in his future. He was not about to be taken down by a woman who couldn't control her impulses or her illegitimate child.

"I worry, my dear, about your future here. I'm afraid you will be humiliated when the parishioners find out. I wouldn't like to see you hurt."

"What does that mean?"

"Perhaps, it would be wise to relocate."

"Relocate?" Katarina was nobody's fool, particularly now that she had a child to care for. "So, I came here wanting to make Peter a member of the Church, and instead, you try to coerce me into moving away?"

"It would be best, I think, for everyone."

"Well, Father, I will not be manipulated. Rising in a fury, Katarina spluttered, "I'm done here," and left the rectory.

Father Favre bounded from his post in case anyone was in the waiting area, damage control on his mind. He caught the back of Katarina's dress as the outside door swung shut. He approached it to watch her through the glass.

Propped upside down beside the building was her blue-and-white umbrella. He stepped outside and scooped it up. The last thing he wanted was the woman returning to reignite that conversation.

He planned to shout her name, but as he watched her slam the door shut on her vehicle and speed away, he knew she was unlikely to return.

He inched the door closed, dropped the umbrella in the stand alongside three others, and said a prayer of thanks complete with the sign of the cross.

FAR FROM THE VILLAGE'S IMPRESSION that Peter's father had all but deserted her, he was, in fact, in frequent touch, but he didn't like returning to Porsel where he could be recognized. That was how they'd met, after all, when he'd returned to the village to visit his parents at their farm four summers back.

Justin had urged Katarina to move out of town where no one knew them, where he didn't have to sneak into their home in the middle of the night like a cat burglar, where they could put a private life together.

So far, she'd refused.

Despite that ongoing battle, they were close, and she loved their small house. It was isolated from others, nearly invisible behind a wild tangle of rose bushes that bordered each side of a narrow stone walkway. They led a quiet life, reading and tending to a riotous vegetable garden. And, of course, there was Peter.

But that was all about to change.

CHAPTER SIX

Outside Rome
Present Day

SITTING IN THE BACKWARD-FACING SEAT, THE STUNNING BUT unforgiving light of dawn wedged Maria's eyes open.

"How come you never learned to swim?" The unexpected question came from the American fella who had no compunction about addressing a sleeping stranger. He jiggled his foot in erratic directions, unaware he was closing in on the folds of Maria's skirt.

She was unsure how to respond to his question or his foot, so out of control so early in the morning.

"I'm just joshing you. What's your name, by the way? Mine's Teddy Weaver. Well, Edward, but ... you know." Teddy's attitude, unlike his timing and jittery foot, was genuine and contagious, and it caused Maria to giggle.

"I'm ... Maria. Maria Caruso."

Beside her, Besina's eyes popped open and shifted to the conversation before her. Whatever this young American man had to say—to a nun from a cloistered convent, no less—she had to hear. She picked up her iPad as cover.

"So, what's ahead for you?" Teddy asked.

"Oh, a job," Maria said.

"Where?"

Usually quick-witted but blanking on a response, she about-faced. "And you? Are you traveling for work?"

"Yes, ma'am. A startup."

"The tech sector is booming in Rome," Maria said.

"You're a techie."

Maria shrugged but added a wide smile.

Besina sat straighter in her seat, her iPad falling onto her lap.

On noticing the article on the screen, Teddy leaned across the space. "Ha." He laughed. "Can you believe that? Hiring a nun to deflect from years of criminal activity."

The woman eyed Maria, who shrank back in her seat, wanting to disappear.

"Ah, yes," Besina tut-tutted. "The Vatican never ceases to amaze me." She lifted her device and hid behind it.

Teddy then stood, rummaged through his carry-on for the latest copy of *WIRED* magazine, which he'd purchased at the station's convenience mart, and inadvertently dropped it in Maria's lap.

"Pardon me, my bad. I bet you'll be glad to see the back of me soon."

"Um, no," Maria said, though it sounded more like a question. She studied the cover, swiping a hand across its shiny surface, and then gave the magazine back to Teddy.

He noted her interest before sitting back down and flipping through it.

"And how about this?" Besina said, emerging again from her device.

Maria braced herself. "What's that?"

"This pretty Valentina Vella, the one who's had so much trouble with the Church?"

"Do you read all the Church gossip, Besina?" Maria asked.

Amazed at her seatmate's cheek, a nun, after all, Besina screwed up her eyes and turned. When she saw Maria's grin, she cackled with laughter. "Yes, all of it." A new round of jollity burst forth, wetting her eyes. She fought to contain herself. "Seriously, she got her science lab back. From the Church!"

"I know."

"You know? I thought you weren't allowed—"

"Well, I am a 'techie.'"

The trials of Valentina Vella and Erika Simone had been a hot topic back in the convent for some time, and evening discussions were spirited, with the house split. Some thought the scientists to be heroines, going up against the Church so that women could finally be seen as equals. They'd proven that a woman had, in fact, held the esteemed role of bishop two millennium back, risking their careers and nearly losing everything. Others found them to be troublemakers.

Maria hadn't often weighed in, but she rooted for Valentina Vella, who seemed to be the spokesperson for the duo, and quietly celebrated when the Vatican upturned the gag order to stay silent about Julia Lucinia. And she'd outright cheered them on—alone in her quarters, but still—when they contributed in the efforts to make the first writings of Yeshua, penned by the Anonymous Scribe, known to the world.

With daybreak came the excitement of a new adventure, and Maria's nervousness had vanished. She sipped her tea and enjoyed the bright morning while her seatmates grew further engrossed in their very different reading materials.

After an hour or so, the train came to a stop.

Teddy was up in a flash, rucksack in hand. "Maria, ma'am," he said, nodding at each lady. Then, he handed Maria the magazine. "A parting gift. *Ciao*," and he was off.

Meanwhile, Besina gawked at the picture that had popped up on her iPad. "Really? I mean, really?" She turned the screen toward the young nun.

It was a headshot of Maria next to an article entitled "The Software Sister to Become Head of Forensic Accounting at the IOR."

There was only one thing to do. Maria batted her eyes and grinned.

The woman guffawed. "Nobody will believe this."

Maria squeezed her seatmate's arm and got up.

Stopping before descending the steps that would put her on the ground, her eyes blanketed the busy scene around her.

Here I am, twenty-eight years old, moving from a place I never imagined leaving for a job in Rome at the Vatican.

CHAPTER SEVEN

Rome

FATHER ORIO RINALDI STOOD IN THE MIDDLE OF A PLATFORM AT Stazione Termini, holding a hand-written sign with *Suor Maria Caruso* on it. All around him, travelers brushed by, hustling toward rumbling trains like gaggles of geese outrunning the fox. He squinted, wrestling the morning sun for a clear view.

The priest arrived an hour before the train was due and prayed he was in the right place. It wasn't easy locating where the train from Palermo would come in. He pestered not one but several on-the-go travelers to show him the way. One of them stopped in exasperation and pointed up. "Just look at the sign," the irritated man had said, before hurrying along.

As he waited, holding his placard, his cassock billowed up, caught by a sudden gust of crisp air. Embarrassed, he flattened his skirt with the sign, looking around to see if he'd become a spectacle.

He didn't know where he fit in anymore, but he resolved to prove his worth by giving this new job his best shot.

Its brakes hissed and screeched as the train spun to a stop.

The priest waited, watching passenger after passenger exit.

Maria, among the last to leave, departed the steps of the locomotive with great care. She spotted the plump priest before he saw her. Seeing him holding onto that sign for dear life caused her to giggle. She hobbled over, cane in one hand, carry-on in the other.

He turned. "Sister Maria?"

She nodded.

"I expected you'd be in full habit, being cloistered away and all." Orio bowed.

"Habit's too hard to travel in, especially with the cane."

The priest placed his hand on his heart. "I," he said solemnly, "am Father Orio Rinaldi, here to take you to your new quarters." He bowed again.

"Father, please, stand up. I'm not the queen. But, here, you can take this." Maria held out her suitcase.

"Of course." He took hold of the bag, dropping the sign. "Your trip?" he asked, crouching to retrieve it, hoping to deflect attention from his clumsiness.

"I'm glad to be on *terra firma* again. "I'm exhausted."

"Well, then, let's be on our way." Orio's first task was to take her for a checkup with *Dottore* Durante Lubrano. "The VAT Mobile is just outside the station," he said, thoroughly enjoying the new moniker he'd given the platinum-gray Citroen C3.

He helped Maria into the car, then squeezed into the front seat and headed out.

On smiling at her for the third time, the peculiar priest asked, "Have we met?"

"Have you visited the convent in Palermo?"

"With all the nuns? All cloistered up? Goodness, no." Orio shuddered at the thought.

"Then, I don't see how we could've met."

"I guess not. But I'm generally good with faces."

"I'm sure you're good at a lot of things."

"Not really."

Maria didn't know what to say to that.

Then, unable to take the suspense any longer, Orio blurted, "So, what's wrong with you anyway?"

CHAPTER EIGHT

Falcone, Sicily
1998

For the first seven years, Maria's twice-monthly transfusions at the clinic twenty kilometers away in Messina had left her able to attend school but unable to do much else. Now, however, Maria faced a critical juncture, and her father and mother struggled to know what to do about it. Without a new treatment for her Thalassemia, she would likely die of iron buildup.

After the three were seated at the dinner table, Carmella surprised her husband by saying, "Maria's been chosen for the six-month study in Palermo."

"What? How do you know this?" Motionless, Faustino's hands curled around a knife and fork, pointing skyward.

"*Dottoressa* Ragni called with the news a little while ago." Carmella's monotone response brooked no joy.

Faustino was always the one to speak with Maria's doctors. He was the one who took charge of his daughter's illness and relayed the news. Carmella never wanted to be involved. Never mind that now. This was a joyous occasion, not to be shrugged off.

"Do you really mean it?" Faustino's utensils clattered as they fell from his hands.

"I'm really going to get better!" Maria shrieked. "Aren't I, *Papà*?" she asked, sounding less sure.

Faustino turned to his daughter. "You're going to get better, Maria. I'm sure of it." Facing his wife, he said, "Did *Dottoressa* Ragni say that, if the new treatment worked, Maria could continue with it?"

"Yes, the drug would have immediate approval." It was not lost on Carmella that her daughter had turned to her father first, but that was not her top-of-the-list complaint. Soon, she'd have to confront her husband, which was never easy. *A Pollyanna, that's what he is,* she thought. *Never worries. If he's not playing with Maria, he's playing with fairies.*

"Luisa's been accepted too." That news completed Carmella's announcement, and she returned, impassive, to her food.

Faustino couldn't understand his wife's attitude. This was a lifeline. He clapped his hands. "You two will get to be together. You and Luisa!"

Maria's smile reached the treetops. Luisa was a year younger than she was. They had met and bonded at the doctor's clinic long ago. Both girls had the signature pale glow of their shared illness, but thankfully, the pigments in their hair hadn't yet turned pearly black—a key feature of Sicilian ancestry—or indeed, they would have looked a fright. They had become best friends. Maria spent the rest of the meal thinking about her bright future.

But that night, as Maria dreamed about climbing trees, she overheard, through paper-thin walls, her parents quarreling.

"Palermo? How do we manage that? We can't move." Carmella waited tables at *La Villa*, owned by a local wine-making dynasty. She'd never make that kind of money anywhere else, especially without a formal education.

"We'll have to relocate. You said the trial requires patients to live close by so they can be monitored daily and cared for in case of emergencies."

"We have no money to move. Our jobs are here."

"I'll drive her there twice a week."

"I just told you she'd have to live close by, monitored daily. So, how does that work?"

Faustino was at the end of his tether. "Tito and I are very close to a patent. Maybe he could loan us—"

"Stop! I'm sick of this computer nonsense."

Faustino knew that a loan was too much to ask of his friend.

After dinner, Faustino searched Palermo on Google, the new search engine introduced on the World Wide Web. He found some helpful statistics but was appalled at the dismal safety factor in the large city. But then he remembered something. "There's a convent there, Carmella. Cloistered nuns."

"Convents don't take in children."

"Maybe this one will."

"A flock of recluses are going to take in a strange child. Your optimism is infuriating."

"It's faith, Carmella, not optimism."

Carmella knew faith was for fools, but she had other sensibilities, and what she lacked in riches, she made up for in chutzpah. For once, her husband might've been right.

CHAPTER NINE

Rome
Present Day

AFTER THE DOCTOR'S STAMP OF APPROVAL, ORIO HEADED TO Casa Veronesi, a seven-bedroom, four-bath, nineteenth-century villa once owned by an Italian family of professionals who, having had no heirs, left it to the Church. It would be Maria's home for the next little while.

Orio pulled into the winding driveway and put the car in park. He turned to her. "What's that you're playing with?"

"This?" Maria looked at the USB drive in her hand. "It's my lucky charm," she said, repocketing it.

"Oh, *splendido*."

Just then, the front door of Casa Veronesi flew open, and a sturdy-looking woman with a long gait barreled their way. "Welcome, Maria. I'm Sister Catherine Benedict, but please call me Sister Cate." She met them at the car and nearly crushed Maria in a bear hug. "I run this place, such as that is." She laughed. "Come, come. We've been waiting for you."

Still nearly apoplectic after learning about Maria's illness,

Orio said to Cate, "She's exhausted, Sister, and she must rest." Then, he grabbed Maria's bag from the back and hustled to catch up. "Her condition is delicate," he added, following them inside.

"For heaven's sake, Father Rinaldi," Maria scolded, "I'm not pregnant."

Cate let go with a hoot.

Orio side-eyed his embarrassment.

Cate took a long look at Maria and remarked, "Breakfast first. We need to put some meat on those bones," and, to the priest, she said, "Join us, Orio."

He beamed with pleasure, unused as he was to social occasions.

Sister "Birdi" Bernadette approached the trio and introduced herself. She wasn't much older than Maria.

Birdi ran a homeless shelter in a sketchy part of Rome. With a nod to the house mother and the priest, she took Maria to her new room. Sister "Lati" Charlotte, her third housemate, had gone to her job teaching in a Church school, but she would be home by the dinner hour. Meanwhile, Orio followed Cate into the kitchen for *un caffè*.

Maria's bedroom was much more extravagant than her cell in Palermo.

This is a grownup room, she thought, as she admired the shelf of books, the burgundy velvet bench at the end of the bed, and the simple but elegant gold chandelier hanging from the ceiling. It was all very dear.

She took off her shoes, unpacked her few belongings into a set of drawers, and set her laptop on top of it. And then she took out the last item from her bag, the copy of *WIRED* magazine. As she went to tuck the parting gift from the friendly American inside the top drawer of the nightstand, something slid out.

She picked up the item, cocked her head, and studied it

curiously. The business card of one Teddy J. Weaver, CEO of Zinq Inc. with his contact info.

So that's the name of his new company.

Her world had collided with that of another, however briefly. The train ride was her first experience looking into the mirror of isolation that had been her life to date.

Holding Teddy's card, she, for some odd reason, was overcome by a wave of perception that was more reaction than the journey deserved. Indeed, everyone had tales to tell when traveling, about the quirks and foibles of the people they met. Still, she couldn't shake this feeling of ... significance. She tucked the card back inside the magazine cover. Then she slid it into her drawer and lined up her meds on top of it.

Feeling contented and hopeful, Maria sat on the side of the bed and said a prayer of thanks.

And that's when it hit her. The only other time she'd moved was with her father by her side, when he took her to the convent in Palermo. She felt a sudden pain in her heart, and at that moment, she missed her *papà* desperately.

CHAPTER TEN

Palermo, Sicily
1998

WEARING A BLUE LAPEL DRESS COAT AND CLUTCHING MIMI, HER beloved stuffed lamb, Maria approached the monastery gate with her father. Beyond the gate lay a small stone courtyard with a graceful, gurgling fountain. Even on this gloomy day, pots of droopy flowers festooned the place.

A black umbrella protected them from the drizzle as they approached the thick, arched entrance door. Unable to hold strong a moment longer, Faustino put down their shield, dropped to his knees, and hugged his daughter tightly as he slipped a tiny pouch into her coat pocket. "Open it once you're inside."

Maria's hand shot into her pocket. She pulled out the velvet bag, loosened its strings, and dumped the rectangular metal device into her palm.

Faustino shook his head smiling. "It's called a thumb drive."

"It's the size of my thumb!"

"It goes inside a port on a computer. There's one inside for you, the sisters assured me. Read the note I left you here," Faustino said, gesturing with a nod. "We'll be pen pals, *cara*. We'll trade when I visit. It's going to be fun."

At that, Maria's tears dried. Faustino rose and reached for the chain. The bell announcing their arrival clanged.

As they stood there, waiting, the rain turned heavy, splattering noisily onto the cobblestones. Then, the wide-planked monastery door swung open to an elderly nun whose face was carved with age. She regarded the man and the child, and her dour expression softened.

"I'm Faustino Caruso. This is my daughter, Maria. I believe you're expecting us."

Mother Superior Antonia could see his heart was breaking. "We'll take good care of her, Mr. Caruso."

As the nun reached out to take Maria's hand, Faustino bent down and wrapped her in his arms again. "You'll be fine, *mi amore*. Just you, *Dio*, and your beautiful mind. And me. I'm always here." He touched her heart. "You have everything you need." Though the words came easy, his smile was forced. There was nothing in the world he adored more than Maria, and his heart, shattered from the notion of not seeing her daily, was stitched together by the thinnest, frayed thread of faith.

Tears trickled down Maria's cheeks as she stared into her father's chocolate-brown eyes for what would turn out to be the last time.

Faustino croaked out a faint "thank you" as the door shut behind his beloved child, and she was led away.

CHAPTER ELEVEN

Rome
Present Day

AFTER A BREAKFAST OF BREAD WITH GOOSEBERRY JAM AND TEA, Maria left Casa Veronesi at 8:45 Monday morning for her first day of work.

She reached the Porta Sant'Anna, where she was checked by Swiss Guards and passed through a security kiosk before entering the round, medieval tower that housed the IOR. Up a few curved steps in the marble dome stood lines of priests in long cassocks and nuns in traditional and modern habits, waiting to deposit cash at tellers' desks. The bank's account holders, under twenty thousand worldwide, consisted exclusively of clergy, religious orders, and employees of the Vatican.

Upon her arrival, the tiny sister was ushered onto an elevator, down another set of curved, windowless hallways reminiscent of the dungeons they once were, and finally into an executive office.

Cardinal Angelico Cacciatore sat behind a heavy wooden

desk, his snowy-white hair thinning at the temples and receding in front. He wore a vacant expression on his pallid face, his thin lips pressed into a straight line, revealing neither curiosity nor disinterest.

Maria gulped. She'd done her best to hold her head high and clamp down on her nerves, but her self-confidence was flagging. She had to resist reaching into her pocket for her good luck charm.

Bishop Archibald Burbidge had placed himself on one of two ornate, turn-of-the-century chairs facing the cardinal. This, he was not going to miss. While he hadn't offered an opinion on the hire—he never would—privately, he had his doubts. But contradicting his boss, well, he'd rather paddle a boat to Sardinia with one oar.

The bishop introduced himself and gestured toward the other chair.

She sat.

The orientation was brief. By the time the cardinal finished with her responsibilities, she was only vaguely aware she'd be handed the books to correct. She was to find inconsistencies or "mistakes," make things right, and update their software. These directives were seriously dumbing down and diluting the job description she'd been given—one that included the terms "forensic accounting" and "cybersecurity." But it wasn't her place to question her higher-ups, at least not on day one.

"Any questions?" Cacciatore asked. "After all, our books are your books."

"Yes, we're an open book." Archibald smiled.

And then, the subject changed, and so did the cardinal's demeanor, a show of importance sparking in his dark eyes.

"As you may know, Sister, the Church values its charitable contributions above all else."

Maria's eyes locked onto the tremor in the cardinal's right hand. "I do know, Eminence."

For the first time, the cardinal considered the woman sitting before him. "And you undoubtedly know the confidential nature of our work?"

"Of course."

"Good, good." The cardinal shifted in his seat. "Along with the duties just described, you will oversee one large account." Cacciatore tilted his head and lifted his brows as if to say, *Are you with me here?*

"Yes, I see, Cardinal."

"And the confidentiality about which I speak applies to this account to an even greater degree."

"Forgive me, Cardinal Cacciatore, but I assume this is the account that is the, er, subject of the embezzlement?" Maria didn't dare mention the erstwhile VP, now in jail.

"That is an impertinent question, Sister." Cacciatore slid his shaking hand back and dropped it into his lap.

"I'm sorry, Eminence. Of course. It's just that the more details I know, the better job I can do. After all, as it was explained to me, I must secure the bank's accounts, all of them, keep them as safe from theft as possible."

Cardinal Cacciatore gave Sister Maria a withering look, designed to make her feel small.

Maria bravely refused to take her eyes off the cardinal's, and they seemed to come to an unspoken understanding.

Drawing a worn leather notebook from a desk drawer, he opened it and pulled out a sealed brown envelope. In a more conciliatory tone—after all, he needed her—he said, "This is a big undertaking, Sister, and we're here to help. Anything you need, anything at all ... come to us." Cacciatore beckoned Maria forward and handed her the envelope. "Your instructions are inside." Having nothing further, he asked again, "Any more questions?"

"Just one, Cardinal. What accounting program are you currently using?"

At that, the new *doretta dei sistemi contabili* for the IOR received blank stares from the pair.

Archibald spoke up, "It's the one everyone uses."

Well, that answered nothing.

"Oh, I almost forgot, Sister, I set up an interview with *La Carta* for this Friday, so the fine residents of Rome can get to know the new director of accounting systems. I would be present, of course."

At that, Maria returned to him a blank stare. "Ah … okay."

"What is it?" the cardinal inquired.

"I, um, wouldn't mind getting my feet wet first, Cardinal Cacciatore."

"Certainly. We'll reschedule for later in the month."

"Thank you, looking forward to it." Maria smiled, even though an interview with Rome's largest newspaper at any time of the month did not appeal to her. She was not the type to draw attention to herself. What would she even say?

As Burbidge showed Maria to her new workspace, a dozen employees, each surrounded by privacy panels, didn't give her even a nod. The bishop set down Maria's bag of personal supplies, then retreated without so much as a *ciao*.

The office was quieter than she imagined and surprisingly sunny. Maria's desk was in the corner with a window on each wall. She could see the ornate Vatican flag out one of them, waving proudly.

She was gratified to see an adequate computer for her needs, a better monitor than she was used to, and a nice, spacious desk, along with a new swivel mesh-back chair. She took out a few supplies, along with a photo of her father and her as a toddler and set them on the desk. Then, she opened the envelope given to her by Cardinal Cacciatore. Inside, she found a bank authorization card and a sheet of directives.

As instructed, Maria took the bank card to the bank's security section, where a clerk fingerprinted her and then pointed toward a notary for her signature.

Back at her desk, she followed instructions and entered the username and three passwords, which opened the IOR's three basic accounts: a business checking account and savings, which seemed straightforward, and another fund, Church Families Charity.

Her eyes fixed on the balance in that account: €125 million.

Maria had never worked with funds totaling such an enormous amount, but it made sense given that the bank's total worth, including acquisitions, was in the eleven-digit field.

According to the instructions, Maria's prime focus would be the infamous charity account.

Deposits came in daily. From that balance, a predetermined amount was dispersed to payees bimonthly.

She began to scroll through the list of recipients and soon discovered that there seemed no end to them. Maria searched payees until she found where it was tallied in the mid-five figures.

"Some charity," she exclaimed under her breath.

She started scrolling through the list—*all individuals, no organizations.*

Further perusal told Maria that the bank paid most recipients on an auto-pay system, direct deposit into a personal bank account, but some were paid by check. No one had written a check back in Palermo since she'd taken over more than a decade before. The system was indeed antiquated. And with a large team running the money, the strong possibility of a human error made it all the worse. Inevitable.

This is how funds were laundered so effectively for so long.

Maria would remedy that.

Item four on her instruction sheet directed her to add and delete names and payment amounts to the charity account based on information sent to her by Cardinal Cacciatore or

Bishop Burbidge. Bi-weekly, she would reconcile the account and send a statement to the cardinal, along with progress on the program shift.

And so, began her "vital work."

Though Maria had created *Convent Counting* back in college, a program that many convents and parishes had adopted from here to Timbuctoo, the Vatican Bank had found a way to use *Microsoft Office Accounting*, even though it was discontinued eons ago in computer years. She couldn't, for the life of her, figure out why the IOR was so outdated.

Maria, though naïve in many regards, boasted a genius IQ and had two advanced degrees from Polytechnic University.

The convent had demanded that Maria complete her education.

Despite many sisters holding master's degrees, even doctorates, many of them worldwide were assigned to work as house cleaners and cooks—performing free labor for everyone from bishops to spoiled young seminary boys who couldn't even manage to wash their own socks. Maria had ducked those duties unwittingly, partly because of her disability, given she could hardly scrub floors. But mainly, it was about her specific skill set. Her programming abilities were evident to all, even the sisters who considered the computer a gift from the devil.

At first, Mother Antonia homeschooled Maria, then, at age fifteen, enrolled her in online classes at the university. Maria breezed through C, Java, Pascal, Peral, Python, and many more courses the way other girls her age breezed through beachside romance novels. She had a master's in programming by the time she was twenty-one, along with her software program. Before starting the overhaul, she wanted to adjust to the new work environment. She opened the first email from the cardinal to familiarize herself. Her eyes widened when she saw the number of adjustments, nearly nine hundred.

She opened the charity fund next. She scanned the list of

payees, looking for a connection to the changes in the email and for commonalities with age, race, gender, and location. There had to be subgroups inside a population this big. She needed to be able to manage the funds while shifting the data to *Convent Counting*. For her convent back in Palermo, that task took her a whole afternoon. But for a fund of this magnitude, it would be the difference between moving out of a studio apartment of fifty square meters and the Royal Palace, which boasted over seventy thousand square meters of space.

She found no patterns but made note to address the matter for clarification, as a hefty amount of money shifted in and out of a charity fund populated "anonymously" and distributed to individual parties exclusively. She could write code specific to the fund to track patterns within the massive client database. She decided it would be her first order of business, as categorizing would make transferring into *Convent Counting* less random and more seamless. It would help to know where the money was coming from, but that was not part of her duties—managing inflow. Anyway, she'd created code with less information to go on in the past, so she'd be fine.

First, she needed to introduce herself formally to her team. Bishop Burbidge had skipped over that part of her induction. She stared out at the cubicles. If she turned her head and focused, she could hear faint fingers tapping the keyboards.

This place needs some Vivaldi in the background.

In Palermo, her work atmosphere was supercharged with centuries' worth of sonatas and symphonies to lift the spirits while working. Classical hadn't appealed to her as a girl, but Sister Delfina would say, "*Musica e matematica vanno di pari passo.*" Music and math go hand in hand. And as she matured, sure enough, so did her taste in music.

To say her first day was turning out to be peculiar was an understatement. Maria felt as if she'd stepped into the role of a glorified bookkeeper at the world's largest and most influential institution. However, she was determined to keep an open mind. Despite her nerves and a seedling of disillusionment, she was still driven by a strong sense of purpose and calm confidence that she was more than capable of helping the Vatican. And, boy, did they need it. Satisfied with her pep talk, Maria grabbed her cane, got up, and walked toward her team.

CHAPTER TWELVE

Rome

MICHAEL LEVIN STEPPED INTO HIS BOSS'S OFFICE AND SLUMPED into the chair in front of the man's messy desk, his ever-present reporter's notebook clenched in his hand, as much a part of him as the slightly rumpled clothes he wore. Fashion wasn't his strong suit, but who needed sartorial elegance when you had stories to chase? "I need a break, even a small one," he said as a way of a hello.

Lou Savinelli's attire never varied. Dark, baggy pants, a wrinkled, white shirt with sleeves rolled up, and a thin tie loosened and hanging slightly askew. The veteran newspaperman aimed to fill his publication with engaging stories gained from old-fashioned legwork, not by the click of a mouse. He'd constructed newsroom workstations—micro cubicles—to be so uncomfortable that reporters would happily spend most of their time in the field. But his number one was in-house doing research again? That meant one thing—it was time for some dialogue. "You've been sitting on this story for months, Mike. You tapped out all your sources over there?"

"This is the one topic they refuse even to give me PR bullshit about, Lou. They're dummied up. I just need one solid lead, a connection to a higher-up that'll get heads turning and, I'm telling you, this piece will find its sea legs and swim the length of the Atlantic by sundown."

"Approach it from another angle," Savinelli said. "Speak to the families. Get them on the record. The Church will have to say *something*, even if it's their usual denial."

"That's just it. A few have spoken out, but running down people who are involved isn't easy. They're hard to find and hard-pressed to talk when we do find them."

"What still gets me," Savinelli said, "is the pope, whichever one he was, announced a new set of guidelines a damn decade ago—"

"Safeguarding for the good of the child. Their right to have both parents in their lives. Their right to affection and education equal to children born to two parents living outside the umbrella of celibacy. It sounds like a whole bunch of garble ... because it is. And what's happened since? Nothing."

"Exactly my point."

"And even with the recent resurgence, that influx of letters Pope Julius received earlier in the year from more than three dozen women claiming to be in relationships with priests who've fathered their children and wanting normal family lives. No one wants to talk about it." Levin ran fingers through his wavy hair. "They pleaded, once again, for recognition from the Church. And the Holy Father, once again, made some flimsy announcement about finally getting around to revisiting the rules surrounding celibacy and illegitimate offspring."

"And nothing." Savinelli said, punctuating his point.

Levin went palms up. "Just another false promise."

"Mike, you know these passion pieces get swallowed by other misdeeds like attempted murder and embezzlement all the time."

"It's almost like they're doing it on purpose."

At that, they both laughed.

Levin went on, "This 'law,' or whatever they keep calling it, forbidding priests to have sex or marry, has been unraveling the lives of mistresses, clerics who've fathered children, and triggering deviant and criminal behavior for—"

"I get it, going on for a century. It's serious and something's got to give." This, Savinelli knew. But he was old and just jaded enough to realize the chance of change was about as likely as his greyhound, Sparky, sprouting wings. Still, the thought of Mike breaking this story—it gave him chills like in the old days.

"And it was Benedict XVI, by the way," the reporter added, shaking his head in aggravation. His boss had the oddest habit of losing names he should have available, given he ran a reputable paper in the heart of Rome.

"These are *our* rants, Mike. Remember, they have no place in your story. No right or wrong. Your job is to tell the story."

"You're speaking to me like you would to that new intern out there ripping pages off the wire."

Savinelli laughed. "Hold on to it. A break will come."

"Lou, I just need the time and the slack to find a current lead that will mean something to the public, to ensure no one questions the story."

"Meantime," Savinelli said, "I'd like you to cover the latest at IOR."

"Ah, Lou, is that why you called me in? Can't you give it to Barbieri? You know I hate that stuff, the latest 'money problems' at the bank."

"Eight figures, swiped from under the watch of the red hats? I'm sorry that's not interesting to you. It's interesting to our readers."

Levin shrugged.

The Vatican Bank losing track of funds was a story as old as the Gospel According to St. Mark. He wasn't interested in reporting more of the same on an institution that had so much money it couldn't bother keeping track.

"Today's news is money laundering, and that's a fact." And news was news. "And as long as you'll be there, we need something snappy on the new hire."

"Don't say it," Levin whined. "It's a snooze."

"You'll make it something more, and our readers will gobble it up. Interview the new head, Sister What's Her Name."

"Maria Caruso. From the cloistered convent at the end of the world. You want me to interview her? She's been written about to a sickening degree."

"Not by you."

"You're killing me."

"You'll survive."

"Will I?" Levin wondered. "Writing about a fragile, doe-eyed virgin hooked on binary code?"

"Look at that, you already got your headline." Savinelli waved a hand, indicating the conversation was over.

Levin dragged his feet out of his boss's office.

Until the Vatican released its next asteroid tumbling toward Earth, it seemed he'd be stuck in Fluff-Piece Hell.

It wouldn't be the first time this long-time investigative reporter was coerced to turn a snoozer into a sizzle piece. He just thought those days were over.

CHAPTER THIRTEEN

Rome

The chaos in the Eternal City had initially overwhelmed her, but Sister Maria had adapted to it and her newfound freedom like a butterfly leaving the chrysalis. Well, not quite. She still felt nearly naked in her new costume, a lightweight navy-blue skirt and ivory blouse ensemble that had replaced her traditional habit. That would take more than a few weeks to get used to.

In the airy, spacious house where she lived, she'd found a family and joy that permeated every corner of the grand, old place. Sister Cate was often off with meetings and other engagements, but Sisters Lati and Birdi spent their downtime caring for the home they loved and each other.

Each morning, the sisters walked together to Chiesa di Sant'Agata for sunrise Mass. In the evenings, after dinner, they'd raid the popcorn machine in the sitting room and trade stories of their "before life," often punctuating them with laughter and silliness. Sister Cate occasionally joined them, but didn't share much from her younger years.

Maria took part, and one evening she shared the story about Tori and her pet bunny and all the secret passages she'd discovered at her old residence. She delighted in that memory, and the sisters seemed to as well. It was a rare night, since Sister Cate was in attendance, dousing the narrative with her hearty laughter. None of the women had grown up in Maria's unusual circumstances. They were all from Rome and knew nothing of the simple, archaic life of a villager from one of Italy's most remote places.

Sandwiched between her daily devotion and at-home time was the workday, and what Maria saw there raised questions about which she had said nothing so far.

The sheer volume of accounting work challenged her and, for that reason, brought her some satisfaction. And she appreciated that she could troubleshoot her coworkers' computer problems. At least they'd started engaging with her when they needed something.

But she had yet to feel welcome at her new place of employment. Maria was left out of all social conversations. She figured maybe it was because of her position as their boss or, perhaps, the limp. That usually caused others to keep their distance. But her concerns went beyond that.

Maria's vibrant curiosity made her acutely aware of her surroundings and the peculiar events at the IOR. The Vatican seemed a place where words masked true intentions, and everyone jockeyed for power. She observed the winks, nods, and subtle maneuvering of the influential, akin to boxers dodging punches. This clandestine palace of intrigue unsettled her. Maria had envisioned her future in a god-centered, prayerful place, but those were not the words she would use now that she had an insider's view. It was no surprise to her that Cardinal Cacciatore wanted to oversee her interview with the newspaper. That, at least, made sense to her now.

While her team worked on their tasks, Maria gave the simple code she'd written for categorizing the payees a test run. She could've used any type of classifier, such as age, alphabetical order, gender, or location, to create subcategories to facilitate the move to *Convent Counting*. She chose gender, as poverty doesn't discriminate in that fashion. A big rule of thumb among coders was never to show a newly written program to anyone before performing basic tests to eliminate defects, and she just wanted to test it for bugs. As she neared the end of her fifth week at the IOR, the program she'd developed with such great care was ready to go.

It was now or never, so she set it in motion.

The recipients broke down into the two columns easily enough. Except an overwhelming number of payees landed under *Female*. Thinking there was a glitch, she reran the numbers, which returned the same result—the charity fund was predominately female.

She looked at the cubicles and called out, "Camille, can I see you for a minute?"

Camille Kingston was a decade older than Maria, even though one couldn't tell by her face, which seemed to be frozen in quizzical disinterest, giving her creamy complexion an even more blank and doll-like appearance. Talking to her made it even more confusing, as her communication skills were below average on a good day. Maria considered that Camille might be on the spectrum. *Aren't we all,* she thought in amusement, discarding the notion.

Camille walked over and tilted her head to punctuate her default expression.

"*Ciao.* Could you take a quick peek at the subcategories for the charities fund? I did a test run using gender."

Camille looked over the stats. "Eighty-six percent of the charities' recipients are female, well, 86.3 percent."

"Yes!" Maria agreed. "Is that strange?"

"As you know, I worked on that code with you, so no, it's not wrong, or *strange*, as you put it."

This is going nowhere. "Thank you, Camille."

Like a windup toy, she pivoted and walked back to her seat.

This time, Maria called out to Paolo Testa, the programmer who was more of the ringleader of the group and the opposite of Camille. "Paolo, excuse me, are you free?"

No response.

Not one to shout, Maria emailed him and heard the quick *ping* on his desktop.

Paolo was up in a flash, striding over. "What's up?"

"I was test-driving the code we worked on to create subcategories, and I was wondering if you could take a look?"

Paolo glanced at it. "Looks good to me."

"Really? Over 80 percent of the recipients here are female."

"Yup." When Sister Maria didn't respond, Paolo leaned closer and, with an arched eyebrow, said, "Well, men can't get pregnant, Sister."

"... Right," she said, though she wasn't sure why.

"... So, it stands to reason there'd be way more female recipients in the 'silent mistress' fund."

"What do you mean?"

Paolo gave her a look, waiting for the light to go on.

"You mean this is not a charity account?"

"Oh, it is, but not in the way you think."

"Excuse me, what did you call it?" Maria asked.

"Nothing. Inside joke." After a beat, Paolo asked, "Can I go?"

"Sure, thanks."

Maria pushed her paperwork aside. *Hmm.* She got back to the tasks at hand.

Twenty minutes later, unable to get Paolo's words off her mind, she called him back. "Really, Paolo, what did you mean when you said 'silent mistress' fund? Did I hear you right?"

"Am I being called out?" He smirked. "If so, I apologize."

Maria motioned to a chair.

Paolo dragged it over and just stood there.

"*Siediti.*" Sit. "Paolo, I just want to know what you meant."

He sat. "Might as well tell you. It won't be long before you learn for yourself."

"Learn what?"

"Well, the truth will find you. It always does."

"Paolo, "Please, get on with it." With one leg carefully crossed over the other and hands resting atop a knee, Paolo began again, "Okay, then. It's common knowledge in our little group that the Church Families Charity account isn't about supporting needy families. You mentioned the number of women in the account."

"Yes."

"There's a reason for it."

"Which is?"

"The account supports women who've had relationships with clergymen ... priests ... and the children produced as a result of that."

The children. Maria thought about that for a moment.

Paolo watched as the light finally turned on ... a thousand-watt bulb! He felt a bit relieved at that. God help him if he had to go into more detail.

Maria stared at the floor, not out of embarrassment, but to quell the wave of shock and revulsion that was churning through her midsection. When she looked up, she was careful not to appear overly emotional on top of her naïveté.

Paolo grinned and breathed a sigh of relief before asking, "Are we all set, Sister?"

Maria's eyes met his for an unspoken confirmation, and he got up and returned to his desk.

Everyone, at least every living, breathing, news-reading

person in the industrialized world, knew this was going on—priests breaking their vows of celibacy. The pope had addressed the situation on the world stage back in February, for goodness' sake, stating that the Congregation of Irish Bishops had updated guidelines regarding priests who fathered children, advising them to face up to their responsibilities in all ways—personal, legal, moral, and financial. The Vatican had created its own document referencing the matter but refused to release it publicly. At the time, Maria had wondered why.

She thought back to their declarations. *I can't remember any remedies being offered.*

The nuns in Palermo had debated the issue over the years, but since Maria was so much younger, she had not spoken up. Through their talks, she learned that celibacy was hard and that being married to God was a sacrifice. On a subconscious level, she felt this herself. But given the circumstances surrounding her disease, she was always grateful for the simpler things in life, such as life itself. For that reason, she didn't consider celibacy one way or the other.

Maria had no idea that a fund like this existed, let alone that she'd manage it. Yet Paolo's comments made it sound like common knowledge. It's Monday. It's sunny. The Church distributes millions annually in "alimony" and "child support." A vast number of women were involved with priests. Or, perhaps better put, a shocking number of priests were involved with women. Paolo had referred to it as the Silent Mistress Fund.

This account is essentially hush money. Wow....

Maria told herself this wasn't her problem to solve. Even if it were, where would she begin?

With the code apparently in working order, she brushed all bias from her mind to focus on the task at hand and opened the list from Cardinal Cacciatore's office.

Cardinal Cacciatore. This information certainly explained his behavior on day one.

Maria's eyes locked on a name near the bottom of the first page: *Luisa Gianna DiCaprio*. Startled, she pushed back her chair. She hadn't seen her childhood friend by that same name in years. Was this her? The name was under the *Delete* category. Why?

Maria opened the Church Families Charity account and searched for it. She clicked on the profile that came up. She saw enough to know that this was indeed her friend. Her date and place of birth were noted as Falcone. It showed that, in 1998, at seven years of age, she'd moved to Palermo with her mother, Elsa. The information ended there. It appeared that Elsa and Luisa were regular recipients of charity funds from the Vatican Bank. Maria couldn't possibly entertain the notion that Luisa and her mother were getting support from this fund. They came from money, old money—that much she knew. They certainly didn't need Church handouts.

Maria needed to know more. Why was her oldest friend receiving money from the Church? Who was she connected to? Maria would have to unlock the secure files to find out. She scanned the room. As usual, no one was paying her any attention.

After three failed attempts to get into Luisa's private file, a word flashed across the screen: *BREACH*.

Maria immediately regretted the rookie move.

MASSIMO PUGIA WAS ON HIS WAY to lunch when his cell phone pinged. Looking down, he opened a text message. "Hacker," he said out loud. Someone was after the office's confidential files. He scrolled through his contacts and tapped in a number.

A minute later, he knuckled the cardinal's office door and entered.

Cardinal Angelico Cacciatore, pen in hand, looked up from his desk.

"Someone's got their head up our ass," Massimo told the cardinal.

"What?"

"Someone's digging through the files, trying to access the private databases. I think you know who."

"Her? You've got to be kidding me?"

"Listen, Angelico, even though you wouldn't expect anything devious, she's the only one with direct access. The breach is in-house. Maybe an accident."

Cardinal Cacciatore dropped his pen from his angry, trembling hand. "Get her in here."

Within two minutes of attempting to break into the secured files of the Church Families Charity fund, Maria found herself being escorted straight to Cacciatore's office by Bishop Burbidge and some other very out-of-place-looking man. It was quite the to-do. And this did attract the attention of her team. She caught Paolo's eye before he ducked behind his monitor.

Bishop Burbidge seemed to serve as the cardinal's assistant as far as Maria could tell. He was always off on some errand or another. But the younger gentleman, well, she had no understanding of his role. Was he the muscle? Though Maria thought it an outrageous notion, she didn't have another word for it. They made the strangest of duos, Burbidge in his cassock, and this other guy in black, too, but jeans and a tee molded to his frame.

The bishop opened the door and motioned her in.

Maria found herself sitting, once again, on the witness stand.

Instead of sitting, the bishop and the muscle flanked her.

Though his reprimand was stated most softly, the cardinal

seethed beneath his mild tone as he reminded Maria to ignore areas where she was not assigned.

Maria played dumb, explaining that she'd started shifting payees *A* through *E* into *Convent Counting* when things went awry. "My computer froze, Cardinal, and I was simply trying to get back into the program."

"Quite understandable, Sister, but stay attentive to your work. And let's remember our oath to the Church and our Lord."

Maria nodded as the room fell silent.

"You may go," the cardinal said with a nod to the door.

His "detail" pivoted on their heels to follow her out when the cardinal said, "Massimo, a word."

"*Sure.*"

When Maria returned home that evening, she skipped dinner and went straight to her bedroom. The surge of emotions she was experiencing could've put Vatican City underwater. So fixated was she with the subterfuge at the IOR, she'd forgotten she was a woman of God first. She should've simply just searched the web for information on Luisa and avoided the entanglements she'd had with the Church. Maria was ashamed on top of every other emotion chugging through her system, and she didn't know where to turn.

She stared out the window at the billowing olive tree in the yard, so graceful and already bearing fruit. "I wish I could talk to you about all this," she said to the tree. "You'd give me the straight story." Maria laughed to herself. She was exhausted. Keenly aware of her medical condition, she realized that her next treatment wasn't for another two days. Perhaps that was part of her fatigue and unease.

Just as she considered a morning call to *Dottore* Lubrano, the front doorbell rang.

She pressed her forehead to the window, wondering who the after-dinner visitor could possibly be. Her heart sprang into her throat as she shot back from view. She'd have been less surprised to be staring down at the peaks of the scarlet-and-gold mitre hat.

CHAPTER FOURTEEN

Falcone, Sicily
1998

Carmella Caruso wanted to keep busy on this day. Faustino had just driven their young daughter away from their home for who knew how long. She would have gone along for the ride but had a shift at *La Villa* that no one would cover. Fridays were the busiest nights of the week, and most of the staff were already working. But, of course, she hadn't asked anyone to switch ....

As Carmella tidied Maria's room, she imagined it becoming a relaxing reading retreat or even an office for Faust, so she didn't have to stare at that clunky computer in *il soggiorno*. But as the daydream grew in detail, guilt flooded her, followed by deep-rooted shame. Her daughter couldn't do anything about her disability. And it wasn't her husband's fault. The stress of a sick child could do terrible things to a person.

There was no true love in her marriage. Was it because of Maria's illness? With her gone, maybe they'd have a chance. She resolved to do better. Faustino was a good man, after all.

After leaving her daughter's room and straightening the rest of the place, Carmella changed into a white, button-down blouse and black slacks and left for work.

Around 11:00 PM, she returned home with a pocket chock full of tips. She poured herself a Campari and soda and collapsed onto the timeworn divan in her work clothes.

The doorbell awakened her at dawn. *Polizie* stood outside to inform her that her husband, along with seven others, had died in the wreckage on the coastal road.

It had been all over the news the night before, and all her coworkers were talking about it. But it didn't occur to her that Faustino was involved. She assumed he'd gone to Tito's, as he did most Friday nights, often coming in past midnight.

Now, it was too late.

Too late to try harder. To be kinder. To start fresh.

Carmella felt the world swallow her up as she walked down two flats and knocked on the door. "Please, can you drive me to Palermo?" she asked her neighbor.

CHAPTER FIFTEEN

Rome
Present Day

CARMELLA CARUSO STUDIED THE SPACIOUS, ORNATE, SQUARE-shaped vestibule of her daughter's new home. She knew money when she saw it, having worked for some of the richest people in Sicily for the last three decades. She wondered what the rest of the house looked like. Taken aback, she'd never considered that nuns could live the high life.

Despite the warm evening, she wore an old khaki raincoat buttoned up to the neck and sturdy lace-up oxfords. Though striking at the still-young age of forty-seven, she looked and felt worn out.

At the top of the stairs, Maria stared down. "Mother?"

Carmella followed her daughter's voice up the curved staircase.

"My goodness, what's happened? Are you all right?" Tightly gripping the railing, Maria hastened, as well as she could, down the staircase and across the tiles to embrace her mother.

"What's wrong?" she said, stepping back to inspect her. "What brings you?"

Maria had never seen her mother more than twice yearly since her father's death. Mother Superior Antonia and Sister Delfina had helped Maria through the intense process of grieving for her father and healing the resentment she held toward her mother. They convinced her that feeling bitter would serve no one. So, as part of her work to become a sister, Maria committed to forgiving her mother.

Carmella slumped against the door jamb. "Can't a mother come to see her daughter once in a while?"

"Well, it's quite unlike you. Why didn't you call or text to let me know?"

"I hadn't time."

"Right. It's an eight-hour trip from Falcone. And you couldn't find a moment to notify me? Why are you really here?"

"I'm having some problems at work. I don't want to talk about it, but it got me upset, so I decided to take a couple of days off, come and see my daughter. After all, I haven't seen where you live and work now. I want to be sure you're being taken care of, and all that."

Like she's ever before been concerned about my living conditions. What twaddle, like most of her accounts.

"Come, Mother," Maria said, "leave your bag for now."

Carmella set her overnight bag down and followed her daughter into the sitting room.

Maria left for the kitchen to start the kettle. When she returned, she said, "You'll stay here, of course."

A flurry of activity ensued as the sisters returned home from their evening out. Birdi took over the kitchen. Lati picked up Carmella's bag and set off up the stairs to ready a room for their guest. Cate was at another one of her meetings.

Maria was grateful for the commotion.

Carmella looked around. "Nice place. Maybe I should become a nun."

Maria cringed, hoping neither sister was passing by the sitting room to hear that comment. "Why, do you need a new job?" she asked, using her mother's backchat to her advantage. Find out why she was really in town.

"What?" Carmella scoffed and looked to the heavens.

Maria studied her closely for signs of some kind of malady.

Carmella felt her daughter's eyes on her and redirected her gaze. She'd had about enough scrutiny. "Yes, Maria, I'm older than the last time you saw me. It's not polite to stare."

"I wasn't. I was ...." This was their opening dance, like clockwork. They'd stumble, step on toes, and couldn't ever hold the beat. Deflecting, Maria asked, "Mother, do you remember Luisa DiCaprio?"

"Of course, I remember Luisa. Most everyone in Falcone does." This eased Carmella's nerves, Maria bringing up Luisa, and saved her the trouble of working it into a conversation—that her daughter's only friend was gone.

"What do you mean? Everyone in Falcone knows her?"

Birdi came in with a tea kettle and cups on a tray. "Here we go." She poured a cup and handed it to their guest. "Oh my, you two look so much alike. You could be sisters. Twins!" She ping-ponged her focus from one woman's face to the other.

"Sister Birdi, if you're looking for a tip, my purse is in the entryway," Carmella commented.

The sister laughed, then poured Maria a cup and added two sugar cubes.

Attire and manner aside, the irony was not lost on Maria that she was the spitting image of the woman, though she had not inherited her mother's darker traits. Maria took the tea with a screwed-up grin, which made Birdi laugh again before retreating into the kitchen.

"Luisa was the talk of the town," her mother continued. "Everyone knew. I'm surprised you didn't."

"Mother, I left Falcone when I was a child. How would I know anything?"

"Yes, well …."

"Well, what?"

Carmella studied her daughter for a long, uncomfortable moment. What she'd come to say was that Luisa's untimely death had spooked her. It was unnatural to lose a child, and she wanted a chance to know Maria before it was too late. But since zero talks with her daughter had ever felt natural, ever gone as planned, she blurted, "Luisa's father was a priest." A bird didn't change their feathers overnight.

"A priest?" So, her mother knew. Six hours earlier, this news would've made Maria fall off the sofa.

"Yes. The whole neighborhood knew. A thing like that … it doesn't stay quiet for long among neighbors." Carmella sniffed and turned her gaze to the window.

"What priest?" she asked calmly.

"Father Mucci."

"Father Mucci!" Maria's stomach flipped. "How could that be? Luisa and I received First Communion from him. I can't believe it. He was so—" She stopped herself.

"Old, yes. Well, anyway, it's all over now."

"What do you mean, all over …?"

"They're all dead."

"Who's all dead?"

"Father Mucci, Luisa's mother Elsa, and now Luisa. They're all gone."

"Luisa?" After her misstep and earlier reprimand, Maria googled this information for verification but wanted to hear the details from her mother.

"Obit in the paper, *Lasicilia*. Luisa's body was found over by Siena Beach. She took walks there. They say she had a heart attack, which stands to reason. She didn't take to the medical trial like you did. She'd been struggling for years."

"I know. I remember ... when we were together." Maria sipped her tea, eyeing her mother over the porcelain rim.

That night, she tossed and turned, the minutes ticking away at her bedside clock, mocking her. Her mind was bogged down with thoughts of the DiCaprio family and from the mysterious activities at the IOR. And now, her mother.

Maria was short of friends or anyone she could talk to. And her mother's presence only amplified that feeling. She hadn't felt this alone since she was a child, roaming those cold, foreign, concrete walls of the convent.

CHAPTER SIXTEEN

Vatican City

AFTER A FITFUL NIGHT'S SLEEP, MARIA SPENT THE MORNING distracted. By lunch, she decided to take a half day. With Bishop Burbidge nowhere to be seen, Maria headed for Cardinal Cacciatore's office to ask permission. Just as she was about to knock on his office door, it opened.

"Sister Maria."

"Sister Cate."

The beat of silence that followed caused Maria a sense of déjà vu, and she tensed up all over again.

"What can we, uh, I, do for you?" Cardinal Cacciatore called out from behind his mammoth mahogany desk.

Before Maria could answer, Cate, lacking her usual joviality, said, "What are you doing here, dear?"

"What do you mean, Sister? This is where I work, as you know. I'm surprised to see you here." Maria silently chastised herself for getting her own hackles up. Bursting out before thinking was a trait she was working hard to quell. Still a way to go. And now, she'd caused another round of uncomfortable silence.

"Of course. I just meant *here, down here.*" Cate gestured erratically in the general direction of the cardinal, signaling to Maria that her housemate's nerves were tightening with each passing moment. "And, well, Angelico, er, His Eminence and I go way back," she continued. "Thought I'd, uh ... stop in. But I must go." She jerked this way and that, settling on "that," and zipped down the hallway, calling out, "See you at dinner." Then she stopped short. "Oh, I almost forgot. Your mother has gone, probably returning home."

"She didn't say anything to me about that last night. She didn't call or text. Did she say why?"

"No, she didn't say goodbye. Made her bed and just, poof!"

Cacciatori cleared his throat. "This isn't the lunchroom, Sister. Did you want something?"

Cate continued her trek toward the exit.

Maria took a long, slow breath. "I'm feeling a bit under the weather, Your Eminence. I was hoping I could work from home."

"Be well, then. See you Monday."

"Yes, Monday. Thank you. And you, too, be well." Maria turned away, wondering why her housemate had gone off her trolley.

In the one-minute walk back from the cardinal's office to hers, Maria's mind was a whirlwind of chaotic thoughts and tangled issues, each one calling for her attention. The CFC, or the so-called Silent Mistress Fund. Her friend Luisa, child of a priest, now dead. Sister Cate at the cardinal's office behaving so unlike herself....

And her mother? Why did she show up unannounced at this particular time for no apparent reason and then suddenly vanish? She'd have to figure that out later.

Maria had to uncover the truth if she was to continue this

Vatican job—and those who held the answers certainly weren't going to help her. *They're deliberately keeping me in the dark, and they're taking me for a complete dummy.*

Determined to unravel everything troubling her, Maria opened the Church Families Charity account. This time, she would be meticulous, ensuring she didn't make any false moves while accessing the hidden data.

With her adrenaline on the rise, Maria grabbed a one-terabyte flash drive from her side drawer. She looked around to ensure her privacy but then amused herself, realizing she could be sitting at her desk dressed in a blue frock and bonnet like Mimi from *La Bohème*, and no one would notice. She inserted the device. which she then used to boot into another operating system, thereby bypassing any trace of her next moves. All she needed now was the password to the secret files.

Ignoring the knot in her stomach, Maria first used a simple tried-and-*sometimes*-true method to access it. She hobbled to the filing cabinets along the back wall and snooped in the paper documents, hoping to spot passwords carelessly jotted down by workers too lazy to secure them. If she was lucky, getting into the digital files, which she was "borrowing" for an indeterminant length of time, would be a cinch.

The Vatican used ridiculously low-level passwords. They were wide open to even the most amateurish hacker wannabees. Maria was far better than that.

Unfortunately, the paper files were a dead end.

Delving into her mind to consider what next, she gazed out the window, staring at the Vatican flag. She nearly laughed out loud when it hit her. *Of course.*

She reached for another flash drive with a password application she'd been working on at her leisure. She entered a list of Vatican search terms, such as purple, gold, papal, 1929, Peter, etc.—until she had over fifty words and numbers—then hit

Submit and waited. One hundred thousand possibilities popped up.

She fine-tuned the search repeatedly until she ended up with twelve possible passwords. She could work with those odds.

With the CFC account open, she used Cardinal Cacciatore's email address as the username and one of the twelve password possibilities to get into the attached secret file.

No-go.

She tried another and failed.

The third password worked. She was in.

She began the download. It would take a while, a couple of hours—so much for taking a half day.

While waiting, she came to another decision and began surreptitiously gathering her personal belongings, quietly adding them to her carryall sac. As she slid the last item from her desk—the picture of her and her *papà*—the download bar flashed. The process was nearly complete.

Maria stiffened. The knot in her stomach spread to a full-fledged burn, radiating up her chest and throat. Panicked, she canceled the download.

With a sharp intake of breath and a tremor in her voice, she whispered, "Devil's delight! What am I doing?" She ripped the flash drive out of the port and chucked it, like a hot potato, into her sac.

This was large-scale criminal activity for which she could go to prison for a long time.

"Pull it together," she muttered to herself as she shook her hands to stop them from shaking.

Exhaling back into her ergonomic chair, she closed her eyes, hoping for a respite from her jitters. Within moments, she sat up, clear-minded and alert. "I'm not leaving with nothing."

She'd already gotten herself a free pass to the subfiles. All she needed now was to see it with her own eyes.

She pulled up Luisa Gianna DiCaprio's file and clicked on her name. A box opened. She used the same combo of letters and numbers to get into the hidden docs, adding *lgdicaprio* to the end of the password she'd just decrypted. She was in. And there it was, proof that Father Mucci was Luisa's biological father. She took a photo on her phone—a much smaller crime should she get caught—and closed out of her late friend's account.

Using the same pattern, she opened a dozen other files and snapped away. When she felt she had enough evidence for whatever came next, she erased her history and wiped the hard drive of the day's activity.

Maria's perception of the Vatican was shattered, and she resolved to defy Cardinal Cacciatore's edict to keep silent about her work.

Drawing a sheet of Vatican stationery out from a cubby, she wrote a note, sealed it in an envelope, and dispatched it via la Poste Vaticane. It was still plenty early for same-day delivery within the city.

The wily nun shut down her computer, stood, and picked up her sac and her silver-handled cane. Lost in a sea of tribulation, she hustled past her team, avoiding eye contact with Paolo on her way out. Rounding the corner to the exit, Maria bumped into a casually dressed thirty-something stranger.

"Pardon me," she said as her cane clanked to the floor and her sac dropped onto the marble tile, bursting open and revealing the desktop photo of her and her father.

"No worries," Michael Levin said as he bent down, scooped up the small frame, and slid it back inside. He placed the strap of her work bag gently back on her shoulder. "Here you are."

She nodded thanks and side-stepped him, heading toward the exit and slipping out of sight.

"There goes my interview," Levin said to himself. "She's fled the building, and it doesn't look like she's coming back." *There's a story here, after all. A hot one.* "Wowzer."

The reporter hot-footed it into the bank.

CHAPTER SEVENTEEN

Rome

MICHAEL LEVIN RETURNED TO HIS DESK IN THE CITY ROOM dissatisfied and suspicious, pretty much the status quo when it came to dealing with the Vatican.

He poked his head into Lou Savinelli's office.

"Let's see it." Savinelli leaned back in his swivel chair, hands clasped behind his head.

Levin slid into a chair and leaned in. "Not the story on the little nun, if that's what you want."

Savinelli's hands fell to his desk, and he, too, leaned in as much as his belly would allow. "Michael."

"Listen, I've been running around after them for a month. Each time I have an appointment, they reschedule. I went there today and bumped right into Sister Maria. Then she beelined around me like I was a marble pillar and left. Something screwy about that, by the way. Anyway ... I headed to Cardinal Cacciatore's, who'd completely forgotten about the interview."

"So, did you—"

"Re-reschedule? No. I'm moving on. Lou, I'd like to go full

force ahead into an investigation surrounding celibacy and the Church."

"What's your angle? It's got to be new."

Levin smiled. "Oh, it is."

Savinelli sighed. "Walk me through it."

"Okay, I'm going to investigate the backgrounds of the cardinals. Obviously, I can't investigate all 230-plus."

"No news station has that kind of budget."

"And no reporter in our field has that kind of time nowadays. So, I've broken it down, way down. I made a list of eight that will turn heads, should one of them be hiding an illegitimate child."

"Eight is certainly manageable but—"

"It's six now. Cardinal Antonio Ricci is dead, and Cardinal Lavoti's in jail. Though, I could likely gain access. So, I'll put him at the end of the list, worse comes to worst. Here's what I've got. He pulled a list from a pocket, unfolded it, and set it on his boss's desk.

Savinelli perused the names before eyeing Levin. "Your passion for the story is impressive, my friend ... reminds me of myself." He turned to glance at the many awards adorning the wall behind him. Turning back, he said, "You're stacking up your own in record time. Pretty soon, you'll pass me by, and I'll have to give you sturdier walls to hang them." A big grin spread across his wrinkled mug as he added, "You have one week to wow me. Now, get out of here."

Back in his micro cubicle, phone to his ear, Levin wasted no time.

"I'm writing a series of feature stories on some of the Vatican higher-ups," he told the man in charge at the Holy See press office. "I'd like to interview a handful of these men about their service to the Church and their lives away from the Vatican.

"So, a slow couple of weeks for you, eh?" Bishop Ennio Batori said. He chuckled over the crackling telephone line.

"Yeah, what can I say? Need to find something to fill the paper."

"Sure, no problem," the bishop said, relieved to be moving on from the embezzlement exploits. He'd be sure to nudge these great men to talk and get the Church back on track. "Do you want me to choose a few cardinals for you?"

"I'm interested in those who are well-known to readers already. Their opinions would grab attention and be most compelling, I think." Levin held his breath for Bishop Batori's response.

"Okay. Tell me who you want, and I'll see if I can round them up."

"Thanks, that would be good of you." Levin had hoped to be put in touch directly, but he'd take what he could get. "Cardinals Abella, Cacciatore, Cleary, Franzen, Parina, and Rondini."

Within the hour, Bishop Batori reported to Levin that five had agreed to the interview. "One refused. Not bad odds, Mr. Levin, if I say so myself."

Expecting Cardinal Cacciatore to be the one to refuse, considering the runaround he'd orchestrated for so long, Levin was taken aback when Batori added, "Justin Parina." The cardinal, with his pristine reputation, who ran the Vatican library.

CHAPTER EIGHTEEN

Rome

DESPITE THE MANY FRAGMENTED THOUGHTS CLUTTERING HER mind for the last thirty-six hours, Sister Maria Caruso walked to Sunday Mass at Chiesa di Sant'Agata with Sisters Birdi and Lati. The nuns were always kind enough to leave a few minutes early to allow for her slower pace. They didn't want to rush her. When they arrived at the visually modern church, built just one hundred years ago, Maria, as usual, excused herself from her housemates and went to sit with Father Rinaldi.

Orio and Maria's friendship began soon after he picked her up from the train station when the two ran into each other at Monsignor Ricci's church for the first time. They often sat together if Orio was not helping with the Mass, and they had enjoyed several meals out.

Maria thought Orio an oddball at first. A real bobblehead. But she'd developed a soft spot for him, perhaps because she was not always understood by others and, therefore, not accepted, as seemed to be the case with her new friend.

On spotting Maria, the priest sat up straighter in his seat.

She always put a smile on his face. And he couldn't wait to share his news. "I've been placed in a permanent position," Orio confided once she sat down.

Maria glanced around to be sure their conversation would not disrupt others. She gave him a sidelong look and whispered, "What do you mean?"

He whispered back, "At the bank. I'll be working at the bank."

"So, a promotion?"

"Sort of."

Maria thought back to their first journey to Casa Veronesi. It wasn't so much that he was an ineffective driver. The issue was more that he never stopped engaging his passengers, only glancing occasionally at the roadway in front of him. "A wise choice given your abilities to make people feel ... welcome."

"Yes, they put me on the welcoming committee for that reason!"

"The welcoming committee?" It certainly wasn't at the top of Maria's long list of changes needed at the IOR, but a friendly face on day one would've been a nice touch.

"Yes. I'll take clients to the officers they're meeting with, making sure they're comfortable with *caffè*, *tè*, things like that. I just finished training, so now I know the layout and where everything is. They gave me a new VAT mobile, too, in Spring Blue. I suppose I'll see you there from time to time."

"I see." After leaving the building early on Friday, she'd told herself to erase the IOR from her memory for the weekend. Unfortunately, her mind had other plans, and she could think of nothing else. Still, she wanted to support her new friend despite not knowing if he'd ever bump into her there. "Are you excited to start?"

"I am, yes. And you? How's work?"

"Fine," she responded with too much pep.

Her tone meant anything but. "What's wrong?" Orio asked.

Before Maria could comment, the music began, and they settled in.

After Mass, Orio asked, "Can you stay for a minute? I want to introduce you to Cardinal Justin Parina. You've met Francesco, haven't you?"

"I have, but I doubt we're on a first-name basis."

"We're best buddies from our seminary days. He's new in town, too, from Ostia."

"Oh, Ostia? Where they—"

"Yes, where the grave is. Julia's grave. The first female bishop?"

"Of course, yes, I know about Julia Lucinia. I may've been cloistered, Orio, but not in Congo."

The priest did so enjoy his new friend's sense of humor. "Well ... the crew stayed with Fran in the parish house. It was so exciting." Orio leaned in. "You know I'm close with everyone from that group. I worked in the Holy Office then, and *Dottoressa* Vella came in and went out all the time, meeting after meeting. She's the one who found Julia."

"Really? It seems there's always news of some kind about Valentina Vella. And, yes, I'd love to meet Cardinal Parina."

They waited for the crowd exiting the church to thin, making it easier for Maria to maneuver up the aisle. As they made their way, Orio noticed that his two friends were engaged in what appeared to be an intense conversation.

"Fran, *ciao,* Justin," Orio said, catching his breath.

"Orio, *ciao,*" Francesco said.

"*Buongiorno,* Orio," Justin said.

"Who's that hiding behind you?" Francesco leaned sideways and peered around his old friend.

Maria was invisible behind the priest's girth. Orio spun around to find her and hustled to the side, revealing the petite, young woman.

"Ah, *Sorella* Maria Caruso. *Buongiorno.*"

"*Buongiorno, Monsignor—*"

"Ah ... no, no. Francesco. That's what everyone calls me, and that's what I like."

"Of course, then. Francesco." Maria turned on her dazzling smile.

"I don't believe you've met the cardinal," Francesco said.

"No, I haven't." Maria's gaze lifted to meet the light-blue eyes of the man towering over her, his deep-brown hair streaked neatly with silver.

"Cardinal Justin Parina heads up the Vatican Library."

"It's very good to meet you, Cardinal."

"She's the new head of accounting at the IOR." Orio bowed ever-so-slightly but righted himself in a flash after receiving Maria's glare.

"I know," Justin said. "Congratulations, Sister Maria. I hope you know what you're getting into."

"I hope so, too, Cardinal."

"I'm Justin to you, Sister."

And enough charm to turn me into his friend, just like that. "Justin ... and, please, it's Maria."

"Hey, what have you two had your heads together about? Plotting another heist of the *Mona Lisa?*" Orio's joke fell flat as a flump.

Justin responded, "I'm sorry. If you'll excuse me," and he was off.

"Well, that was strange," Orio commented. "He's usually so cordial. I'm sorry, Maria, I don't know what his problem is. Fran, do you know what his problem is?" Orio asked, fishing for information.

"I do, Orio." Francesco was ready to clobber his comrade, who always managed to spout inappropriate words at the absolute most improper times. "His problem is cancer. Prostate cancer."

That shut the priest up.

Maria and Orio stepped back from Francesco, allowing others to greet him. She thought briefly before asking, "Do you have plans, Orio?"

"No, I don't. Where shall we go?"

"Oh ... you choose." Maria caught the attention of her housemates and, with a signal, let them know she would not be accompanying them home.

Orio chose Trattoria Terra, a favorite, and headed for his shiny, new car.

Maria hesitated. "Let's walk."

Orio relented. "Can you make it?"

"Got my cane here."

They were quiet on the ten-minute walk over.

Orio was consumed with thoughts of Cardinal Parina. He scolded himself for the gossipy way he'd behaved before he knew about his friend's illness. At the same time, he couldn't stop thinking about the photos. What if the cardinal *did* have a family? And now he might die?

This new picture weighed on him.

CHAPTER NINETEEN

Rome

ORIO USHERED MARIA INSIDE TRATTORIA TERRA when they arrived at the eatery just off a busy piazza. Grazia, the manager, greeted them effusively and led them toward a corner table.

Maria was more than preoccupied, and she ignored the menu.

Orio assumed it was because of her mother. He knew enough about that relationship to know it wasn't an amicable one. Still, to ask directly seemed rude, and he was well beyond his quota for the day. "Are you okay?"

"What?"

"You're a million miles away."

The server arrived. Orio ordered for them both. For Maria, he chose her staple dish, *spaghetti al pomodoro,* and for himself, *arrosticini.*

After the server left with their menus in tow, Maria took a decent drink of water and then blurted, "I've done something unthinkable, horrible actually."

Unable to resist the latest budding scandal, Orio leaned forward with wide-open eyes. "Tell me."

Maria decided caution was the best policy, and she didn't tell all. "In the account I oversee, the payments aren't going where I assumed they'd be going."

"What do you mean?"

"And I sent a letter about it to someone," she confessed. "I probably shouldn't have."

Orio inhaled and let out an audible breath. "Wait ... a minute. What?"

The server returned, set hot plates down, and left. Orio tucked in.

"Okay. I'm running a special account that, on the surface, seems well and good. But I discovered something really, uh ... well, far from well and good. It's *brutto*. Very bad ... unethical."

Orio wiggled his knees. "How?"

"Well, a certain amount of money is supposed to be disbursed to a specific group of Church members and organizations. But the funds are going somewhere else entirely, and it's all under the table and a big secret."

"How do you know?"

"Encrypted files. I got in, and that's what I saw."

Confusion wrinkled Orio's face. "What? If they aren't going where they're supposed to be going, where are they going? For heaven's sake, tell me."

"I can't." Maria's eyes slid to the side, avoiding her friend's. A crumpled face and an untouched plate of pasta told of her distress.

"Maria?" Orio's knees picked up speed. "Look, the fact that you've told me this much means you do want to confide in someone. And you want this, ah, whatever it is, to be heard."

Maria took a breath, closed her eyes, and then exhaled. "I oversee an account called Church Families Charity. Supposedly, it's been set up to support members of the Church who live in poverty. That's what Cardinal Cacciatore and Bishop Burbidge told me, and I had no reason to doubt them. Then, as I began working on the account, I bumped into some strange stuff. The money in the charity fund is not going to Church members in need at all."

"Okay," Orio said, "then where is it going?"

Maria paused and looked directly into Orio's eyes. "It's going to the mistresses of priests."

"Ah, come on," Orio said. "That sounds unlikely. What do you mean?"

"I mean that the Church is paying off women who are *romantically* involved with priests."

"*Romantically* ... do you mean, like, uh ...." Orio's ears burned red.

"Sexually. Yes, Orio. That's what I mean. They sleep together."

"All right. All right. I get it." Orio raised his palms as if to say, *Enough*. Then he leaned in. "But, why?"

"I don't know, maybe to keep them quiet. I don't know the whys and wherefores. I just know the money's going out to them. There are thousands of women and, obviously, thousands of priests involved with them. It's massive amounts of money being sent all over the world."

Orio tensed and sat up straight in protest. "No, that could not be."

"It could be, and it is happening."

He stared at her. He knew she was no dummy. "What evidence do you have?"

"Encrypted data. I told you I found it."

"Found ...?"

Maria could tell she'd lost the priest. "There's a subsystem on the account where hidden data is stored. I accessed it. It spells out the priests' names, the women they're linked to, and the names of their offspring. I saw it all."

"Surely not." He kept rebutting her, but the black-and-white photo of a young Justin Parina flashed on the screen in his mind with a large question mark hovering over it.

"I can give you an example. I have a friend, had ... Luisa DiCaprio ... she just passed away." Maria took a breath to rein in her emotions. "Her mother was receiving money from the Church. And Luisa was too. The information in that encrypted file identified a priest as Luisa's father. One that I knew as a child. And my mother verified it."

"Did you go to your boss?"

"Definitely not. There's an alarm on the subsystem. It's standard, and I should've known better. When I accessed it the first time, they knew, and Cardinal Cacciatore called me in and dressed me down."

Orio turned pale. "I still think you must be mistaken about all this." His mind went to the photos again, but he didn't speak of them.

"That's what I thought at first. I figured what I found must be an anomaly. And even after I knew it wasn't, I tried to convince myself that I dreamed the whole thing up. But this is no glitch. This is real, and it's a nightmare." Maria scooched closer. "And I have the tangible evidence with me."

"You what?"

"I broke into the files again, but I took care not to get caught the second time. And I began to download them, but then I realized the legal trouble I could be in, so I scrapped that plan and took photos of some of the pages instead."

"With your phone?"

"Of course." Maria glanced around and curbed her voice. "Here's the thing, one thing anyway. The Church dictates that priests must be celibate. But when they err, it turns a blind eye ... then the girlfriends, or women ... it pays them off. It's a massive deception and a rotten situation. The Church isn't supposed to be supporting them. It's deceitful! They even call it the Silent Mistress Fund."

"Great holy God," Orio's brain could burst out his ears by this point, so he began, "When I was packing up Cardinal Ricci's office—he's Fran's uncle, did you know that?" Orio looked quizzically at his friend.

"Uh, I wasn't aware of a Cardinal Ricci."

"Anyway, I found a few keys that nobody was supposed to find, at least it looked that way. One was rattling around inside a locked box in the back of his top drawer, and another was taped to the underside of a pencil case."

Maria felt her eyes glazing over. "Get to it, Orio."

"I had no idea what to do with the keys until I found a safe hidden behind the cardinal's bookcase, in the back of his desk. I tried the keys and one of them fit. Guess what was inside?"

"I can't imagine."

"Nothing, except an envelope with bank account records inside—transfers from a priest's private account in the late nineties into a woman's account, along with two old photos of them together with a child."

The server returned, quieting them both. He frowned at Maria's nearly full plate and whipped it away, promising a quick return with dessert.

"You know who the man was with the woman and the child in the photo?"

"Well, obviously, I don't, Orio." Maria huffed a little.

"Cardinal Justin Parina."

"The man I just met, head of the Vat?"

"Let me tell you something, Maria, if he's fathered a child, a man as kind and devoted as he is, heck, anyone from a country deacon to the pope himself could've done the same!" Orio took a sip of wine to temper his excitement.

The server kept his promise and dropped off two servings of his favorite-above-all dessert, *zabaglione*.

Orio motioned Maria to eat. "Fran said to leave it alone, but it's all I can think about." He smiled as he watched his friend dig into the creamy, frothy custard and stab at a fresh peach slice.

"So, how many clergy have fathered children in your account?" he asked.

"It's hard to say."

"Ballpark?"

"Okay. Well, the payees are in the five figures, so—"

"Mother of Mary, Maria!" Orio said, choking on his last sip of wine.

"Sorry."

"Next time, build up to it." The priest scratched his head. "We don't make that much money. Even the higher-ups are under six figures annually. You'd think that would be a deterrent. Between all the charity work and travel, there's hardly anything left over."

Maria went quiet.

"What is it?"

"Nothing."

"Maria." He studied her. "What are you hiding?"

"You missed the point, Orio. Priests aren't supporting these children," she said. "Parishioners are. Everyone that donates to any Church anywhere. The *payers* are from all over the world, individuals, not businesses looking for tax write-offs and certainly not the priests themselves."

Orio slumped in his seat, letting this sink in. "Except Justin."

"What do you mean?"

Orio trained his eyes on some invisible spot. "I can't know this for certain, but the money paid to this woman came from his account. It looks like Justin was using personal funds to support her." He pursed his lips and drummed his fingers on the tabletop. "I knew he was a good guy!"

Maria gave him a look.

"Compared to what you're saying, he's looking pretty good."

"We'll see …."

"Well, what do you intend to do about all this?"

"I told you … I sent a letter."

"To?"

"Well, we've been talking about her."

"Oh, no. Not—"

"Valentina Vella."

"Oh, boy. Can of worms now …."

CHAPTER TWENTY

Rome

CHECKING INTO VALERI LABORATORIO DE CONSERVAZIONE, before heading home after a three-day weekend in Mallorca with her fiancé, Luca, Valentina Vella, not surprisingly, faced a pile of letters. She knew how much her business partner, Erika Simone, hated opening the mail. Spotting a package addressed to them both, Valentina pulled it gently from the middle of the stack. The return address was Paula Kirkpatrick, her nemesis. She opened the package and removed a small packing envelope along with a note:

Returning this to its rightful owners. I'm relieved to see you both back on top.
I'm sorry for everything.

Paula

Valentina thought back to those miserable days. An invitation to speak at Oxford: Cyber-Archaeology in the Holy Land.

She and Erika had set up their slide presentation and stepped onto the stage. And then a switch of the slides exposed the top-secret grave of Julia Episcopa. The rest was history.

What remained a mystery was who had sent the flash drive for Paula to reveal to the world.

Valentina never even thought to set her eyes on the stick. Now that she had it in her hands, her desire to know who was to blame for the fiasco came roaring back.

She scanned the handwriting on the label out of habit before setting it down at the edge of her desk. Her business partner was visiting her brother Edmond, an ICU nurse, in Genoa—she could wait to tell her about this strange twist.

She flipped through several more pieces of mail and then came to a letter with a Vatican City postage stamp. There was no return address. She slit open the envelope with a manicured nail, noted Friday's date, and read the handwritten message.

Dear Dottoressa Vella,

I've made a significant discovery at the Vatican Bank where I work, and I need to share it with someone. As a woman of God, I'm contacting you because of your bravery in addressing the Church's stance on women. Honestly, I don't know where else to turn.

Could we meet so I can share what I know? I'll be at Pizzeria Bellavigna at 6:00 PM on Monday and hope you can join me there.

Perhaps it's silly, but I wish to wait until we meet before identifying myself.

MC

Since discovering the woman bishop, Valentina had received many letters, some congratulatory, some critical, and others enlisting her help in some matter. *Here we go again.* That was her first thought. Her second was that this note had a different ring to it.

She picked up her phone and made a call.

"To what do I owe the pleasure?" Yigael said in place of hello.

"A couple of things. Chez Nous? In two hours?"

VALENTINA SEATED HERSELF in a corner booth opposite Yigael, the amber lighting adding shine to his smooth, bare head.

Yigael had ordered a bottle of Chateau something. She was grateful he'd remembered how she loved the red blends, and Chateau anything meant the wine was distilled from a combination of vineyards. This generally brought out the best in each grape. Yigael had already poured her a glass.

They hadn't spoken in weeks. Since up-and-coming archaeologist Kara Maggi discovered dozens of scrolls near the boat caves in Ercolano—written by the Anonymous Scribe—and the "okay" had been granted to recover the Jewish treasure from the Saint-Denis Cathedral, they'd both been tied up.

Yigael missed Valentina and felt a sense of rightness in the world that she'd called.

Valentina took a sizeable sip of wine.

After a minute of comfortable quiet in each other's company, Valentina reached inside her Italian canvas tote and produced the package from Erika's ex. Mood lighting was not a scientist's friend, but before handing over the "evidence," she studied the address label one more time, noting the connecting strokes, word spacing, pen lifts, consistency, and slants.

"What's got your brain in knots? I can practically hear the gears cranking up over there?"

She placed the package in front of Yigael.

He inspected the address and turned it over and back again.

"What?" Yigael said, glancing up.

"Just open it," Valentina urged.

He did and dumped the contents on the table. "Ah ...." He picked up the flash drive, looked at the envelope again and the box, and then he packed everything back up. "I'd like to dig into this. Okay with you?"

"More than okay. Do you think it's possible to find out who sent it to Paula?"

Yigael locked eyes with her and, with a wry smile, said, "Perhaps." Between his history as a top spy for Mossad, a Who's Who in the Israeli military, a famed archaeologist, and with his contacts worldwide, if anyone could find out who sent the stick, it'd be this tough, burly man. He slid the "evidence" into an inside jacket pocket and changed the subject. "So, how about that Vatican?"

Valentina shook her head. "What could possibly happen next?"

"Exactly."

"Poor Pope Julius, working so hard to bring unity to the world with the news of the Diary of Yeshua, penned by the Anonymous Scribe, and the IOR rains all over it with embezzlement charges. Do you think Lavoti might be behind everything?"

"Maybe, but he was in jail when the police cuffed and carted off the veep and his executive assistant."

"That doesn't mean he wasn't behind it."

"Facts."

"I wonder if they're all rotting in the same cell."

A hearty laugh escaped Yigael. "Now, that's an image ... speaking of the Vat, I read up on the nun. What do you think? There's a lot of press on her."

"Indeed. Sister Maria Caruso. What do you think?"

"She's a distraction, a pawn. I don't believe a word of it."

"Of her story?"

"Of the Vatican's intentions," he said, emphasizing the word intentions. "I'll tell you one thing: The world is reaching the end of its rope with the Church. Even God above will be reluctant to 'forgive' if they do anything shady where this young woman is concerned."

"Well, that's my cue if ever there was one. Look at this." Valentina reached inside her bag again and extracted the letter from MC.

Yigael read it, then turned the letter over and back again. "Oh, boy!" He read it a second time. "Sister Maria, of course. And she's scared. So? What are you going to do with this?"

"Forget about it."

"Oh, right. You aren't the least bit curious."

"I am. But I can't run away fast enough from controversy with the Church. You, of all people, should understand that."

"Still afraid of the Vatican, are you?" Yigael probed.

"Not afraid, but I do have cold feet. Why get into all that turmoil again?"

"Excellent point."

"It is?"

"Absolutely. Do what you want. Do not get involved."

Valentina stared at Yigael, searching for an answer. "Well," she said, palms up. "I kinda didn't expect you to say that. What is your opinion? Hit the gas or not?"

"Exactly." Yigael sat back and released his second genuine laugh of the evening. Oh, how he missed their repartee.

CHAPTER TWENTY-ONE

Morcote, Switzerland

ASIDE FROM A FADED PHOTOGRAPH AND A FEW SCANT REFERENCES to the village he now found himself in, Michael Levin's background search had unearthed almost nothing about Justin Parina's personal life. So, relying on little more than a notion, he swung open the door to Berta's Bakery and eyed the temptations in the pastry case. Unable to resist, he ordered an apricot-filled *bombolone* and *un caffè*.

"*Buon appetite,*" Berta Hoffman said, gesturing toward a round table in a corner window. "Where are you from?"

"Rome." Levin set down his doughnut and espresso.

"You here on vacation?"

He was used to playing along. Many women openly flirted with the good-looking guy whose sandy hair always looked windblown and whose gray-green eyes held an irresistible intensity.

He finished his pastry and approached the owner at the counter.

"What? You cannot resist my *bomboloni*." She laughed.

"They're delicious, *Signora*, but I'm all set for today." Levin withdrew his phone from his pocket and showed the shop owner an image of Justin Parina from more than a decade back. It had taken some digging to find one without his Roman collar.

"Do you know him?" he asked.

Berta half-closed her right eye and looked at him suspiciously. "Why do you want to know?"

"I want to talk with this man for a story I'm writing for my newspaper," he said.

"A reporter? Never seen him." She snuffled, convinced reporters were snoops up to no good. "Did you check Facebook?" Then she turned her back on him.

Levin breathed heavily and headed for the exit. "Thanks anyway ...."

"That's Robert Molinelli," she said to his back. *Maybe just a question or two.* "What's he done?"

Robert Molinelli? Ah ... Levin lassoed his excitement before turning. "Why do you think he's done something?"

"Because you're here asking about him. He comes here several times a year, stays a while, then leaves."

That tracked with what Levin had dug up. Why? That was the question Levin figured he was about to find the answer to.

"I think he's a spy."

Levin raised his brows. "Really?" Amusement formed on his lips.

"Let's just sit down here. Another *caffè*?"

At Levin's nod, Berta heaved a sigh and prepared two shots of the rich, aromatic liquid.

Within the hour, the loquacious middle-aged shop owner had given him what he came for. Levin looked down at his notebook to verify the address and began his hike up the hill. A faint pant informed him he was glad to reach the top. Up some steps, and then he knocked.

The door opened.

A striking woman with wavy, ginger hair peered out. She carried a pair of fine Gingher sheers.

"Yes?" she said.

"Sorry to intrude," Levin said, "but do you know this man?" He reached inside his jacket pocket for his phone and showed her the photo.

The woman blinked but stood stock still. "No," she said in an even tone. "Who are you?"

"My name is Michael Levin. I work for *La Carta* in Rome." He fished out a card from his pocket and handed it to her. "Are you Katarina Silva?"

"Please, go," the woman said, closing the door.

Levin could hear the click of the lock. He knocked once more, before departing.

KATARINA HAD MOVED to Morcote and the hillside house when Peter was five. She intended to maintain a low profile, and she did, but eventually, the village proved monotonous and stifling.

With Peter at school, Katarina went in search of a career change. Her degree in business had secured her a job in an accounting firm straight out of college. She was always assured of work in that field, but it certainly didn't feed her creative nature. And single motherhood came with something most people didn't talk about—its fair share of isolation. Katarina was lonely. If she couldn't have an everyday family life, she was determined to find fulfillment elsewhere.

She had trained as a seamstress at an early age and developed a fascination with textiles, but she hadn't picked up a pair of scissors in a long time, since high school. Despite that, she found a side job mending for a local dry cleaner after she could show him that she was still nimble with a needle and thread.

This part-time work, coupled with full-time employment and parenting a youngster, kept Katarina busy to say the least. But it was worth it to keep her mind off the fact that the man she loved had visited her only once since she'd arrived in Morcote ten months back.

Just as her emotions threatened to wallop her on one particularly difficult day, an idea struck.

She bought a piece of fine, white linen and crafted a simple, summery, A-line dress with a large pocket. She appliqued a bright, multi-colored dragonfly to the pocket and hand-stitched a trim of silk ribbons on the neck and hemline. She took her creation to the owner of Piselli Dolci, Morcote's shop for young girls.

"My dresses are one-of-a-kind," Katarina told Sweet Pea's owner. "The dragonfly is my logo, and no two will ever look alike."

Mia Grunder, the shop owner, was impressed with the fine quality of Katarina's work and enchanted with her whimsical trademark. "What made the dragonfly buzz into your life?" she asked.

"I didn't expect anyone to ask me that question." Katarina laughed. "Well, the dragonfly symbolizes change, transformation, and adaptability, emphasis on adaptability. I try anyway ..." she said blithely.

"Yes, don't we all." The light exchange struck Mia deeply—she saw a hint of pain in the young woman's eyes—but she hid her reaction behind a simple smile. "You've got an eye for what will sell, Katarina." Mia knew she had a market for such excellence. She bought the dress and asked for three more. They all sold in no time, and Katarina Silva was in business.

When Mia suggested she corner the Asian market, Katarina declined, deliberately keeping her business small lest her secret life become known. As it was, she had a dozen buyers in France, Italy, and her homeland of Switzerland, so small was a relative term.

After closing the door on the reporter, Katarina walked through to the backyard gazebo, where her visiting mother was reading. "The past has come back to haunt me, *Mutter*."

"What?" Greta Silva asked, looking up from her book.

Katarina felt the heat rise in her neck. She approached her mother, sitting on the bench beside her. "A reporter just came by with a picture of Justin."

Greta had known for years that her daughter's secret would one day be revealed. It seemed to her that it had been a long time coming. "Have you told Justin?"

"Not yet. I'll call him. But," she shivered, "I feel like this is an omen. It feels like everything's going to change."

"Everything *is* going to change for you ... I mean with Justin so ...."

Katarina's eyes glistened with emotion.

"Maybe it's time, then, *liebling*," Greta said.

"Time for what?"

"Time to unburden yourself." Greta placed a hand on her daughter's knee.

"No, I couldn't." Katarina felt the tears rise and spill out, as they'd done so many times in the past. Despite her intention to live with grace and calm, symbolized by the dragonfly, she was often overwhelmed by embarrassment and shame and another familiar feeling—grief. What would she do without him? The pain was too much to bear.

"Come here." Greta held open her arms, and Katarina collapsed into them as if she were a child and not a woman in her fifties.

As she cried, she imagined life without Justin in her world. At the same time, she wondered what it would be like to get her awful secret off her back. She was tempted to talk to the reporter.

Almost.

CHAPTER TWENTY-TWO

Rome

CARDINAL JUSTIN PARINA ARRIVED FIFTEEN MINUTES EARLY AT the offices of Vicente & Fabbro Avvocati on Via Flaminia. Ernesto Vicente, a well-known attorney, was recognized for serving the legal needs of many religious figures in Rome.

Justin hesitated before going in as a wave of emotion washed over him. Guilt that he had for years lived a secret life, regret that he'd cheated on the Church, and heartbreak that he'd seen so little of Katarina and their son Peter. They were familiar feelings, unwelcome and unpleasant.

Dressed in civilian clothes, he breathed deep and slow to quiet his nerves before stepping inside the attorney's outer office.

I found it impossible not to love her. Just as strong, though, was my ambition in the Church.

And here we are.

"Signor Vicente, *per favore*," he said to the receptionist, whose dangling pink earrings tinkled as she looked up from her computer screen with a faint smile. Justin glanced at his gold Bvlgari watch, his only luxury possession, before adding, "I'm a bit early."

"Cardinal Parina, he'll be just a moment. If you'll have a seat." The receptionist turned her eyes back to her screen.

Justin rarely allowed himself to consider too profoundly what he'd done twenty-some years ago. But, when he reviewed his financial arrangement for Katarina with his attorney, he was forced to face his choices. And now, since he'd learned of his illness, he could think of nothing else.

The cardinal decided he'd failed on both counts. He had not served either his mistress or the Church honestly.

Ernesto Vicente appeared in the waiting area. "Cardinal, this way."

Justin stood, and the two shook hands.

Entering through a heavy wooden door, the cardinal took a brief sweep of the attorney's office, once again noting its quiet richness of leather and wood.

"Please, sit down." The attorney gestured to a chair in front of his desk, and then he sat on a high-backed swivel chair. A neat stack of paperwork covered the center of his desk.

"Cardinal, we met just recently for your annual review. Has something come up?" Vicente dipped his chin and raised his brows.

Justin got straight to the point. "My life is ending, and I want to be sure my financials are in order ... that my arrangements for Katarina and Peter are complete."

Vicente had for years managed the cardinal's trust and could rattle off to the penny how the ups and downs of the money market affected it. If the news Vicente had just learned surprised him, it didn't show.

"Let's take a look. "Has anything changed? Have your assets changed? Have you added stocks or other property since we last met?" He lifted his eyes in a dispassionate way.

"Not added. The farm in Switzerland, Porsel, has been taken over by the bank. I no longer own it."

"Too bad," Vicente said.

Justin felt the need for explanation, "When my parents left me the farm, I rented it out. Unfortunately, the renters left it in bad shape. I couldn't recover and support it."

Vicente refrained from additional comment. "Any personal valuables?"

The cardinal glanced at his watch and gave Vicente a rueful smile. "Only this, a gift from my mother. I would like for Peter to have it."

Vicente sat back in his chair. He rested his elbows on the arms, a pen held high in his right hand, which he twiddled between his fingers before slapping it down on the desk. "As you've requested, upon your death, the principal will be distributed in its entirety. To Katarina, 80 percent, and Peter, 20 percent, including the Bvlgari. Is there a change there?"

Justin shook his head and whispered, "No."

"I know, Cardinal, that when you came to me years ago, you rejected participation in the Church program that would've paid a monthly stipend to Katarina for Peter's care, preferring instead to support him with your own income. The same stipend is available to her upon your death. If you've changed your mind and are now interested in participating, a nondisclosure agreement must be signed by Katarina. She would then be prohibited from confiding this arrangement to anyone."

"No, Ernesto, Katarina will not need funds from the Church. What she will have from me is sufficient ... she has her own company, which does well."

"Okay, then." Vicente drew forward the paperwork and looked up. "How long do you have?"

CHAPTER TWENTY-THREE

Rome

At 6:00 pm sharp on Monday, Valentina Vella opened the door to the well-known pizzeria and looked around. It hadn't taken her long to overcome her resistance, and, besides, her curiosity had gotten the better of her. She wanted to meet this woman.

The evening *passeggiata* was already on. Families, friends, and acquaintances, all dressed in their finest, strolling through the streets, greeting each other, gawking through store windows, and deciding what to do next. Either home for dinner or out. Valentina knew the restaurant would fill up soon.

She scanned the nearly empty place and spotted her target, who gave her a subtle wave.

"You must be MC." Valentina flashed a warm smile and sat down. "I must admit, you've aroused my curiosity."

"Thank you for coming, *Dottoressa* Vella." Maria absorbed the scientist's sophisticated presence.

"Please. Valentina." Never one for small talk, she got to it.

"You indicated in your letter that you have no one else to turn to. Surely, your mother superior? Someone?"

Of course, the brilliant scientist knew who she was. Maria flushed but refused to feel foolish for signing her message with initials. "When I tell you what I know, you'll understand why there's no one in the Church that can help me. Although, I have shared this information with one friend."

Valentina wondered what this young woman so new to Rome could have to say. "Why don't you start at the beginning and tell me what's on your mind."

"First, I want to explain ... because you'll be wondering like everyone else. I have a medical condition that requires periodic blood transfusions and has kept me from growing fully. As you can see, I'm limited in what I can do physically. And the cane is from an incident as a child. So ...."

Valentina's empathy vein nearly burst. "Oh, I'm sorry. She couldn't help herself and took Maria's hand. "I never thought ... no ... please, you look just fine to me. *Bella, giovane donna minuta.*" Beautiful, petite, young woman. Valentina's compassion toward other women had grown exponentially since she learned about Julia and her search for equality way back in the first century.

Maria relaxed. "I'll start at the beginning."

"Please, do."

"I took my vows in Palermo and lived in a cloistered convent until recently. I moved to Rome because of a job at the bank. At the time, I was suffocating at the convent. Mother Superior recognized that I needed a break, and then this job opportunity turned up. Apparently, I have some relevant expertise, and I guess the powers that be thought they could use me. Now, based on what I found out, I think they brought me in as a figurehead, someone who would never question the goings on and would never *be* questioned."

"Wow," Valentina said in a whisper, "that sounds intriguing, and it sounds like they made a wrong choice, Sister Maria."

Maria's face contorted as if she had bitten into a lemon. "I sure didn't ask for it."

"I read your story in *La Carta* and about your programming skills. *Convent Counting*, yes?"

"Guilty." Maria smiled.

"A friend of mine installed it a while back. A priest. Monsignor Ricci. He uses it now at his church."

"Really? That's the church I go to."

"Oh? Well, congratulations. You've made quite a name for yourself."

"Thank you, but that's not really why I'm here," Maria said.

"Okay, go on." Valentina rearranged her skirt and sipped the Chianti a server had brought moments ago.

Maria's glass of red sat untouched. "When I got to Rome," she said, "I was placed in a secure unit with a team under me and told to make sense of the 'books.' Basically, to update the program they were using, which is old, antiquated actually, and to keep better track of things since the ...."

"Embezzlement. Go on." Valentina lowered her glass.

Maria told her about Church Families Charity—about being told the fund existed to support Church members in need, its nine-figure balance, and the recipients numbering in the mid-five figures.

"Whoa."

"The budget is off the charts."

"*Sono scioccato*. I'm shocked. You must've been too. But the Vatican certainly has the resources."

"That's not even half the story. Most recipients are female, and one of the men on my team hinted, well, he more than hinted, that there was a reason so many women were on the roll—"

"And?"

"The account I'm working on has nothing to do with those living below the poverty level or in homeless shelters or orphanages," Maria explained.

"What do you mean?"

In a tone that Valentina could barely hear, Maria said, "It's really a payout to mistresses of priests."

"The entire fund?"

"Yes ... all over the world."

Valentina worked to keep her calm. "How do you know?"

"I accessed a secret sub-file that linked recipients to priests," Maria said. "In many cases, several women are linked to a single priest. And it's not all women. Their children are documented too "Unfortunately, my first break-in breached security, and Cardinal Cacciatore called me to his office. He was furious."

"*Oddio*. What'd you do next?"

"I went home."

Valentina laughed quietly.

"But in the morning, I went back to my desk and broke in again. "

Valentina's face froze in disbelief, then relaxed into a loud peal of laughter. Containing herself, she leaned back in her chair. "Huh?"

"I gathered evidence in a way that wouldn't land me behind bars. That was Friday afternoon." Maria, dry-mouthed, took a sip of her wine, eyeing Valentina to get a read on her. With no clue as to whether the renowned scientist believed her, she set down her glass and announced, "Apparently, there are varying degrees of wrong."

"Oh, the Vatican will be the first to tell you that." Valentina scoffed just thinking about how easily they bow and bend the line between right and wrong to suit their needs.

Maria exhaled and shook her head, still shocked by her act of defiance. "Well, they haven't come after me yet. I don't know what they're planning, but I know I can't go back there. I don't want to go back. I called in today, but that'll only work for so long, despite my stellar excuse."

Valentina was not innocent about the ways and means of the heavyweights and thought the young nun was right in being cautious.

"Well, I've always believed that the number of priests straying was larger than most of us imagined. But the fact that the Vatican is keeping track and paying ... it's a business. The Church just doing business. Ye gods."

The two women from very different worlds sat there for a moment, united in silent solidarity.

"But why come to me?"

"You faced down the Church before. I figured you might want to know about this."

Valentina mumbled, "Truly, there's nothing more I want to know about what the Church is up to." Her breath whooshed out.

Maria ignored Valentina's protestation. "The way I see it is millions of people, some of them in need themselves, are donating their hard-earned money to the Church to help the poor. But that's not where their money's going. I may not live in the 'real world,' but I know that biological parents are responsible for their offspring. People who give their life to the Church and take vows don't do it to get rich, but that doesn't mean those from congregations worldwide should be paying, actually *paying,* for the misdeeds of the clergy."

And that doesn't even touch the issues of celibacy or molestation or rape, Valentina thought, *if all this is true.* She grasped the irony immediately. "Oh, dear God. Payoffs. Well, nothing surprises me."

"Can you do something? Can we do something?" Maria asked.

"Sister—"

"Please, call me Maria."

"Maria, look," she said, not without sensitivity, "I don't know what anyone could do about this, really. The magnitude. What are you asking of me?"

Maria looked down at her napkin. She was losing to her emotions. "I've lived a sheltered life. There's no question of that. I try every day to live Yeshua's principles ... and I've followed the rules of the Church." She dabbed her eyes. "I guess I want it exposed. Contributors should know what the Church is doing with their money. But they also need to know about the ethics of the men they hold in such high regard. But who am I? Who would listen to me? But you ... you're ... you."

Valentina pressed her lips together to squash an incoming smile. "You sell yourself short, Maria." Valentina found herself growing endeared to the woman. Her own story was the same as Maria's at one time. She had lived a life of obedience and loyalty to the Church ... and it had been followed by disillusionment.

Returning to practicalities, Valentina asked, "You have some evidence of all this. You said so earlier, yes?"

Maria thought better of showing Valentina the evidence on her phone. *Not here. Not in public.* "I do. How should I get it to you? We can't do it via text or email, and I don't want to put anything in the post.

"Tell you what," Valentina said, "take it to Francesco and tell him it's for me."

"Okay, I'll be going to Vespers on Wednesday. I'll give it to him then." Monsignor Francesco was confirmed trustworthy by the only two people she dared to confide in, which was good enough for her.

The server, in a rush as the café was filling up, dropped their tab onto the table and sped away.

"I've got this," Valentina said, digging into her handbag for cash.

"Oh, no," Maria said. "I should—" Looking at the scientist's stern expression, she backed down. "*Grazie,* Valentina."

"Ask Francesco to call me when he has your evidence. And how can I reach you?" Valentina asked.

"I live at Casa Veronesi. It's close to Francesco's church. Here." Maria handed Valentina a blue sticky note with her mobile phone number. She did not want to be presumptuous and ask for Valentina's number.

Valentina took it but raised both hands, palms out. "No promises, Maria, but I'll take a look. Meantime, I need to use *il bagno.*"

"And I must get home."

"You calling for *un taxi*? I could drop you off."

"No, I'll walk. It's close. *Grazie* for coming, Valentina. I hope I will see you soon."

Valentina stood and looked around. When she spotted the café's public restroom, she stooped and planted *baci* on Maria's cheeks.

Maria grabbed her cane and stepped toward the door.

"*Ciao,* Maria," she said, and off she went.

Valentina washed her hands, pulled out lip gloss, and applied a quick swathe. She ran fingers through her shiny chestnut hair, longer now, with some bend, and swinging free when she whirled in surprise. Satisfied with her appearance, she headed for the front door. Nearly there, a woman with an espresso set down her empty cup and scooted back in her chair, smacking Valentina in the knee.

"Ouch." Valentina's handbag flew off her shoulder, its contents scattering onto the shiny, black-and-white floor.

The woman murmured, "*Scusa,*" and exited.

CHAPTER TWENTY-FOUR

Rome

MARIA TOOK A STEP OUTSIDE PIZZERIA BELLAVIGNA.

The street was clear except for a large, black SUV with blackout windows parked on the next block where she was heading.

Two men wearing dark suits, crisp, open-neck shirts, and spit-polished Derbies leaned against the vehicle. One of the men sported a Fedora, the other gnawed on a toothpick.'

As Maria approached the corner and turned, head down and deep in thought about her conversation with Valentina, an alternate thought pierced her sensibilities.

Hey, wake up. Pay attention.

And then, when she looked up, she stopped breathing. The men's apparel was unlike the casual street-style khakis and jeans familiar around neighborhood *trattorie*. More significantly, they were staring straight at her, not away like everyone else, when she caught them gawking at "the young nun with the cane."

Maybe her imagination was running wild, but she didn't think so.

I need to get out of here.

She wasn't going to outrun them, and the café was too far back, but maybe she could turn onto the side street just ahead, and somebody might be there to help her. Sweat broke out along her brow line as she questioned her crazy notion that bad guys hired by the Church were hunting her down.

That said, as she rounded the corner, her rationale wasn't going to change the fact that heavy footsteps from behind were gaining on her, and there was no sign of help on the side street.

What have I gotten myself into? And Dottoressa Vella? *Is somebody after her too?*

The summer sun was setting late, creating an awful glare. Maria had only one option and just seconds before it was too late. She dove into her purse with her free hand and got a hold of her phone.

Too late.

The man grasped her thin arm with a meaty paw, sliding it downward and snatching her cane. Simultaneously, the SUV squeaked to a stop beside them. Maria let the phone fall from her grip, hoping it landed out of sight in the shrubbery lining the side of the building.

A scream was building, out of instinct more than anything, but as soon as her lips parted, the man in the hat wrapped a hand around her face, pressing against her nose and mouth.

Having rammed the vehicle into park, the one with the toothpick shot out, rounded the back, and propped the door open for his partner, a devious smile fixed on his prisoner.

Her captor turned her toward the humming SUV and forced her into the back seat, joining her, while the other circled back and got behind the wheel. The vice grip around her face was released, and she gasped for air, choking.

Before she knew it, she was blindfolded and restrained by a

rope attached to her wrists. Then her captor hopped out, slamming her side door as he jumped into the front seat.

The driver sped off.

In under an hour, the car braked, the engine shut off, and her captors pulled her out.

A warm shower had begun to pelt down.

CHAPTER TWENTY-FIVE

Rome

ORIO HAD BEEN WORRIED FROM THE START. HE HADN'T LIKED that Maria was going alone to a public place to speak with the beleaguered Valentina Vella. Not with what she knew. Maria had promised to contact him right after. That was over four hours ago. Usually, his return home to La Dimora, a lushly green apartment complex housing priests, was a relief after a fretful day at the Vatican. He could commune, however briefly, with others and enjoy an excellent meal cooked by Polish nuns.

But now he was troubled. Pacing the length of his small apartment, he hadn't the faintest idea what to do. *I've got to do something ... what?* he wondered.

While Maria divulged her suspicions about the bank fund to the famed archaeologist, the priest had been sipping tea and indulging in cannoli at Pasticceria Unica. He had long resigned himself to the fact that, as a priest, he must give up many things, but sweets would never be one of them. So, as one hour ran into two, and two cannoli turned into three, with no response from Maria, the priest had texted Fran twice and called Sister Cate multiple times, with no response. Finally, Sister Lati picked up at Casa Veronesi. She said Maria wasn't home yet and promised that she would walk down to The Corner Bookstore to see if she'd stopped there. He didn't hold out much hope, though, as he imagined Maria was more of an e-book kind of gal. He imagined Lati would not find her perusing the bestseller shelf this late on a workday. And his suspicions had proved correct.

Frustrated and still unnerved, Orio returned home and brewed another tea to calm down. He sat at his quaint kitchen table for two. Today's *La Carta* sat untouched on top of a pile of mail. It always served as a good distraction—the latest stories on the Church. Reporter Michael Levin often had a juicy tidbit for him to chew on.

Levin and the priest had a bit of history together. They'd crossed paths during the Julia search, and twice, the priest had passed along a small bit of information that landed in the morning paper.

That's it! Orio thought before he'd even unfolded the periodical. *He's the one.*

He texted Michael Levin.

SOS. We must meet tonight. Orio Rinaldi

It was after 11:00 PM, and he didn't expect the reporter to respond. But he was wrong.

What's up? Levin texted back.

I have a major story for you. It'll be worth your time. Orio directed Levin to meet him at a public park halfway between his residence and the newspaper's location. *I don't want to be seen by anybody.*

This better be good.

The park was shrouded in darkness, the only light coming from two murky lamp posts in the parking lot. When Levin finally spotted the priest's outline sitting on a bench, he said, "This is a little over the top, don't you think?"

"Well, I didn't think it would be this dark. Why don't they put more lights out here?"

The reporter stifled a groan. "What have you got?"

Orio feared the repercussions of Fran even more than the Church. But he and his old friend hadn't seen eye-to-eye from the start. He hadn't even responded to his earlier texts, either, and his worry over Maria trumped the consequences of his subsequent actions.

"It all started when I found a file folder in Cardinal Ricci's office with ... another cardinal's name posted to it. It was locked in a safe," he began. "Inside, was a list of bank deposits to a woman ... outside Rome. I didn't know what it meant. I showed it to Fran—Monsignor Ricci—and he was also clueless. There were photos, too, of a ... personal nature." Orio swiveled his head in one direction and then the other. Nothing but stagnant shadows.

"Personal nature, you say? What kind of personal nature?"

"What?" Orio asked. "Oh, not that kind of thing ... just what looked like a family on holiday."

Levin motioned with a wave of the hand for the priest to continue.

"Right. And then, just the other day, Sister Maria Caruso revealed something she'd found at the bank along these same lines ... with accounts and women. And things started to add up."

The priest's recitation about his discoveries had been riddled with stops, starts, digressions, and holes, and usually, Michael Levin would've interrupted the man several times to fill in the blanks or quit wasting his time. But, as the nervous priest prattled on, Levin was dropping names and places into his mind like puzzle pieces.

Justin Parina.

Child support payments.
Katarina Silva.
A photo of them together—likely blackmail.

So much adrenaline was surging through his system that the reporter had difficulty maintaining his signature casual stance.

Levin preferred to come off as underwhelmed in these situations. It was the best way to pull more of a story out of those who thought they had one to tell, and it was the most effective way to appear unbiased. But not two hours off the plane from Switzerland, he found the awkward, portly priest—who always seemed to be on the periphery of the action—verifying the story Savinelli had given him one week to pull together. The story of a lifetime if he did his due diligence and got it right. It could be enormous.

"I'm sorry," the priest said, misinterpreting the reporter's silence for disinterest. He wiped a hand across his brow. It felt like he'd worked off one of those cannoli in the telling of that story. "I know I'm not making a whole lot of sense. I just—"

"You are, Father Rinaldi. Your timing is ... immaculate."

They both cracked a smile at Levin's ironic word choice.

"You mean to tell me," Levin went on, "these are all active relationships in the files the nun found?" *A potential cornucopia of evidence.*

Orio was hesitant because he hadn't seen the proof. But he believed his friend. "Thousands of them."

"Can you verify?"

"I can't, frankly. Sister Maria can, but now she's missing, and I'm sure the story she told me is tied to her disappearance. I thought if we, well, if you .... Can you publicize this? Maybe that'll be enough to scare them into letting her go."

Oh boy, this guy doesn't get it, Levin thought. "Not without some digging on my part, verification. Has a missing persons report been filed?"

Orio shook his head.

"So maybe she's not missing."

Michael Levin saw the truth in his eyes. Missing or not, the priest believed Sister Maria was gone and in some kind of danger. That's when he thought back to bumping into her on Friday. Her sac had fallen, and a picture had tumbled out of what looked like a father and young daughter. When he placed it back into her bag, he'd spotted some pens and flash drives. He hadn't thought too much of it then. But now?

She'd packed up her office. Sister Maria had been running scared then.

None of this, unfortunately, changed the reporter's next move. "I can't put out a story I can't verify."

"I understand."

"But I'll look into it." Levin was excited about the story possibility, but he couldn't give the priest false hope. "Stay in touch. I mean it. And let me know when you hear from Sister Maria." Despite popular opinion, he was human, and he was now worried about the nun too.

Orio nodded but sat frozen in glum desperation, believing the reporter wouldn't help him, and he didn't know what else to do.

"I'm sure this will all work out, Father Rinaldi." Levin forced a smile and left with the first real beginnings of the story he'd been scraping together for years.

This could change everything.

CHAPTER TWENTY-SIX

Rome

IT WAS LATE MORNING WHEN MONSIGNOR FRANCESCO RICCI heard heavy, incessant rapping at his door. He sped from his room and clipped down the hallway toward the front entrance to his private quarters at Chiesa di Sant'Agata. Swinging it open to the sight of his frantic friend, he said, "Orio, you know they can probably hear you inside the Sistine Chapel."

"I'm sorry. Do you have Valentina Vella's phone number?"

"Sorry? You raced over here for a phone number?"

"I have to talk to you too. It's important. Her number, please?"

"That's a funny one. When have you ever needed Valentina's phone number? I didn't think you liked her."

"I never said that." Orio huffed.

Francesco persisted, "You didn't have to. You stay a mile away from her any time she's around."

"Well, I've not seen her since your uncle's death, and remember, she caused the cardinal more than his fair share of trouble. She might even have caused his heart attack," the priest dared to suggest.

"Orio. That's an awful thing to say. Valentina did no such thing."

"Well, she did set his red cap spinning when she discovered Julia."

Francesco chuckled. "That she did."

"Hey, can we get back on track here? What's her number?"

"Why do you want it? Is this about Maria? Your messages last night didn't make a whole lot of sense."

"Well, I couldn't help it. I was out of sorts. Actually, I was worried to death. I *am* worried to death. Fran, something's wrong, very wrong. She's gone missing."

Orio hadn't slept a wink. Nor had he heard from Levin, who he now considered a dead end.

He filled Fran in about Maria's meeting with Valentina. "And she hasn't been seen or heard from since. Valentina saw her last, at least I think so. And I also think she's been taken by some evil people. Her boss, Cardinal Cacciatore, is likely behind this. That man creeps me out. Or Lavoti, maybe he's puppeteering from his jail cell. I wouldn't be surprised!"

Francesco stopped him right there. "Orio, you're leaping to outlandish conclusions, based on what? Maria not going directly home after dinner? Maybe she went home, then got up early and went for a walk. Maybe she's at The Corner Bookstore. It's open twenty-four hours."

"Fran, she never came home. Lati checked the bookstore last night. And Sister Cate called me this morning. She's been trying her constantly too. Maria's not answering either of our calls or texts. Before you write this off, understand why I'm so worried. She has no friends. Doesn't know the city all that well. She needs regular medical care! Today, in fact. Oh, and I stopped at *Dottore* Lubrano's, and—"

"Orio, that's enough." He put a hand on the priest's shoulder. "You've convinced me. Something's wrong. Valentina's number is on my phone. I'll go get it."

Francesco retrieved his phone and scurried back to the vestibule, pulling up Valentina's number for Orio. He was impressed at the speed with which his longtime friend concluded that the whereabouts of the young nun was in serious question. She'd taken over the highest position at the IOR that a woman has ever held. If Orio's instincts were right, the Church would have hell to pay. This would be high profile.

Dammit! the monsignor thought. He knew it was too good to be true. When Cardinal Cacciatore announced her hiring, he'd gotten a bad feeling. He couldn't believe how open-minded the higher-ups had become—overnight. He'd praised and thanked God for the blessings and the bright future of the Vatican Bank with Sister Maria Caruso steering the ship, but his intuition had told him that something was off.

Francesco had initially intended to have lunch with Cardinal Parina. However, he invited him to the church instead, bringing him up to speed and hoping for his support. After deciding, Francesco returned to his office and called his longtime, trusted friend.

ORIO'S VOICE SHOOK when Valentina Vella answered his call. "*Dottoressa* Vella, this is Father Orio Rinaldi. I'm sorry to bother you, but do you happen to know where Sister Maria is? Maria Caruso?"

That question came out of the blue, but Valentina's sharp mind instantaneously linked it to her conversation last night. "Uh, would it be imbecilic of me to ask how you could be aware that I know anything about Sister Maria? If you know we met yesterday, you must be the one she confided in."

"Yes, and now she's missing," Orio said.

"Missing?" The chaos as Valentina tried to exit the pizzeria flashed in her mind. "No, she isn't with me, and I don't know where she is." Anxiety pierced the edges of her stomach.

"Do you know how she planned to return to her house after your meeting?"

"Yes, she walked. I left practically on her heels, well, not exactly. I had to pick up some things off the floor ...." Valentina's voice faded away.

"What? You swept the floor?"

"No, I was, this woman spilled an espresso. I couldn't get out. Never mind. Anyway, I was delayed, but she was nowhere in sight when I finally made it out the door."

Valentina waited for the priest to pick up the conversation, but his heavier-than-usual breathing was the only hint that he was still on the line. "She has a lot on her mind," Valentina went on. "Also, she's not well. Maybe she got sick on her way home."

"I already checked with her doctor."

"Maybe she ended up in the hospital. Tell you what? I'll call hospitals, and you—" Having second thoughts, Valentina said, "Where are you?"

"Fran's church."

"Francesco knows about this?"

"Yes."

"Who else?" Valentina asked.

"No one, except Sister Cate at Casa Veronesi, because she's been calling and calling Maria too." Orio thought better of mentioning Michael Levin.

"Father, I know someone who, I believe, can help us. Let me make a call, and then you and I will meet up and put our heads together."

Yeah, I know exactly who she'll bring in, and I'll be on tenter-

hooks. But he said, "See you at Fran's. Oh, *Dottoressa Vella*, wait. Where did you meet with her?"

"Pizzeria Bellavigna."

Orio clicked off.

CHAPTER TWENTY-SEVEN

Rome

Valentina Vella stood as Monsignor Ricci entered his own office. "She hasn't turned up in any of the hospitals I've called, Fran."

The monsignor's brows wrinkled, creating lines of worry. "Follow me. I have a feeling we're going to need more space."

He directed her toward the conference room in his new parish, which was far from large but roomy enough to fit an oval oak table with six chairs surrounding it. As they made their way down the hallway, they met Yigael, who'd just arrived.

"Oh, good, you're here," Valentina said offhandedly. "Oh, and Orio Rinaldi called in a while ago … he found no trace of her around the pizzeria. No one in any of the shops saw her. But he's sticking around there for a while, just in case."

"And hello to you, too, Beloved Woman."

"Yigael," she murmured coyly.

He grinned and landed kisses on her pinky-red cheeks, then turned. "Fran, how's it going?"

The two shook hands.

They all took a seat at the table, and then it was all business.

"That blithering idiot Rinaldi. Is there anything he doesn't get his nose into?" Yigael had been duly unimpressed with the priest on the few occasions the two had crossed paths. One time, in Yigael's presence, Orio had nearly knocked the pope to the floor!

Yigael Dorian and Orio Rinaldi lived at opposite poles. The ex-Mossad was focused and fastidious, while the priest was impetuous and slapdash.

Valentina, who'd never been a fan of the ill-fated priest, surprised herself when she said, "If it hadn't been for him, we wouldn't know Maria's missing."

"*Hmph.*" Yigael pursed his lips.

Valentina's phone rang. "Yes?" Several moments later, she added, "Bring it over."

Yigael posed his question by raising a brow.

"Father Rinaldi. He just found her phone."

Yigael's eyes turned into slits. "I'll believe that when—"

Valentina cut him off with a glare.

Ten minutes later, the priest bustled in, huffing and puffing.

He put the phone on the table and tried to fly back out, but Yigael stopped him. "Wait."

Orio's eyeballs rolled up, but the rest of him froze, his usual stance kicking in at facing the terrifying ex-spy.

"Where are you going in such a hurry?" Yigael asked.

"I'm late for a tour, but that's the least of it. I'll try to find out what I can about Maria at the IOR."

"You work at the bank too?"

"Uh, yes, and as I said, 'I'm late.'"

"You're going to be a little later because you seem to be ground zero, and *I'm* late to this little party."

The flustered and winded priest didn't dare defy Yigael Dorian. He took an open chair at the table.

"So, as I understand it, the crux of the matter is this: Sister Maria oversees a fund where she discovers payoffs from the Church to women, ah ... mistresses of priests and their children if they have them. She tells you about it and says she has evidence." Yigael nodded at the phone sitting in the middle of the table.

Orio nodded back. "Yes. I didn't see it, but she said she took photos."

"So ... then she has pizza with Val, er, *Dottoressa* Vella here—"

"For heaven's sake, I'm Valentina to everyone in this room."

Orio retrieved a handkerchief and dabbed at his forehead, amazed at his elevated status.

"And then she disappears into thin air."

"Well, that's boiling it down, but yes," Francesco said.

"And you went to Pizzeria Bellavigna and found this phone, her phone ... in a bush outside the restaurant?"

"Around the corner from it."

Yigael stared at the priest, puzzling this all together.

"She'd never go anywhere without her phone," Orio said. "She's a techie. It'd be like me leaving the house without my collar. Also, her phone is her lifeline, literally. She's about one med between life and death."

Yigael's eyes clamped shut. After several seconds, they opened. "Dammit," he whispered.

Orio gulped before continuing, "Plus, Valentina said something about getting held up when she left the pizzeria. It was odd." He turned to Valentina. "Did I hear you right about the espresso and you sweeping the floor?"

"What?" Yigael turned to Valentina.

"Tell you later."

"Well, was that an accident or deliberate?" Orio turned back to Yigael. "And it got me thinking. If this is a worst-case scenario, and she was tailed and then taken, she'd ditch the phone." He slumped in his seat just thinking about it. "She couldn't have outrun them."

Everyone grew heavy-hearted. His point was a strong one. Assuming Maria tossed the phone, well, it punctuated their suspicions that she was kidnapped and wanted someone to know.

"So, you think she separated herself from the evidence before vanishing into thin air."

"I do," Orio choked out.

"You think she had the forethought to do that?"

"I do. Yes."

Francesco jumped in. "Unfortunately, the phone is locked, so we can't see the photos."

"Fran, this add up to you?" Yigael asked.

"Yes. Inasmuch as Orio has explained it to me, it's the most plausible scenario."

Yigael shook his head. *There's never any telling. Here I am without a clue, and the do-nothing priest Rinaldi comes up with the goods. Some things I don't understand.* His respect for the wayward priest upped a glimmer.

"I have to go."

"Okay. Stay in the loop."

Orio turned toward the door and bumped into Cardinal Justin Parina. "*Ciao, amico.* See you soon." And out the door, he went.

"I'm sorry. I got here as quickly as I could. I had a doctor's appointment," Justin said, taking a seat. "Thank you for contacting me, Fran."

"Everything okay?" Valentina asked.

"Yes, Val, thank you. Oh, and Erika's back. She's got you covered at Valeri."

"Great."

"How can I help?" he asked.

After they filled Justin in, they broke for coffee and reconvened around the table.

As Francesco sat back down, his phone rang. "Orio," he said. "Yes? Yes, calm down. Yes, I know you're good with faces—"

Yigael motioned for the phone.

"Orio's at the bank. He says he ran into a woman he saw just last Sunday at the cantina."

"That doesn't mean anything."

Francesco handed over the phone.

"Rinaldi, Yigael here. What's up?" He listened briefly, then said, "Text Francesco the name, and we'll look into it." Yigael hung up. But before he handed the phone back, a text came in.

Pepper Pugia. It was followed by a better-than-nothing photo the priest must've taken on the sly.

Valentina slid behind Yigael to peek at the screen. "Oh, *merde.* She was at the pizzeria, too, yesterday."

"You're sure? Is she the one who barreled into you at the restaurant?"

"She sure is."

Francesco put a hand on her shoulder and gave it a squeeze.

Just then, Jacques Ignatius and Anna-Marie Mannes walked in.

"Made good time." Yigael did not look at his operatives, staring at the photo instead.

"It's not so far from ... oh, never mind. He's lost in space," Jacques said to no one in particular.

"From Paris, did you say?" Yigael stood, clapped Jacques's back, and kissed Anna on the cheek. While Yigael had left the ranks of the Mossad, Jacques remained a valued operative and a close friend. Anna also left the fabled agency to run Ruja's Rare Antiquities, Yigael's shop in Jerusalem. Now, she was *always* at his disposal.

After greetings—they all knew each other—Yigael took the stage. "Given the evidence and behavioral patterns to this point, we must assume the worst. Sister Maria Caruso's been kidnapped to silence her about the fund, the payoffs the Church has been distributing to mistresses in exchange for their silence. We don't know their intention, whether they just want to scare the wits out of her to get her talking or something more ... uh, worse."

"Father in heaven," Francesco said under his breath. He could barely fathom the Church being involved in this kidnapping scandal. But payoffs and the possibility of murder? Was there no limit to the wrongdoings this institution he'd devoted his life to was willing to commit? All to serve their so-called greater good.

"Are you all set?" Yigael asked Jacques and Anna.

"The Israeli treasure is 95 percent wrapped and packed. Philippe and Carol are finishing up, so we're all yours." Yigael's team of four had been removing stolen Jewish treasure, hidden for centuries in the basement of the Basilica of Saint-Denis just outside Paris, and returning it to Israel.

Yigael gave Jacques a pointed look before turning Francesco's phone screen toward him.

Jacques leaned in and studied it, then took a step back. "Is that ...?"

"Dara Damahdi," they said in unison.

"Goes by Pepper Pugia now. Rinaldi said he saw her Sunday at Trattoria Terra, where he and Maria were dining. And he bumped into her just now, literally, smacked right into her on his way into the bank. She works for Cacciatore. *And,* she was spying on Val and Maria last night at the pizzeria right before Maria went MIA."

"Somebody, catch me up," Justin said, breaking the tension.

"Catch us all up," Valentina added.

"She's ex-Mossad, dirty as they come," Jacques said.

Yigael laughed. "I've wondered where she's been hiding the last few years. Of course!"

"At the IOR," Francesco said, shaking his head in disbelief.

"God help us all," Justin added.

"Jacques, Rinaldi said it looked like she was leaving. In a hurry."

"Cacciatore in on this too?"

"Deep as can be, it looks like," Yigael responded.

"On it," Jacques said, busting out the door.

"Chat soon," Anna said, in tow.

CHAPTER TWENTY-EIGHT

Rome

Yigael looked out the window with a grim expression. The urgency to find Maria was paramount. She was confronted with dual peril, one from her abductors and the other, her medical crisis.

A brooding Valentina, lost in thought, mindlessly tapped her index finger on the arm of her chair.

Justin stepped outside for a walk.

Francesco sat at his desk, working on his Sunday homily. Having no success, he pitched his pencil into the holder and dropped his face into his hands.

Just as Justin returned, the *ping* of Francesco's phone steered everyone in his direction. He stared at a number he didn't recognize and picked it up. "Francesco Ricci speaking."

"Monsignor Ricci, this is Michael Levin at *La Carta*."

The color drained from Francesco's face.

"I've discovered some information about a missing nun. Sister Maria Caruso, the new bank executive. She might be in possession of a file that could potentially harm the

Church. I'm seeking more details and found that she is a member of your church. Can I swing by, ask you a few questions?"

Francesco covered his phone and said, under his breath, "*La Carta,* Levin." And then he put the call on speaker. "I'm ... sorry, but what is this about?"

Levin said again, "Sister Maria Caruso, the bank's new forensic accountant is apparently missing. Can you answer some questions?"

"I don't know anything. I don't really have ... uh ...?" Francesco glanced at Yigael. "There's really nothing I can tell you." His eyes darted here and there in a show of discomfort.

Well-versed in handling the press, Yigael reached for the phone. "Levin, this is Yigael Dorian."

Well, well, well, Michael Levin thought. *Yigael Dorian.* There was story here, *di sicuro.* For sure.

"Long time, Yigael. Welcome back to Rome." Yigael had granted Levin a rare interview when the top spy decided to break with the Mossad and enter private life as an antiquities dealer.

"It's 'no comment' unless you agree to an embargo." Yigael had decided it was better to talk to the guy, keep him in check, rather than turn him loose to discover more and run with the story.

Levin thought that something was better than nothing. "On my way over," he said.

At that, Justin said, "I really must go." With that, he darted out the door again.

Valentina drew in breath. "What was that about?"

Francesco murmured, "Don't know," but his thoughts were elsewhere.

Yigael seemed deep in thought, too, and remained that way, even as they shifted locations into the rectory, until the reporter's arrival some twenty minutes later.

"Valentina," Levin said in greeting. Levin knew her from countless previous interviews.

He nodded at Yigael and Francesco.

"Have a seat, Michael." Francesco swiveled a chair beside his desk and gestured for Levin to take it.

"There must be something going on to bring these two together at a church," Michael Levin said dryly to Francesco as he faced the somber-looking group of three.

Before Levin could get the upper hand, Yigael took the lead, "We're aware that Rinaldi's filled you in." He recalled his fury when Francesco gave him the tip on that news. "We don't know why or where, but yes, Maria Caruso is missing. We can confirm it."

Levin's face maintained a mild expression. "Do you mean to convince me that Yigael Dorian has come to Rome to look for a sick nun?"

"She's in danger. And I was here."

"Polizia?"

Yigael gave Levin a scornful glower. "I told you she was in danger."

"And you work alone ...."

"I've made a career of finding people."

"Right. And what about the other half of the story ... the secret bank account and the payoffs?" Yigael groaned and looked away. *Rinaldi.* He spent twenty minutes answering Levin's questions, giving him the exact details Orio had. That's all they had, really.

"What can you tell me about a link between Cardinal Justin Parina at the VAT and a woman named Katarina Silva?"

Yigael opened his mouth to speak, but Monsignor Ricci decided to take this one.

"I did come across the Silva name in my uncle's files," he said, "but I have no idea who that person is and no inclination to find out. No ethics violation has ever arisen regarding my uncle, Cardinal Antonio Ricci, or Cardinal Parina, for that matter. Both are held in the highest esteem and are beyond reproach."

The monsignor feared that Justin speeding away told another story, but that was speculation he would keep to himself.

No newbie to dealing with the press, Valentina jumped in, "Look, you must hold the story. She could ..."

Levin recalled his encounter with the nun. They were nose to nose, picking up her belongings less than a week back. "Look, I'll hold the Sister Maria story, but you have to promise me an exclusive on the rest."

"Just as soon as we can give it to you," Yigael said. "My word on that."

Levin nodded a quick confirmation and left. The truth was, they didn't have any more information than what the priest had given him, and he couldn't write a story on conjecture. But at least he knew there was one. And when the time came, it was his to tell.

Jacques and Anna picked up the trail as Dara Damahdi rounded the southeast corner of St. Peter's Square in a most surprising vehicle.

"Holy hell, what is that thing?" Jacques said. "What she's driving ... Dara's probably pretty well off, but I don't think *that* well off."

They tailed her until she arrived home, parking the opulently outfitted auto inside a locked garage. They staked out the building, taking turns napping after sharing pasta from the food mart down the block. Small talk filled their awake time. "Registered to Cardinal Angelico Cacciatore," Anna said, fumbling with her tablet.

"What?" Jacques said, cranking his eyes open and rubbing his face.

"The car, the Mercedes ... belongs to Cacciatore. And it matches the pope mobile."

"How do you know that?"

"*La Carta*. They printed a story on it because it was so controversial. They called it a '*highly irregular and ostentatious move*' for a cleric."

"You can say that again. Why is Dara driving it?"

"No idea, but maybe 'Cacciatore,'" Anna said with emphasis, "wants to get it out of the line of fire, remove it from the gossip mill."

"Or," Jacques tossed in, "well, he would never actually *drive* it, so he leaves it with his, ah, chauffeur ...?"

"Who knows what her title is these days." Anna giggled.

The lights went on in Dara's flat at 6:00 AM. By 7:30, she was out the door and back in the customized Benz.

She pulled out, and Yigael's duo tagged along.

Dara stopped to pick up Massimo Pugia, where they paused at a *bar* for *due caffè*, then headed north toward the Vatican, but she didn't stop there. Bypassing Vatican City, she crossed the River Tiber and drove into a quiet neighborhood of wide avenues and elegant buildings. She turned onto a narrow leafy street of lavish residences, all with front gardens, and stopped in front of a nineteenth-century Art Nouveau-styled palazzo. Cardinal Angelico Cacciatore appeared from a side door. He slid into the vehicle. She reversed the route, ending up at the IOR.

Several hours later, she and Massimo stepped back out and took off in the Mercedes. An hour later, outside Rome, they stopped.

After shadowing them, Jacques and Anna pulled into a thick belt of stone pine where they could maintain surveillance. They watched as Massimo went Inside. Dara stayed outside.

What was this place? An old convent? It seemed so.

A while later, Massimo joined Dara outside, and they left.

"So," Anna said.

Jacques eyed her. "Yep."

This had to be Sister Maria's location.

They headed off, following the "cousins" back to Vatican City.

CHAPTER TWENTY-NINE

Velletri

THE TINY ROOM WAS SPARE. TWO HIGH-SET WINDOWS OFFERED A scrap of light onto dull gray walls. The only furnishings were a wooden desk, a single bed, and a straight-back chair. A small cross hung on the wall above the desk.

Maria had spent two sleepless nights staring at the water-stained ceiling, thinking of the events of Monday evening. It was only just before the break of dawn, the inky night sky turning a hazy purple through her tiny windows, that she'd dozed off. And both nights, she dreamed of her father, awakening her to his comforting words she believed were intended to soothe her fearful soul.

She heard a noise outside her confines.

The door unlocked, and a nun appeared, carrying two small towels and a meager meal of rusks, marmalade, and tea, the same breakfast as the day before. The nun set down the tray and handed her a towel.

Maria knew the drill. She followed the nun out the open door, using the wall for balance.

She made note of the guard that flanked her cell—the driver that had kidnapped her. They were, apparently, tag-teaming each other for guard duty. She stepped into the lavatory, two doors down from her quarters, and washed up as best she could with no shower, using the small sink, an abrasive bar of soap, and a hand towel. Maria shot the nun a look after that, and the middle-aged woman moved closer to the entrance, tipping her head down as Maria relieved herself.

"You can't keep me here," Maria said on exiting the toilet area. "I need medical care."

The nun shook her head and motioned Maria out. She left the facilities and returned to her room. Just as the nun shuffled out, the guard locked her back in. Maria noted that at least the jittery woman acknowledged her for the first time. *Progress.*

She blinked a few times, tears of frustration letting go. Her focus shifted to her medications. She needed day-to-day drugs to stay alive. How long could she survive without them? That theory had never been tested.

By midmorning, she'd finished her prayers. With nothing else to occupy her time, she thought about her dream from earlier, her sweet life in the convent, and her angel, Sister Delfina. *How would she feel about this? I wish she were here.*

Exhausted, Maria fell into another restless sleep. She was roused by a vibration on the other side of her door. "Who else have you talked to about the account?" the low, angry voice asked.

She couldn't recognize the voice but was sure it wasn't either of the men who'd grabbed her outside the pizzeria. If she had to guess, she'd pin it on the Massimo person who'd dragged her into Cardinal Cacciatore's office for a chewing out five days ago, even though she'd heard him utter only one word, "Sure."

She sat up in bed and saw his shadow outside the door.

Maria knew that no matter what she said, it would be nowin. And not answering this one question might be the only thing keeping her alive.

"I'll be back," the man growled, and his aggressive footsteps faded.

They'd conducted a detailed inspection of her attire and taken her purse, her cane, and her lucky charm. How disappointed they must've been when they opened the flash drive to discover years' worth of messages to her late father.

By the true grace of God, they hadn't noticed her drop her phone. But inside that bleak cell, Maria faced a critical turning point, and she dared to think what she never would have, not in her wildest imagination.

I'm not going to get out of here alive.

Then she thought of her *papà*. *Oh, yes, I am.*

CHAPTER THIRTY

Rome

Trying for a lead to Maria earlier, Yigael had spoken with several contacts who worked in Vatican City. One had for years laundered money for Israeli criminals. Another had, ironically, investigated the very same illegal money laundering for which the Church had been recently outed. Still, he'd come up empty.

Locked down, he thought. *Where to next?*

His phone rang. Anna.

On hanging up, Yigael formulated a plan.

Turning his attention back to the group, now seated and quiet, each processing what had happened, he said, "We've had a break. Jacques and Anna have found her in a convent south of here. Il Convento di Santa Veronica Giuliani. It's in Velletri. That's our best info, anyway."

"Thank God," Valentina said.

"It usually pans out," Justin said, having returned shortly after Levin's departure, bearing gifts of fruit and a *torta alla crema*. "With the bad comes the good. Right on the heels. I've seen it time and time again."

Yigael wasn't so sure. There hadn't been much good to come after his wife and young son were killed in a terrorist bombing in Jerusalem so many years ago. He turned away.

Valentina knew exactly what he was thinking—Yigael's grief endured and arose unexpectedly at its own choosing—and she ached for him. Yet it was she who had helped bring him back from the brink by dragging him into the field again to dirty his hands in a dig. Eventually, he came to, enough to feel the thrill of finding an ancient artifact of value.

Yigael turned back, refusing to meet Valentina's gaze. "It is essential for you all to go about your routines as if nothing has happened. Justin, go home and get a good night's sleep. I want you at work tomorrow, business as usual. Francesco, same for you. And, Val, if everything goes well, I figure Maria will be safe in our hands by midday tomorrow, and I'd like you to be around. She'll need you."

The four of them then went silent, each absorbing this latest development and feeling relieved that Maria would soon be out of malevolent hands.

Orio rounded the corner into the conference room just then, and, in unison, they turned their attention to the priest.

Picking up on the vibe, he asked nervously, "Hey, what's going on? Why's everybody acting like I just survived a plane crash? Oh! Is it Maria, did you find her?" He clasped his hands together.

Just as Justin was about to respond, Yigael broke in, "Rinaldi, we *believe* we've found her."

"What? Truly? Oh, my ... oh, oh, oh, what a relief."

Without a hint of a smile, Yigael added, "But you need to leave town."

"Leave town ... leave town?"

"You're too close to her. They'll come after you if they have to."

Orio paled. "Oh."

"Don't do anything more. I mean it. Where does your family come from?"

"My family? Well, I have heaps of brothers and sisters … I haven't seen them in forever … everyone lives in Bari."

"Great, going south, and it's far enough away. It's the best place for you. Look, Orio, it's 'out of sight, out of mind' with these guys. You'll be fine once you're no longer visible to them."

The priest nodded.

"When Jacques and Anna get back here," Yigael said, "they'll take you over to your place to pack up."

He nodded again and rose to go.

"By the way, Rinaldi," Yigael said, stopping him, "you've done more than anyone could've asked or expected, quite frankly. We wouldn't have any leads were it not for you. You found her phone, and that single snapshot of Dara Damahdi …. You have my thanks."

"You have the thanks of all of us, old chum," Francesco said, clapping him on the shoulder.

Overcome with emotion, Orio dared not say anything, but those words were just the nudge he needed to stay on task. For Maria. "I'll just go upstairs for a bit, if that's all right, and wait on your … operatives." He needed space.

"You go ahead," Francesco said.

"Well, I guess that's it for now," Yigael said, after watching Orio go. "I've got a bit of work to do yet."

A bit? Valentina knew better. "I'll be off then too. You know where the key is when you wrap for the night here."

With everyone scattered, and Yigael awaiting the arrival of Jacques and Anna, he spent some time on that other matter, as promised to Valentina.

Soon after, they walked in.

Yigael, Jacques, and Anna hovered over blueprints they'd discovered in a public records system online showing the interior construction of Convento di Santa Veronica Giuliani, a sprawling religious community in Velletri.

"Here's what I need now. First, I need you to take Father Orio Rinaldi to his flat to pack and then the bus station." Yigael handed them a list of the preparations needed to get Maria out, along with a photo of her. "Then, set these things up. And after that, sleep for a few hours."

Jacques and Anna perused the list, exchanged a secret smile, and then burst out laughing.

"What?" Yigael asked as his bushy brows drooped.

"Sleep? With this lineup?"

CHAPTER THIRTY-ONE

Bari

Despite zero warning, Father Orio Rinaldi arrived in his hometown that evening to a welcome fit for a visiting dignitary. All his brothers and sisters and their assorted children waved and shouted as he pulled into the bus station.

He barely remembered his hometown, having been back but twice since his seminary days. He'd always been terrified of his parents, his mother in particular, but they were dead and gone now, and, for the first time, he was eager to pick up again with his siblings.

The visiting priest stepped off the bus unsteady, his legs prickling from the long journey. Nieces and nephews rushed forward and nearly knocked him over as they crowded around, pulling on his cassock and jumping up and down.

A loud voice that belonged to his eldest brother, Leonardo, named after his father, shouted, "That's enough! Go on now." Leo flapped his arms at the youngsters, and they all scrambled. Turning to his brother and patting his shoulder, he said, "You'll stay with us, Orio."

Leo, at age fifty, was a jovial fellow who worked in city maintenance. It was plain to the priest that his eldest brother had taken their father's place as head of the family.

Back at Leo's, with a mix of savory nibbles and sweet confections on a platter before him, despite his worries over Maria, he dove in enthusiastically.

A barrage of questions rushed him, which he'd anticipated and liked answering, but, after a time, thoughts of his friend intruded again, and he was hard-pressed to pay attention.

"Orio?" Leo boomed, sensing his brother's fatigue and getting to his feet.

"Yes?"

"Let's go out for a bit while the kids settle down for bed."

The two walked into old Bari where tight-knit locals lived a free and easy way, with open doors and women visible inside making pasta. Up ahead, stood the town's famous eleventh-century church, the Basilica di San Nicola's. Under the twinkling stars, it was even more overbearing and majestic than he recalled.

Orio nodded toward the church as they passed by. "I don't feel I belong there anymore."

"I wonder whether you ever did." Leo cast a furtive glance at his brother. "Here, let's sit," he said as they came to a bench in front of a *panificio* with a *For Sale* sign in front.

The two brothers got reacquainted, and the mutual affection put Orio's heart at ease, if for a moment.

That evening, Orio slept soundly in a room with lace curtains and knick-knacks on every available shelf.

Waking with his mind buzzing, he dressed and met his brother and sister Isabelle at the breakfast table. Leo's wife, Eleanora, stepped in from the kitchen *con caffè*.

"*Buongiorno*, Orio," she said, dropping a sugar cube into her cup.

"How long will you be staying?"

To that, his response was, "Do you know how far Palermo is from here?"

And to that, the room of chatty loved ones fell silent.

CHAPTER THIRTY-TWO

Velletri

At noon, a freshly painted van with Enel Gas & Electricity emblazed on each side pulled onto the off-the-beaten-path to Il Convento di Santa Veronica Giuliani. Velletri was a good-sized town fifty-nine kilometers outside Rome, but no one seemed to pay any attention to this relic if the grounds were any indication. An overgrown field of wildflowers encircled the brick building, interspersed with dry patches of dirt. If not for the intermittent activity yesterday, the place would look abandoned.

"Here we go," Jacques said, taking off.

The mood inside the truck was quiet, with natural tension, though Jacques and Anna were not nervous as such. They'd worked on many of these assignments and considered this one routine. An unknown was if they'd be confronting Maria's captors. Another was whether the young nun was even there. That had not been verified.

The truck came to a stop at the front entrance. Jacques got

out. Dressed in a tan jumpsuit with an *Enel* logo on a pocket flap, he rapped the knocker at the convent door.

As he waited, Anna hopped out, similarly dressed but donning a canister that appeared to be an aerosol fire extinguisher in a carry strap. In plain sight was her preferred method of operating. She walked to the corner of the building that was upwind and released a few short spurts from her hose. Then she posted up behind Jacques and let another go for good measure. Her canister did not contain an extinguishing agent but a solution of less than 2PPB (two parts per billion) of mercaptan—the odorizing agent in gas that was not harmful at that level. Most of what they did involved a fair amount of persuasion. People were quick to believe and easy to spook. They were banking on both.

When the door opened, they faced a young nun. "Gas leak, Sister. Emergency. Please, direct me to your prioress. We must get everyone out. Hurry."

The young nun took one sniff of the air, turned, and ran back inside, yelling, "Mother Margherita, Mother Margherita. Where are you? *Emergenza!*"

The unflappable abbess peered out from her office doorway, rimless reading glasses perched on the tip of her nose. "What is it?"

"Mother, the gas company is here. There's a leak ... gads, I can smell it! Can't you? Could we," she turned toward Jacques, who was right behind her with Anna in tow, "have an ... explosion?"

"Calm down, Sister Lorna," Mother Margherita scolded. "You're making matters worse." She turned toward the utility workers. "Now, what have we here?"

"Truly, Mother, there is no time to waste," Jacques said. "The fumes are becoming noxious. We need to get everyone out."

"I understand," Mother Margherita said. "Sister Lorna, go ring the emergency bell three times. Go now."

At the sound of the warning bell, nuns rushed in from all corners of the convent—the kitchen, chapel, and workrooms—and moved swiftly in tandem toward the main entrance.

Jacques rounded them all up. "Check the basement," he directed to Anna. "Gather about fifty meters back," he yelled to everyone else, ushering them outside.

Scrutinizing each nun, Jacques could see that Maria was not among them. He wasn't surprised. Nevertheless, he asked Mother Margherita, "Is that everyone?"

"Yes, of course," she answered, the lie sending high color to her cheeks that Jacques did not miss.

CHAPTER THIRTY-THREE

Velletri

The stripes of warm, fuzzy light the morning sun had created across her cold, dank walls were gone. *Must be close to noon*, Maria thought. It was a beautiful day somewhere beyond her cell. The nun would shuffle in shortly to replace the breakfast tray with lunch, and Maria would ask for another bathroom break. But then she'd be alone, again, for the duration.

The solid wood door to her cell was locked and guarded, and two high-set windows made her options for escape seem dismal.

Turning an eagle eye on every object in her sightline proved fruitless, but driven by desperation, she kept at it. The floor vent was far too small, and even with the chair, the windows were too high and narrow for her to squeeze through. The door was the only way out, but she couldn't force it open.

Maria no longer feared that someone would kill her—at least not before learning what she had and what she knew, or she'd be dead by now. She figured they would just wait her out until desperation broke her.

Footsteps coming fast up the hallway sent her adrenaline flowing. It couldn't be the nun that fed her, for she shuffled her feet in a soft, sweeping motion. And it wasn't the man with the angry voice, Massimo, the one vying for information. He had a long, forceful gait.

The lock on her door clicked. She backed into the corner opposite and waited.

She heard the footsteps retreat even faster.

Still, she waited.

But no one entered.

It was unusually quiet.

The stillness became even more pronounced with each passing second.

She stood in the corner, staring trance-like at the doorknob.

The spell was broken by the blare of an alarm.

Maria approached the door, straining to listen. She heard a flurry of footsteps then, mostly echoing away from her direction, but that was it. So she wrapped her hand around the knob, made the sign of the cross, and turned.

It opened.

She peeked into the hallway. She could hear voices, but they were far off too. Maria shot out of her room and scanned for an exit. That's when it hit her that not just her cell, but the hallway, was identical to her home in Palermo. This was revelatory.

The stairwell.

To her chagrin, the one at the beginning of her wing led to the first floor and a basement door that was locked.

Think!

Okay, yes.

A laundry chute. That'd be her best chance for escape.

Find it.

Maria scurried back up the stairs, down the hall, and into the lavatory, where she studied it for the first time. Under the sink, she found some nearly invisible seams. She pressed around them, but nothing gave way. Disappointed but refusing to give up, she thought there had to be another way out.

As she turned to leave, she saw behind the bathroom door a white ventilation grate mounted to the wall. It was huge, and it sagged. Maria dropped to her knees. She inspected the grate and tried removing it.

It rattled, and she froze.

Hearing nothing in the hallway—no one within earshot—she twisted the top two screws with great care and placed them on the tile floor. The grate bent open, but not enough for her to crawl in. The bottom screws were rusty, stuck.

She was starting to sweat, and her heart was, once again, thumping in her chest when her father's voice broke through the chaos. *"You'll be fine, mi amore. Just you, Dio, and your beautiful mind."* She closed her eyes to clear all thoughts and let an idea come, as her father had instructed.

She dashed back to her room, her limp now a secondary concern, if that.

She spotted the butter knife on the breakfast tray and snatched it up. On her way out, she closed the door. It would only add seconds more to her escape, but every bit counted.

With great care, she used the edge of the knife as a flathead screwdriver and twisted until both screws jiggled free. The grate dropped down, and she faced a large hole.

The upper-floor rooms in her childhood home had used chutes to lower linens and garments to the basement, just like this one. It still did, only this one had fallen out of use.

Giving silent thanks for her slight frame for the first time, Maria climbed into the basket, still in place, as if waiting on towels and sheets to fill it up.

Inside her escape route, she frowned at the hole in the wall, a dead giveaway as to how she'd gotten out, but nothing she could do about that.

This was not the first time Maria had taken a ride such as this. As a young girl in Palermo, she'd pulled herself up and down various chutes for entertainment in her early somber circumstances. She recalled how Sister Delfina and her beloved Tori knew of her antics but had kept her secret from the reverend mother.

Maria reached for the pulley rope and, hand over hand, began to lower herself. Moving fast, the lift hit the bottom with a *thump*. She listened for sounds. Hearing none, she opened the chute door into the basement.

Sunlight, thick with dust, flooded her line of vision. The commotion upstairs had died away, leaving the convent as silent as the grave. The musty smell was overwhelming and caused Maria to cough and wrinkle her nose.

Now what?

Time was of the essence. She prayed the basement held her path to freedom.

"You, Dio, and your beautiful mind ...."

A tunnel.

She scanned her surroundings, hoping to find it. The priest hole was an ancient escape route for persecuted priests on the run. While many monasteries had them, some had been sealed off in modern times.

Maria first had to locate a concealed doorway that would open to the underground tunnel and then hope it would lead her to freedom.

She inspected the area, feeling all around the walls, pushing in as she went. She came upon an old, rickety wine rack set below a window. She ducked to keep out of the sightline and jiggled it, finding it wobbly. She pulled. The wine rack slid sideways, revealing a short staircase behind it.

There it was—a lump formed in her throat.

"Now or never ...."

ANNA-MARIE MANNES mounted the steps to the second floor where Yigael had predicted Maria would be kept. The first room she entered appeared to be an office—an out-of-place one with shiny, up-to-date hardware. She'd come back to that. She searched every other room, all bare. There was but one left.

As she approached the last door on the right, she lost hope when the knob turned but peeked in anyway.

An unmade bed, two used towels, and a tray of half-eaten food told her the room had been occupied.

But of Maria, there was no sign.

She looked around the empty cell for more conclusive clues. Anything.

Finding nothing of value, she exited at full pace, sped down the stairs she'd just come up, and swerved onto the main floor landing.

Running up and down the other hallways, Anna found nothing. The windows in every room were not built for a human to fit through, even a small one. *No escaping the nunnery,* she thought. The kitchen did have giant windows for better ventilation. That was it. But Maria couldn't have made it there unnoticed, she reasoned.

And Jacques, who was up front by the van, hadn't confirmed that he had her.

Maybe the bathrooms?

She ran back toward Maria's cell and into the closest lavatory. The windows were all intact. It looked like they hadn't been opened in decades. She swept the room and then figured she'd better check each stall rather than just peek under them. In the end, finding nothing, she turned to exit.

Whoa! The hole in the wall. The unhinged grate. She knelt and peered down into it. She took in the metal contraption at the bottom, the *laundry chute.*

Man, Anna thought, *did she train with the Mossad?*

She pushed through the door that took her to the stairs leading to the main floor.

From there, she found a door that was locked and required a key, like all the other ancient doors. It had to go to the basement. It made the most sense. She considered kicking it in when she heard sirens.

Police? They weren't part of the plan.

CHAPTER THIRTY-FOUR

Velletri

MARIA SLIPPED INSIDE HER ESCAPE ROUTE, PULLING THE WINE rack as tight as she could so as not to leave an overt clue. One would have to know the tunnel existed to find it. She imagined a couple of nuns did, the older ones, but doubted her captors would.

The tunnel was high enough that Maria didn't have to stoop but pitch black, much darker than she recalled from her childhood. And as she felt her way through, she noticed the walls were so damp they dripped. Her former sense of whimsical adventure was replaced by an adrenaline-powered survival instinct, which had her nerves fraught with tension.

She tried to conjure up the image of her father again to assuage her fear and couldn't do it. But as she trudged along, Tori and Pippi the bunny popped into her head.

She relaxed a bit as she remembered the day she learned of the tunnel, and her old favorite nursery rhyme flooded her mind. "*Batti batti le manine ... Che son belle e piccoline ... Son piccoline come te un, due, tre ....*

"... *Un, due, tre!*" Finally, the toe of her shoe met a wall, stopping her forward movement. What was she facing? Maria felt around. A door. A slatted, wooden door. She fumbled for a latch. Finding it, she pulled the door open to seven steps up and her first slit of daylight.

Maria entered the small stairwell, closing the wooden door behind her. She climbed the steps. Unlike the covering to the priest hole back in Palermo, this lid was more solid and twice the size. Luckily, she was too. She raised her arms and pushed up with all her might. It opened, falling to the right with a bang.

The sun blinded her.

She crawled out and, still on her knees, pushed the heavy lid back over.

She was free.

A field of lavender shot out in every direction. She was at the backside of the convent but far enough away take in a 360-degree view of everything. She could see the hullabaloo out front, nuns gathered, a utility vehicle. And the police, sirens blaring and blue lights flashing, they were among the mayhem.

With no time to dwell, she tucked several errant strands of her sweaty, sable hair back into her hairclip and started crawling. She stayed low in the field, creeping in an arc away from the convent.

Eyeing the tree line about a hundred or so meters ahead, she scrambled toward the woods.

CHAPTER THIRTY-FIVE

Velletri

THE NUNS, MUTTERING AND MOVING AMONG THEMSELVES IN front of their convent, had come to a complete stop in a long silent tableau by the time the *carabinieri* screeched to a halt.

Jacques Ignatius gaped at this setback. *All we need.*

Four uniformed federal soldiers bound out of their vehicle and took in the scene. Three *carabinieri* had weapons drawn.

Mother Margherita stepped forward as the one in charge approached. The nuns broke their tableau and huddled closer to each other so they could hear the exchange.

"What's this about?" Mother Margherita looked down at the mustachioed officer.

"We're investigating possible drug operations going on here." The *carabiniere* uncharacteristically took off his cap.

Mother Margherita's nostrils flared as an audible gasp arose among the sisters. "Why on earth would you think that?"

"A neighbor reported seeing two swarthy, suspicious-looking men arrive here earlier in a vehicle that appeared, ahem, out of the ordinary. They say it's been ongoing as of late.

And now, with this … well, what *is* happening here?" The carabiniere gave Jacques and the Enel gas van a once-over and waved his hand around, pointing to the convent and then at the sisters and the truck.

Mother Margherita stared blank-faced at the officer.

Jacques saw his chance. "Officer, we had a report of a gas leak and had to usher out the sisters. We found the problem. It's been fixed, and we'll be on our way."

Just then, Anna exited the building on the heels of a straggling nun. She gave a barely perceptible shake of her head.

"May we get the sisters back inside, please?" Jacques asked.

The lead officer narrowed his eyes, not quite believing the story. Nevertheless, he said, "Okay, get going."

As the Jeeps moved off, Anna returned to the truck, and Jacques ushered the nuns back into their sanctuary.

"You're in good shape, Mother. It was a small leak, and it's fixed. You should have no further problem." Jacques smiled, and, after the last nun disappeared inside, he jogged back to the van.

"Nothing?" he asked as he jumped into the passenger seat.

"No sign of her here," Anna said as she pulled away from the curb.

"They may've taken her to a second location." Jacques shook his head in frustration. "And now, between nosy neighbors and the authorities' radical reaction—"

"No, they don't have her, but she was imprisoned here," Anna said. She explained about her open cell door, the grate, and the laundry chute.

"Okay, so she's on her own. With no money and no transportation, no meds."

"I'm not so sure about that. She basically just escaped from *Château d'If*."

"…Right."

"*Chateau d'if*. From *The Count of Monte Cristo*? It's a real prison off the coast of Marseille?"

Ah, yes. She'd brought him back to his college days with that comment, but it got him thinking. "So, where would she be? And by the way," Jacques added, "that head nun ignored Maria in the face of danger, didn't get her out. Turned ten shades of red when I confronted her."

Makes me sick. Anna looked out her window. "But somebody helped her. The door to her cell was open. Maybe it was the mother superior, defying the Church, and that's what had her so nervous."

"We'll think about that later," Jacques said, pulling away from the curb. "For now, we'd better scour the streets. Maybe we'll get lucky and spot her."

CHAPTER THIRTY-SIX

Velletri

Maria shot to her feet and began running through the woodlands while silently thanking God for the police cars that had captured everyone's attention. She'd been able to get farther away than she thought possible. But not able to keep up the pace, she stopped, smoothed her wrinkled skirt, dusted herself off, and began to walk. It wasn't until she stopped, hands on knees for a breather, that she realized this was the longest she'd gone without thinking about her limp. She'd never so much as left a room without her cane before this week. That made her curious, but there was no time to dwell on it.

The sun was a beast. She was thirsty, and a bite to eat wouldn't hurt. What she wanted to do above all, though, was find a phone and call Orio. But she knew better than to entertain that idea. She had to strategize.

Who knew how many people were involved with this Silent Mistress Fund and her kidnapping? She determined it was best not to contact anyone at the IOR or Casa Veronesi. And certainly not Valentina. She'd put her in enough jeopardy just by asking her to meet. She prayed that *Dottoressa* Vella was not harassed or harmed by their brief interaction.

That didn't leave many options.

Calling Monsignor Ricci crossed her mind. Orio said he could be trusted. And Church lines weren't bugged as standard. As soon as she got to a town and found a phone, that would be her best bet. Yes, that was what she would do—call Francesco at Chiesa di Sant'Agata.

Emerging from the woods, when she felt safe enough, she stopped a young girl in uniform who must've been on her way back to school from lunch break.

"*Mi scusi*, I've been visiting the convent and must've taken a wrong turn. Can you tell me where to catch the bus?" Maria had no idea where she would be heading. She just had to get out of this neighborhood. She'd take the first bus to come along.

"*Certamente, suora.*" Then she took a good look at the young nun. "But are you all right? There's blood on your face and your clothes—"

"I'm fine." Maria forced a smile. "Just took a tumble in the woods. I'm fine," she repeated. She wanted a phone, but she needed privacy, too, not to be overheard.

"If you're sure ... well ... the girl pointed out directions and said, "I would take you there, but I must get to class."

"God bless you, *bambina,* thank you."

"Not at all*, Suora.*"

When Maria reached the bus stop, she realized she had no money and would need €6 to board. She gulped back her shame and ventured forth toward a friendly-looking young woman who appeared to be of college age.

"I'm so sorry," she said, "but I left the convent forgetting my coin purse. I'm terribly embarrassed to ask, but could you provide the fare for me? I must get, uh, back." Maria's ears reddened in mortification.

"I'm sorry, Sister," she said, "but I have no extra change." The girl looked around at the others waiting, three women and an older gentleman. She hoped they hadn't heard the exchange because she felt self-conscious about refusing a nun. But they had taken in Maria's appearance and, thinking her a liar or worse, turned their backs.

Trying to assuage her guilt, the young woman justified her refusal. *A sister asking for bus fare? She sure doesn't look like one.*

Maria didn't know what to do next. She turned to leave when the only man in the group came forward.

"Sister, where are you from?"

The man was in his sixties, wearing an open-neck shirt and a flat cap with a herringbone pattern. He held his bus ticket in his hand.

"From Sicily, sir," Maria said. "I was born in Falcone."

"You don't say. Thought I recognized your accent. I have people near there. Carini."

"Ah, yes." Not knowing what else to say, Maria smiled.

"I'll get your ticket. Allow me," the man said. He gave a scathing look to the young girl who'd refused to help and walked to the ticket vending machine. He returned and handed Maria her ticket. Then, he removed a pipe from his shirt pocket and cradled it unlit between his teeth.

"I'm very grateful, sir." Maria's relief showed.

Noting her general appearance, nervousness, and pale visage, he asked, "Are you all right?"

"Oh, yes, of course. Don't mind me," she said. "I was minding some children at the convent. I'm afraid I got too involved with their playtime in the sandbox. And then, I was running late and had no time to, uh, freshen up."

The man in the flat cap nodded.

The bus arrived, and he ushered Maria up the steps.

It eased away from the curb but came to a sudden stop as an Enel Gas & Electricity van cut them off.

Must be a leak somewhere, Maria thought.

CHAPTER THIRTY-SEVEN

Velletri

Mother Margherita had reported the mayhem at the convent to Massimo Pugia as soon as the police had left the premises.

Massimo had screamed in fury, "Lock the place down!" The man had snapped.

He'd arrived at the convent in record time.

Furious with the slow-witted nun who answered the door, he pushed her aside, stomping toward the room on the second floor. From her office, the mother superior saw him pass by and ran out to follow.

Massimo took the stairs two at a time with Mother Margherita not far behind.

"Who unlocked this door?" Massimo demanded of the head nun, who was breathless from the run up the stairs.

"No one did." She withered under Massimo's scrutiny. "She must've done it herself." She was racking up lies as if it were peak blooming season, and her purple fields were ablaze with golden tulips.

Massimo entered the room. Giving it a quick scan and seeing nothing helpful, he banged back into the hallway, opening the door next to hers, then dipping his head into the lavatory. He scanned it and wound a look around the door. The grate on the floor. The hole in the wall. He examined it more closely and stomped back out. "Take me downstairs."

Once in the basement, Massimo saw nothing out of sorts. It was a moist, dusty space with old shelving, empty canning jars, old cans of food, likely expired, some rusty garden tools that hadn't been touched in what seemed like decades. And a rickety wine shelf, which was off kilter. He moved to it like a bear on the prowl and shoved open the door to the tunnel. "What's this?" he asked the nun.

"It's an old priest hole."

"In English," he barked. What she'd said was plain enough. But nothing he'd ever heard of.

"It's … it's an old escape route for persecuted—"

"There's an escape route built into the building?"

"No one knows it's here. Please—"

"She did! And that's how she did it." For an instant, he took his hat off to the tiny nun for her brazen feat. But then he wrinkled his nose in distaste. "What's that bloody smell?" he asked.

Mother Margherita hadn't quite recovered her senses, astonished as she was by Maria's audacity, but she said, "Gas leak. We had a gas leak earlier. It's fixed now."

"Gas leak! What do you mean?"

The abbess filled Massimo in on the earlier events as they both mounted the stairs.

On the ride back into the city, Massimo knew he had no choice but to report the screw-up to his boss. While Cardinal Cacciatore didn't know—didn't want to know—the details of Maria's capture, he did insist on being kept abreast of trouble.

Not knowing any way around the mess, Massimo made the call.

Having explained everything else, he wrapped it up. "And the gas leak was bogus."

Cacciatore listened in silent fury to the upshot of the day's events. "So, someone figured out where you took her," he said.

"Yes, but we can't be sure if someone helped her escape and is holding her or whether she did it alone and is somewhere ... else." Massimo sounded calm, but wild trepidation about this turn of events attacked his stomach. Life was cushy at the IOR, and Pepper appreciated the shelter the Church provided. He didn't want to aggravate her any more than the man paying their salary.

At the end of Massimo's recitation, the cardinal said in a steely tone, "Find her."

CHAPTER THIRTY-EIGHT

Velletri

With some distance between her and the wacky scene at the convent, a *servito* came into view. Sister Maria decided she'd better get off and find a phone. When the bus stopped, she waved at her kind benefactor and exited the public transportation.

Maria looked down at her attire as the bus pulled away. Her appearance seemed to have worsened, if the disparaging looks from attendants pumping gas were any indication. She was covered in sweat and dirt—and was that blood on her blouse? She had no money, no phone, and looked affright. Who else would possibly help her?

The limp seemed to enhance her overall lack of appeal. She dusted off the white blouse and navy skirt again and wiped the sweat from around her hairline. *I'm going to be okay,* she told herself. She reiterated this mantra as she held her head high, moving inside the Autogrill and passing by its cases full of mouth-watering, paper-wrapped meat and cheese sandwiches and delectable pastries. Maria allowed herself a moment of self-pity. She could use a sandwich but had neither time nor money to indulge. *But at least I'm alive, even if not well and good.*

She was banking on her charm from this point on, as it was all she had left.

As she approached the cashier, she received everything from wide-eyed stares to scowls to pouty faces struck with pity. This made it more difficult to act normally and blend in.

"Dov'è il bagno?" she asked the cashier.

He eyed her, deciding if he wanted her in there.

"I fell off my bike, and I'm supposed to meet a date here," she said, gesturing to her attire. "And now look at me!"

He directed her to the restrooms.

As soon as she entered and relieved herself, she washed her hands and scooped up water from the tap, quenching her thirst. She wiped her chin and studied her reflection in the mirror. No wonder she got all those looks. In addition to dirty and disheveled garments, blood was streaked above her left eye. Surface scratches, thankfully. She recalled they were from a branch when she stood to start running. She blotted the wounds with a towelette until the dried blood flaked off, most of it anyway.

As she shrugged at the image staring back at her, she saw a woman in her early twenties enter the facilities. Dressed like a celebrity with a plunging neckline and hair piled high with sparkly combs holding it all together, she was talking to herself while texting.

Maria turned and deliberately bumped into her. "Excuse me. Oh, I'm so sorry," she said. "May I ... borrow your phone?"

The young woman took a step back and regarded Maria. The diminutive, grimy woman was not from her world, and she didn't know what to make of her.

When it didn't seem like this would bend Maria's way, she struck a casual pose and added, "You should see the other guy."

The young woman snorted, which made Maria release a chuckle.

"I'm Maria, by the way." She figured a name would create more trust but adding "Sister" would've taken it too far.

"Um, Chiara. You need my phone?"

Maria nodded. "Just for a second."

"*Sì.*" Chiara handed it to Maria, staying between her and the door, à la guard dog.

Maria went to a web browser app and plugged in Chiesa di Sant'Agata, then stared at the number as panic set in.

She looked at Chiara. "*Uno momento per favore,*" she said, apologizing for the delay. Then, she pressed the phone to her heart, closed her eyes, and focused. A few seconds later, she opened them.

Maria plugged in a number and put the phone to her ear.

CHAPTER THIRTY-NINE

Rome

TEDDY WEAVER HAD JUST ORDERED A SECOND LILITH, HIS favorite craft beer, when his phone vibrated. *Unknown Caller,* but a local number. Huh. It was Friday, five o'clock, and the Texan was ready to relax. But something told him to answer.

"*Ciao,*" he said.

"Teddy. Um, hello. I doubt you remember, but ... this is Maria, um, from the train." Her voice rose as a question. "We met on the way to—"

"Maria, of course." He gave the two gentlemen he was with an *excuse-me* gesture and stepped outside the fenced-in patio area. "What took you so long?"

Teddy's warm and welcoming voice stirred the heavy emotions she'd been keeping at bay, and she sucked down her tears. "I need a favor. It's a big—" She cut herself off to gain control of her quivering voice.

He picked up on it. "Hey, Maria, what do you need? Anything ...."

"A ride," she said, adding that she'd text him her location but wouldn't be able to contact him after that, because the phone she was using wasn't hers. She didn't release any other details but promised to fill him in later, in person.

Teddy told her to sit tight. He was on his way, and he hung up.

Maria sent him the location via text through the MAPS app.

He confirmed, and she handed the phone back to Chiara, who was no longer on guard. She was, in fact, outside her own head for the first time in months.

"May I?" Chiara asked, dropping her phone in her bag and going for the barrette in Maria's hair. Before Maria could respond, the young woman removed it and was combing through the nun's hair with her fingers. "Give it a little shake."

Maria shook her hair out and ran her own fingers through it as Chiara had done.

Chiara then dug into her purse, searching for something to no avail. She snorted again and took the sunglasses off her head. "Here, they'll help with the, um ...." She placed them gently on Maria. "Look at that. You're a whole new woman."

Maria turned back to the mirror. The oversized designer sunglasses—Jimmy Choo butterfly frames—combined with her loose and untamed hair, had, in fact, hidden the scratches from the tree branch and transformed her. Her new look did appear purposeful. Almost. "Thank you, Chiara, but I couldn't take your expensive eyewear."

"I have three more in the car. Please, it won't get me into Heaven, but it's the least I can do." Chiara wasn't in the business of doing good deeds as standard.

"I do look different," Maria commented, relaxing her shoulders a bit.

"Which I'm guessing is the point. You take care," Chiara said, heading toward a stall.

"It could, by the way," Maria commented at the door.

Chiara turned. "What?"

"Get you into Heaven." Maria smiled and left.

CHAPTER FORTY

Rome

Yigael Dorian stood in front of the conference room window at Chiesa di Sant'Agata, gazing out. He'd covered every base to secure Maria's well-being, including putting *Dottore* Lubrano on standby. He had expected to whisk her away when she was rescued and brought back to Monsignor Ricci's church, but now?

No Maria.

After his team delivered the ominous news, Yigael had Jacques and Anna stay in the Velletri neighborhood and check out transit stations and rental agencies even though Yigael imagined she had no means to pay. But who knew? Maria had proved herself capable of surprising things. If she could bust out of a convent where she was being held prisoner, she could probably sweet-talk her way onto a bus or into a rental car.

Another thought took hold for Yigael. It wouldn't be long before a lack of food and medication would put her in danger equal to what her captors might deliver if they found her first.

He had to locate her.

Yigael glanced at a brooding Valentina. They'd arrived together this morning, and she was back on the phone, checking hospitals for any woman close to Maria's description having been checked in.

Francesco sat at his desk working on his Sunday homily with little success. He finally stood, frustrated, and looked in on Yigael and Valentina in the conference room.

"Excuse me," he said. "I'll be upstairs."

Valentina looked up from a notepad where she'd been crossing off the hospitals she'd called for the second time that week. "Of course, Francesco."

The monsignor had been avoiding this, not wanting to face the truth. But, with the mission to rescue Maria unsuccessful, extreme measures might have to be set in motion.

He went upstairs to his bed chamber. There, having found a more secure home for the elusive evidence discovered by Orio in his late uncle's office, he pulled out the bottom drawer of his nightstand and removed the envelope. He dumped the contents on the bed.

Francesco gathered the bank account info and two photographs. The afternoon sun cast a warm glow across the top image of a young Justin Parina and the woman in question. This one was taken from a closer range than the other.

Francesco had kept his promises of celibacy and obedience since his ordainment almost twenty years ago. His heart belonged to the Lord. He never questioned it or crossed a line. It hadn't always been easy, but it wasn't impossible.

He never wanted to cast judgment on a man he thought he knew. But someone, whoever the photographer was, had captured a connection between Justin and this woman that had him doubting that his friend had kept those same vows.

Francesco would never betray Justin. Despite that, this was the only proof they had of a possible silent mistress. She appeared to be receiving funds from Justin's private account, but there was much more to this story and maybe a chance this information was the line between some dots they couldn't yet connect. Possibly to the fund in question, the reason they were all together. He had to do something. With the envelope in hand, he hustled downstairs.

Francesco was nearly out of breath when he rounded the corner into the conference room. He stretched out his hand with the paperwork.

Yigael turned from the window. "For me?"

"Uh ... uh, no."

"Fran, you okay?" Yigael asked. He nodded toward the envelope.

"Yes. I'm okay." Francesco looked down at the envelope in his hands. Then, to his own surprise, he said, "I need some air," and he headed out.

CHAPTER FORTY-ONE

Velletri

After what felt like the longest wait of her life, Maria watched a red Volkswagen T-Roc cruise into the parking lot of the mart, slow to a roll, and veer in her direction.

She headed toward the car.

Teddy knew it was Maria straight away, mainly by the navy and white outfit, though it was a disheveled mess. But the trendy glasses too large for her and hanging lopsided—not to mention her wild hair and the limp—did not resemble the woman he'd chatted with on the train.

She stepped in.

Teddy peeled out, heading, for lack of instruction, back toward Rome.

They were silent for a bit, and he tried to study her from the corner of his eye without being obvious. That's when he noticed the scrapes on her forehead. "Are you okay? Should we be going to a hospital? Your eye."

"It's nothing. It's okay."

"And your limp. What about your ankle? Do you think it's broken?"

"Yes. But that happened in the second grade. I don't think there's much they can do for it now." She gave him a shrug.

"Okay," he said. Confused and not quite knowing how to respond to this woman in his car, Teddy relied on his default mode and cracked a thin smile. "Oh, I brought you water. It's right there and half a sandwich. The other half is, well, gone." He patted his stomach and then handed her the baggie.

"Thank you, Teddy." She dug into it with vigor but found that, after a few bites, she was too wound up to eat. "Thank you so much for coming. You won't understand this, but I had no one else to call. Well, that's not true. It was between you, Valentina Vella, and the pope."

"The famous Valentina Vella? The archaeologist?"

"The same." And she leaked her own little smile.

"Well, I'm honored," the gentleman in him said, but he wasn't nearly as honored as he was confused by the quip. "But I'm a stranger. Forgive me. I'm happy to see you, but you're right, I don't understand."

Maria sighed. She drank some more water and then some more, finishing it off. "I know," she said. "Okay, okay. It's just hard to know where to start."

"You don't have to tell me anything. But I do need to know where I'm taking you."

"That's one question I don't know the answer to," she said. A burst of tears flooded her cheeks and dripped off her chin.

Teddy leaned forward, unsure what to do. He craned his neck her way and looked to make eye contact, but her head was bowed low and twisted away from him. "Hey, hey there, it's going to be okay."

Maria raised up. "That's enough," she said to herself. Then she heaved a breath and began, "Okay, one second I was working, minding my own business, just trying to do my best and follow the path—"

"I get it. Coding can be tricky like that. Were you working on a pattern program? Maybe I can—"

"No. I don't mean ... I mean the path of God. Although, the Vatican Bank was not what I'd imagined, and Cardinal Cacciatori was not the warmest of bosses, and I'm not sure who in that establishment is following the path of God or any—"

"Whoa, slow down, Maria. The Vatican Bank, a cardinal's your boss, and what?"

"Teddy, I hate to have to tell you this, but I'm *Sister* Maria Caruso. The person the Vatican hired to 'distract' from their latest scandal." She was quoting him from their first and only encounter on the train.

"Oh." Teddy shook his head as if to readjust the suddenly askew perception in his mind. "Okay, I'm going to need a minute." Then he turned his head and stared right at her, trying to find a nun behind those pouty pink lips, dazzling eyes, and silky, tousled locks of wavy, caramel hair.

On the heels of that, he admonished himself for thinking any of those things. "Sister Maria. I'm sorry. Wow, so you're a nun. A nun? You're *the* nun." He felt himself break out in a sweat, basically everywhere. *Am I in shock? Is this what it feels like? Just focus on the road.*

"Hey, Teddy, it's okay. I'm an ordinary person ... but I admit this is out of the ordinary."

"I'll say."

"And call me Maria. Please."

"Absolutely, Maria. Maria. Maria's easier, that's for dang sure."

"I don't know where I'd be right now if not for you. So, while you adjust to all this news, just know that I'm grateful." She tried to hold a smile, but it faded fast from stress and exhaustion.

She turned and looked out the back window. It didn't appear anyone was following them.

Teddy was in deep shock. People didn't surprise him very often. He thought back to the train ride, to his remark regarding the nun the Vatican had hired. He wanted to take the snarky comment back. *Let the past lie.* He reminded himself to, once again, focus. "So, you weren't kidding about phoning the pope. Do you, like, have his direct line?"

"No, but he follows me on Insta."

"Really?"

She gave him a look.

"Funny." Teddy shook his head. "Um, so you don't have your phone on you. I don't see a purse or pockets, and you called on my private line, an unlisted number. How'd you find me?"

"You slid your business card inside the magazine on the train before you gave it to me. It fell out when I was unpacking at Casa Veronesi, where I currently reside."

"... And you memorized it?"

"No, Teddy, I didn't memorize it." She laughed a little at that. "I recalled it to memory."

"I knew it!" He knew the moment he met her, she had more than her share of natural talent. "I knew you were a damn genius, and I wanted you working for my company. My instincts were dead on."

"Were they? Dead on?"

"No." He laughed. "They were not. He could not have imagined for all the chicken fried steak in Texas that he'd been mildly flirting with a nun—a woman of God—on his train ride into Rome.

Well, the icebreakers served as a distraction from Maria's colossal problems and gave her some time to get her head together and her heart rate normalized. But with those out of the way, no options in sight, and no one to trust, she told Teddy everything.

She started with her disease, then told him about the death of her father and the distant, hostile relationship with her mother, which kept her in a life at the convent. Then she told him about creating *Convent Counting* at fifteen and her two degrees in information technology, which led to her job at the IOR. And then, discovering the truth about the Church Families Charity fund, being kidnapped, and her escape. He was up to date.

It was a lot to take in. Even to her, it sounded more like she was pitching a movie concept to Giuseppe Tornatore, her favorite film director, than recanting a short synopsis on the story of her life. The fact that Teddy didn't have any questions was making her anxious. What if he thought she was lying? Or crazy?

They drove in silence for a bit.

Then, he said, "Well, I'm a boot-wearing, rodeo-going Texan with a Southern drawl that sticks out here like a banjo in the Sistine Chapel. I'm the oldest of four, all brothers, I graduated from A&M, and I'm a Protestant to boot."

"Okay …" Maria said.

"And you're an intelligent, sophisticated woman, a nun who's a native of Italy and works or worked for the Vatican and—"

"Teddy, where in the world are you going with this?"

"You can stay at my place. No one would be crazy enough to put us together. No one will look for you there. It's the perfect hideout, at least until we come up with a better plan."

"Just like that, you believe me?"

"My mother raised me to rely on my instincts, to always act the gentleman, and to have faith."

Maria gave him a slight nod. She certainly understood

about instinct and faith, even though she fell short when she tried to think about anything her own mother had taught her.

"You only met me the one time, too, Maria, and you're trusting me with your life story. Heck, with your whole life. I won't let you down."

Despite the tornado of circumstances that had swept her old life up and away, Maria could still see God at work. He was keeping her on her toes, that was for sure, but she felt safe. For now.

"Thank you, Teddy," she could barely choke the words out. "Your place. Thank you so much."

Maria relaxed back on the headrest and closed her eyes, feeling a small measure of peace for the first time in three days or, possibly, since moving to Rome.

CHAPTER FORTY-TWO

Vatican City

It was well after business hours, but with all the time spent at medical appointments, Cardinal Justin Parina had catching up to do. He'd just finished reviewing requests from scholars seeking access to the Archives. Even though a routine matter, he paid strict attention, as he was always conscious of protecting his baby, the VAT.

The cardinal replaced his fountain pen in its holder, set aside the thin porcelain cup that held the remnants of his favorite Earl Grey tea, cleared the workload from his honey-hued desk, and stared out his window as the smoky blue of twilight leaked in, softening the atmosphere.

He would've typically taken his customary walk and gone to dinner in the bishops' elegant dining hall by this hour. But he'd been in the mood for neither.

Justin rose and opened his wine cabinet instead as he contemplated the crisis ahead.

Unanswered calls from Michael Levin to Justin's private

phone over the past forty-eight hours had put him on high alert. Then, when Katarina rang to tell him about Levin's visit to her in Morcote, he knew for sure that the secret he'd kept all these years had caught up with him. A newspaperman was bang on to reveal his other life for all the world to see.

He crouched with his nose in the temperature-controlled cooler when a knock sounded on his ajar office door.

Monsignor Ricci poked his head in.

"*Ciao.* Come in, Fran," he said, standing, a dry, fruit-forward red from northern Italy in hand.

"You sure? Do you have a minute?"

"Of course. Have a seat. I was just about to uncork this Valpolicella Classico."

Francesco sat down, envelope tucked under an arm, wondering how to begin.

"You'll have a glass, yes?" the cardinal asked, sensing his unease.

"Yes, why don't we? You're okay to indulge?"

"A little wine won't be what kills me."

Justin uncorked it, poured two glasses, set them on his desk, and sat back down. "I was hoping for news of Maria, but your mood tells me otherwise."

"Unfortunately, we haven't found her yet." Without further ado, Francesco placed the envelope on the desk between them, taking up his wine glass for a sip before saying, "I don't know who else to talk to about this."

Justin stared at it for a moment without reaction. Then he took it and unfastened the clasp, letting the contents fall out.

After a short review, he looked up from the photographs. "I'm not a perfect man, Fran."

"None of us is, Justin." Francesco pressed his lips together in a tight line.

"Who else—"

"Orio found these things in my uncle's office. He won't say anything." Francesco knew he had to be totally transparent. "But ...."

"Levin." Justin gave him a look of acknowledgment. He hadn't wanted to roll in the recent intrusion of Michael Levin into his life. Things were complicated enough, but it was too late. The reporter had been to Fran's church. He was on a moving train now.

"He doesn't actually know if there's a story." Hesitantly, knowingly, Francesco asked, "Is there?"

Justin sighed heavily and took a second look at the pictures. "Odd. I've never seen these. I remember the day, though. Katarina and our son, Peter, years ago."

The cardinal confirmed what Francesco knew in his heart to be true. "Then you don't know the story behind them," the monsignor surmised.

"I sure don't. And I have no idea who could've taken them. It looks to me like my uncle was holding on to these to blackmail you."

"Blackmail? Why?"

"You mean, other than the obvious? Maybe because you got the position at the VAT, and he didn't. I hate to think of my uncle as spiteful, but he must've intended something."

"Oh, my position was a bone of contention, all right. We got over that, but you've clearly been misinformed about the relationship between Antonio and me."

"Then, tell me about it, please."

"He couldn't have been blackmailing me. He was my mentor, my *confessor*, my helpmate."

Astonished, Francesco coughed a laugh. "Your mentor?" The monsignor sat back in his seat, taking it in.

The cardinal was lost in an avalanche of memories. "Antonio knew all about my deception. When I found the courage to confess to him, I had my resignation letter in hand, certain he'd force me out. But your uncle amazed me by urging me to stay."

"He didn't want you—"

"—to resign? No. The most important thing to your uncle was the Church. Everything he did and every decision he made was intended to boost the image of the Church. I imagine he was thinking of the scandal he'd incite if he forced me out."

"Yes, I can see that," Francesco said. "The Church was his ... ah, well ...."

"'Mistress,' were you going to say?"

"Sorry, clumsy of me." Francesco clamped his lips together in regret, and then the thought struck him. "This might've been the time for you to walk away. Many priests have."

"Oh, I wanted to stay. I loved the Church, and I loved my position in it. My ego was consumed by the VAT."

Of course, it was. Francesco was not blind to the attention—the adulation—this Adonis commanded.

"The Church was equally as important as my, um, family," Justin said. "I wanted both because I loved both and didn't want to have to choose."

"And Katarina?"

"She's always seen the Church as the other woman. Always been bitter about it. And painful as it is, the issue has stood between us."

"And yet, she's stayed?"

"Yes. In the beginning, I had things to work out," Justin continued, "Peter was born, and I needed to make his support legal and consistent. That's when your Uncle Antonio told me about a Church fund for women involved with priests. Of course, it was, is, a secret fund, but secrets spill out, and I didn't want any part of my secret to become known. It would've meant giving up too much."

"Wait!" Francesco sprang forward like an arrow from the

string, nearly knocking over his wine. "You mean you know about this Silent Mistress Fund? It *is* real?"

"Oh, certainly. I understand it has a healthy clientele. Antonio referred to it from time to time, usually griping about a troublemaker. But I chose to use my own funds, which, fortunately, I had in a trust. Antonio sent me to an attorney who handles legal affairs for clergy, and he helped me set up my personal account and promised to manage it. It would all be very quiet and private. And it has been."

"Justin," Francesco said, a frown clouding his face, "you knew about this fund when all of us, Yigael, Valentina, Orio … we were all discussing it two days ago, yet you said nothing …."

"Fran, when I heard 'outsiders' mentioning the fund, I feared if I spoke up, the investigation would bend in my direction, and my double life would be discovered."

Francesco sat straight and still as a lamppost, waiting for Justin to go on.

"I'm in shock, if you want the truth. Until this week, Antonio and I were the only ones who knew about Katarina and Peter. They risk exposure too. With Maria having evidence of the fund, it'll all come out. I was trying to protect my family for a little longer."

Justin took a beat to compose himself, as he'd been more emotional as of late with his diagnosis, and now this. "I'll write my resignation letter in the morning."

"What? No. That's not why I came, and this changes nothing between us. I respect you now as I always have."

The cardinal's eyes glossed over. "I was weak, Fran. I had an overwhelming attraction to her, and I fell in love." He imbibed more wine.

"Do you, can I ask … do you still love her? Do you have a relationship with them still?"

Justin's hair caught the light, highlighting his deep-brown locks and contrasting strands of silver that gave him an air of experience and sophistication. "It's hard to explain my relationship with Katarina to a man of the Church."

"*You* are a man of the Church. Don't think otherwise."

"I'm a hypocrite, standing alongside men like you and Orio. I have a woman in my life and a child and to answer your question, the initial spark between us never died. Yes, I do see her, if not as often as she and I would like. Peter's away at university, so, seeing him? No, not lately." The true nature of the relationship with his son was another story for another time.

Justin's face darkened and when he spoke again, bitterness dimmed his tone. "Celibacy has crippled the cleric and, by default, the parishioners, but it is the way things are. I've defied this unwritten rule, and I suppose it's been the cowardly way. But, in truth, I don't know what the remedy is, or rather, I do know, but bloody hell if I know how to put it into practice. With the world changing as it is, it might be right around the corner ... or eons away."

"Justin, listen to me. I hope you'll put this resignation idea behind you. You need to get hold of yourself, if I may be so frank. The Church needs you. You're a good man."

Jailed by guilt and shame for so long, Justin's emotions erupted, and tears finally wet his eyes. "I've been plagued by this secret for so long, I often wonder if it's affected my health." He rose and moved to the window, gazing out.

His friend's palpable pain struck Francesco. Yet, he wasn't clear how he felt about Justin's "family life." The cardinal sure wasn't going to give up Katarina and Peter. *Could* he stay in the Church? Francesco had a lot of thinking to do.

"What do you want to do?" he asked the older man.

Justin turned around. "I'm not sure," he said. "If I resign, I will at long last be honest with myself and my Church family. I don't think I can go to my grave unless I shed this burden. And Katarina's reaching the end of her tether. She's sick of living in the shadows. Wouldn't it be better for us to step into the open and discuss the toll it's taken to live secretly because the Church refuses to abolish archaic rules that have no place in Christian life? Perhaps, it's my destiny to come forward. Perhaps, that's the legacy I'll leave."

Francesco stood and joined Justin at the window. He put an arm around his friend.

CHAPTER FORTY-THREE

Palermo, Sicily

As they passed the guide sign announcing sixty kilos to Maria's hometown. Father Orio Rinaldi congratulated himself on devising a plan to help her without flouting Yigael's demands to stay out of Rome. The aging spy hadn't said anything about his traveling elsewhere, so, as far as Orio was concerned, he was still technically following orders.

It was a drive to Falcone from Bari, but no matter how broken the relationship between mother and daughter was, Carmella would undoubtedly want to know that Maria was missing. Maybe she could help. Maybe—and this was a long shot—Maria had contacted her. Then, at least, Orio would know his friend was alive.

As much as he'd wanted to linger with his family and get to better know the children, all he could think about was the young nun. And Isabelle had immediately volunteered to drive him.

He and his dear, sweet, older sister had gotten in the car and out on the road before the breakfast plates had been cleared. Orio remembered that Carmella Caruso worked at a fancy establishment, mainly nights. If traffic cooperated, he'd catch her before her shift. It was a weekend, so, barring an accident, he should be fine.

They talked pleasantly to this point. But nearing their destination, Isabelle felt overcome by emotion and voiced her heartfelt thoughts. "We've missed you, Orio."

"You've all been so kind," he responded.

"You went away so young."

The priest looked at his sister, surprised.

"Times were different then." Isabelle touched his arm. "Their *genitori* ... they struggled. They did the best they could. Unfortunately, well, with so many children ..." her voice trailed off.

Orio counted as number five in a line of seven children.

When you became an altar boy, our mother was ecstatic," Isabelle said. "And when you hung around the parish to do odd jobs for the nuns, she insisted you had a calling for the Church."

"I only stayed around the church because I didn't want to do chores or play soccer," Orio admitted.

"We know." Isabelle had known outdoor activities had held little appeal to Orio. "But then, good Lord, our mother sent you to seminary when you were only twelve."

Orio dropped his head. "I remember."

"Well, I guess you could say we've always missed you and, well, we love you. I want you to know that."

Touched to tears, he and his sister began really talking, and suddenly, every life experience seemed to total up and spill out. It felt good to share his journey with someone who loved him. Isabelle disclosed her stories, too, some of them hilarious. She had Orio roaring with laughter and wishing he'd been around for all the fun when her children were small. She swore she was awake for the first two years straight with Enzo, her second son.

Right away, he loved her back.

Coming into Falcone, he searched for Carmella Caruso's address and, given what he already knew from Maria, found it easily. They made good time and arrived just after two in front of her apartment complex.

He smiled at his sister as he exited her car, then he found Carmella's flat and knocked.

"Coming," a voice rang out.

Carmella opened the door. On seeing a priest, she said, "I don't want any," and tried to slam it shut.

"*Signora* Caruso!" Orio called out, stifling a yelp over the pain in his left foot from sticking it between the door and the frame. "I'm Father Orio Rinaldi, Maria's friend. I'm not selling anything." He pushed the door open a bit more to peek around.

Carmella stepped aside to let him in, looking this way and that down the walkway for her daughter.

Orio stepped inside and stopped short as she shut the door and turned to him with a questioning shrug.

"My word," he said. "No doubt you're Maria's mother. She looks just like you."

"Uh-huh. So, what do you want? And where's Maria?"

Wanting to let Carmella down slowly, he responded, "I was visiting family ... nearby. How about *un caffè*?"

"Okay, then." She pivoted. "Follow me."

Orio took a seat in the kitchen and glanced about. Young Maria had lived here once. Was there any trace of her? None that he could see.

Carmella set down the hot drinks and sat across from him.

The priest briefed her on Maria's job at the IOR, explaining that she oversaw the Church Families Charity account but then discovered the true nature of the fund.

"Oh? And what is this true nature?"

Carmella looked confused or possibly bored. She was a hard person to read, and Orio took a sip of the bitter beverage in front of him. He dared not ask for sugar or cream as he proceeded with care.

"Maria discovered the money goes to mistresses of priests. They call it the Silent Mistress Fund."

"Say that again?"

"Oh, it's just the way they refer to it at the IOR. They call it the Silent Mistress Fund."

"You don't say."

Orio pursed his lips and nodded his yes.

"Where are you going with this?"

"*Signora* Caruso, I'm sorry to say your daughter is missing. We believe she's been kidnapped by those who run this fund. If word got out about it—"

Carmella got up abruptly and left the room.

Five minutes later, she was back, a small suitcase in hand. "Let's go."

"What? Where?" Orio asked as she stood erect in the archway of the kitchen.

"To the train station. We're going to find my daughter."

"Um, my sister. We need to tell her. She's in the car at the end of the street."

"Better yet. We don't have to walk. I'm riding shotgun."

"What?" the priest rose, turning three shades of confused.

"What do you mean, 'what'? We're going to Rome to find Maria. And you're sitting in the back seat 'cuz I called shotgun."

"But I'm not supposed to go—"

Carmella gave him a hard look.

"Oh, okay, then. To Rome." He scurried behind the feisty woman, wondering how he would explain all this to Yigael Dorian. Of course, he'd have a whole night on the train to figure it out.

CHAPTER FORTY-FOUR

Rome

Jacques Ignatius and Anna-Marie Mannes arrived back at Monsignor Ricci's church early Saturday morning. They'd scoured the outskirts of the city, looking everywhere imaginable through the night. They'd come up empty. It wasn't the news Yigael wanted to hear.

Having lost all hope, Valentina suggested, "Doesn't one of the nuns at Casa Veronesi run Casa di S. Antonio, the homeless shelter?"

"You think Maria would involve another sister, possibly put her in danger?"

"I don't know, but she doesn't know anyone else."

"Hiding in plain sight right in the city in the safety of a homeless shelter? It's a long shot, but let's go," Yigael agreed.

Valentina grabbed Sister Maria's phone and slid it into her bag. "If we find her, we're not coming back here, right?"

"Right. We'll keep you posted, Fran. Jacques, Anna, you two grab a bite, rest. You can't go on forever."

"Righto," Anna said, and she and Jacques followed Yigael and Valentina out.

Fifteen minutes later, Yigael parked and barreled into Casa di S. Antonio—a once-white-but-now-gray-with-age building—leaving Valentina in the dust. He noted the line of hungry men, women, and children waiting for a meal. He scanned the room's perimeters, then moved toward the only interior door he saw and pushed through.

There, in a small office, sat Sister Birdi, tending to the scraped knee of a little boy.

"Hello. Can I help you?" she asked Yigael.

Valentina inched past him, knowing she'd be more equipped to handle this. "Hi, are you Sister Birdi?"

"Yes. Are you …?"

"I'm Valentina Vella."

Birdi placed the bandage on the boy's knee and said, "All better," and he scampered out. Then, she looked at them with tears in her eyes. "She's not visiting her mother, is she?"

"We were hoping she was here."

Birdi shook her head.

"Who told you she was visiting her mother?" Yigael asked.

"I thought, um …." Birdi diverted her eyes and shivered.

Her turmoil was not lost on either of them.

"When did she mention—"

Valentina pressed her hand on Yigael's arm. "Anything you could tell us would be most helpful, Sister. We're trying our best to find her."

"Sister Cate told me she went to visit her mother. But Maria's mother was just here. And Maria didn't pack, well, anything. I've had a feeling something's wrong, but I didn't know what."

"If you hear from her, Sister Birdi, will you have her call me? Please." Valentina scratched her phone number without a name on a sticky note, put a pin through it, and stuck it on the bulletin board among a hundred others. She held her eyes on Birdi's in unspoken understanding. "And, please, not a word to anyone."

Ashen-faced, the nun nodded soberly.

Back in the utility van—her Alfa Romeo was too tiny to hide Maria should they locate her—they sat slumped in defeat.

"Sister Cate," Yigael said through his teeth. "She's involved. She told Sister Birdi nonsense about Maria going home."

"I wonder how much Birdi knows about Cate," Valentina said.

"If we don't come up with Maria in the next few hours, I intend to grill her," Yigael said. "I'm figuring she knows quite a lot about Cate's comings and goings, what she's up to. Why or how she could be wrapped up in all this."

"We're not going to get anywhere with her," Valentina said. "You saw how scared she looked."

Yigael gave her a look that said he wanted to go right back into the shelter and give Birdif the third degree.

"A young, frail, *attractive* nun traveling on foot—limping—just disappears? How is this possible?" Valentina asked.

"It's not. We're missing something. She didn't have any hobbies where she made a friend she might've contacted?"

"We've been over that already."

A knock on Valentina's window jolted her into a tiny scream.

"My God! Are you serious?" Yigael said.

"I'm jumpy ... sorry," Valentina said, whipping her head around. "Oh, Birdi, it's you. It's Birdi, Yigael."

Yigael smiled secretly at how cute Valentina was when flustered. He motioned for the nun to get in the back seat.

She did, closing the door behind her.

"What is it, Sister Birdi?" Valentina asked.

"Um, I'm no Sherlock Holmes, but maybe there's something

useful in her room. I know she keeps her laptop there. Though, I can't imagine how anyone would get into it."

"Leave that to us," Yigael said.

"Okay. Well, her computer, it's still there on her dresser. Her toiletries are there too. Her suitcase is sitting beside the armoire."

Valentina noted Birdi's strange demeanor. She'd seen it before when a panic attack came on. As Birdi pressed a hand to her chest, Valentina took her other, and the nun relaxed a little.

"No one will be at Casa Veronesi for a couple of hours. I have a spare key." She handed it to Valentina. "Hers is the last bedroom on the second floor, opposite the bathroom."

"We'll bring your key back."

"Just give it to Maria," her voice caught, "when you find her." With a small nod, Birdi hopped out.

"Let's go," Yigael said.

Hiding inside the utility truck was a stroke of brilliance. Within ten minutes, they were parked outside the Casa Veronesi with no worries of anyone questioning their presence.

Valentina dumped the contents of her tote onto the back seat, leaving room for Maria's belongings. She was out the door and inside the house in a flash.

In the last bedroom on the second floor, she spotted Maria's laptop right away. Then she grabbed underwear and a change of clothes. Searching every compartment before exiting, she found Maria's meds in the nightstand drawer. Fumbling with the prescription bottles in her nervousness, she finally secured them in her tote and noticed *WIRED* magazine underneath. She picked it up, studied the cover for a beat and then opened it.

With renewed energy, she stuffed it in her bag and high-tailed it out.

Valentina lunged back into the car. "Drive!" she said, slamming the door behind her.

"Calm down, this isn't a diamond heist." Yigael pulled out and drove off. "Anything of note?"

Valentina peered into the bag. "Meds, clothes, laptop, oh, and this magazine. I don't know why I grabbed it. It was under her pills in the nightstand drawer. I guess it spoke to me."

"Ha, thinking like the Mossad. What'd you find?"

Valentina opened the front cover and lifted the business card that was tucked inside it.

Yigael snatched it out of her hands. "*Teddy J. Weaver, CEO, Zinq Inc.,*" he said, studying the card.

"My phone. Where's my phone?"

"Back seat."

"Right." She grabbed it. "You think we found a friend?"

"Worth a shot."

As Valentina took back the business card to plug the number into her phone, it rang. The incoming number was the one she was about to call. She turned her phone to Yigael.

"Answer it."

Valentina hit *Accept*. "Teddy?"

"Miss Vella?" Teddy responded.

"Yes! Is she—"

"Oh, boy, I'm mighty glad to be in touch with you, ma'am. Yes, she's here. Sleeping, been sleeping all day. She's breathing, though. I've checked 'bout a hundred times. She said to leave her rest and to contact no one. She was adamant. But I had to call someone, and it was between you and the pope."

"You chose wisely, Teddy J. Weaver. Address?"

"2367 Ovest Quinta Strada. Pull into the garage. I'll close it behind you."

"See you shortly."

CHAPTER FORTY-FIVE

San Paolo, Rome

Cardinal Justin Parina stood before the impossibly tangled ironwork that curled like branches up the glass doorway, joining the extravagant flowers and shoots, sprigs, sprays, and fronds of vellum and gold leaf that decorated the upper windows. *Trust Cacciatore to live in a fancy palazzo,* he thought. *Pretty, though.*

Justin was not an intimate of Cardinal Cacciatore's, though he'd had plenty of battles with the ultra-conservative red cap, as they took opposite sides on most issues to be decided by the Curia. Otherwise, Justin saw him rarely, but, by reputation, the older man's choice of neighborhood and style of accommodation did not surprise him. Cacciatore had held himself apart and above for as long as Justin could recall.

He appreciated the flowing lines of the ornate knocker before reaching for it and giving the door two taps.

A young nun with fair skin and hazel eyes opened it and smiled. "Why, you're—"

"Justin Parina."

"I recognize you, even though you aren't dressed ... I mean, you're surely dressed, just not ... oh me, what am I saying? Well, you're practically famous."

Justin chuckled, thoroughly enjoying the nun's discomfiture. "And your name is?"

"Sister Joella."

"All right, Sister Joella. Is the cardinal at home?"

"Why, yes. Is he expecting you?"

"No, he ... might I come in?"

"Oh, certainly, Cardinal Parina, forgive me." Joella opened the door wide, and Justin stepped inside. "Please, if you would, wait here. I'll be right back."

"Of course." As Joella retreated on footsteps light as a night whisper, he moved from the foyer into *il soggiorno,* a living room that could only be described as opulent.

He looked up at the frescoed ceilings and down at the marble floors with Persian carpets. There seemed no end to the tapestries and gold-framed paintings, to say nothing of the life-sized sculptures seizing space in the great room. *This is a museum. So much for humility and modesty.* Then he had a fleeting, cynical thought that perhaps all the riches were meant to intimidate anyone entering.

Sister Joella appeared at the top of an ornately carved wooden balustrade and gestured him up the stairs. "His office is up here. He'll see you now."

Justin followed her.

"Cardinal."

"Well, if it isn't the distinguished Cardinal Parina." At Cacciatore's arm wave, Justin sank into an overstuffed armchair.

The cardinal was at his desk, computer fired up, which was atypical of him during this early evening hour, but it'd had been a strange week all around.

"Nice digs."

"What would you know about it?" Cacciatore growled. "You

in that dumpy little flat with all the other do-gooders. So, what are you doing here? What do you want? I'm busy."

"I'll bet," Justin agreed. He carefully folded one leg over the other.

"Well?"

"I'm here on two matters."

"I have a few other things on my mind."

"I know."

"What do you mean 'I know'?"

"Maria. Where is she?"

Cacciatore shook his head. "I figured that's why you were here. Why would you think I know where she is? I don't. If I did, she'd be here now. I'm worried sick about her."

"And I want to discuss the Silent Mistress Fund."

Cacciatore controlled a gasp but couldn't contain the shaking in his right hand.

"I know all about the fund, Angelico. I've known for years."

"How? It's confidential. It's a tightly held private matter."

"I was offered an opportunity to use the fund."

Cacciatore's surprise was real. "You mean you had—"

"And still do. I have a family, a lovely woman and a son."

"Well, I admit I'm flummoxed. So, our pretty boy is not so spotless, is he? Well, I'll be—" Cacciatore erupted in a cruel laugh. "I haven't come across your name."

"Because I didn't want any part of it."

"Too good for it, eh?"

"Hardly. I intend to resign. Justin held up the envelope containing the letter of resignation from pastoral office that he would present to the Curia's Dicastery for Bishops. And if you don't come clean about the fund and tell the truth about it, I will."

"Justin," the old man shook his head, "no one will believe you, whatever kind of evidence you have … listen, friend," he scoffed, "the Church is bigger than a man and his mistakes.

And the institution will be protected. The parishioners rely on the strength of the Church. You can't take it down, and you're ignorant to think otherwise."

"I'm not trying to take down the Church, Angelico."

"No? Then, what are you trying to accomplish? And what are we supposed to do about this mammoth situation, anyway? We're providing for the women and offspring. Have you come in here with a better solution? Or to point a finger at your brother? As if your sin is smaller? Is the degree to which one sins what matters now? Little sins and medium sins don't count anymore? You're a great man for caring for your family on your own, but I'm a monster for protecting the Church? *Our* family? Is that what you're saying?"

"That's exactly what he's saying," Yigael said, barging into the room. "Where's Maria?"

Yigael had come here after informing Francesco of Maria's safety and learning of Justin's intentions. He merely wanted to stop the cardinal from sacrificing his career now that Maria was okay. But the earful he got while standing outside Cardinal Cacciatore's office was enough for him to take another approach to his unexpected visit. "Where is she?" he demanded.

"What? I have no idea. She wanted to take a half day on Friday, and then Sister Cate said she fell ill over the weekend."

She told Birdi that Maria was traveling home for a few days. Sister Cate's chock full of explanations about her whereabouts. Yigael tucked that information away for later. It incensed him that the Church felt so impervious to punishment that they didn't even bother syncing up their cover story.

"You're lying, Cardinal," he said with a hard emphasis on "'cardinal."

"Yigael, please," Justin said.

Cacciatore knew Yigael Dorian by sight and reputation and as someone to fear. Some believed the ex-Mossad had used his muscle to see Cardinal Lavoti off to jail for conspiracy to murder.

The cardinal stood and walked closer. He would not be bullied. "I have no idea where the girl is," he hissed. "So, I'm just as worried as you are, Dr. Dorian, if, as you say, she's missing."

It took everything for Yigael to control his rage.

Justin stood and approached them both. "Angelico, please, release Maria."

"He won't! What's this?" Though Yigael knew exactly what it was, he gestured to the envelope in Justin's hand.

"My resignation let—"

Yigael snatched it and turned back to Cardinal Cacciatore. "This isn't over. You better pray she's okay, or you'll share a cell with your buddies. If there's any room left."

"Are you threatening the Church?"

"Just you." Turning for the door, Yigael nearly barreled into the "cousins" on their way in.

"Dara," Yigael said with a knowing nod as Massimo and Pepper Pugia walked past him.

"Yigael," she responded and blanched, showing a tinge of panic that turned her pale cheeks blood red. He'd called her by her name, a moniker she hadn't heard out loud in over six years, and yet, it felt right, ex-Mossad to ex-Mossad.

Yigael turned back to the cardinal. "You don't even know who you have working for you." Then, to Cardinal Parina, he said, "Justin, let's go."

Without a word, the cardinal followed him out.

Outside, on the way to their cars, Yigael handed back the folder.

"I can explain."

"Fran gave me the highlights, that's why I'm here." Then under his breath, Yigael added, "Do not react to what I'm about to say."

The cardinal agreed with a nod.

"She's safe. And Val is with her."

"But you just told Angel—"

Yigael stifled the rest of that sentence with a shift of his eyes, and Justin was not about to argue ethics with the man. He gave another slight nod, which looked like a goodbye, and split away from Yigael to go to his car.

As he got in with an exhale, his lip curled up in one corner, displaying the faintest of smiles as he said a silent prayer of thanks.

CHAPTER FORTY-SIX

La Giustiniana, Rome

MARIA STOOD IN THE ARCHED DOORWAY OF THE HALLWAY LEADING to Teddy's *soggiorno* her eyes fixed on her new friends. They relaxed comfortably, engaging in light-hearted conversation, as if the world outside held no troubles. But Maria felt a heaviness within, an unshakeable fear of looming trouble, possibly even legal issues.

Her gratitude swelled as she reflected on their steadfast support. What would her fate have been without them? They'd found her phone, gotten into her home to gather her essentials—clothes, meds, her laptop—discovered Teddy's contact information, and then hunted her down. They'd replaced her cane and coordinated with her doctor to ensure she had everything needed for a full recovery. She marveled at their tenacity.

She waited for a lull in the conversation and then stepped forward. *"Ciao."*

Valentina, the only other woman present, expressed her joy with an audible sigh on seeing the young nun showered and fresh-faced. "Oh, Maria, you look lovely and brimming with health. How are you feeling?"

"So much better, thank you, Valentina." She smiled, making eye contact with the others—Yigael, Cardinal Justin Parina, and Teddy.

A knock on the door rerouted everyone's attention.

Teddy opened it to Monsignor Francesco Ricci.

He entered to greetings all around.

The group had been waiting for Francesco to wrap up his Sunday post-Mass obligations so that he could come for *il pranzo*. Lunch.

Yigael had suggested a conclave to sort out the matters at hand—Maria's kidnapping and the fund. And he and Valentina had also taken charge of their midday meal, ordering from their corner café an *antipasto, insalata grande, lasagne agli spinaci,* and plenty of *focaccia*. This was just the ice breaker Maria needed, breaking bread with friends as a prelude to a conversation she'd never participated in nor imagined being part of.

It had taken combined efforts to prepare Maria to sit at this table.

Her long sleep had been followed by three extended visits from *Dottore* Lubrano to attend to her medical needs. While blood transfusions were usually done in a formal setting, the doctor had no problem setting up a private clinic at Teddy's home. He left earlier this morning, confident his patient had fully recovered physically.

Emotions were a different story.

Three days ago, she'd never felt more alone and terrified, fleeing for her life through the hidden priest hole at the convent in Velletri. Now, she was about to dine with five compassionate comrades she could trust implicitly. They were committed to helping her move forward, ensuring she no longer faced her challenges alone.

So, despite the kaleidoscope of heated emotions reflecting

off each other and creating a dizzying effect, Maria also felt blessed. Yes, the Vatican had kidnapped her—well, it was a high-ranking cardinal who'd ordered it, but others were in the know—and yes, her previous perception of the Church needed recalibrating. Still, as she put on one of the fresh blouses Valentina had packed from Casa Veronesi, Maria said a prayer of thanks for her returning health and the flurry of allies. She would not be alone in whatever came up next.

When she met Teddy Weaver on the train ride from Palermo to her new vocation at the IOR, Maria could not have imagined she'd be hiding in his home by summer's end. And she certainly couldn't have dreamed her place of refuge would be a fancy, two-story Romanesque-style villa in northern Rome with terra cotta floors, chestnut-beamed vaulted ceilings, fashionable furnishings, and rare antiques.

Teddy had placed Maria in the first-floor primary bedroom to ensure her comfort and ease of movement. He was staying on the second floor.

Maria had followed her vows to a T. She'd worked her whole life to be a good person, to share her natural gifts in God's name, and to rise above adversity—her illness and the contentious relationship with her mother. She'd been practicing the art of forgiveness her whole life since the day her father died, the day that nearly broke her. In that regard, she was ready for whatever life threw at her, including this.

Still, she felt anger rise again, as it had all week. She took a slow, deep breath and counted to five before releasing it.

CHAPTER FORTY-SEVEN

Rome

CARMELLA CARUSO STORMED TOWARD THE OLD VILLA, LEAVING Father Rinaldi in the dust to pay the cab driver.

On hearing a vehicle in the drive, Sister Lati had peeked out the front window. Now wide-eyed, she held the door open while the enraged mother raced through it.

Exhausted from Carmella's all-out determined pace—and hungry from a morning lacking his usual cornetto (or two) and wake-me-up espresso—Orio dragged his feet along the walkway toward Casa Veronesi.

"Come in, Father, and sit here." Lati gestured to the reading chair just beyond the vestibule.

He sank into the divinely comfortable down-filled cushions. He could sleep forever. After a bite. But serious matters pressed.

It had struck him on the train ride that when he'd found Maria's phone outside the pizzeria and scrolled through her list of unopened notifications, all twenty-odd texts and phone calls were from him.

Not one was from Sister Cate. Yet, she'd said that she, too, had been trying to reach Maria.

My God, she was in on it ... maybe, he'd remembered thinking. But for once, he'd kept his machinations to himself. *Well, at least until I get back into Rome and in touch with Yigael,* he'd promised himself. Still, the way Carmella was all wound up, he wasn't sure his efforts weren't in vain. She was ready to set Casa Veronesi on fire to purge from it any secrets that might lead to her daughter's whereabouts.

"Where's Carmella?" he asked Lati.

Lati shrugged and gestured to the whole villa with open arms. "Somewhere."

Circling back after giving the main floor a quick scan, Carmella barked, "Where's Maria?"

"I thought she was with you," Lati squeaked.

Carmella shot Orio with a confirmatory glance.

Sister Cate Benedict, returning from morning Mass, hustled through the still-open front entrance. "What's this? Carmella, you here again?"

The frantic mother all but pounced on her. "Yes. Where better to start searching for Maria."

"You have no right to storm in here like a ram butting the china. Calm down!"

"I will not. My daughter's gone missing. And what's this one talking about?" She nodded to Sister Lati. "Why would she think Maria's with me?"

Cate said nothing.

"Where is she?"

Orio rolled and lifted his way vertically in case of trouble. Well, there was trouble. He side-stepped to the vestibule where Sister Lati was standing.

Cate looked from Carmella's dagger eyes to Orio's helpless shrug, unsure how to proceed.

"He filled me in." She pointed an angry finger at the stout priest standing frozen beside the statue-still Lati.

"Well then," Cate said, "I'm sure what … Orio said is accurate."

Orio drew a hanky from a pocket and mopped his face, though he couldn't do much about the rest of his body. "Sister Cate, I don't actually know anything." Well, he knew one thing. Maria was nothing like her mother. And he was second-guessing his latest lark to roll the woman into the mess. Thank goodness he hadn't let her in on his suspicions about Cate. There was no telling what she might do with those tidings. The muscle of a distressed mother topped all.

"She's sick, though," Orio added. "Of course, you know this, Sister. The stress alone—"

"I don't know where she is. I swear," Cate bit back, raising her voice. "I'm as concerned as you are. And I understand her physical limitations and the danger she could be in."

"The danger she could be in. What do you mean about *the danger she could be in*?" Carmella crept closer to the tall nun.

"Carmella," Orio said against his better judgment. "Let's calm down. Sister Cate is referring to Maria's illness. She's just as worried as we are." He smiled at the nun.

"I don't know where Maria is. I'm sorry I can't help you."

"Now, listen to me, Sister. I'm not too fond of your answers. They're making me think you do know. And I don't care if I die looking for my daughter. I won't stop, so stick that in your pipe and smoke it."

Cate and Carmella plunged deeper into the old villa as their battle progressed. Orio hugged the vestibule wall, inching toward the ensuing drama as Lati shot up the stairs.

"No, you don't understand. I *really* don't know where she is." Cate covered her face with her hands, shaking her head. "We don't … she isn't …." Finding a chair, the nun gripped the back and sat. She looked from Carmella to Orio and back before collapsing in on herself. "She's escaped."

Orio slapped a hand over his mouth, and Lati let out a small cry from the top of the stairs.

"What?" Carmella shrieked, pulling up a chair and taking a seat, knee to knee and nose to nose with Cate. "So, you did take her ... and then ... you lost her? Is that right? Did you kidnap my daughter? And then you lost her?"

Cate squirmed and then leaped out of the chair and launched into a frenzied pace.

Well, we're getting somewhere anyway, Carmella thought. "So, you did take her?"

"Please, understand our position. With the information she's upturned ... well, she could take down the Church!"

"There are worse ideas!" Carmella sneered, standing.

"Tell that to the thousands of men running the institution! And to its billions of followers."

"I don't care about any of that! Thousands? Billions? I don't give a tinker's curse. How about *one*," she spat. "That's what I do care about, my daughter. She'd better be alive. And that's all I've got to say." Carmella heaved a breath out and crossed her arms fiercely across her breasts.

Cate was struck by so much bottled-up emotion that she went flush.

Carmella could see that the woman might faint, and she took a step toward the sideboard, grabbed a magazine on top, and waved it in Cate's direction, fanning her to ensure she remained lucid. Now might be her only chance to scoop up as much information as she could. "You're not being clear with me, Cate. So, you took her where? And why? To scare her?"

Orio watched as the nun turned fire red. "Sister Cate, can I get you a glass of water?"

"She's fine, Orio." Carmella eyed the priest. "Sit."

He sat. The priest knew better than to speak again. But for

mercy's sake, he also needed to water his dry mouth. He couldn't believe what he was hearing. While his theory about Maria's whereabouts was validated, he had hoped secretly he was imagining it all.

"I think so, Carmella. To scare her into returning anything she may've taken from the bank. However, I honestly don't know." Cate didn't know what the grand plan was. And now, she didn't want to think about any of it. Unfortunately, she had to. Carmella was like a stubborn bulldog.

"So, now you've, what? Misplaced her?"

"Looks like it," Cate said nonchalantly. "Oh, I didn't mean that. No, not really."

"Not really what? She could be dead."

"She's not."

"How do you know?"

"I just know."

Carmella stepped closer, fists clenched.

Though taller and bigger, Cate knew she was no match against the enraged mother before her. "Because I just know."

"What does that mean?"

"She's very resourceful, your girl."

"You're talking in riddles, and I'm not above using force to get answers. Do you hear me?!" Carmella stopped just short of cold cocking her.

"The Church doesn't know her whereabouts. She escaped. I'm certain of it."

"Expand!"

"When Maria first came to us, she told us about the convent, her bunny, her gardener friend … and the priest hole."

Carmella's brows snapped together, and she loosened her crossed arms. "The what? What did you say?"

"I believe she said priest hole, Carmella," Orio blurted. "Priest holes are secret passageways underneath some monasteries and convents."

Cate looked at the priest with something akin to gratitude.

Orio nodded but then, catching onto Cate's implications, added, "Oh!"

Cate returned his nod and picked up where he left off, "They were built in medieval times as escape routes for persecuted priests. Maria knew all about these tunnels. She played in the one in Palermo as a child. So that's what she did. She found the tunnel. And got out."

Orio could barely believe what he was hearing.

Carmella sat back down.

"Cardinal Cacciatore and Cardinal Lavoti, before he went to jail," the nun continued, "used a convent not far from here to manage some of their affairs that needed discretion. Maria was taken there. I didn't know about it at the time. The cardinal called after the fact. Anyway, fortunately, this convent had a priest hole."

"I'm not following you … exactly."

"I had no idea this would get so out of hand. May God forgive me. But that's where they took her … to the convent in Velletri. They wanted information. They wanted to know what she had on them. You see, she'd breached the system and had damning evidence regarding a fund she was overseeing."

"I know all that. The Silent Mistress Fund. Get on with it," Carmella fumed.

"The what-did-you-call-it fund?" Cate gasped.

"You never heard it called that? The crooked little so-called family charity fund?"

Cate had never heard such a delineation, but the accuracy of the label demoralized her. She sank and let out a howl so loud it echoed through the empty halls, reverberating off the walls and filling the space with a mournful cry that embodied all her pain and despair.

Orio, thoroughly shaken, found himself flattened against a far wall.

Carmella was having none of it. "Get with it here, Cate. We're not done. Go on from where you left off."

"Well, okay, they knew, and they'd been following her. Then, when she left the bank last week, taking her personal belongings, that really got the cardinal sweating. And he made his move.

"When I found out, I drove out to Velletri to see what I could do. I know the mother superior there, Margherita. She's a friend, and no one would question my presence. But then, there was a gas leak. It was mayhem."

"A gas leak? And you left her there? You wretched human being," Carmella cried out.

"No. It wasn't like that!"

Orio had never seen someone from the Church confess to wrongdoing so overtly.

"Anyway, when I arrived back here at Casa Veronesi later, the cardinal called to confirm what I already knew, that Maria had gone missing. She found the priest hole in a tick, I'm sure of it, and tunneled her way out."

"She could be dead on the side of a road or still in that tunnel!" Carmella knew that was unlikely. Though sheltered, she knew how strong her daughter was. Just like Faustino had been. The thought brought a tiny smile to her heart.

"She's not in the tunnel. Trust me on that."

So, the sinister nun had not left her to die. She must've circled back and checked. At least there was that. With a tilt of her head and a lift of her brow, Carmella sought Father Rinaldi's opinion.

Orio cleared his throat. "Carmella, Maria is certainly not dead. She has a brilliant mind. She's somewhere safe. We need to get to her, though."

"Orio?" Having released her sins, Cate felt her blood pressure dip for the first time all week. "I'm sorry, where are my manners? Do you ... are you hungry? Carmella?"

Despite the abrupt pivot, neither of them said no to that.

"Well, okay then, I'll put something together." Cate called out to Lati.

At the large dining room table, over cold cuts, cheese, a crispy loaf of sourdough bread, a bowl of fruit, and a surprisingly light but spicy French red, the three of them worked individually to process the situation.

After three slices of Pecorino Romano and a hearty sip of wine, Carmella said, "Hey, I'm curious. How much are they paying you to be part of the boys' club and do their dirty work?"

That was a question Orio hadn't expected.

"No one pays me. Some things aren't about money. Orio knows."

"Oh, I really don't, Cate," he responded. "I'm just wrapping my brain around all this. And, honestly, no one normally tells me anything."

"I can see that," Carmella said, sizing him up. "But they should. You're nice and a good listener."

"Um, thanks."

"Listen, Cate, what's your story, anyway?"

The nun fidgeted with the stem of her glass, circling the wine. "I suppose mine is the same as anyone's in our vocation, Carmella. I love our God above and wouldn't make it a day in this world without his love and forgiveness. Protecting what we love, as you well know, comes at a price."

"Unbelievable," Orio said mainly to himself, the fires of anger burning in his belly.

"Sometimes, Orio, you must weigh your sin against your greater purpose. 'The thief comes only to steal and kill and destroy. I came that they may have life and have it abundantly.' John 10:10."

"That is not what that verse means, all due respect. You cannot think that kidnapping Maria was for the greater good."

Carmella studied the nun. "You're hiding something."

"I'm not."

"Said the magician to the spy. But take your time." Carmella sipped her wine. "We're not going anywhere."

Orio made a noise, something of a grunt, and began to rise.

Carmella admonished him with a sharp glare.

He sat back down. Now all he could do was watch as the typically strong and domineering nun, exposed by a desperate and astute mother, looked down to hide her shame.

She fixated on the untouched glass of wine in front of her until the wellspring of heartbreak let loose, and she sobbed.

Neither Carmella nor Orio moved to comfort her, but they did sit patiently to give her time to recover.

After a bit, having not uttered a word, Cate wiped her face and retrieved her phone from a pocket. She dialed 112, tapped the speaker button, and set it on the table.

"*Polizia*, how may I direct your call?"

CHAPTER FORTY-EIGHT

La Giustiniana, Rome

Teddy Weaver's backyard was the secret garden setting of fairy tales, with a wood-burning barbecue and a gothic masterpiece of a table where the six of them now sat, all framed in a canopy of green. The abundance of exotic plants provided Maria the privacy and comfort to recuperate. But with the meal complete and the afternoon sun in an azure sky dancing on the branches of Himalayan cedar and cockspur coral trees, the assorted bunch was antsy to start talking.

Where to from here?

Though it hadn't been easy, Yigael had kept his thoughts under lock all weekend. Even the seasoned ex-Mossad knew it wasn't his place to determine Maria's next steps forward. After all, he'd just met her and knew she was still getting used to him. The short, thick-set man to whom most would accede their authority came a with a steep learning curve. This, he knew.

Valentina had appreciated Yigael's willpower and had noted it all afternoon with an occasional smile of approval. A pro in nonverbal communication, she raised an eyebrow in her new female friend's direction, her idea of a nudge.

Maria nodded and stood at the head of the ornate table. Her audience turned, enrapt before she'd spoken a single word.

"I imagine you're all wondering why I've gathered you here," she began.

Though on a one-second delay, the laughter was loud when it came, and days' worth of tension washed away like the rough edges on tumbled sea glass.

She sat back down.

Teddy took a moment to dash off to collect two carafes of Chianti Classico Riserva di Montemaggio. He'd purchased them on a quick trip to Florence and had set them aside for a special occasion. He'd be hard-pressed to find an occasion more epic than this, and so he'd decanted them earlier. He set the glass pitchers on either end of the table.

"To begin," Maria said, "and I hope you can understand, my mind is driving me crazy. Literally. This ... event in my life has taken it over. It's in every nook and cranny of my brain. I keep reliving this past week over and over, and I'd like for it to stop. I want to forget about the entire ... thing, but it won't go away. And I'm just so angry—"

"Maria, if I may," Valentina interrupted, "you have every right to be livid over what the Church has done to you."

Maria had talked with Valentina about her unique upbringing, the loss of her father, and the contentious relationship with her mother, one she'd struggled to make peace with, and the scientist was sure Maria was feeling old anger spun in with fresh fury over what the Church had done. Maria was at a crossroads, a life-defining moment, and those always drudged up unresolved issues from the past.

"I'll be the first to say it, *if I may*," Francesco intervened, "From an ethical standpoint, the Church must take responsibility for its heinous response to you discovering the true nature of this fund. What they did, may God forgive them, is criminal, and it endangered your life. It could well have ended it."

"I second that." Teddy nodded at the monsignor.

Justin nodded, too, though he wasn't comfortable partaking in the discussion. He felt lucky that no one would question his silence. They'd pass it off as fatigue from his cancer treatment.

"I believe the question is," Yigael said, "what's the next best move? Do you go to the police?"

"The press?" Valentina said.

"The pope?" Francesco added.

"And if so, when?" Yigael asked. "Do we keep you hidden and make the Vatican sweat some more?" Yigael's lips curled at the idea. "And then we use your 'unknown whereabouts' as leverage to coerce them to do the right thing and admit to the account?"

Though a valid idea, Francesco wasn't the gameplay type. He glanced at Justin to see if he could read his thoughts about the notion.

Maria was all too aware that this round-table discussion could end in a face-off between clergy and laypeople. They were divided. "Could we table the idea of taking vengeance on the Church momentarily and talk about the bigger issue?" she suggested.

"Bigger than the Church acting like the Sicilian Mafia, manhandling a woman and endangering her life?" Teddy asked with sarcasm.

Maria smiled at him. She could never repay her new American friend for all he'd done in their brief time getting to know each other.

"I think what she's referring to, Teddy, is the Silent Mistress Fund," Justin said audibly enough for everyone to pause, but surprising no one more than himself.

Maria locked eyes with the cardinal, and they shared a

moment of understanding. "I'm thinking about the thousands the Church has wronged, and that's just counting the mistresses and offspring that were born from their ... relationships. What about all the women who've never stepped forward? What about the victims who didn't willingly participate? What about the offspring who've no idea who their real father is?" Maria shuddered. She was out of her depth but believed in the Divine Creator and trusted she was placed here for a reason.

Valentina could feel the heat of the emotion permeating Maria's skin. It blanketed everyone, and the table grew solemn.

Maria made a point of sitting taller and continued, "And there's the issue of parishioners worldwide. For decades, they've donated freely to a 'charity' fund under false pretenses. Yes, the use of charitable donations is at the Church's discretion. But what it's done, *is doing*, is deceitful on such a grand scale that it, that it—" Maria cut herself off.

"Takes your breath away," Valentina said. "I know how you feel." The Church had taken her voice away with a gag order over the discovery of the tomb of Julia Episcopa, the first female bishop in the Church back in Yeshua's time. And the Church had stolen her lab Valeri out from under her over the discovery of the *Secret Temple Scroll*, the oldest document on Yeshua, depicting his life in real time.

The Church did not take kindly to change.

Francesco looked across at his oldest friend before turning back toward the head of the table. "Maria, if I may, priests have been practicing celibacy in the Church since the year 1,100, when the rule came into effect. But the Vatican wrote it as a discipline, not doctrine, which means Julius Africanus can lift it, just as any pope before him could have."

Justin was taken aback by his friend's progressive statement, which strongly insinuated that he was for change.

The look the two men of the cloth shared did not go unnoticed by anyone.

"I like your line of thinking, Fran," Yigael said, "though I'm a little surprised."

"Well, I wasn't just writing sermons all weekend, Yigael. I, too, know how to surf the net."

His comment elicited laughter all around.

"And I spent some time in the library too. The list of popes who've had sexual relationships before and after being ordained is in the mid-double digits. The Bishops of Rome!" Francesco raised his hands in defeat. "A decade back, when new guidelines were set for offspring of priests, Pope Francis was quoted as saying, *'Never say never,'* and this right here might be why."

"Pope Francis said it was a question of discipline, not faith, Fran," Justin said. "And that he was ultimately in favor of celibacy." Decades of guilt fed the cardinal's counterpoint.

"Well, of course, he was, Justin. The undertaking to change this rule is bigger than any one man, or woman," Francesco looked at Maria and Valentina, "and he likely did all he could."

"Which was little more than nothing."

"Yigael," Valentina scolded.

"He's right, Val," Francesco said. "He did nothing. Offspring of clerics still live in hiding, ashamed and stigmatized. Civil laws ensure every child has a right to know both parents, but canon law trumps that in the eyes of the Church. Our higher-ups make their own rules. The rest of the world be damned. At the most recent conference, the bishops laid out principles to prioritize the best interests of the child, and still—"

"Nothing's changed," Yigael interjected, and Valentina didn't stop him this time. "But we're off topic. We need to tackle the most imminent issue first," he looked at Maria, "your kidnapping."

"I can't agree with you this time, Yigael. I line up with Francesco," she said. "With the thousands of mistresses and victims of assault and offspring of clerics living in silence, they must take priority over my situation."

Maria saw they were surprised by her candor. "My best friend's mother was a victim," she admitted. "I never knew until my mother visited this last Thursday to tell me Luisa had just died."

That made everyone's eyes but Valentina's—who knew of the story—get wider.

"And then the subject of Luisa's mother came up. My mother told me that Elsa DiCaprio was just seventeen when Luisa was born. Her father turned out to be the priest at our local parish in Falcone. Father Mucci. He was twenty years older than Elsa.

"How could that relationship have been … consensual?" Maria bowed her head to find the right words. "Luisa's death led me to this fund and her true paternity.

"I've done so much thinking about this, obviously. And I realize women and kids are living in shame and secrecy because their fathers are clerics. Some don't even know who their fathers are, yet they carry the crushing weight of inexplicable guilt, and it darkens every relationship they have."

"Not to mention," Francesco dared to say, "the clerics— some of them anyway—living in silence because they've acted on the human emotion love and the need for contact and connection. They, too, are suffering."

Justin flushed. But no one noticed as Francesco had dropped the mic with that comment.

Clearing his throat, Yigael said, "Fran, your points have been … surprising." Then he cracked a wry smile, adding, "something you want to tell us?"

That cut the tension.

Francesco laughed out loud and shook his head. "No, Yigael, my vows are intact. This situation has caused me a great deal of contemplation, however."

Nods all around.

After a beat, Maria said, "This fund has spent hundreds of millions of parishioner dollars over decades to protect a discipline that, to be kind, is not working."

"The understatement of the century," Yigael said. *"Literally."*

"Even as a little girl," Valentina began, "I questioned why our parish priest didn't have a wife or children. Everyone around him did, and he seemed all alone. I got the stock response *'because that's how it is'* constantly, until I finally stopped asking."

Justin ventured, "What everyone seems to be saying here is there are victims on both sides of this misguided rule."

"That's where we're all in agreement, Justin," Yigael said.

As the cardinal nodded at the ex-Mossad, Francesco could swear he saw a weight lifted from his longtime colleague's shoulders.

"So, as you can see, my kidnapping is way down on the list of issues that needs addressing."

Everyone thought on these points.

"Sounds like what you're saying, Maria, is that you'd like to first speak to the pope directly," Teddy said, adding, "Boy, I never thought I'd be saying that."

Valentina smiled at the young man. She had to give it to him. He was steady as a rock.

"Maybe there is a divine order we could be following here," Yigael said. "You speak with Pope Julius first, tell him about your kidnapping and why it happened, and then show him proof of the Silent Mistress Fund. And lean into him about your concerns with the growing list of victims. Then we go to the police under the pope's guidance. After that, we contact the press, Levin, of course. That way, you're in control of the narrative."

"This is so ... huge." Maria looked flushed and tense.

"It is," Yigael said, empathizing through his own experience of jittery nerves when meeting with esteemed individuals. "Are you up to it?"

"I am, yes."

"I do think Yigael's plan makes sense," Valentina put in.

He nodded, and so did everyone else as they relaxed, sipping their wine.

After a long beat, Yigael focused in on Maria and Teddy. "If you go to the pope, you'll need hard evidence. More than those images you snapped on your phone." Yigael had, in fact, broken into the device and reviewed them, before giving it back to her, along with Birdi's key, the minute he'd arrived at Teddy's. He dipped his chin and raised his brows. "How about it?"

Maria and Teddy's heads spun toward each other.

"We can get it," they said in unison.

Francesco interrupted the mood with an "uh-oh," as he was stared at his phone.

"Fran?" Yigael asked, though it wasn't a question.

"Orio just texted."

"I knew he couldn't keep his mitts out of this." Yigael wasn't angry ... yet. After all, he'd done a lot.

"What is it, " Valentina asked Francesco.

He looked up after perusing the message, all eyes on him. "I'm just going to read it. *'Back in town with Carmella Caruso, long story.'"*

"My mother's here?"

"The text goes on," Francesco said, motioning to his phone and clearing his throat. *"'Sister Cate called in a missing persons report on Maria, told them her last known whereabouts, a convent outside Rome.* Polizia *asked her to come by the station, see if there was anything more she could tell them. She left a while ago. I would've texted sooner, but ....'* And the rest is Orio rambling."

"Sister Cate knew where I was? At the convent? How's that even poss—" Maria stopped herself and thought back to when she'd bumped into the nun in Cardinal Cacciatore's office the morning after her mother's surprise visit. She knew then something was going on.

"Velletri's under an hour away from here," Teddy said, rising.

Teddy made his way to the sliding glass door. "Imma fire up the laptop and turn on the flat screen. If the police are there, this is going viral." And he was off.

"So, going backward, it looks like police, the press, and then the pope," Valentina said to lighten the mood.

"Still need the proof." Yigael glanced once more at Maria.

"Worry not." Maria tried and failed to sound relaxed, though hacking into the IOR's computing system wasn't what had her stomach stirring.

"Maria, are you okay?" Valentina asked.

She nodded. "I'm fine." But she wasn't. It was one thing to conceive of a pack of older, conservative church leaders—driven by custom, stature, and the male ego—lying, cheating, and kidnapping in the name of the Church. It was another to imagine a nun being involved.

Teddy stepped back outside, laptop in hand. "*Viva Roma* has an article online already."

"Of course, they do. The bottom feeder of news outlets."

"They're not *The New York Times* ... or *La Carta,* Yigael, but they're in business 'cuz they deliver the news faster than a hot knife through frozen butter. And sometimes they even get it right." Teddy set the computer in front of Valentina.

The others gathered around as she read.

"'Il Convento di Santa Veronica Giuliani, Velletri, is under investigation after a missing persons report was filed on Sister Maria Caruso. This old convent was the last known location of the sister, who recently made history by becoming the head of forensic accounting for the IOR, the highest position a woman has ever held at the Vatican Bank. She was reported missing Sunday evening after ...."'

CHAPTER FORTY-NINE

San Paolo, Rome

Cardinal Angelico Cacciatore was back at it shortly after an unsuccessful cat nap that he'd tagged with an equally unsatisfying shot of whiskey to quell his nerves. Nothing he did could push his heart rate back down into double digits.

What more news was blossoming about the little nun who'd escaped his clutches? With that singular stressor monopolizing his brain space, he sat back down at his grand home office desk.

Clicking away to find the latest update, he discovered that the hastily compiled missing persons reports had tripled in the last two hours, but the story itself had stalled. However, phrases like *"whereabouts unknown ... police are searching"* repeated like a runaway wheel.

So much wind. At least they haven't linked me ... yet. He peered out his office window at the street below. No reporters.

His phone buzzed again—Massimo. The cardinal was in no mood to talk to his henchman. He let it go, as before.

Cacciatore saw through the reporters' conjectures and speculations to two possibilities. Maria was either safely in hiding, or this was an inside job—one of his own had gone rogue and knew her whereabouts.

"His own" had been dwindling, with his colleagues at the bank—save for Bishop Burbidge—in jail. He reasoned that if Maria were in hiding, she would not likely be tipping off the press. His intuition landed on the one person who could've come clean and reported to the authorities. However, he couldn't be sure.

A tapping at his front door evolved into a wrapping that further tested the cardinal's fragile nerves. If it didn't quit, he'd have to answer it because Joella was off on Sundays. Thoughts of her distracted him for a moment. He couldn't fathom why that "cute little thing" wanted to be a nun. Switching gears in a blink—he had no time for wild contemplations—he stayed put in his office chair, still dressed in his bathrobe and fine, Italian-made leather slippers he'd changed into after his nap. He did not have the energy to deal with Massimo and couldn't fathom how the string of unanswered texts had not made that clear.

The wrapping turned into a brutal *thwack*.

In a temper, he rose, tightened his sash, descended the stairs, and went to the door. "Cate?" he said on opening it. "I'm not dressed."

"I can see that." She pushed her way in.

Yanking his robe closed further and carefully screening her worried, red-rimmed eyes, he said, "It's like you've seen a ghost. What brings you here on a Sunday, for heaven's sake?"

Sister Cate was unsure how to answer. Could he indeed not have a clue? Evidently, she'd have to spell it out for the old boot. It had been a rough few hours. She figured it was best to be direct.

"Angelico, it's over," she began, though she was mainly speaking to the marbled entryway while wringing her hands.

"The fund. It's going ... public. Within a few days, Church Families Charity will be known everywhere."

"Don't be ridiculous. Calm down. It's going to be fine." The cardinal watched as Cate fidgeted. He'd never seen her behave like this before. "This is probably all Maria, you know. Her doing. I bet it is, too smart for her own good, that damn little nun. I don't know what we were thinking, hiring her. *Ehi, un caffè*? Or how about a Campari? Come." He turned for the kitchen.

Her feet remained rooted in place. "We have to be prepared to face it."

He pivoted back toward her. "This will blow over. Look at me," he said with authority, although his costume diminished his sense of superiority. "Cate, I said look at me."

Reluctantly, she met his eyes.

"The point of everything we do is to protect the Church. It's our vocation. And protect it, we have."

"Have we?" she asked.

"Yes. And we'd do it again. Whoever found Maria probably called the police. Unfortunately, the press got hold of it. They're toying with us, don't you see?" The cardinal started pacing. "Because if they really wanted this to explode in our faces, the police would be at my door. But they're not. You are. Because we're right, and they know it. They're just trying to spook us."

"Angelico, we're not—"

He cut her off and faced her directly. "What we've done is protect the Church from chaos and calamity. And we've sent a message. You don't mess with us. That's what this says. We're servants, and we took vows of obedience, which means we're soldiers if need be. We must follow and protect the laws of the Church, to keep it strong, to—"

"Angelico!" she shrieked. Cate had never raised her voice to him like that. But it did the trick, and he quieted down. "It's illegal to kidnap," she shouted, at the end of her rope. "The laws of the Church would never support that. Besides, we could've killed her. Don't *you* see?" She prayed he was grasping the gravity of their deeds.

Cacciatore had no plans to kill the young nun. The scheme was intended to persuade her to return what she had stolen and keep quiet. Some people needed nudging more than others. And Maria, as it turned out, was bullheaded.

What the cardinal really wanted to say in response to Cate's babbling was that had the goal been to kill the new head of forensic accounting, well …. But he didn't give voice to that sentiment. Instead, he let out a grand sigh that echoed in his entryway with its elegant, high ceilings bordered by floral ornamentations.

The tired-eyed cardinal stared down his narrow nose at his longtime friend. She wasn't just a colleague. She was part of his inner circle. Softening his features to feign understanding, he gathered his thoughts. "We didn't hurt her, though, did we? Maria's fine."

"How do you know she's fine? She's missing, and she could be dead."

"Believe me, she's out there, orchestrating everything. And, quite frankly, I fear what her end goal may be. We need to get in front of this." He realized he did need to rout out Massimo and Pepper. His henchman's female counterpart made him downright uneasy. Yet there was no doubt she was the brain behind that duo.

Cate shook her head. "She's just a girl, Angelico. She was doing what she thought was right too. And God only knows what kind of irreparable psychological damage we did to that poor—"

"Dammit, Cate, this isn't about her." The old nun was the fly atop a *porchetta* sandwich, and the cardinal was on his last slab of patience. "This issue is bigger than you or me. And I don't appreciate you coming here and confronting me like this. We have history!"

That's all it took for Cate to stomp her foot. "Indeed, we do. And here's the way it is for me. Going forward, I will not live out the rest of my days shackled to our history, Angelico. You know how grateful I am. I've paid you back with my servitude, even though I'm the victim here. *I'm the victim!*" Cate bent at the waist, palms on her knees, hyperventilating. "Oh, what have I done? Unforgivable," she managed to spit out between short, choppy breaths.

In a panic, the cardinal dragged a club chair from his sitting room. The last thing he needed was a nun splayed out half-dead on his hand-painted, porcelain tile. He knew CPR, but he had no plans to perform it. "Here. Sit."

She did.

"Cate." The cardinal was out of his depth, just as he had been decades back when he'd first met the broken girl. But he had to do something. Weakness was unbecoming, and he never had the patience for nonsense like this. He needed his team, such as *that* was, to stay the course at any cost.

The cardinal dug deep and asked for guidance. "Just calm down, Cate, and don't be so irrational. Of course, you're a victim." He held a false smile until she looked up and acknowledged it. "And think about it. Without compassion from the Church, where would you have ended up? Church Family Charities exists for that very reason. And the Church gave you purpose, and you have been a dutiful servant. Draw from that strength now, Sister Benedict. Let's pray together."

She ignored him. "The charity fund shouldn't have to exist. Don't you see that? The 'reason' it exists is what's wrong with the Church, and Maria recognized that." Cate dropped her reddened face into her hands. She was so tired, so wrought with guilt and grief piled on top of a lifetime of shame.

"Cate?" The cardinal felt the back of his neck grow hot with irritation. *Women can be so dramatic.* "What exactly are you saying?" He knew what was coming, and he wanted to kick himself for ever trusting any woman with serious matters of the Church.

She looked up, her plain face unruffled for the first time all afternoon. "I'm saying it's done, Angelico."

That statement felt like a baton to the shins. "What? What do you mean? What have you done?" He seethed while realizing he didn't really have to ask. He knew. She'd betrayed him. She'd called in the missing persons report, just as he'd suspected. Coming here was just a courtesy. A thank you and a "get stuffed" all rolled into one. But he wanted to hear her say it, nonetheless. "What have you done?!"

Cate drew strength from her Creator as she stood on weak legs and squared off with the domineering cardinal. "I did what was right, and you should too."

And with that, she turned and left.

CHAPTER FIFTY

La Giustiniana, Rome

"You know what this means," Yigael said, as the group minus two filed into the house from outside to continue their talks. Justin and Francesco had gone, leaving Valentina, Maria, Teddy, and himself to finalize the end game.

"Beg your pardon?" Teddy asked. "What 'what' means, Yigael?"

"The fact that Maria's kidnapping is now public business means we must call the police and let them know she's safe. And we'd better do it *rapida*. If we delay, there could be trouble. The police aren't fond of searching for kidnap victims who've already turned up."

Maria and Valentina shared a look.

Yigael asked softly, "Do you want to press charges against those you think took you? You'll be asked that question. Either way, it's okay … yes or no."

"Who would ever believe a cardinal kidnapped me," Maria responded. "It sounds ludicrous. No, I don't want any part of it. I'm safe now." *I hope I'm safe*, she thought.

"You will be interrogated, though."

"Yigael, do you have to use such a user-*un*friendly word? Tsk." Valentina brushed off an invisible bug from her shoulder, a habit she drew on when irritated.

"Story, then, you'll have to tell your story," Yigael corrected himself with a sour look at his longtime friend.

"Yigael," Valentina persisted, "can't you put the lid on this so that Maria doesn't have to talk to the police?"

"No, I cannot put a lid on it, as you say. This is local. There's nothing I can do." Yigael trod carefully but had to speak his mind, "These men have to be prosecuted, no way around that. Even if you don't want to press charges, the police will investigate. Look, we don't have much time to hash this out." Do you need a few minutes before we call?"

"Just a question … will I get in trouble for taking the silent mistress evidence?"

"What you did is out of their jurisdiction. That happened in Vatican City. Rome PD can't touch you."

Maria's gaze took her to a cluster of petite, exotic plants on stands flanking the fireplace, landing on a gorgeous magenta orchid. It calmed her beating heart. Several moments later, she said, "Go ahead and call. I'm ready."

Yigael was out of his seat like it was on fire, phone in hand.

Maria headed for the kitchen. "I need a *Spuma*."

CHAPTER FIFTY-ONE

Campo Santo Teutonico, Rome

Sister Cate Benedict thrust herself into her aging, bright-blue Smart Fortwo Coupe 450 and sped from Cardinal Cacciatore's to the burial site adjacent to St. Peter's Basilica, where she tried to still her mind and pray. Failing that, she sat on a bench outside the *polizia di stato*, reevaluating her life choices and steeling herself.

One event, one singular event had led to this moment, and, in hindsight, it seemed as clear as the tranquil Lago de Bracciano this time of year.

Rome, 1978

Leaving choir practice *at St. Joseph's church ten minutes earlier— she was to solo on Sunday—fifteen-year-old Catherine Assini had forgotten her schoolbooks. Circling back to pick them up, she called for Sister Margaret, the organist, but got no reply.*

Hurrying up the double flight of stairs to the music room just off the balcony, she scooped them up from under a chair. Turning to leave, she was startled by her priest, Father Stefano Aurelio, standing by the stairs.

"Oh, I'm sorry, Father. I didn't hear you come up."

"Catherine, don't ever apologize for coming to church."

She laughed. "Have a nice night." She moved to step around the priest and head downstairs.

He sidestepped in front of her. "You look pretty today."

"Thank you." Catherine, with the alluring red hair and pale complexion of the Irish, was used to compliments. But ... it was something in his tone ... and an uneasy feeling took hold.

He stepped closer, and she smelled ... cloves? Did the priest smoke? It was a strange thought wedged into so many others.

Catherine had never had a first date, nor had she ever been kissed. She wasn't entirely sure of Father Aurelio's intent, but instinct told her she needed to get away.

She darted to the side, but he grabbed her, pulling her into his chest. She pushed against him, but he clasped harder. "Truly beautiful," he said, inhaling the scent of her hair. He pulled back and caught her eyes briefly before pivoting and pressing her into the wall. That's when her books—her only shield—slid from her arms and hit the carpeted floor with a thud.

She was trapped.

Catherine's dreams vanished in the organ room of St. Joseph's that fall day.

Later, back at home, she skipped dinner, blaming it on cramps.

The following week, she bowed out of the solo in the Christmas concert, explaining to Sister Margaret that her school load was too intense for extracurricular activities. By the end of the quarter, the As in her college prep courses had collapsed to Cs, and she hadn't bothered with an excuse for that swing downward.

By the new year, her parents despaired daily over what had become of their daughter—a point that Catherine confirmed when she finally announced to the heartbroken duo where her vocation would lie. But life often fell out of the groove. Of that, Catherine had convinced her young self, and so she marched on, shoulders back, as one did when fate took everything but one's breath.

IT WAS TRUE that Cardinal Cacciatore had been her savior, taking in a wayward pregnant teen without much of a story to tell. He'd shown her compassion, given her a new way. But she was done answering to him. Done toeing the line and shouldering the wrongs of others. Done suffocating from shame.

Cate knew less about police procedures than she did pop music. But for the baby whose face she never saw, whose skin she never touched, whose name she'll never know, she was done hiding.

"It's over," she said to the Almighty as much as herself as she stood and walked toward the police station to turn herself in for aiding and abetting in the kidnapping of Sister Maria Caruso.

CHAPTER FIFTY-TWO

La Giustiniana, Rome

Detective Domenico Loria stood outside Teddy Weaver's residence. The detective had seen it all in his thirty years on the force. Not much surprised him anymore. But this one was a whopper, a nun kidnapped. He was eager to learn what more he could.

He rang the bell.

Yigael answered.

"You?" Detective Loria said, taking a half step back.

Yigael Dorian was well-known in police jurisdictions all over the city. He'd influenced many local cases when it interfered with Mossad investigations. As the last word, often, he was both loved and hated. "Detective ... come in." Yigael led Loria to where the three others were gathered.

"*Un caffè*, Detective?" Valentina stood, already heading for the kitchen.

"This is Teddy Weaver." Yigael gestured toward the young man.

The detective looked questioningly at Teddy. "You're American."

"Why, yes, but I didn't say. You didn't even get a whiff of my accent yet." Teddy smiled warmly, lightening the tension.

Loria merely smiled at the young man's comments before turning to Maria. "*Ciao*. You must be Sister Maria."

"*Ciao*, yes, indeed," she said with a nod. His manner immediately put Maria at ease.

The detective turned back to Yigael. "And you know her how?"

"Friend," Yigael said.

"That it?"

Yigael shrugged, sat, and gestured for Loria to do the same.

Valentina returned with *il caffè*.

"Who's she?" Loria asked.

"Why don't you ask her?" Yigael said.

"Madame?"

"A better friend," Valentina said.

"Name?"

"Valentina Vella."

"I thought you looked familiar. And why are you two here?"

"We're friends," Yigael and Valentina said together.

Yeah, and Yigael Dorian has probably coached the victim to within an inch of her life, he thought.

Detective Loria looked around the well-appointed room, then focused on the nun. His voice softened. "Well, Maria, my full name is Detective Domenico Loria. I understand you've been through a difficult ordeal. I need to ask you some questions. Will that be all right?"

"Yes, Detective. I'll do my best to tell you what you want to know, but I do not wish to press charges."

The detective's eyebrows pitched upward, and his head tilted. "Oh?"

Maria didn't elaborate.

"May I ask why?"

"I don't want any more involvement than I have right now. I want to forget about … the ordeal."

"Can you tell me about who kidnapped you?"

"They were two men I've never seen before." From there, Maria recounted details from exiting the pizzeria to being locked in a room at the convent to her escape and the call to Teddy.

"And you know Mr. Weaver … how?"

If Maria was embarrassed by the question, she hid it well. She figured she'd been through enough and didn't have to cave to a police officer asking a probing question. "We met on a train."

Loria's tilted head dipped. "And why do you suppose you were kidnapped?"

Maria's eyes slid toward Yigael.

He gave her the barest nod.

Returning her eyes to the detective, she said, "I … I came across some information that could be detrimental to the Church. I think they wanted to silence me."

"What information was that?" Loria asked.

"It was a … banking discrepancy."

"This discrepancy … what was it about?"

"Discrepancy is perhaps the wrong word, Detective. I came across a file that was meant to be kept secret. It was about some activities the Church is engaged in that could be considered questionable." Maria was doing her best to keep the heart of her story hidden from the police. At least for a while, until she could tell it herself, publicly.

"What is the nature of the information contained in the file?"

"Detective Loria, I cannot speak to this right now."

"Why is that?"

Maria sat straighter, pursing her lips, refusing to respond.

"Then, just how did you come to possess this secret information?"

Maria released her breath audibly. *This isn't going to look good.* "I broke into the banking system and discovered the file. It contained data that might put the Church at risk if it were to become public knowledge."

"And the file is where?"

"Right where I left it."

"I'd like you to turn it over. Digital or hard copy, we'll need to see it."

"I don't have it."

"Oh? Who has it, then?"

"The Church has it."

"You didn't take it?"

"Uh, no."

"Why not?"

"It wasn't mine to take." Maria squirmed but didn't reveal the photos she had on her phone. And Yigael, Valentina, and Teddy sat stone-faced, safeguarding the secret.

"That's enough for now," Detective Loria said as he left.

Maria gave Teddy a quick peep of relief.

Valentina stood up to return the cups to the kitchen but stopped short when she heard the detective's following words.

"Oh, I wanted to mention … a sister you know, Cate Benedict, turned herself in earlier today … confessed to aiding and abetting in your kidnapping. She's sitting in a jail cell."

Figures. Yigael grimaced.

The news crushed Maria. *So, she* was *in on it.* Her whole body turned in on itself.

Valentina dropped down on the armless chair by the kitchen door.

"Who's Cate Benedict?" Teddy asked.

The detective turned to the young American. "She's the one who unlocked Maria's cell door."

CHAPTER FIFTY-THREE

La Giustiniana, Rome

Sister Cate's involvement with her kidnapping had turned Maria's stomach and kept her awake for most of the night. But as her feet hit the cool tile, it woke her up just enough. She and Teddy had work to do.

Two hours of plotting and coding reminded Maria of one of the reasons she loved computer programming—and it wasn't because of the math. It had the effect of sweeping her up, up, and away, so her mind could focus on nothing else.

It was a Godsend this morning.

"Okay, pal, this is it." Sister Maria said to her desk mate, surprised by her casual talk to the man a man she'd spoken to for only a scant five minutes, never mind she'd been living with him unchaperoned. "You know we're breaking the law here."

"Aw, heck. In for a penny, in for a pound." Teddy might've used naughtier language, which he expressed on occasion, but he was sitting next to a nun, the reality with which he, honestly, had yet to come entirely to terms.

"Maria laughed. "I haven't heard that one."

"Needs must when the devil drives."

"What? Nor that." She giggled.

"You, dear Maria, haven't heard of many things." He gave her a wry side-eye.

"Seriously, Teddy, I know we've talked about the consequences that might come, and we agreed on what we want to do, but now, well, this is it. In a few more minutes, we can't turn back."

"Let's go. Let's break into the Vatican Bank."

Maria shuddered and then took a deep breath.

The pair of techies sat side by side at the workstation in Teddy's home office, she on her laptop, the Texan on his desktop. Overnight, an idea had come to Maria about just what might work for the break-in.

After discussing the system's software and the makeup of her IOR team with Teddy, they decided to use old-school clone phishing emails to gain access.

The hack required the attackers—Maria and Teddy—to replicate an email message sent routinely from a recognizable party. The sender's email address and body of the message would look legitimate and familiar, which was vital. The aim was to trick the recipient into opening the email.

Once the unsuspecting recipient did so and clicked on the link inside it, malware-embedded code would be downloaded, breaching the security system. The type of malicious code they wrote could not be detected by commercial antivirus software —and the intrepid, able hackers would then gain broad entry into the Vatican Bank files.

They'd spent the better part of the morning creating the virus. It was ready to go.

Now, it was time for Maria to craft the perfect message from a known sender to transport their creation.

Who to send it to? Someone who wouldn't suspect anything. Someone who wouldn't question a routinely fielded update. She addressed the email to the hardworking and meticulous but blank-faced Camille Kingston.

In the subject line, Maria typed in *Software Update for Convent Counting.*

When Camille spotted the email from dan@xpsolutons.com—the company that now owned and operated *Convent Counting*—she would think nothing of it. And hopefully, she wouldn't notice the typo and would open it out of habit. When she installed the update, it would override the previous program. None would be the wiser, and a whole new vista would open for the two techies turned hacktivists.

Maria's own program—how about that?—would be her entry into the Vatican Bank.

Maria didn't know when the system would be checked for malware, though. She had to pray that Paolo Testa, the point person for her team, would not spend his morning doing just that. In her short time with the IOR, she'd noticed that Paolo wasn't really a Monday kind of guy, and so she was gambling that he wouldn't check for spyware on the first day of the week.

Camille took her lunch break from 12:30 to 2:00 daily and had never strayed from her schedule for even a minute. She and Teddy would take over the machine while she was away.

It was just after ten in the morning. With the email written, and the malware attached, they were ready to go.

She hit *Send*, and they sat back and waited.

Valentina popped through the doorway. "How are you going? Getting into the system?" she asked.

"You don't want to know," Maria said not taking her eyes from the screen.

Valentina laughed. "You go to it, then." She popped back out.

Two hours later, Maria's screen came alive with all she needed. With a few clicks, the silent hack was complete.

Next, she and Teddy hacked into the hidden subsystem

using Cardinal Cacciatore's username and password. The cardinal hadn't bothered to change it since her breach—she'd been banking on that. Teddy had set up a cloud-connect remote printer, which meant they could print from the bank to Teddy's kitchen, where he'd moved his printer as a convenience to all.

Maria sent the printer statement after statement from the encrypted subfiles of the Church Families Charity account.

The whir of the machine at work, as it spit out page after page, indicated all systems were a go.

After stopping in the kitchen to check the files, Maria ventured out back for some fresh air. She settled into a cushioned lounge chair on the patio. The warm sun shining down did nothing to comfort her, though, as her insides were buzzing, so she revisited her risk.

She was breaking the law, committing a felony. They'd never prosecute her, though. Even so, she couldn't imagine what was next. She certainly didn't have a job to go back to. Silent hacking, even into the billion-dollar organization, was like a child pocketing a *caramel* at the neighborhood market compared to kidnapping.

Teddy, lagging, joined her outside. He handed her a glass of *caffè shakerato*, the icy, sweet espresso he'd just made, and took a seat in the chair beside her.

Maria took a sip and cringed. "I've never liked this. Sorry for your trouble."

"Aw, no trouble, and no worries."

"I'm wondering what to do." She sighed.

"Suffer through it or give it to me. I love *shakerato*."

"No, I mean, I'm wondering what I'm going to do when this is over ... with my life?" She shifted away from the sun. "I'm not like everyone else."

Maria never had dreams, never had options. She'd always just followed the narrow path that was laid before her without question. What was she supposed to do? Just walk away from everything she'd ever known? She wished Orio were with her. He was her closest friend in Rome, but Yigael had asked her not to contact him or anyone just yet.

Teddy Weaver had recently reinvented himself, leaving a cushy future in Austin—a steady job at the hundred-plus-year-old family business for the great unknown. Still, a connection to what his new friend was going through was a shallow one at best.

Her circumstances were so foreign to him. Living with a life-threatening disease. Being raised by nuns in Sicily. He'd always had options and opportunities. He was, as every woman in his family had put it, *"a strapping young chap with the world at his feet."*

Armed with an arsenal of charm and wit, not to mention family money from a trust, Teddy not only didn't know how to respond to Maria, but he couldn't even pretend to understand her quandary. Still, he felt close to her, though he couldn't pin down why. "You can always come work for me. I meant it when we first met, and I mean it now."

Maria took another sip of her espresso and wrinkled her nose. "Despite your terrible taste in beverage, you're too kind."

"Think about it."

CHAPTER FIFTY-FOUR

La Giustiniana, Rome

AT THE KITCHEN TABLE, YIGAEL AND VALENTINA PORED OVER THE pages-long printouts of NDAs.

"Well, she was right." Looking up, Valentina removed her reading glasses.

"Good thing for all this trouble," Yigael griped.

"Well, she *was* kidnapped," Valentina said indignantly.

"I just love getting your hackles up."

Valentina put her glasses back on and took a more concentrated look at her copy. "Bishops, countless higher-ups. Cardinal Bellevue ...."

"Didn't I meet him at that ta-do with you?"

"What? Oh, my God. New Year's. Yes."

"So many. Right here. Black and white."

"I can't believe it. And look at this. Bishop Remmi. I've chatted with him time and again at conferences. Valentina sat back and emptied her breath. Then she began turning pages again. "These names are all over the map, all over the world."

Yigael raised an eyebrow. "An interesting conundrum."

"You usually have more to say about such things."

"Well, you see the problem, don't you?"

"You mean what exposing this would do to ... everyone?" Valentina asked.

The politics of the situation was far from lost on them.

"The Church has more than one billion followers," Valentina said. "Releasing what we have here could cause the entire machine to crumble."

"Cacciatore wasn't wrong about that." At the mention of his name, Yigael felt like he'd taken a gulp of bad wine. "And then what happens to those who were bound together by the structure? Where do they go? And I speak not only of the members but also of clergy right up to the top. A chaos I, frankly, can't imagine."

"I'm surprised you have such empathy for another faith, the Church, specifically." Valentina considered Yigael in a new way.

"It's the same thing. You don't want to see the structure topple, perhaps shored up but never done away with. People need their outlet for worshipping, no matter what religion they're part of." Yigael got up and peered out the window at Maria, still on the lounge chair. "And she's at the core of this."

CHAPTER FIFTY-FIVE

La Giustiniana, Rome

"Let's go." Yigael motioned Valentina to follow him outside to join Maria and Teddy.

"Maria, do you want your story to go public?" Yigael asked, pulling up a seat.

"Seems it already has," she said. Maria was back to trying to absorb the latest bombshell—Sister Cate's involvement—now that her brain had left hacker mode. The image of Cate in a jail cell disturbed her considerably.

"Yes, your kidnapping has, but why it happened is still quiet. This is a chance for you to get out in front of the 'silent mistress' story before reporters get on it and begin speculating. This way, the first information out there will be the truth. You'll only have to do it once, and that'll be the end of it."

"What would I have to do?" Maria's naiveté stood out like a red poppy in a field of daisies. "We could call a news conference where a group of television and print reporters will ask you questions," Yigael said.

"Oh, no, not that," Maria said emphatically. "No TV."

"Or," Valentina said, "we could arrange a newspaper interview. We know a reporter from *La Carta* who's shown himself to be fair in the past."

"The fund is what I want people to know about," Maria said. "I don't want to talk about the kidnapping. I don't want any story to be about me."

"You won't have to talk about your kidnapping," Valentina said. "We can dictate what's fair game."

"Whoa, there," Yigael interjected. "You can't dictate to the press what they can and cannot ask, and they will ask. However, it's not a problem because you'll say that police have asked you not to discuss 'the ongoing investigation.' An easy out."

"Yes, I see," Maria said. "So, I can tell the reporter about the fund, and that'll be enough, right?"

"This story is sensational," Yigael explained to Maria. "After *La Carta* prints it, the press will fall all over themselves to get their chops around it. The fact that the Church has a system in place to pay off women to remain silent ...."

Maria cringed. "At first, I thought that people contributing to the Church should know where their money's going. And I still do think that ...."

"Well then?" Valentina asked.

"Now, though," Maria continued, "I realize there's more to consider. After all, it's helping the women and children who've lived in silence, fear, and shame for so long."

Valentina sat at the end of Maria's chaise lounge and took her hand. "I can be with you every step of the way."

"So," Yigael said, "it has to be your choice to call this reporter."

"I want to do the right thing," Maria said. "On the one hand, people who give to the Church are being duped. On the other, women and children might be put at risk. Or end up destitute? It all seemed so simple at first. Now, I just don't know."

Teddy, who'd been sitting silently by, wondering how in the world his life had come to this, finally found his words, "Hey, if I may, Maria's life was in danger just a few days ago. Her life matters. Aren't we concerned that it's too dangerous to put her on display for the whole world to see? Yigael?"

"Once the players are exposed, the secret is out, and the risk to Maria is over."

Teddy's expression didn't change. He looked dubious.

"Do you want some time, Maria?" Yigael asked.

Maria scanned the grounds, admiring the bell-shaped cockspur coral trees and sweet-smelling oriental sweetgums. Their tranquility made her feel small in the scheme of things and gave her courage. Several moments later, she said, "I want to do this. Go ahead and contact the reporter."

"I'll connect with *La Carta*," Valentina said, "and you better get your game face on." She smiled at Maria before pressing Michael Levin's number.

"I'm going to get something else to drink. If you'll excuse me," Maria gave her *shakerato* back to its rightful owner with a quirky smile and headed into the kitchen with her cane.

She pulled a bottle of Spuma from the fridge, grateful Teddy'd stocked up on her favorite soft drink, and poured the cola over a glass crackling with ice.

Waiting for the fizz to die before sipping, she scanned the mass of papers the printer had spit out onto the square craftsman table. She flipped through several of them when a name on an NDA snared her attention.

She drew the printout closer. At the bottom of the page, it read:

Name of child: Maria Allegra Caruso
Date of Birth: 01 June 1990
Mother: Carmella Allegra Caruso
Father: Martino J. Mucci

The fluted glass slipped from Maria's hand, splashing soda over her legs and shattering in all directions as it struck the terracotta floor.

As her mind swam in a sea of memories, searching for an anchor, she registered the sound of a door opening.

She looked up to meet Cardinal Parina's eyes.

Time stood still as Justin took in the scene—the shattered glass, the puddle of cola, the printout in Maria's trembling hand, and the silent scream he read in her eyes—and he saw plainly that something dreadful had taken hold. To the cardinal, she seemed in shock.

"Maria," he said. "Let me help you." Justin reached out and clutched her shoulders, hoping the contact would jar her out of wherever her mind had taken her.

Maria's expression remained unchanged. Whatever trauma had enwrapped her, it had stolen her words.

"Don't move, or you'll cut yourself." Quickly rummaging through kitchen drawers until he found the dish towels, he mopped up the soda, gathered the glass into a pile, and pushed it into a corner away from her. *At least she won't get hurt now.*

Then he gently took Maria's arm and directed her to a seat.

She looked up at him with wide eyes that wet her tawny cheeks in a steady stream of salty tears.

He'd never seen anyone cry without making a sound before, but thank God, *she's was responding.*

Justin pulled up a chair beside her. "May I?" he asked as he took the printout, intuiting it held the cause of her pain. His eyes landed on all that mattered—her name and the names of her mother and father, her biological father.

He let out an audible breath.

The young nun was not only at the center of the Silent Mistress Fund as the head of forensic accounting at the IOR, but she was also embedded in it. Her mother was a recipient because Maria's real father was a priest.

It took a lot to shake Justin, but he was out of his depth. He felt his hands trembling, too, as sweat broke out along his hairline. "Let me get Valentina for you."

Maria touched his arm. "No." She turned toward him, tears dripping off her chin and soaking into the collar of her blouse. "Sit with me for a minute. Please."

He nodded and put his hand over hers. He knew better than to speak.

CHAPTER FIFTY-SIX

La Giustiniana, Rome

Cardinal Justin Parina looked around for reinforcements. He glimpsed out the back window, trying to catch the eye of Valentina or Yigael, even Teddy—anybody—but a young cypress blocked his view. Given his past with his son Peter, he felt inadequate to comfort Maria.

Peter had suffered growing up, seeing his father come and go. They'd barely be getting to know each other when it was time for Justin to leave again, cutting their budding connection short—his duty to the Church prevailing over all else. They had never attained a father-son bond where they could talk heart-to-heart and express their feelings about their eccentric circumstances, just dull, meaningless chats about nothing that mattered.

When Peter's resentment peaked in his mid-teens, he stopped speaking to his father altogether. After he went off to college, the relationship, such as it was, collapsed completely.

Justin hadn't seen his son in six years.

For the first time, seeing Maria in despair, the trauma of his own choices hit him fully. He wanted to run away but found it impossible because Maria, sobbing uncontrollably, held a surprisingly firm grip on his arm. She was in her pain, feeling it fully.

Justin couldn't imagine what was going through her mind. He knew of her history, though. He'd read *La Carta's* profile on the new hire about her late father and their shared love of technology. And he knew of Faustino Caruso's tragic death when she was just a girl.

What could Justin say that would quell her shock and grief?

"I—I'm so sorry, Maria," he stumbled on the words. "If there were anything I could do to turn back time and set things right, I would."

"My friend …."

Justin didn't feel like a friend, but he responded, nonetheless, "Yes, Maria, I'm your friend."

"I mean my friend, Luisa. I mentioned her last night—"

"Yes, I recall."

"Luisa … I just realized … she was my, my sister. I didn't know it, but she was." Maria twisted a strand of hair between her fingers and studied it. "Our hair. The color and everything." How had she not seen it? "And Thalassemia. We both had it. Father Mucci passed this disease to us, to both of us. He was our father."

This time, her sobs were lifting the rafters, and Justin couldn't believe the others weren't rushing the kitchen. Teddy's walls must've been insulated with steel was all he could imagine.

"Luisa died just last week," she hiccupped, "and I knew nothing about it … because we hadn't spoken in years. We just … lost touch."

"Maria, you mustn't blame yourself because none of this is your fault."

"I should've been there for her." Her mind spun with

memories, Luisa popping up at the center. Every moment they'd played together, sat alongside each other at the clinic, ate tasty *crostatas* afterward ....

Her heart somersaulted into a new kind of grief. She hadn't lost an old childhood friend but a sister with whom she'd never share another smile—her only sibling.

Feeling unsure but acting anyway, Justin wrapped an arm around Maria and pulled her into a comforting embrace, something he'd only ever dreamed of doing with his adult son.

Maria was surprised by how easily she collapsed into his arms. Physical touch was not common for her. But her defenses were down. The canvas that had told her life story in muted pastels had been painted over with heavily pigmented tones she didn't recognize. Where had her simple existence gone? It had been there just a minute ago.

Her eyes dragged along the sticky tile floor to the tiny hill of shattered glass and syrupy soda in the corner. There was her old life, unrecognizable and in a million little pieces.

Her heart pivoted to her father, whose loss she carried daily. It ached with wonder. "Had he known?" she caught herself saying out loud, "He must have."

"What's that?" Justin asked.

"My father. He had to have known ... I wasn't his." Maria pulled back and looked up at the cardinal for answers. He was around the age her father would've been. And he had an energy about him, a kindness that reminded her of her dear, sweet *papà*. Or maybe she was imagining it.

Justin smiled through his perceived shortcomings. "I promise you, he loved you just the same. You were every bit his, Maria."

"He was ... everything to me."

"He was a lucky man who raised a beautiful daughter."

Maria smiled faintly at his thoughtful sentiments before fresh tears reappeared. She rested her cheek on his chest.

"My family was always broken. I felt it, and I never knew why."

Daring to speak aloud about what he had carried with him for more than twenty years, he said, "I'm broken, too, Maria."

She looked back up at him, and he wiped tears from her face as he smiled down. "We all are."

She pressed her cheek into his chest again.

"Maria? Michael Levin's on his way!" Valentina called out from the *terrazzo*, popping into the kitchen moments later. "Oh, there you are."

Valentina stopped short as she took in Maria's discomposure. "What's going on? What happened?" She looked at the cardinal. "Justin?"

"Valentina." He shook his head. "Here." He picked up the document and held it out to her. "At the bottom."

It didn't take Valentina but a second to get up to speed. "She slapped the printout back onto the table and knelt before the nun.

Justin let go as Valentina wrapped her arms around Maria and said fiercely, "You are not alone. I'm here, and I'll be by your side. We all will. We'll get through this. You have all of us to help you, Maria." She pulled back, lifting Maria's head by the chin and cupping her face with warm hands. "I'm so sorry." She looked at Justin, her face pinched with concern that shifted to gratitude.

A knock at the front door, and the drone of male voices rumbled into the kitchen.

Teddy entered first, followed by Yigael. They took in the trio, Val leaning into Maria, Parina looking tortured.

Teddy, feeling like he shouldn't be in his own kitchen, said, "I was just grabbing a drink for the reporter. I'll be out in two shakes." He ducked inside the fridge and back out, and he was gone.

Yigael didn't scare so easily. He wanted—no, needed—

answers. He saw the tiny tower of shattered glass and the cola-soaked dish towels in a corner. But he saw no blood on the floor or in the sink. No one was injured. "Val?"

Valentina swept her thumbs under Maria's eyes, clearing that round of tears, and said, "I'll take care of this, okay?"

Maria nodded.

Valentina stood and handed the printout to Yigael. "At the bottom."

They took a couple of steps away.

Yigael read it over. The plot just thickened to the texture of cement. He gave Valentina a look only she could see. And at a temporary loss for actual, out-loud words, he mouthed, *What the hell?*

"We'll just tell Michael that she fell ill, right?" she said in a lowered voice. "We can do that. Recovery's been 'touch and go,' given all she's been through. You go tell him and give him something, a nugget, to hold him over while we figure this out."

"A nugget? He's not a puppy, Val, a treat won't do. And besides, he doesn't want to hear her story from me. He's a reporter. He lives and breathes news, and we contacted him." Yigael looked past Valentina to the nun. "Don't worry, Maria, we'll figure something out in the next sixty seconds." To the cardinal, he said, "Justin."

"*Ciao*, Yigael," Justin said back.

"Good timing." Yigael nodded, noticing the comfort the cardinal's presence was providing Maria.

Justin almost laughed at the irony. But he was doing everything he could to keep his emotions contained as they'd always been. They were banging on the door that housed his real persona, though. The one he'd locked away half a lifetime ago. And they wanted out.

"Okay," Valentina said, palms up. No solution had been proposed at the last minute, but it didn't change either fact—that Michael Levin was waiting or that Maria was top priority.

"I'll take her to her room, and you go talk to Michael. You have to," Valentina ordered once again. "Just postpone him the best you can."

"You know he's not going to—"

Justin cleared his throat and stood. "I'll go talk to Levin." His collar had strangled him for far too long. It was time.

"Justin, I can handle this," Yigael said, slightly insulted.

"No, I mean, I'll step in for the interview."

"Ah, yes, let's swap out intel on the Silent Mistress Fund for what's new with the Dewey Decimal System. I'm sure Levin will be thrilled."

Justin gave Yigael a pointed look. "He's been trying to pin me down … on a related matter."

Yigael and Valentina swapped glances. He knew what that related matter was and would fill her in shortly.

Justin placed a comforting hand on Maria's shoulder. "I, well, I can take your place, Maria. I will. It's the one thing I can do for you right now."

He gave her a reassuring squeeze as only a loving parent would, as her father had done a million times in their short time together. And with that gesture, she knew.

Justin looked at each of them in turn, stealing his courage. "I have a phone call to make first, but it's time I told my story."

CHAPTER FIFTY-SEVEN

Vatican City

"I'm sorry, Cardinal Cacciatore isn't available," Bishop Archibald Burbidge said from his small room outside the boss's office.

"I'm calling for comment on a series of stories that will run, starting in tomorrow's edition, concerning celibacy among clerics ... and the Silent Mistress Fund." Michael Levin knew that would get his attention. "Will you have him call me, please?"

"If you'll hold for a moment."

I thought so.

The cardinal's soft voice was barely audible when he said, "Levin?"

"Cardinal Cacciatore?"

"What can I do for you?"

"*La Carta* is printing a story in the morning edition about the existence of a secret fund that pays mistresses of clerics to remain silent about their relationships."

A long pause followed before Cardinal Cacciatore said, "Off the record, please."

Levin rarely granted off-the-record interviews. He figured that what was suitable for him to hear was fit for his audience to read. However, if he thought his source could further his story, he sometimes relented. "All right," he said.

"There is no truth to what you say. This sister you name is a maverick and a troublemaker." The cardinal's voice rose in tone and intensity. "She was fired from her position at the bank and, for some reason, has utterly disappeared. And believe me, there is no such account. Never." He paled, his mind scrambling. "Whatever you have is fraudulent. Sister Maria had plenty of time to cook up whatever file she wanted to, her way of causing trouble."

"Cardinal, I never mentioned Sister Maria Caruso. The article is about a cardinal who has first-hand knowledge of the true nature of the Church Families Charity fund. As for its fraudulent nature, well, evidence of this fund is on my desk right now. I'm looking at a printed copy of the names listed on the account and the cleric associated with each one. Are you accusing one of your peers of lying?"

In a whisper more malevolent than a scream heard in St. Peter's Square, the cardinal said, "If you print this so-called story, I'll have you fired and your paper shut down! Are we clear?"

"I assume you have no comment, then, on the record, Cardinal?" Levin said in a dispassionate voice.

Cacciatore slammed down the receiver.

CHAPTER FIFTY-EIGHT

La Carta
Sacred Vows Shattered: Vatican Cardinal Reveals Double Life
By Michael Levin

Rome—*Yesterday, in an unprecedented move that sent shockwaves through the Vatican, Cardinal Justin Parina, the esteemed curator of the Vatican Library, resigned. The ecclesiastical leader for three decades stepped down from his high-ranking position and requested to be laicized, a rare step for a cardinal of Parina's stature. The move would allow him to disengage from clerical duties and live as a layperson.*

The request for laicization comes amid revelations that Parina intends to live openly with his mistress. This woman has been his enduring companion in a relationship forbidden in the clergy due to the vow of celibacy.

Cardinal Justin Parina, a revered figure in the Church of Rome, has been leading a clandestine double life. Not only has he served as a cardinal, but he has also been a father and life partner to a hidden family under the pseudonym Robert Molinelli, with identification papers to verify it. After concealing this secret for more than two decades, Parina finally reveals the truth about what he describes as a flawed system, one that may have broken him. This revelation comes at a poignant time, as he has recently been diagnosed with early-stage cancer, though he declined to specify the type.

Enforcement of the celibacy mandate began in the Middle Ages. However, multiple popes have overlooked this discipline from then to now. Rather than being compelled to abandon their vocation, clerics who stray have been encouraged to maintain silence about their personal circumstances, which extends to their partners and children. In the 1970s, a fund was established as the most robust approach possible to safeguard this silence.

To my first question about the recently discovered Silent Mistress Fund, he declared, "I am not here to discuss the so-called fund," subtly acknowledging the swirling rumors. "Nor am I here to delve into the alleged abduction of Sister Maria Caruso following her unearthing of this fund.

"I wish to speak about the Church, which needs introspection and reform. The Church is neither impervious to change nor irreparable, provided it musters the courage to move forward and act honestly. So, I'm here to blaze that trail by addressing the contentious issue of celibacy within the Church through my personal journey."

And so, nestled in a quaint flat in the heart of northern Rome, a goblet filled with an exquisite 2015 Amarone della Valpolicella—a remarkable vintage—by his side, Justin Parina embarked on his candid revelation.

"I was twenty-nine at the time, and a bishop, sitting on the bank of a tiny lake in Switzerland, near Porsel, contemplating how quickly I'd risen to my position in the Church when I saw her emerge from the mountain trail.

"She was striking, tall and lithe. Her long, wavy hair echoed the color of cinnamon. She was clad in a gauzy dress that danced with the wind as she moved. Of course, I noticed her.

"She walked straight toward me, her cheeks flushed from the climb, and sat down. Then she turned and smiled.

"I felt compelled to tell her straight away that I was a priest, but she was way ahead of me.

"'Hello,' she said, 'I almost didn't recognize you ... out of uniform.'"

"I was wearing khaki shorts and boots. She told me that she knew me when, some years back, I visited my parents, who owned a farm in Porsel. Her face suddenly clicked into place, not as if no time had passed but as if we'd known each other all along.

"That's when I knew I was in trouble. I didn't know what to say. Somehow, it's always been awkward, a priest being alone with a woman. So, I blurted out the first thing that came to my mind. She was wearing sandals, and I said, 'How did you ever get here in those?'

"She just laughed, this glorious, throaty sound that was so joyous and infectious that she made me laugh, too, and I felt such freedom then.

"I'd brought a sack lunch, pulled out a sandwich, and offered her half. I felt a bit more comfortable by then, so I said, 'Go on, you must be hungry after that trek. I didn't realize how treacherous it is. One misstep, and I'd have tumbled down the mountainside.'

"She laughed again and looked at me in a way that took me all in, and she said, 'Hmm, you look fairly steady to me.'"

"I was taken aback. Again, I didn't know what to say. So, I said nothing. Instead, I looked around at the majestic mountain peaks rising all around us and the small herd of ibex grazing in the distance, and at us side by side, amiably munching on our shared sandwich ... and I felt a stirring I had long suppressed ... starting with my years in training at the seminary.

"That was the beginning."

This is the first in a series of investigative reports on the widespread breach of priestly celibacy.

CHAPTER FIFTY-NINE

Vatican City

Within a minute of Cardinal Angelico Cacciatore arriving, he hadn't even situated himself at his desk yet, the office phone rang. The call was internal. The cardinal stared in disbelief. "Yes," he growled.

Cardinal Germain LaChapelle identified himself and said, "Angelico, please, come up. His Holiness is waiting for you."

The cardinal's sharp intake of breath pointed to his surprise. "What is this about?" He'd never been summoned to the pope's office, though he surely knew what it was about. As promised, that vile reporter Levin had posted the article about Justin Parina.

"I can't say."

The cardinal dared not refuse to meet with the pope, but he needed time to work out what he would say. "Can you tell His Holiness that this isn't a favorable time for me to come? Perhaps later—"

"I'm afraid not, Angelico. You had better get right here." The pope's secretary hung up.

The cardinal buzzed for his underling.

Bishop Burbidge walked in seconds later.

"I'm going to meet with His Holiness, and I'm afraid this meeting will not lead to anything good. We may've been found out. Wait for me here. I'll figure out a way to pick up the pieces."

"Cardinal," the bishop said with a placid face and a slight bow.

Cacciatore swept past him, exiting his office for the five-minute walk to the Papal Palace.

His hand quivered when he entered the papacy.

The Bishop of Rome stood at the window overlooking the gardens. A cloud floated by, casting a shadow on his favorite rose bushes. On hearing his door click shut, Pope Julius turned and faced his visitor.

"I am not happy to have summoned you here, but I suppose you have guessed why?"

"I …."

"You are fired, Angelico. You will remove your belongings within the hour and be escorted to the Jesuit house until permanent reassignment is made."

"Holy Father, I—"

"Angelico, I am sorry, but more, I am ashamed for you and ashamed and embarrassed for our Church that such shady dealings have gone on here and will be made public. The severity of this crisis, and it is a crisis, cannot be overstated, but I mean to set things to rights."

Dazed, the cardinal said, "Your Holiness, I only learned about this when a reporter called to tell me minutes ago."

"Do not insult my intelligence. Your prints are all over that fund." The pope turned once again to the garden.

He'd learned from Yigael Dorian and Sister Maria just that morning that the cardinal's email address was the username for access to the subfiles. He'd seen them for himself. They were lying on his desk.

Cacciatore dropped his head and grabbed his shaky right hand with his left, massaging it futilely to assuage his nerves.

"Can I assume you had no hand in the nun's kidnapping ... at least that?" The pope knew better but wanted the cardinal to come clean.

"What? A kidnapping? I know nothing of that."

"Coincidental, isn't it, that Sister Maria Caruso was kidnapped after coming across the true nature of this fund." The Holy Father stared at the cardinal, who reluctantly lifted his eyes. Fear shrouded them.

"A kidnapping, you say. Surely not. No, no, I know nothing about anything like that. I don't." He could now add an upset stomach to his list of ailments.

The pope gestured toward a tapestry chair. "Please, sit. I want some answers."

The pope sat beside him. "Let's start with the file. Did you create this account for secret payouts?"

"Certainly not, Holy Father."

"You know it's not too late to redeem yourself to some extent by answering my questions honestly."

The cardinal sagged in his chair, lowered his head again, and began to sob in silence. He put up his hands as an unmoved Pope Julius handed over a handkerchief.

"I didn't create the file. I took it over when the previous overseer retired," he confessed. "And when our vice president was caught for embezzling, I hired Sister Maria to keep the books straight. I hired her!"

"When was this account begun?"

"I don't know, Holy Father. From what I gather, it's been in existence for decades. All I know is that I was to continue it. Cardinal Ricci, before he died, knew about it, and others did too. I've guarded this account with my life. I figured I was serving the Church by doing so." His misery was complete.

For a moment, the pope's natural compassion stirred for the cardinal. He was one of so many others doing misguided service for the Church.

"At first," he continued, "after I was appointed to the position, I was appalled to learn of this fund. And then, it wasn't long before I was put in charge of it. I didn't like it, but there was no way out. I couldn't tell anybody because it was secret, and there would be hell to pay if word got out. Given that, I did some research and found that the arrival of celibacy a millennium back also marked the beginning of priests breaking their vows, taking lovers and fostering children. The actual numbers in the archives are enormous. So, given the nature of Church teachings, I figured I could help by keeping things quiet and supporting the, ah, families. I thought it was the thing to do."

The pope shifted. "Tell me more."

The cardinal became animated. After all, he was an expert on the subject. "Church records go back to the late eighteen hundreds," he said. "Many women then claimed a liaison with a cleric, but their claims were swept under the rug because nothing could be proved, and the priests involved simply denied their dalliances. But somewhere along the way, it became clear that to keep the women quiet, the Church would need to pay them. Thus, this account. And then, DNA changed everything. Paternity could be proved, and more women came forward asking for help to support themselves and their children, some threatening to expose their liaison if we didn't … help.

"Now, not all women know about this, er, program, but word spread and, more and more, they began to understand they could get something from the Church. And according to Italian law, a child who has not been recognized by one or both parents can petition the Court and file a lawsuit. It's called a 'petition for judgment of paternity/maternity.' Can you imagine the mayhem if this started happening? I'm protecting the Church from collapse!"

The cardinal's words had left His Holiness reeling, but he remained calm. "I am sorry you see it that way, Angelico, but I cannot alter what I say here today. Please, prepare to take your leave."

In a last-ditch effort to save himself from humiliation, Cardinal Angelico Cacciatore dashed back to his outer office to confer with Bishop Burbidge. Maybe there was some way to get out of this trouble.

But when he arrived, he found his minion gone and two gendarmes removing their computers.

CHAPTER SIXTY

La Carta
Arrests Made in High-Profile Kidnapping Case
By Michael Levin

The Vatican—*Two aides to Cardinal Angelico Cacciatore were taken into custody on Tuesday for their involvement in the kidnapping of Sister Maria Caruso eight days ago. Bishop Gregory Alistair and Massimo Pugia were apprehended in Cacciatore's office.*

Meanwhile, Polizia di Stato Detective Domenico Loria says the search for additional suspects is ongoing. Two unidentified men, believed to have ties to the Mafia and considered the actual kidnappers, are still being sought. A female suspect, identified as Dara Damahdi, is wanted as an accessory in the alleged kidnapping. She had severed ties with the Mossad and assumed the name Pepper Pugia, posing as Massimo Pugia's cousin for six years. Often seen in the company of Pugia and Cardinal Cacciatore, it seems now she has slipped out of Rome.

"Our investigation names Cardinal Angelico Cacciatore as the mastermind behind the plot to kidnap Sister Maria,"

Detective Loria said. "Cacciatore's motive was to keep the Silent Mistress Fund secret, but after Sister Maria discovered it, he feared she would release the information, making it public knowledge. Just hours after learning he'd been fired, Cardinal Cacciatore bolted to safety, taking a midnight flight to Zurich, where he owns a terraced chalet. Italy has no extradition treaty with Switzerland.

CHAPTER SIXTY-ONE

Rome

MARIA STARED OUT THE CAR WINDOW AT THE SAME COOL HUES OF summer she'd so enjoyed on the train ride from Palermo. But her journey north was a lifetime ago, a memory that may as well have been cataloged alongside the death of her father. It was fuzzy, distant.

She was a different person back then—six short weeks ago. But summertime at dusk didn't disappoint, and so she said thanks for the verdant fields with the frosting-pink horizon spread atop. She could still count on that.

Maria felt Valentina's eyes on her, protector that she was. She turned and offered her a thin smile of reassurance.

Valentina gave her hand a squeeze. "You ready to be back home?"

Home?

Casa Veronesi in the Eternal City—with all its ancient history from the Colosseum to the Sistine Chapel to the uncorrupted body of Pope John XXIII and the tomb in Ostia of the first female bishop in the Church—was it home?

Maria never imagined God's plan would include adding her name to Rome's colored and epic chronology. She was no one from nowhere ... until she took the highest position a woman had ever held at the Vatican Bank, uncovered a secret fund paying mistresses of priests hundreds of thousands for their silence, and became a victim of scandal. It would take some time to adjust to her new story. But as for home? She no longer had one as far as she was concerned.

And what of my mother?

Maria's brain went into overdrive trying to perceive that for what it really was.

Had she come to tell me ... the truth?

Had Luisa's death prompted it?

Maria's mother was neither a happy person nor an easy one to love. Was this why? Had Maria just cracked the code? All these years, she'd asked herself how someone could be like her mother. The embodiment of anger. Born without the ability to experience joy was how Maria had finally chosen to think of her to forgive her for all her shortcomings in the parenting department. Meanwhile, her mother was one of thousands the Church was paying to keep silent.

Her childhood was a testament to the dark effects—the secrecy, the shame, the resentment—the fund had over a person. Her mother was living proof. Did this revelation make her feel compassion toward the woman? Was she angrier? She'd been lied to. Denied the opportunity to know the truth. Denied the essential bond between a mother and child. Her father had been denied too. Did she know her mother at all?

She did not.

But this wasn't all on the woman who'd given birth to her. Maybe she'd played a role, but the Church held the load of responsibility. The secret had unraveled the fabric of their family dynamic. They were frayed from the start. There was no foundation from which to erect a life. They never had any hope of mending.

"Home. Yes, I think I'm ready," the young nun fibbed.

Valentina cocked her head with a knowing sigh, and Yigael peeked in the rearview mirror, picking up on her intonation and the quiver in her voice.

"Maria? I have something for you." He swung an arm into the back seat with a closed fist.

Maria held her cupped hand under his, clinging to a whisper of hope that it might be ....

Yigael opened his fingers, and a tiny plastic pouch fell into her palm.

Maria felt her breath catch. Her lucky charm. The flash drive and her lifeline to the man who had been, and always would be, her real father. Tears glistened as she clutched the device and pulled it to her heart. "Thank you."

"Yes." Valentina smiled wide. "Thank you, Yigael. Do we dare ask—"

"You do not."

At that moment, Maria knew she'd pick up her life from there, wherever it may lead.

"I have something for you, too, Val," Yigael said, one eye on her, one on the road. "Chez Nous, say, eight?"

An animated man, she knew his facial expressions well, second only to her own. He knew who sent the flash drive. She'd ruminated briefly on those strokes and slants and loops on the address label but was sidetracked shortly thereafter to help manage Maria's rescue mission.

Valentina's heart slumped with her shoulders. *Now is not the time*, she told herself. "I'm looking forward to it after I help Maria get settled," she said.

Yigael nodded with a thin smile that didn't reach his eyes.

As they rounded the corner to Casa Veronesi, Maria let out

a small gasp, and a tear let loose. She swiped it from her cheek, pocketed her lucky charm, and turned to Valentina.

Her eyes were wet too. "This city ... it has its moments." The archaeologist shook her head as she caught Yigael's eyes. "Just when you want to give up on it."

"Tell me about it," he said wryly.

There were several dozen gatherers forming a half circle around the villa. In proper ceremony form, they'd created a wall of candles, keeping the press behind them.

As Yigael pulled into the drive, ready to manage the throng, he saw they were maintaining a respectable distance. They were merely there to support Maria in untainted solidarity, doing what fellow Romans and parishioners of the Church do, welcoming her home with convivial cheers.

And they weren't the only ones.

Maria looked beyond the revelers to Orio, standing on the steps outside the front door, and then to the woman racing down the walkway.

Valentina motioned for Maria to exit.

She barely had both feet out of the vehicle before her mother enveloped her in an embrace.

CHAPTER SIXTY-TWO

Rome

IN A DIMLY LIT CORNER OF CHEZ NOUS, THE SAME *RISTORANTE* where Valentina had handed Yigael the flash drive two very long weeks ago, the ex-Mossad spy turned antiquities dealer sat nervously, tapping his fingers against the wood tabletop, his expression a mix of concern and hesitation.

When Valentina entered—late, as usual—the air was thick with the murmur of hushed conversations.

"What is it, Yigael?" she asked, sliding into the booth beside her friend, noting the Campari Spritz he'd already ordered for her. His was a Negroni.

It hadn't taken him long to answer the puzzling question about who sent the flash drive to Paula Kirkpatrick that had unraveled Valentina and Erika's professional lives.

"I have an answer, but it'll be a tough one for you to swallow."

"Ah, *sì*? Yigael, you make it sound close to home like it could be Luca, for God's sake." Valentina chuckled.

Yigael's lips twisted.

"Well, who?"

"Closer than that." He skipped a beat. "Erika."

The words hung in the air, heavy and suffocating. Valentina thought back to the script on the envelope, which bore but a loose resemblance to her business partner's. Her mind raced knowingly, but her heart spoke for her, "No, that can't be true. Erika would never do that. Impossible."

"It wasn't Erika alone."

"You mean she and Paula were in it together?"

"No, it was Erika and her brother Edmond."

Valentina lifted her glass, barely managing a sip as the bright-red liquid threatened to spill over the edge.

"For what it's worth, she's devastated," Yigael said.

"So, you've talked to her, and she's admitted it, and she knows I know? Would that be right?" She scoffed. "How could she? What was she thinking?"

"Maybe her emotions got the best of her. It happens."

"Don't defend her, Yigael."

"I'm not. I'm just saying people make mistakes. It's human nature."

"And Edmond? Honestly, I didn't know the guy had it in him to pull something like this off. How'd you find out?" Valentina asked.

"When you handed me the package, part of me knew. I saw the way you were studying it. I could tell the penmanship looked familiar to you."

"Yes, but without going into tedious detail … we both know handwriting style is not attributed to genetics," Valentina said.

"And that's what was tripping you up. That and your heart."

"I overlooked it because I didn't want to know?"

"Yep."

Valentina shook her head. The man was right.

"The postmark was a giveaway, a little town not far from

where Edmond lives. That and the script ... after I found a sample of hers and compared it, I decided to talk to her."

"So, you strong-armed her?" Valentina's strict grimace relaxed, but she did not smile.

"Strong-arm Blondie?" He laughed. "I think not. She'd lay me flat in *un secondo*."

"I doubt that."

"I think she's relieved to have it out in the open. Listen, you have to talk with her. There's a lot at stake for you both."

Valentina was not ready to see Erika. She had the emotional mountain of betrayal to hurdle before she could even think of sitting down with her business partner and closest friend. Her hurtful and damaging behavior was beyond understanding.

But it had to happen eventually.

CHAPTER SIXTY-THREE

Rome

ON RETURNING TO HER HOME, SISTER MARIA HADN'T EXPECTED that words would suffice for everything they'd all been through, and she'd been on point in that regard. But Sister Cate, whose demeanor had been contrite and yet contrastingly unburdened, had taken great care with the meal. And with the help of Sisters Lati and Birdi, it had been quite the party with *minestra di verdure, legumes and frutta, risotto alla Milanese,* and Orio's special *tiramisu* in plentitude, not to mention the wine and aperitifs.

Maria's mind and heart had been 90 percent present for the homecoming, but the remaining ten had stayed tucked inside her pocket beside her lucky charm.

Yigael had no idea what he'd done for her by retrieving her most precious possession. It had felt as if she'd lost a piece of her father with news of her true ancestry, and the device had somehow given it back.

On second thought, maybe the man did know.

Cozied up in her bed hours later, her mother but a hallway

away, Maria propped her laptop on a pillow. She inserted the flash drive into an adapter and opened the single document saved to it all those years ago.

She always read her father's one and only message before adding a new one, a habit she'd formed on his passing, a ritual she'd grown accustomed to as a way to end her days.

Tonight, she'd pick that habit back up.

My darling Maria,

Surprise! Welcome to the future. It starts here, with you and me.

You are growing into a beautiful, young lady. I am so proud of how you're handling your circumstances. Your strength gets me through every day. Your sense of humor? Well, you may not realize it, but that's from your mother, and it lights up my heart. But your love of computers? That's from me. We will always have that. I look forward to hearing back from you.

I love you,

Papà

Maria scrolled down through the pages after reuniting with her father's words, through years of responses to his one sweet goodbye, and then entered today's date and began.

Dear Papà,

You won't believe the story I have to tell you ....

CHAPTER SIXTY-FOUR

Rome

Father Orio Rinaldi leaned over the kitchen sink, clad in dad jeans, a black shirt with a clerical collar, and Mrs. Molise's frilly apron, which hung loose, its ties trailing to the floor. As he washed the dishes from his latest culinary creations, a heavenly aroma wafted from the oven while a *puttanesca* sauce bubbled on the cooktop.

At Fran's invitation, he'd arrived just last night after reuniting with Maria. Seeing her safe and sound at Casa Veronesi filled him with satisfaction. He knew she still had much to sort out with Sister Cate and her mother, though, so he'd wait patiently to catch up in private. In the meantime, he decided to make himself useful, and baking was therapeutic, a refuge away from his own troubles.

Unfortunately, Mrs. Molise disapproved of Orio's presence in her kitchen, and she'd made her stance known in sniffs, snorts, and stomps. Convinced his culinary skills were no match for hers, she wanted rid of the portly priest. The sooner, the better.

She lugged a bag of groceries inside and plopped them on the counter. "What's that smell?"

"Just some baking this morning," Orio said.

"What?"

"Cookies."

"What kind?"

"*Cuccidati.*"

"What?"

"*Cuccidati.* They're stuffed with figs. They're a little complicated to make, so I got up early—"

"I know what *cuccidati* are," Mrs. Molise said with a wrinkle in her brow. "My mother used to make them."

"This is my mother's recipe. They're just about ready to come out of the oven. Do you want to try one?"

"I'll try one after they've cooled."

Is she really going to eat one? The priest plunged his hands into the dishwater, thinking silence would be the best course of action.

"And move away from that sink. I'll take over. You tend to your cookies." Mrs. Molise sniffed, but this time, it was not in disdain. *Maybe he's not so bad,* she thought. Or maybe that was her nose talking. Her kitchen smelled divine.

As Orio bent over to remove his first batch from the oven, Monsignor Ricci popped through the kitchen door. "Orio, can you come here?"

Orio brightened at the sight of his friend. "Fran, just smell this sauce. We'll serve it over spaghetti. *Delizioso.*"

"You and I must talk. Come on into the office."

He put down the wooden spoon he was using to stir and sheepishly said, "But the sauce ...."

Mrs. Molise turned her head skyward. "God in heaven," she muttered.

"Mrs. Molise will have that well in hand. Come on."

Francesco lifted his eyes skyward. "And take off that apron," he ordered.

Orio looked down at the ruffled apron themed with big, red cherries. He flushed and pulled it over his head.

Settling in the study, Francesco said, "Have you thought about what you will do next? You're welcome here, of course, and take your time. But you cannot stay forever. You know that."

Orio had yet to think about such things and didn't want to.

As a man who'd been a part of the Church since adolescence, he didn't know how to consider what was next. All he knew was the institution he'd devoted his life to had disappointed him to an irreparable degree. He imagined this was what a marriage felt like at the beginning of a divorce, when one spouse discovered he never really knew the other at all.

He dropped his head into his hands.

"Orio."

"I know," the priest admitted. "Mrs. Molise says I'm just escaping my problems here." He gave his friend a bleak look. "I feel like I'm living on some other planet. I've lost my way and don't know how to find it back."

"Orio, I cannot tell you what to do. No one can. You're the only one to have the answer, and it's time for you to be looking for it. Pray. Listen to God. You'll come to know what's in your best interest, what you really want in your life."

"What do you mean, 'what I want'? I've only ever followed the instructions of others from as far back as I can remember."

"I know," his friend said with empathy, "but perhaps it's time that you listen to yourself."

"I never thought of that."

"Sure, you have," Francesco smiled. "Look at what you've done for Maria. You followed your heart, your gut. It's in large part due to you that she's safe. You were under no one's directives. I thought you were overreacting initially, but you pressed on."

Orio looked unsure.

"Take your time, my friend," Francesco said, rising from his chair. "The answers will come."

"I hope so, before a quarter of a century passes like with Justin."

Francesco cocked his head, wondering if that was a passive-aggressive attack on their friend.

"You know what I mean. He suffered all those years in silence, incapable of choosing. I feel like I'm going berserk, and it's only been days." Orio shook his head. "How is he, by the way?"

"Justin? Good. I just saw him. I think," Francesco thought for a moment, "I think he looks taller."

"His burden has truly been lifted?" Orio asked, hoping to draw inspiration from the cardinal's story.

"I believe so. And yours will be, too, Orio. Keep the faith."

CHAPTER SIXTY-FIVE

La Carta
Revelation: Cardinal's Mistress Speaks Out
By Michael Levin

Rome—*The Vatican is in turmoil following explosive revelations regarding payouts to women allegedly involved with clerics. Cardinal Angelico Cacciatore, recently dismissed from his position at the IOR, has remained silent about the so-called Silent Mistress Fund. Bishop Ennio Batori, Director of the Press Office, denied any knowledge of such an account, assuring that all Vatican Bank accounts are legitimate. Despite their terse rebuttals, one woman is speaking out.*

Katarina Silva is a lively, copper-haired woman in her fifties who lives in Morcote, Switzerland. She is a business owner, a mother, and has been the lover of former Cardinal Justin Parina for over two decades—and she has a bone to pick with the Vatican. Silva claims her relationship with the well-known cleric began when he was on the fast track to a higher status in the Church. She came forward to share her story, one she insists is not unique. We met at a small hotel in the city where she was staying.

"We just fell into it," Silva said. "Had I known the consequences for myself, Justin, and our child, I might've had better sense. But I loved him, and that's never changed."

Silva moved away from the small Swiss hamlet of Porsel to the waterfront village of Morcote when their son was a toddler, the cardinal seeing them for short stints throughout the year.

"It was difficult and lonely. Justin urged me to stay out of the limelight. For that reason, I tried not to form close friendships. He was desperate to keep our lives secret, from the Church and the public. The thought of his 'other life' being exposed to parishioners sent him into a tailspin. He claimed he loved me, but I knew his devotion to the Church overshadowed that.

Silva said she received funds monthly for more than a dozen years. While she refused to name the amount provided, she maintained that it was not from the secret fund, of which she was aware, but from the cardinal's modest income.

"Justin doted on our son when he was here and was loving toward me, but in the final days of his visits, he became distant, his attention returning to the Vatican, and I knew he was lost to us once again. That was the saddest time of all … when he disengaged. And then, after he left, we were alone again until the next time. My mother knew. She never approved, but over the years, she softened to our relationship. At least I had her to confide in."

Silva says that her life in the shadows became so uncomfortably small without real friends that, at one point, she sought help by combing the internet for stories like hers. She found a support group for women in relationships with priests called Hearts in Conflict and attended a meeting.

"The gathering was close to where I do business in Milan.

The women I met were activists, and when they mentioned 'going public,' I left, thankful that I hadn't given them my real name. If Justin had known I was about to let the world in on our secret ... I hate to think what it would've done to him. I would've ruined his life. He's not a selfish man. He's the best man, in truth."

After a lifetime of keeping their secret, she and the cardinal are now speaking publicly, hoping it might help other women in the same situation.

"As for me, I am disgusted that this Church forces its servants into a lifestyle—celibacy—that is unnatural and cruel. You can't put restrictions on love. The Church refuses to recognize that. Its position has ruined so many lives, those of the priests, the women, and the children, especially the children."

The Vatican refused to comment on Silva's story.

This is the second in a series of investigative reports on the widespread breach of priestly celibacy.

CHAPTER SIXTY-SIX

Vatican City

Julius Africanus had served his church in relative obscurity as an archbishop in Atlanta, Georgia, before being appointed by the previous pope to the Vatican's legislative body, the College of Cardinals, at age fifty-eight.

Pope Gregory Augustine had met the Atlanta archbishop during a trip to the United States and found him to be an energizing presence. After the new cardinal's move to the Vatican, Pope Augustine sought him out often and lent an enthusiastic ear to his open-minded progressivism about the future of the Church.

His peers saw the wiry, unassuming cardinal differently, though. To them, Julius seemed laid back and without opinions. Therefore, they mistakenly assumed their power and conservative values could easily control him. The cardinals erred further in presuming that, because the man had hearing loss and wore aids in both ears—caused by a traumatic brain injury when he was hit by a car while riding his bike—he would miss on the "finer points" and therefore be no threat. Julius Africanus was to them, then, an inconspicuous figure.

Perhaps for these reasons, in the wake of Pope Augustine's untimely death, the Curia elected the cardinal on the third ballot to become the next Bishop of Rome.

The upheaval that Pope Julius Africanus was shaping on the heels of the revelation of the Church Families Charity fund was stunning Vatican watchers, followers, and, especially, its insiders.

And it came not without his deep conviction about the role of the Church.

The pope's unwavering ethics demanded, first and foremost, his obedience to God, only then to his conscience, and lastly, to Church authorities. When he saw that the Church existed in reverse order to this ideology, he decided to shake things up. And news of the outrageous fund became the perfect place to start.

"I cannot live in contradiction to my principles, and if I cannot, neither should anyone else," Pope Julius explained to his predecessor, Pope Emeritus Alexander XIII, who had retired before Augustine's papacy and lived on Vatican grounds in a four-story convent surrounded by a sizable fruit and vegetable garden. Pope Emeritus reportedly enjoyed the marmalade made from the garden's oranges.

The two sat outside in a small flower garden as the sun shimmered with thin light and the dahlias bobbed in a mild breeze. The Pope Emeritus wore a simple white cassock, having given up his red mozzetta, the cape he favored as pope. He had also handed back the pontifical ring he had worn.

Glancing at the bishop's ring that had replaced it, the pope wondered whether his predecessor missed it.

"You will throw the entire Church into chaos," Alexander said. The glitter in his nut-brown eyes registered sorrow.

"Perhaps," the pope considered. He remembered that

Alexander had been unable to point the Church in a new direction and had decided to retire and let someone else take over. "The Church has failed miserably," he reminded him.

"Surely, you can shore up this matter of the fund and leave the rest of it," Alexander countered.

"It's not just Cardinal Cacciatore and the fund. It's all of them. Sister Maria Caruso just brought it all to magnificent light. I'm telling you … you pull the yarn, and the great pillars of the Church unravel. Your plan will end the Church as we know it."

The pope stared at the teapot resting on the glass-top table between them. He topped off his tea and that of his companion before asking, "Isn't that the point?"

"Be careful what you wrought," Alexander warned, picking up his cup and sipping to avoid further eye contact.

CHAPTER SIXTY-SEVEN

Vatican City

ONE WEEK AFTER SPEAKING WITH ALEXANDER XIII, THE cardinals poured in from their posts around the world, summoned to the Holy See by Pope Julius Africanus.

With no clue to the purpose of this unusual gathering, the gossip mill was rife with juicy tidbits churning out faster than a blender on high speed. With no leaks, one could only imagine what Pope Julius had up his sleeve. Could he be announcing his resignation as had Alexander not so very long ago? More than a handful of cardinals were breathless with that kind of anticipation.

The mood turned sour, though, when the pope's secretary, Cardinal LaChapelle, advised the others that, instead of being housed at the Vatican, they would be put up at several low-budget motels outside Vatican City and would double up. The pope wanted to give the prelates a taste of how the other half lived.

"This is detestable," eighty-year-old Cardinal Joshua

Martins of Naples complained witheringly to his new roommate, fifty-two-year-old Pedro Agnelo of Mexico.

"Outrageous," Agnelo agreed.

The two cardinals squeezed into the narrow lane between two single beds, their cassocks swishing and bumping like a pair of kittens in a dance-off as they put down their travel bags in the small economy room.

They were further annoyed not to be welcomed into the Sistine Chapel or the beautifully marbled Clementine Hall at the Apostolic Palace for their meeting but, instead, at the plainer Saint Martha's House adjacent to Saint Peter's Basilica.

How important could this meeting be? Many of them wondered. *What are we really doing here?*

It didn't take long for them to find out.

At eight o'clock in the morning, one day after the last arrival had touched down in Rome, Pope Julius stood at a small lectern facing his more than two hundred cardinals shifting around on simple wooden chairs, hard surfaces they were entirely unused to.

The sun streamed through windows half-covered with shades. The staccato clip of a hand shear broke the silence outside as a gardener pruned some nearby shrubs.

"What I have to say today gives me no pleasure," the pope began. He scanned his audience and saw curious faces looking back. He took a long, silent breath.

In the minutes that followed, Pope Julius delivered a searing condemnation of those whose job it was to serve him. He accused the prelates of living duplicitous bureaucratic lives, of failing to serve God, of back-stabbing each other, and of blindly ignoring the needs of their parishioners.

"You have used your positions to muscle your way to power, control, and riches," he said, "and you are mindless of the harm you to do humanity." The pope's agony in making such pronouncements was evident in the set of his jaw and in the moisture giving a sheen to his forehead. Though the harsh rebuke was a long time coming, the pope had no illusion that his words would change anything. No, the old guard would simply ignore him and continue the status quo. They controlled the money, and they would not let go. That's how it had always been and why more drastic measures had to be taken now.

Looking again over his audience, he saw curiosity turn to stone.

What the pope would say next was known to no one other than his predecessor.

"I am taking a step, which is unprecedented in the history of our Church," he told the group. "But it is a needed one."

The word *unprecedented* brought about movement and a rustling of garments before the men settled, giving His Holiness their absolute attention.

"Today, I am dissolving this legislative body. The Curia will no longer serve this pope as decisionmakers. You no longer have authority here."

Audible gasps rang out and chairs creaked and scraped as the red caps turned to one another in shock. Several wobbled to their feet in indignation, one with his fist pumping upward and his chair falling back.

When the clatter ceased, Pope Julius said, "The church is upside down. I intend to turn it to rights."

As the words "outrageous," "impossible," and "he can't do this" began to reverberate among them, the pope's voice cut across theirs.

"I am not finished," he said. "While this Curia is dissolved, I will select twelve men to help the Church out of its strife."

All eyes slipped from each other back to the pope.

"In the meantime, you would all be well advised to pray for forgiveness, atone for your sins, and become the holy men of God you signed on to be."

Pope Julius stepped away from the lectern and moved forward to greet his former cardinals individually, to show them no malice.

Those who now doubted their future might've turned away from the pope, refusing his blessing. Instead, the thought that he'd pick twelve new advisors to steer the Church's future led each to think he might be one of those.

With smiles, however forced, they accepted his hand.

CHAPTER SIXTY-EIGHT

La Carta
Cardinals Stripped of Their Scarlet Robes
By Michael Levin

The Church stands at a pivotal crossroads. In a stunning twist, reported in La Carta's Special Edition *yesterday, Pope Julius Africanus dissolved his Curia and dismissed his cardinals, referring to them as power-hungry careerists undeserving of their esteemed roles.*

Rome—With a special Vatican pass, I gained access to private Vatican grounds to document the exodus of over 200 cardinals. A curious Vatican gardener joined me, and we watched in disbelief as the former princes of the Church streamed through a side door and stepped outside the Vatican walls, to embark on lives reduced in stature and circumstances. They exited in a downpour that matched the gloom on their faces. This upheaval has left millions in shock and fear, wondering: What comes next?

The plan for the newly demoted men was set in place even

before the pope addressed them. While they lost their cardinal status, they won't be entirely without a title. A news release, meticulously prepared by Bishop Ennio Batori, Director of the Holy See Press Office, states that all cardinals have been demoted to the office of bishop. Those over eighty years of age will be cared for in Church housing, suited to their varying health conditions. The younger ones living in Vatican City will serve in vacant bishop positions within dioceses. The rest will return to their dioceses but with reduced authority.

His orders don't end there.

Pope Julius has ordered a complete overhaul of the Church order. "We have always operated as a hierarchical system with the laity at the bottom of the stack. No longer," His Holiness declared.

Effective immediately, the pope is establishing six-member lay councils in each diocese. These bodies will hold equal authority with priests, bishops, and deacons in determining the use of funds, shaping local Church policy, and addressing clergy misconduct. Each council will consist of three men and three women, elected by their peers and by non-office-holding members of the congregation.

Vatican observers believe the pope's actions are carefully timed to reassure congregants worldwide that their Church remains steadfast. In the pope's words: "There is no need for any God-fearing congregant to believe that their Church does not stand behind them as it always has. It is steady, and you may remain faithful to it."

The world now waits for Julius to name the thirteen individuals—twelve men and a woman—who will assist him in leading the Church into the future. Very little is known about this plan, leading to speculation and competition.

Surprisingly, the pope indicated that the Silent Mistress Fund was the catalyst for his determination to scale back and start over. "If such a monumental deception could persist for so many years, the urgency for a new moral authority becomes undeniable."

This is the third in a series of investigative reports on the widespread breach of priestly celibacy.

CHAPTER SIXTY-NINE

Rome

With all eyes on the Vatican capers, Valentina Vella eventually slipped away from Church politics to meet with her business partner. Erika had sent her several text messages after Yigael exposed her, all of which Valentina had ignored. Hanging in the balance was their partnership, their beloved lab Valeri, and most of all, their long friendship.

Erika Simone arrived first at Impronta, a pop *ristorante* steps from the swanky Via Veneto. She ordered quickly from the Latin American menu, hoping a fancy starter would lure her partner to stay and not duck out after expressing her fury.

Valentina arrived to a platter of scallops with passion fruit and avocado, served on a colorfully designed stoneware dish. A covered ceramic tortilla warmer sat to one side, and a bottle of Santa Margherita Pinot Grigio tipped out from a frosty ice bucket. One perfectly groomed brow lifted at the sight.

"Val," Erika said as her partner neatly sat in the chair opposite. "Thank you for seeing me."

"Yes ... of course."

"How's Maria? I mean, I know she's physically okay. I read the news. But how is she?"

"She's a strong, young woman. And she's going to be fine."

"Good."

Silence.

Erika had chosen the dry but refreshing white wine, hoping Val would think it paired well with the seafood and fruit dish. She took a sip and was herself surprised by the nice apple finish.

Valentina did the same, landing an eye on her partner but remaining silent.

When she and Erika discovered Julia's grave, the Church shuttered the find and forced the two to sign a gag order preventing them from publishing their findings, even speaking about the first-century leader.

When word of the find went worldwide, through no fault of the Valeri women—or so she thought—the Church retaliated by confiscating their lab, destroying their livelihoods, and, above all, ruining their reputations. From Valentina's perspective, that's what Erika's betrayal had cost them. The two had climbed back, but regaining the trust of the scientific community had been tough.

Erika fumbled for a starting point but found none she thought could dampen the fires of Valentina's rage. When she finally drummed up the courage to say something honest and direct, "I'm sorry" was all she could muster.

Valentina's eyes remained smoldering.

Erika shifted in her seat. "I wasn't trying to hurt you. I couldn't see beyond what they'd done to us, Val. I wanted revenge. No, not revenge. I wanted justice. For us, for Julia, for every woman in between."

"You should've talked to me."

"I know. I talked to Edmond instead."

"And talked him into mailing the flash drive?"

"Yes, I wanted to confess a thousand times. But things just kept happening. There seemed to be no opening. The *Secret Temple Scroll* took center stage, and then all those scrolls dropped in Herculaneum. And then the pope gave Valeri back to us." She stopped for another sip of wine. "And then, suddenly, things were back to normal. And I thought—"

"You thought the subject would never come up again."

"By that time, I thought I'd lose you if I confessed to what I had Edmond do. When we got our lab back, I took it as a sign to leave it alone. Let the past lie."

"But what about Paula? You broke up with her over this. You were as angry as I was."

"I didn't think she'd go that ... public."

"What?" That logic was lost on Valentina.

"I thought it would be a slow leak, a balloon with a tiny puncture, one you didn't notice until it was too late. And then the Church wouldn't, *couldn't*, retaliate."

"That's naïve, and I'm being generous with that term. It was bound to be a huge story wherever it was leaked, on the net, in a newspaper, by a broadcast reporter ... or at the International Conference of Patristic Studies in Oxford in front of 1,200 of our peers." Valentina was getting heated all over again and stopped to catch her breath and recenter.

"I had no idea she'd do that, I swear. The drive was sent before we were even booked for that conference." Erika hung her head. Either she was mending fences the more she divulged or building a cement divide between her and Valentina to last forever. "Paula and I ... it wasn't in the cards for us. And maybe, after witnessing the catastrophic effects of my actions, I just didn't want to face her anymore either."

"Does she—"

"Yes, she knows. I went before that firing squad right after speaking with Yigael." Erika shook her head and then added submissively, "She responded after three texts."

Valentina was unreadable. And quite frankly, Erika had no expectations. She was just relieved her partner hadn't up and walked out.

"You're my best friend, Val, not just my business partner. Can you, please, forgive me?"

"I need more time."

This wasn't what Erika wanted to hear, but more than she could've hoped for, and she had to accept it. "I understand. Thank you for coming."

Valentina made a move to rise, but then she sat back down.

"So, Paula really didn't know who sent her the package? You two dated for what, two, three years. The handwriting is remarkably like yours. There's no denying it."

"Everybody's not you, Val."

"It's more than hard to believe she didn't notice."

"Yeah, well, she wasn't paying attention. She didn't pay attention to a lot of things."

"Well, you dodged a bullet there."

Erika laughed out loud. Unexpectedly, Valentina did too.

As the laughter died between them, what remained was years of hard work and commitment. The two women shared the same passion for ancient societies and human behavior. They'd embarked on parallel paths until they'd one day intersected. That crossing had created Valeri. It unearthed the first female bishop in the Church. It found the very first writing about the life of Yeshua. It fought the Church … and won in the end. They were seekers of truth and, together, worked to better the world for all humankind.

Valentina picked up her spoon, scooped up a scallop, and set it on Erika's plate. Then she helped herself and lifted her glass.

CHAPTER SEVENTY

Rome

CARDINAL JUSTIN PARINA CAREFULLY PACKED HIS CIVILIAN clothing into a spinner bag on his bed. He zipped it closed and flipped it to the floor, then walked to his wardrobe, opened a drawer at the bottom, and removed a small safe.

He unlocked it, took out his forged ID, slipped it into his wallet, and put the wallet into his jacket pocket. He placed the now-empty safe in his carry-on and added extras, including books and a tiny silver box trimmed with silk ribbons, a gift. The remainder of his belongings had been boxed and shipped.

Taking one last look around the flat he'd called home since arriving in Rome as a young priest, he silently thanked his past self for choosing a place just outside the gates of St. Peter's. Although it was only a short walk to his office in the VAT, it offered the privacy and escape he craved from after-hour gatherings. And after Katarina entered his life, his choice paid off even more, shielding him from the spotlight as best he could manage.

He gathered his bags, opened the front door, and walked

out, wearing khakis, a crisp, blue-and-white striped shirt that accented his pale-blue eyes, a navy pullover sweater, and brown calfskin loafers. No trace that he had been an ecclesiastical prince of Rome.

He dropped his bags in the foyer and exited. Justin walked the few steps from his apartment to the Vatican Library and entered through a private door to his *suite di uffici*. Bypassing the office workers' unoccupied desks, he zeroed in on the copy room and stopped in front of the shredder. Reaching into his jacket pocket, Justin retrieved his false ID and shot it through. He watched as his micro-cut document disassembled into unidentifiable confetti that trickled into a receptacle. He was not interested in opening the door to the private office where he'd spent so many hours. He'd removed all personal items, which had turned it into a generic space.

His phone rang. Glancing at the display, he was not surprised by the caller. "I'll be right out."

Justin emerged to the sunshine and the waiting car. He glanced at the back seat of the Fiat Panda and saw his luggage. "Thanks, Fran," he said, hopping inside.

Monsignor Francesco Ricci had insisted on taking Justin to the airport.

As he pulled onto the Autostrada A91, it was surprisingly quiet inside the car. Perhaps they'd exhausted all the words that mattered between them. It was inevitable that from this point on, their pathways would diverge. Justin on his way to a freedom he'd never known ... him evermore tied to the Church in new and unfamiliar ways.

When Francesco pulled up to the Swiss Airlines terminal, he got out, retrieved Justin's bags, and set them on the curb.

Awkwardly going through the motions of parting, Justin patted himself down. Did he remember his boarding pass, wallet?

Francesco bending over the luggage, inspected the locks.

There was no putting it off any longer. As their eyes met, their hearts shattered, grief written on both their faces like a tragic verse inked in sorrow.

"Fran, you will come ... on your vacation ...." Justin's voice faltered, and he could not hold back his tears. It was likely he would not see his friend again.

As he grabbed his pocket-handkerchief, Francesco, tears misting, clutched him tightly.

As they broke apart, the monsignor said, "*Stammi bene,* Justin." Take care of yourself.

"*Anche tu, mio caro amico.*"

CARDINAL PARINA BOARDED a Swiss Airlines flight from Rome at noon. An hour and a half later, he touched down at Lugano. When he stepped off the plane, the tall, striking man shook off the residue from his false identity as Roberto Molinelli and his former identity as the cardinal in charge of the Vatican Library and became Justin Parina.

He boarded the ferry for a short distance to Morcote and went to an isolated spot at the bow. Justin reveled in the landscape ahead, its green hills lush with olive and cypress trees, happy he would never again have to consider this trip a visit.

He had yet to share the best news with his family. He was responding well to hormone medication that could potentially extend his life by five years plus. The most remarkable part was that he now experienced no side effects and felt like his old self again.

Arriving in the center of the village, he smiled as he took in the familiar, quaint streets of Morcote, the colonnades, and pretty boutiques.

He picked up his bags and began his walk, passing by a newspaper kiosk with the monthly *Morcote Press* front page screaming the headline "Vatican Cardinal ...." Justin didn't bother to look at the rest. He chuckled just as someone drew his attention away. A woman stood outside Berta's Bakery, waving the newspaper about.

Berta Hoffman. *Well, now she knows.* Justin raised his hand in acknowledgment, then turned onto a narrow path and started climbing toward the brick house overlooking the Mediterranean.

Arriving at the long, narrow staircase, he took the steps hurriedly. Reaching the top, the entrance door swung open, and the two people he loved most stood inside, side by side, their arms outstretched.

CHAPTER SEVENTY-ONE

Rome

"Funny, with all that's happened, we should find ourselves back here," Sister Maria said, sitting beside Father Orio Rinaldi as if nothing had happened.

It was a Sunday morning at Mass, and together, they would enjoy it as they had many times before, with Monsignor Francesco Ricci guiding the sermon.

The church overflowed with expectant congregants at the edge of their seats wanting to know "what next?" after the pope's astonishing announcements. Folding chairs crowded every available space in the aisles and vestibule. The atmosphere was electric as they waited.

This occasion marked the first genuine conversation between Maria and Orio since her return to Casa Veronesi and his return from Bari.

"Well, you know what they say," Orio said, "The more things change, the more they stay the same."

Maria gave her friend a wan smile.

"Can we go to lunch after?" he asked.

Then she grinned. "Of course. Trattoria Terra?"

"As long as you don't have news like the last time we were there." Orio looked to the heavens.

"No. Not this time."

Maria's downhearted voice caused the priest to ask, "What is it?"

"Not really anything. We'll talk later."

"I have something I want to tell you too."

Francesco surprised his congregants when he did not immediately start the Mass, but instead, stepped down from the altar to be level with them. For several moments, he took in his audience. He loved each member there. To him, they represented family, and he lamented what he was about to say.

"I wanted to be the first to tell you," He began. "This will be the last Mass I will celebrate here."

The congregants looked at each other and then back to the priest they adored and appreciated for his honest and heartfelt ministering.

"As you know," Francesco continued, "Pope Julius announced a little while back that he would appoint twelve men to act as advisors as he transitions some of the Church's policies and practices into new ones that are more befitting for these times."

At this point, the Church members understood where this talk was headed, and rustling could be heard throughout.

"Well, His Holiness has appointed me, though for what reason I have yet to understand." Francesco's humility was reflected in a sheepish grin as he also sought to lighten the mood.

The congregation laughed together.

"But that means I must leave my place here." He looked down at his folded hands as the crowd's displeasure registered.

But then, there was an abrupt shift in mood, and his audience leaped to their feet and erupted in cheers and applause.

Francesco was under no illusion about what was ahead. He would soon be moving into Saint Martha's House for an indeterminate period—to join twelve men and one woman—to undo much of what had taken over one thousand years to build.

Whether he was up to the task, he didn't know. But he had asked himself what Yeshua would think of the Church now. Would he appreciate that it was alive with two billion members across the world? Or would he be troubled that his teachings had been distorted and turned into a rigid, rule-oriented bureaucracy?

His belief in the answer would steady him for the work ahead.

AT TRATTORIA TERRA, Maria turned to Orio. "I had no idea. Did you?"

They'd waited in a long line before being seated at the busy café. But now they had their familiar corner table.

"I suspected it. I was there when he got the call," Orio said. For once, the priest had kept what he knew quiet.

"So, what is this news you have to tell?" Maria asked.

The din in the small place made it difficult for them to hear each other, but they managed to talk over it.

"You first," Orio said. "How have you gotten on so well since, well, everything?"

"You know, if it hadn't been for you, I don't know what would've happened to me. You knew I'd been taken, and you found my phone."

He flushed and sought to minimize his contribution. "Well, I was just nosing into things, as usual," he said, shifting his hefty girth about in his chair.

"Well, thank you. You saved my life."

Uncomfortable with the appreciation he still wasn't used to receiving, the priest averted his eyes before asking, "Well, what now? You aren't going back to the bank. What will you do?"

"I've been helping Sister Birdi at the shelter, but I'm just filling in, and I can't see myself staying there. So, I'm unsettled ... which makes me a little stressed."

"What do you feel called to do?" he asked. "What do you want?"

"What do I want?" Maria echoed.

"Yes," Orio said. "Fran asked me that a while back, and the question surprised me because I had never considered it. I always did what I was told. But as I thought about it, the idea came to me that what I want could be what God wants too."

Maria raised her eyebrows. "If you put it like that, I'd have to say that I most want to return to the abbey, my convent in Palermo."

"Running away?"

"I've asked myself that," Maria said, "but the abbey is where my heart is. They took care of me after my father died." Maria paused, searching for the right words.

"What is it, friend?"

"Did you know the ... fund is why they took me in?"

Orio did know her biological father's name was used to secure Maria a place in the convent. He'd spent more time with Carmella in the last few days than Maria likely had in years. "That's nothing to be ashamed of. Your life was at stake, and your mother did what any mother would do."

"I always thought my father got me in because they argued about it, but after he convinced my mother, she pulled the strings. The sisters didn't want to let me in. When they finally agreed, they treated me with so much affection and respect." She forced a smile. "The life I thought I was meant to live has been rewritten. Where do I go from here?" She shrugged and added casually, "I don't know. I'm surprised I was able to suggest where to eat."

He laughed.

"But you know what they say .... You can never return home."

He shook his head and said softly, "You can *always* go home."

Maria's eyes widened with the thought she'd rejected.

"In fact, that's exactly what I'm doing," Orio confided.

"What do you mean?"

"I'm going home. I'm leaving here, the priesthood, and returning to Bari."

Maria's mouth dropped open. "I'm amazed."

"When I visited my family there," he explained, "I saw a bakery shop for sale, and I had this wild idea that I would like to buy it ... and work it."

"Go on." And just like that, Maria's eyes twinkled in fascination.

"My brother Leo has backed me," he explained, "and I'm going." The priest removed a cloth from the slit in his cassock and blotted at the tears gleaming.

Maria's face reflected the wonder she shared with her friend, along with confusion and deep thought. "Could I really?"

"Maria, you can always go home," her friend repeated.

CHAPTER SEVENTY-TWO

Murattiano District, Bari

"Ah, Signora Cabrera, you are here for Jemma's cake, *sì*?" Orio Rinaldi stood behind the pastry case, wearing a bright-white shirt, an impressive toque, and a big smile. Though only a few months after his grand opening, he felt right at home.

"*Sì*, Father." She beamed.

"Ah, ah, ah." Orio waggled a finger good-naturedly at his customer. "None of that now. I am no longer a priest."

"And so, you are not, Father … I mean, Orio," *Signora* Cabrera said. "But, please, indulge me once in a while."

In truth, Orio indulged his customers more than occasionally. They were enthralled to have a man of the cloth in their midst, even if he was only a *former*. Many of them refused to part with his clerical title.

"It's hard to believe little Jemma is turning sixteen," he said. "Now, tell me, is that young man she has started to see coming to the party?"

The *signora* raised a brow in astonishment. "How do you

know about Gianni, Father? I mean, Orio. I say, you seem to know the news before anyone else does."

"Don't worry, *Signora* Cabrera, my lips are sealed." He drew a finger across them in a locking motion, but his smile told of mischief.

Turning around, Orio collected the chocolate cream cake from the countertop. Inspecting the dusting of cocoa powder, the gold leaf, and edible flowers on top, he nodded in approval and handed over the cake. This invention was his house specialty, and he called it Torta Dolce di Suor Maria. Sister Maria's Sweet Cake.

"Jemma will love this," he said with assurance.

"She will. Thank you, Father." *Signora* Cabrera balanced the cake with both hands and scurried out before he could remind her once more.

When Orio returned to Bari back in the fall and took over the bakery on Via Argiro, his brothers helped splash on new paint inside and out. He installed a commercial juicer and placed a tall glass canister filled with oranges on the counter. The back wall displayed an espresso machine and, next to it, a panini press.

Orio had taken the required training for licensing and decided to offer a small but superb wine selection. The reds filled a polished wooden wine rack set out of the way of the counter where customers could browse. The white and sparkling wines stood front and center in a stainless-steel refrigerator with glass doors.

When all was ready, Orio set up small tables with colorful chairs inside and out. Only then did he unveil the new sign: *Pasticceria Famiglia Rinaldi*.

His nieces and nephews had been all too eager to step in as servers. In their black jeans, white collared shirts, and green serving aprons, the crew helped as if they owned the place, which someday they might.

Customers lined up to buy Orio's little gems, his bakery case emptying of cakes and pastries, tarts, cookies, and strudels each day. Business boomed from the start.

In the meantime, Orio had his eye on a café for sale a stone's throw from Via Argiro along Bari's waterfront, the Lungomare. Lined with palm trees, historic buildings, alluring shops, and stunning sea views, Orio felt he could showcase all his culinary skills and make a real mark in his hometown. He could almost smell his *sugo di pomodoro* as he thought about it. Ristorante Famiglia Rinaldi ... link the two shops.

Orio had created two of Maria's Sweet Cakes on the day *Signora* Cabrera had come in. After she left, he returned to his kitchen to slather icing and the finishing touches on the second, then boxed and posted it to Abbazia di Santa Lucia in Palermo.

He hadn't seen or heard from Maria since he'd left the Eternal City, and he knew he wouldn't because she again lived behind cloistered walls. But he missed her and sending a cake every now and then let him keep in touch as best he could. It also told Maria that he was doing well.

Orio had put Rome behind him. When he expressed a brief thought, perhaps of regret, his brother Leo told him, "The past, if we learn from it, illuminates a path to a brighter future."

That it had.

CHAPTER SEVENTY-THREE

Palermo, Sicily

The small graveyard lay in a grassy plane behind the monastery's vegetable garden. Maria approached the wrought iron gate and turned the latch. Stepping inside, she scanned the identical stone markers lined up precisely and then moved toward the mound of rock and dirt. This burial was new. The grass had not yet covered the grave.

She knelt and prayed for several moments, then touched the earth and stood. The headstone had yet to be set in place.

With tears brimming, she turned back toward the gate. As she stepped out, she saw Salvatore, the gardener, rounding the corner. He carried his familiar rake and a small, brown paper bag. Maria raised her palms as if to say, *It's all so terrible.*

"She will always be with you, you know," Salvatore said as she reached him.

"I know," she replied. "And I do feel her presence, her guidance. But it's not the same. I owe her so much. She gave so much to me when I came home."

Maria had returned to the convent in a frazzled state. Mother Delfina Bouvier, her friend and mentor, had been the encouraging presence, standing by as she took one step at a time to come to terms with where she'd been and what it had cost her. The sisters of Abbazia di Santa Lucia had been there too. Even the walls of the convent seemed to hum with solace, their melodies alive with Vivaldi's *The Four Seasons* and the soaring works of Hildegard von Bingen. Music, which had once felt like an irretrievable part of her, became woven back into her daily life.

And though it had taken months, she pulled through.

"It was just so sudden," Maria said, her voice breaking. "One day, she was here, and the next, she was gone."

What began as a routine stomach infection spiraled into sepsis, claiming Delfina's life in just a matter of days.

"You can call on her whenever you want, and she will be there."

"I know," Maria whispered, her words weighted with grief. "I just, I thought we were in this together." A harsh laugh, mingling with tears, caused her to hiccup.

"You've come through much, and you will do so again, Maria." Salvatore propped the rake against the stone walls of the monastery and turned to face her squarely. "To have trials, to hurt ... this is what living is."

A distant car engine drew their attention, but the gardener's words lingered in the space between them.

"Follow your heart, let your joys and sorrows be your guideposts, just as Delfina told you to do when you got on that train headed for Rome."

She looked down past her gray, knee-length skirt at her sensible black shoes, well-worn from use at the convent, and nodded.

Salvatore touched Maria's chin and brought it up so he could look into her eyes to check that his words had sunk in.

"Here." He held out the little baggy, a twinkle in his eye. "A slice from the cake that arrived while you were out back."

She took the treat. A swell of emotion prevented her from saying thank you, but he saw it in her eyes.

Salvatore nodded and headed back to the garden patch as Maria made her way down the cobblestone path, her cane and brown bag in one hand, a small suitcase, weathered and utilitarian, containing her few belongings, in the other.

Just beyond the monastery grounds, a Sicilia Orange Fiat 500 idled. Michael Levin stepped out, squinting as the sun cast highlights onto his sandy hair and the breeze pushed it into his eyes.

He met Maria at the gate and took her suitcase. Placing it in his trunk, he turned to her, his easy smile both reassuring and infectious. "You ready for this?"

ACKNOWLEDGMENTS

Thanks to everyone on the *Silent Mistresses* team who helped us get this little baby from Start to Print and beyond.

To our Italy connection, Shaun Loftus, publicist extraordinaire, deep, deep thanks. Her magic has allowed us to reach readers across the globe.

From the UK, much appreciation to our great award-winning, ever-patient cover designer, Jane Dixon-Smith.

Thank you, Jazz Weaver, for the dragonfly illustration—the cherry on top.

THE VATICAN CHRONICLES

The Mystery of Julia Episcopa
The Anonymous Scribe
Silent Mistresses

Know What's In Your Plate

A Real Food Guide to Vitamins, Mine

Are you always tired, bloated, or f(
you're "fine"?

This book reveals what your body is missing... and how real food can help you feel human again.

by
Sachin Gothwal
Founder, Gud Life Sciences

Know What's In Your Plate
Fix Your Health with Nutrition and Food

Copyright © 2025 by Sachin Gothwal
All rights reserved.

No part of this publication may be reproduced, stored in a retrieval system,
or transmitted in any form or by any means—electronic, mechanical,
photocopying, recording, or otherwise—without the prior written permission
of the publisher, except for brief quotations used in reviews or articles.

Published by Gud Life Sciences
First edition, 2025
ISBN: 979-8-2840-3809-3

This book is intended for informational purposes only.
It is not a substitute for professional medical advice, diagnosis, or treatment.

Always consult with your physician or qualified health provider regarding any health condition.
The author and publisher disclaim any liability for adverse outcomes from application of information in this book.

To those who've suffered in silence —

the ones told "your labs are normal" while your body screamed otherwise.
This book is for you.
For those who choose to fight back —
not with fear, but with food.
With smarter choices, better habits, and the belief that healing is possible.

You're not broken. You're just missing something.

Index – Know What's In Your Plate

1. Index 4
2. Introduction 6
3. Potassium 8
4. Magnesium 13
5. Calcium 18
6. Sodium 23
7. Phosphorus 28
8. Iron 32
9. Zinc 37
10. Selenium 41
11. Chromium 46
12. Copper 49
13. Manganese 57
14. Vitamin A 60
15. Vitamin D3 64
16. Vitamin E 68
17. Vitamin K2 MK7 72
18. Vitamin C 75
19. Vitamin B1 (Thiamine) 81
20. Vitamin B2 (Riboflavin) 85
21. Vitamin B3 (Niacin) 90
22. Vitamin B5 (Pantothenic Acid) 94
23. Vitamin B6 (Pyridoxine) 99
24. Vitamin B7 (Biotin) 103
25. Vitamin B9 (Folate) 108
26. Vitamin B12 (Cobalamin) 113
27. Glutathione 117
28. CoQ10 122
29. Alpha Lipoic Acid 127
30. Lutein 131

31. Zeaxanthin 136
32. Resveratrol 140
33. Curcumin 145
34. Quercetin 150
35. Lycopene 155
36. Astaxanthin 159
37. Amino Acid Summary 164
38. Leucine 167
39. Isoleucine 172
40. Valine 176
41. Lysine 181
42. Methionine 186
43. Phenylalanine 190
44. Threonine 195
45. Tryptophan 200
46. Histidine 205
47. Carnitine 211
48. Glutamine 211
49. Glycine 212
50. Tyrosine 213
51. Choline 214
52. Antioxidant Power 219
53. What To Do Next 222
54. You Did It 224

"Know What's In Your Plate: A Simple Guide to Vitamins, Minerals & Antioxidants"

✅ Introduction: Why Micronutrients Are the Foundation of Health

Your body is like a high-performance machine — and it runs on **micronutrients** like vitamins, minerals, and antioxidants. These small compounds don't give calories or protein, but they control almost everything else — from your energy levels to

immunity, bone strength, digestion, mental clarity, skin health, and heart function.

🍃 What Happens When You Don't Get Enough?
Many modern health problems — like fatigue, poor sleep, anxiety, frequent illness, hair fall, or joint pain — **start with silent nutrient deficiencies**. These symptoms are often not due to age or stress, but due to missing micronutrients that the body desperately needs.

⬤ Long-term deficiencies can lead to:
- ❌ Arterial calcification (lack of Vitamin D & K2 MK7)
- ❌ High blood pressure (low Potassium or Magnesium)
- ❌ Osteoporosis (calcium imbalance and low Vitamin D)
- ❌ Weakened immunity (low Zinc, Selenium, Vitamin C)
- ❌ Cognitive decline (B12 and Omega-3 deficiency)

✅ This Book Will Help You:
✓ Understand what each nutrient **does** in your body
✓ Identify **natural food sources** (with visuals)
✓ Learn **timing** and **combinations** for better absorption
✓ Avoid harmful **food clashes**
✓ Prevent or support recovery from **chronic conditions**
✓ Use the **nutrient tracker** to stay consistent

🧠 You'll Also Learn:
✓ Nutrients that clash or work together
✓ Gut health, sunlight, hydration influence
✓ When food is enough and when supplements may help
✓ Long-term planning with simple tools and visuals

⚡ Potassium — The Silent Fix for Fatigue & Bloating
"Why do I feel bloated, tired, or foggy — even with a clean diet?"

You're eating well, drinking water, maybe even cutting back on salt — but your belly still feels puffy, your energy crashes by noon, and your heart races when you're stressed. These aren't just signs of "aging" or "stress." They could be symptoms of a **hidden potassium deficiency**.

Potassium is your body's **cellular balancer** — it keeps your fluid levels, blood pressure, energy, and muscles in harmony. But here's the catch: over **97% of adults in the U.S. don't get enough.** And the symptoms are sneaky.

💪 What Potassium Actually Does
Potassium works in every cell, but especially in muscles — including the heart. It doesn't get media attention like sodium or magnesium, but it plays a central role in:
- Regulating blood pressure and fluid balance
- Reducing bloating and water retention
- Supporting nerve impulses and muscle contraction
- Balancing blood sugar and insulin sensitivity
- Calming the nervous system under stress

When potassium drops, your body holds on to sodium — and that leads to swelling, tightness, and fatigue.

⚠ Signs You Might Be Low on Potassium

Let's look at the real-world signs — not lab numbers. Many of these symptoms are so common, they're often ignored or misdiagnosed.

Physical Signs	Mental/Emotional Signs
Bloating or puffiness	Brain fog or lack of clarity
Muscle cramps or weakness	Anxiety or restlessness
Fatigue, especially mid-day	Mood swings
Irregular heartbeat	Low motivation
Constipation	Feeling overwhelmed easily

🔲 How Much Potassium Do You Need?

Before reaching for supplements, let's understand what *real-life potassium goals* look like. Most of it should come from food — supplements are tightly restricted (by law) and not effective alone.

Group	Functional Daily Dose
Adults (Men & Women)	3,500–4,700 mg/day
Athletes	4,700–5,500 mg/day
Low-carb/keto diets	~5,000 mg/day

⚠ FDA limits supplements to ~99 mg per pill — so **food is the only practical way** to meet potassium needs.

🥑 Best Food Sources of Potassium

Let's bust a myth: bananas aren't even close to the top potassium foods. The real stars are leafy greens, beans, squashes, and avocados — and they support heart, muscle, and gut health, too.

Food Item	Potassium per serving
Avocado (1 medium)	975 mg
Sweet potato (1 medium)	540 mg
Spinach (cooked, 1 cup)	840 mg
White beans (½ cup, cooked)	502 mg
Coconut water (1 cup)	600 mg
Butternut squash (1 cup)	582 mg
Salmon (3 oz)	425 mg

✅ Tip: Combining potassium-rich meals with **magnesium and fiber** enhances absorption and supports gut function.

🔄 What Helps or Blocks Potassium?

You might be eating potassium foods — but your body could be **losing it** due to stress, sugar, or caffeine. Let's look at what helps you **absorb and retain** potassium — and what drains it.

Boosters	Blockers
Proper hydration (with minerals)	High-sodium diets

Boosters	Blockers
Whole plant-based meals	Diuretics (coffee, alcohol)
Magnesium-rich foods	Refined sugar and stress
Exercise + post-workout recovery meals	Overuse of processed foods

🟢 Remember: It's not just what you eat — it's what your **body keeps**.

💀 Long-Term Risks of Deficiency
Low potassium over time doesn't just mean cramps or puffiness. It silently increases risks that build up over years.
- **High blood pressure** (especially with high sodium intake)
- **Heart arrhythmias**
- **Insulin resistance and type 2 diabetes**
- **Kidney stress or stones**
- **Chronic fatigue and muscle breakdown**

And yet — potassium is almost never tested in routine checkups. You have to **pay attention yourself.**

📊 Weekly Potassium Food Tracker
This tracker isn't about being perfect — it's about staying consistently close to your daily goal. If you build plates using foods like these, you'll naturally support hydration, energy, and heart health.

Day	Avocado	Spinach	Sweet Potato	Beans	Coconut Water	Salmon	Estimated Total
Monday	✓	✓		✓	✓		~3,800 mg
Tuesday		✓	✓		✓	✓	~3,700 mg
Wednesday	✓		✓	✓			~3,900 mg
Thursday	✓	✓		✓	✓	✓	~4,300 mg
Friday		✓	✓		✓	✓	~3,600 mg
Saturday	✓	✓		✓		✓	~4,100 mg
Sunday	✓		✓	✓	✓		~4,200 mg

🎯 **Target:** Try to reach 3,500–4,700 mg/day from food. A few shifts in your weekly menu can make all the difference — for your heart, your energy, and your focus.

🌙 Magnesium — The Mineral That Calms Everything
"Why do I feel tense, tired, and wired — all at once?"

You lie down to sleep, but your legs twitch. You're exhausted, but your mind won't stop spinning. Or you wake up after a full night... and still feel like you were hit by a truck.
If this sounds familiar, your body may be missing its **calming conductor** — magnesium.
Magnesium doesn't hype your system — it **grounds** it. It relaxes muscles, eases tension, steadies heart rhythm, and lowers the stress load on your nerves. But here's the problem: over **50% of adults in Western countries** are deficient, and most never realize it.

💪 What Magnesium Actually Does
This is one of the most multitasking minerals in your body. It quietly powers over 300 enzyme reactions, especially the ones that:
- Calm the nervous system and relax muscles
- Improve sleep quality and circadian rhythm
- Support steady heartbeats and lower blood pressure
- Aid in blood sugar balance and insulin sensitivity
- Boost mood and reduce inflammation

Magnesium is like the oil in your engine — without it, everything grinds and tenses.

⚠️ Signs You Might Be Low on Magnesium
Before diving into dosages, let's connect this with daily life. You don't need a lab test — your body tells you loud and clear.

Physical Signs	Mental/Emotional Signs
Muscle cramps or twitches	Anxiety or panic feelings
Fatigue or low stamina	Brain fog or memory lapses
Headaches or migraines	Mood swings or low resilience
Constipation	Trouble sleeping or staying asleep
Tingling or numbness	Feeling overwhelmed easily

🌑 Magnesium supports both physical calm and **mental clarity** — especially during high-stress periods or hormonal shifts.

🏁 How Much Magnesium Do You Really Need?

Now that you see the signs, let's get clear on what "enough" looks like — because the RDA is a floor, not a goal. You likely a need **more** if you exercise, drink caffeine, or deal with stress regularly.

Group	Functional Daily Dose
Adult Women	320–400 mg (elemental)
Adult Men	400–450 mg (elemental)
Pregnant Women	350–400 mg
Athletes / Stressed	Up to 500 mg

⚠ Look for **elemental magnesium** on supplements — not just "magnesium citrate 500 mg," which might only contain 90 mg of usable magnesium.

🥜 Best Food Sources of Magnesium
Before you pop a pill, try your plate. Magnesium is rich in seeds, greens, beans, and even dark chocolate — nature's anti-anxiety food.

Food Item	Magnesium per serving
Pumpkin seeds (1 oz)	150 mg
Spinach (cooked, 1 cup)	157 mg
Almonds (1 oz)	77 mg
Black beans (½ cup)	60 mg
Avocado (1 medium)	58 mg
Dark chocolate (70–85%)	64 mg per square
Tofu (½ cup)	37 mg

✅ Tip: Cooked greens are better than raw for magnesium absorption. Light steam, don't boil.

🔄 What Boosts or Blocks Magnesium?

You may be eating enough — but losing it faster than you think. Here's what supports your magnesium retention... and what drains your tank.

Boosters	Blockers
Vitamin B6 and D	Alcohol, sugar, and stress
Adequate protein	Diuretics (coffee, meds)
Hydration and fiber	Overuse of calcium-only supplements

🔄 Magnesium also supports **potassium absorption** — so balancing them together can improve muscle and heart function.

💀 Long-Term Deficiency Risks

When magnesium runs low for too long, the body shows deeper signs of imbalance — not just in energy, but in heart, brain, and bone health.

- Heart arrhythmias and high blood pressure
- Type 2 diabetes and insulin resistance
- Chronic fatigue and inflammation
- PMS and hormone-related mood shifts
- Migraine, tension headaches, and sleep disorders

Magnesium isn't a quick fix — it's a **foundational stabilizer**. Without it, things fall apart quietly.

📊 Weekly Magnesium Food Tracker

You don't have to hit perfection — but getting close to your daily goal, most days, can change how your body and mind feel in under a week.

Day	Pumpkin Seeds	Spinach	Almonds	Avocado	Beans	Dark Choco	Total Est.
Monday	✓	✓			✓	✓	~350 mg
Tuesday		✓	✓	✓			~300 mg
Wednesday	✓				✓	✓	~280 mg
Thursday	✓	✓	✓				~330 mg
Friday			✓	✓	✓	✓	~310 mg
Saturday	✓	✓			✓	✓	~360 mg
Sunday		✓	✓				~250 mg

🎯 Aim for **at least 300–400 mg daily** from food. Use supplements for top-up — not the foundation.

🦴 Calcium — Strong Bones or Silent Risk?

"Why do my joints ache, nails break, or muscles twitch — even when I take supplements?"

You've probably been told to "get more calcium" since childhood. And maybe you are — through milk, yogurt, or even pills. But if your bones still feel weak, your muscles cramp, or your body seems stiff and brittle — something deeper is going on.

Calcium isn't just about quantity — it's about direction. It needs to go to the **right place**. Because the wrong calcium in the wrong place? That's how you get **hardened arteries**, kidney stones, and painful joints.

💪 What Calcium Actually Does

It's not just a bone builder. Calcium is a **signaling mineral** — a sort of internal communicator that supports:
- Bone density and tooth enamel
- Muscle contractions, including your heartbeat
- Nerve signal transmission
- Blood clotting when you're injured
- Hormonal balance and cell metabolism

But calcium is also a double-edged sword — powerful but potentially harmful if mismanaged. That's why this chapter goes deeper than "drink more milk."

⚠ Signs You Might Be Low on Calcium

These signs are more common than most people realize — and they often overlap with magnesium or Vitamin D deficiency.

Physical Signs	Mental/Emotional Signs
Brittle nails or dry skin	Mood swings or irritability
Muscle cramps or spasms	Trouble focusing
Numbness or tingling	Low stress tolerance
Tooth decay or weak enamel	Feeling "fragile"
Weak bones or slow healing	Anxiety or restlessness

🔎 Note: If you're supplementing with calcium but still experiencing these symptoms, it could be a **cofactor deficiency** — not enough magnesium, Vitamin D, or K2 to help calcium absorb and travel correctly.

🧮 How Much Calcium Do You Really Need?

Let's make the numbers work **for you**, not just as a checklist. Most adults get far less than needed from diet — or far too much from supplements.

Group	Functional Daily Dose
Adults 19–50	1,000 mg
Adults 51+	1,200–1,300 mg
Teens / Pregnant Women	1,200–1,300 mg

📌 **Important**: Always track **total daily intake** (diet + supplements combined). Overshooting without cofactors increases calcification risk.

🔎 **Best Food Sources of Calcium**

Let's step beyond milk and find **real food sources** that deliver bioavailable calcium — with less digestive stress and more nutrient synergy.

Food Item	Calcium per serving
Fortified almond milk (1 cup)	450 mg
Collard greens (1 cup)	260 mg
Greek yogurt (¾ cup)	200–250 mg
Tofu (½ cup, calcium-set)	250–300 mg
Canned sardines (with bones)	325 mg
Chia seeds (1 oz)	180 mg
Broccoli (1 cup)	43 mg

✅ **Tip**: The combination of **calcium, magnesium, and K2** in meals ensures proper uptake without side effects like gas, cramps, or plaque buildup.

⚠ What About Arterial Calcification?

This is the part most people — and even many doctors — miss.

Excess calcium with no guidance in the body can settle in **arteries, joints, and kidneys** instead of your bones.

That leads to:
- **Atherosclerosis** (artery hardening)
- **Heart disease**
- **Kidney stones**
- **Joint stiffness and inflammation**

The solution? **Vitamin K2 MK7** — it activates a protein called *Matrix GLA*, which directs calcium **away from arteries and into bones** where it belongs.

❗ Taking calcium without K2 is like sending cement into your bloodstream without a construction plan.

🔄 What Helps or Blocks Calcium?

The next time you hear "drink milk for calcium," remember — absorption is a team sport. You need the **right players** to move calcium into the right tissues.

Boosters	Blockers
Vitamin D3 and K2 MK7	Excess caffeine, soda, or salt
Magnesium	Oxalates in raw spinach (limit excess)
Physical activity	Antacids and proton pump inhibitors
Healthy fat with meals	High phosphorus (from sodas/meats)

💀 Long-Term Deficiency or Misuse Risks

Calcium deficiency is serious — but **improper use** is even more dangerous. Here's what happens if your calcium isn't managed well:
- **Osteoporosis** (bones literally weaken from within)
- **Tooth decay** and gum damage
- **Arterial calcification** (heart attack risk)
- **Kidney stones** and calcium deposits
- **Joint pain** or "aging body" symptoms in mid-life

🪨 Balanced calcium = bone strength + heart safety. Don't let it go rogue.

📊 Weekly Calcium Food Tracker

If you're not tracking your calcium, you're probably **under** or **over** without knowing it. This tracker helps you hit your sweet spot through a mix of dairy, greens, and fortified sources.

Day	Almond Milk	Yogurt	Sardines	Tofu	Greens	Chia	Total Est.
Monday	✓	✓	✓		✓		~1,200 mg
Tuesday	✓			✓	✓	✓	~1,100 mg
Wednesday		✓	✓	✓			~1,250 mg
Thursday	✓	✓	✓		✓		~1,300 mg
Friday	✓		✓	✓	✓	✓	~1,350 mg

Day	Almond Milk	Yogurt	Sardines	Tofu	Greens	Chia	Total Est.
Saturday	✓	✓		✓	✓		~1,200 mg
Sunday	✓	✓	✓	✓	✓	✓	~1,450 mg

🎯 Aim for 1,000–1,300 mg/day — and never forget the **K2 + D3** partnership if you're supplementing.

🧂 Sodium — The Misunderstood Mineral
"Why do I feel light-headed, foggy, or drained after sweating?"

You're trying to eat clean. You cut out processed foods. You've switched to low-salt snacks. But suddenly, you feel dizzy when standing up, your brain feels fuzzy, and your workouts leave you wiped out instead of energized.

This may not be dehydration — it could be **low sodium**.

For decades, sodium has been blamed for high blood pressure and heart disease. But that's only one side of the story. In reality, **too little sodium** — especially in active or low-carb lifestyles — can lead to exhaustion, mental fog, and poor recovery.

💪 What Sodium Actually Does
Sodium gets a bad reputation — but it's **essential for life**. It works in tight balance with potassium to:
- Maintain fluid balance and hydration
- Regulate blood pressure and blood volume

- Support nerve impulse transmission
- Enable muscle contractions (including the heart)
- Help absorb nutrients like glucose and amino acids

If your sodium levels dip too low, the entire electrical system in your body slows down.

⚠ Signs You Might Be Low on Sodium

These symptoms are often mistaken for burnout or low blood sugar. But they can come from sodium depletion — especially if you sweat a lot, eat low-carb, or avoid salt entirely.

Physical Signs	**Mental/Emotional Signs**
Headaches or light-headedness	Brain fog or forgetfulness
Muscle weakness or cramps	Irritability or low patience
Salt cravings	Anxiety or inner restlessness
Dry mouth or nausea	Trouble concentrating
Fatigue after workouts	Feeling "flat" or unmotivated

🪙 If you've ever had "keto flu" or post-sweat dizziness — this is likely low sodium in action.

🧂 How Much Sodium Do You Really Need?

Let's make sense of the numbers. The government recommends limits, but in reality, your body's sodium needs depend on your lifestyle, sweat, and diet.

Group	Optimal Daily Range
Sedentary adults	1,500–2,300 mg
Physically active adults	2,300–3,000 mg
Low-carb / keto diets	3,000–5,000 mg
Heavy sweaters / athletes	Up to 5,500 mg

⚠ 1 teaspoon of table salt = ~2,300 mg sodium. Most processed foods over-deliver — but clean eaters often **under-consume.**

🧂 **Best Food Sources of Sodium (the Clean Kind)**
Sodium isn't just in chips and fries. When done right, it's in bone broth, fermented foods, and real salt — and your body welcomes it.

Food Item	Sodium per serving
Sea salt (½ tsp)	~1,150 mg
Bone broth (1 cup)	300–600 mg
Pickles (1 medium)	570 mg
Olives (10 small)	420 mg
Cottage cheese (½ cup)	400 mg
Sauerkraut (½ cup)	330 mg
Smoked salmon (3 oz)	700 mg

✅ Tip: Use **sea salt or pink salt** in cooking — they often contain trace minerals like magnesium and potassium.

🔄 What Supports or Sabotages Sodium Balance?
Your body doesn't just need sodium — it needs to **hold onto it** during stress or heat. Here's what helps keep it balanced.

Boosters	Blockers
Drinking electrolyte-rich water	Overhydration with plain water
Balanced potassium intake	Excess caffeine or alcohol
Healthy fats + protein meals	Diuretics, certain medications
Fermented, unprocessed foods	Processed junk (adds volume but not value)

💭 Low sodium often shows up during **fasting**, after intense workouts, or in hot climates. Think of it like mineral insurance.

💀 Long-Term Deficiency or Imbalance Risks
Sodium imbalance — whether too high or too low — leads to issues. But most clean eaters and athletes risk the **low** side.
- Chronic fatigue or burnout
- Low blood pressure or dizziness
- Electrolyte imbalances during exercise
- Confusion, poor cognition
- Muscle breakdown or heart stress in extreme cases

It's not about "avoiding sodium" — it's about **getting the right kind from the right sources**.

📊 Weekly Sodium Food Tracker

Track your sodium from real, whole-food sources — especially if you're avoiding processed meals or doing intense activity. You'll feel clearer, stronger, and more energized.

Day	Sea Salt	Bone Broth	Cottage Cheese	Olives	Pickles	Salmon	Est. Sodium
Monday	✓	✓		✓			~2,100 mg
Tuesday	✓		✓		✓	✓	~2,500 mg
Wednesday	✓	✓	✓				~2,200 mg
Thursday	✓	✓			✓	✓	~2,600 mg
Friday	✓		✓		✓	✓	~2,800 mg
Saturday	✓	✓		✓		✓	~2,700 mg
Sunday	✓		✓	✓	✓	✓	~3,000 mg

🎯 Healthy goal: ~2,300–3,000 mg per day if active or sweating often. And never skip salt if you're eating low-carb — it's the **missing link** to feeling good.

🔋 Phosphorus — The Energy Behind Everything
"Why do I feel sore, stiff, and drained — even after resting?"
You sleep well but wake up sore. Your muscles ache after light exercise. Your brain feels slow, and your recovery just isn't what it used to be.

It's tempting to blame age, stress, or sleep — but often, the real culprit is **low phosphorus.**

Phosphorus is essential for **making energy at the cellular level.** If calcium is the structure, phosphorus is the electricity — powering muscles, bones, and even your DNA.

💪 What Phosphorus Actually Does
Phosphorus is found in every single cell — but we rarely talk about it. Here's what it does behind the scenes:
- Supports ATP production — your body's energy molecule
- Builds strong bones and teeth (second only to calcium)
- Repairs tissues after exercise or injury
- Maintains acid-base (pH) balance in blood
- Supports growth, metabolism, and DNA formation

Without phosphorus, your body can't heal, repair, or *function at full charge.*

⚠️ Signs You Might Be Low on Phosphorus
Low phosphorus is often overlooked because the symptoms mimic common problems. If you feel like you're "just not recovering" — this may be why.

Physical Signs	Mental/Emotional Signs
Muscle weakness or fatigue	Brain fog or low alertness

Physical Signs	Mental/Emotional Signs
Bone pain or stiffness	Lack of motivation
Joint soreness post-exercise	Mild depression or irritability
Tingling or numbness	Poor concentration
Loss of appetite	Feeling drained despite sleep

⚠ Vegans, alcohol users, and people with blood sugar issues are especially at risk for phosphorus depletion.

▰ How Much Phosphorus Do You Need?

Let's break down the range. Most adults get *some* phosphorus from protein — but not all of it is absorbable, especially from grains or processed food.

Group	Daily Functional Dose
Adults (19+)	700–1,200 mg
Teens / Pregnant	~1,250 mg
Active / Injured	1,200–1,400 mg

⚠ Too much **inorganic phosphorus** (from soda and processed meat) can damage kidneys — but food-based phosphorus is safe and beneficial.

🔍 Best Food Sources of Phosphorus

You don't need fancy superfoods to get your phosphorus — it's hiding in your pantry already. Protein-rich whole foods are your best bet.

Food Item	Phosphorus per serving
Salmon (3 oz)	270 mg
Chicken breast (3 oz)	210 mg
Eggs (2 large)	180 mg
Lentils (½ cup, cooked)	180 mg
Pumpkin seeds (1 oz)	280 mg
Greek yogurt (¾ cup)	200 mg
Quinoa (1 cup, cooked)	220 mg

✅ Tip: Soaking or sprouting lentils and seeds makes phosphorus more bioavailable. Avoid colas and meat preservatives that overload your kidneys with artificial phosphate.

🔄 What Helps or Hurts Phosphorus Levels?

Your phosphorus levels are tied to your **protein quality** and **magnesium balance** — but they're easily thrown off by modern junk food.

Boosters	Blockers
Whole protein-rich meals	Soda, soft drinks with phosphoric acid
Magnesium and Vitamin D	Highly processed meats and cheeses
Proper digestion (enzymes)	Overuse of antacids or calcium-only supplements

🔄 Phosphorus works best with magnesium and Vitamin D — think of them as the "energy trio."

☠️ Long-Term Deficiency or Excess Risks

If phosphorus drops too low, or is absorbed in the wrong form, long-term damage sets in.
- Poor bone mineralization (osteomalacia)
- Chronic muscle fatigue and soreness
- Delayed recovery after exercise
- Insulin resistance and blood sugar swings
- Kidney stress from excess inorganic phosphate (soda, lunch meat)

👍 Balance is everything: **Too little** phosphorus weakens you. **Too much** from the wrong sources inflames you.

📊 Weekly Phosphorus Food Tracker

You're likely getting some phosphorus already — this chart helps fine-tune your intake from whole food sources, not synthetic overloads.

Day	Eggs	Yogurt	Lentils	Salmon	Quinoa	Pumpkin Seeds	Total Est.
Monday	✓	✓		✓	✓		~950 mg
Tuesday		✓	✓		✓	✓	~1,000 mg
Wednesday	✓		✓	✓			~1,050 mg
Thursday	✓	✓		✓	✓	✓	~1,300 mg
Friday		✓		✓	✓	✓	~1,100 mg
Saturday	✓	✓		✓		✓	~1,200 mg
Sunday	✓	✓	✓	✓	✓	✓	~1,450 mg

🎯 Ideal range: 700–1,200 mg/day from food. Prioritize **clean protein**, not cola cans.

💧 Iron — The Oxygen Carrier You Can't Live Without
"Why do I feel breathless, weak, and pale — even with rest?"

You climb the stairs and feel winded. Your hands and feet are cold. You wake up tired even after 8 hours of sleep. Maybe your skin looks dull, or your hair feels thinner.

These aren't just signs of "aging" or stress — they're classic symptoms of **iron deficiency.** And if you're a woman, an athlete, or plant-based, your risk is even higher.
Iron is what helps carry oxygen to your cells. When it's low, **nothing in your body can work at full power.**

💪 What Iron Actually Does
Iron doesn't just sit in your blood — it moves oxygen, builds stamina, supports hormones, and sharpens brain function. You need it for:
- Making hemoglobin (the oxygen-carrying part of red blood cells)
- Supporting physical strength and energy production
- Preventing dizziness, fatigue, and cold sensitivity
- Boosting brain alertness and memory
- Strengthening hair and nail growth

Without enough iron, your cells can't breathe — and your energy suffers at every level.

⚠ Signs You Might Be Low on Iron
These signs are common — but dangerously easy to ignore. If you're experiencing even two or three, it's worth paying attention.

Physical Signs	Mental/Emotional Signs
Fatigue or low stamina	Brain fog or poor focus
Pale skin or dark under-eyes	Anxiety or low resilience
Hair thinning or brittle nails	Feeling low or "meh" often

Physical Signs	Mental/Emotional Signs
Cold hands and feet	Poor stress recovery
Shortness of breath	Irritability or low patience

🚺 Women lose iron monthly through menstruation — and pregnancy increases needs by up to 50%. If you're female, low iron could be stealing your vitality.

How Much Iron Do You Really Need?

Iron needs vary widely based on gender, age, and lifestyle. Here's a guide to optimal daily intake:

Group	Functional Daily Dose
Adult Men	8–10 mg
Adult Women (18–50)	15–18 mg
Pregnant Women	27 mg
Postmenopausal Women	8–10 mg
Vegans / Endurance Athletes	18–25 mg

⚠ Iron is harder to absorb from plant sources. Pair it with **Vitamin C** to boost bioavailability.

🍖 Best Food Sources of Iron

Iron comes in two types: **heme (animal-based)** and **non-heme (plant-based)**. Heme iron absorbs better — but both have a place when combined with smart food pairing.

Food Item	Iron per serving
Grass-fed beef (3 oz)	2.1 mg
Chicken thighs (3 oz)	1.1 mg
Spinach (cooked, 1 cup)	6.4 mg (non-heme)
Lentils (½ cup, cooked)	3.3 mg (non-heme)
Pumpkin seeds (1 oz)	2.5 mg
Tofu (½ cup)	3.4 mg
Dark chocolate (1 oz, 85%)	3.3 mg

✅ Pro Tip: Add **lemon juice or bell peppers** to plant-based meals. Vitamin C can **double or triple** non-heme iron absorption.

🔄 What Affects Iron Absorption?

Getting enough iron is one thing — **absorbing** it is another. Many healthy habits can actually block iron if not timed right.

Boosters	Blockers
Vitamin C (citrus, berries)	Calcium-rich meals (e.g., cheese)
Eating meat with plants	Coffee and black tea (with meals)

Boosters	Blockers
Cooking in cast iron pans	Phytates in raw grains and legumes
Fermented foods	Antacids or acid blockers

🍲 For best absorption, take iron-rich meals **separately from dairy, caffeine, and high-calcium foods.**

💀 Long-Term Deficiency Risks

Iron deficiency anemia isn't rare — it affects nearly **1 in 3 women worldwide.** Long-term depletion causes serious system-wide problems:

- Reduced oxygen to muscles and brain
- Hormonal imbalances and fertility issues
- Poor immunity and slower wound healing
- Increased risk of premature aging and fatigue
- Mood disorders and depression

⚠ Never self-diagnose with supplements — excess iron can be harmful. Test before supplementing.

📊 Weekly Iron Food Tracker

This tracker helps you build iron from food first — safely, slowly, and with the nutrients that help it get absorbed.

Day	Beef	Spinach	Lentils	Pumpkin Seeds	Tofu	Dark Choco	Est. Iron
Monday	✓	✓		✓		✓	~15 mg
Tuesday		✓	✓		✓	✓	~17 mg

Day	Beef	Spinach	Lentils	Pumpkin Seeds	Tofu	Dark Choco	Est. Iron
Wednesday	✓		✓	✓			~16 mg
Thursday	✓	✓		✓		✓	~20 mg
Friday		✓	✓	✓		✓	✓	~19 mg
Saturday	✓	✓		✓		✓	✓	~21 mg
Sunday	✓	✓	✓	✓		✓	~22 mg

🌀 Aim for 15–18 mg/day from meals — especially if you're female, athletic, or plant-based. Supplement only with medical guidance.

🔧 Zinc — Your Body's Silent Repairman
"Why am I breaking out, getting sick easily, or feeling a little... off?"

You wash your hands, eat clean, maybe even take supplements — but still, your skin breaks out, you get that one cold everyone else dodges, and cuts take forever to heal. It's not random. It might be **zinc** — the behind-the-scenes mineral your body depends on for **healing, immunity, and hormone balance.** But here's the kicker: it doesn't get stored easily, and stress burns through it fast.

💪 What Zinc Actually Does
Zinc plays a quiet, crucial role in keeping you strong, sharp, and resilient. Without enough of it, your body's ability to **repair, defend, and grow** slows down.

- Speeds up wound healing and skin repair
- Boosts immunity and shortens duration of illness
- Supports testosterone, sperm health, and fertility
- Maintains healthy skin, hair, and nails
- Enables proper taste, smell, and vision

Think of zinc like your **internal handyman** — fixing small problems before they become big ones.

⚠ Signs You Might Be Low on Zinc

Let's decode the red flags. These everyday annoyances are often your body's early alerts — and they point right to zinc.

Physical Signs	**Mental/Emotional Signs**
Frequent colds or infections	Brain fog or forgetfulness
Acne, eczema, or poor skin	Mood dips, especially under stress
Slow wound healing	Low motivation or drive
White spots on nails	Loss of taste or smell
Hair thinning	Irritability or fatigue

Zinc is lost through sweat, stress, and poor gut absorption — so if you're active or under pressure, your needs are higher.

▥ How Much Zinc Do You Really Need?

It's not a "more is better" game. Zinc works best in the **right range** — especially because too much can mess with copper and immunity.

Here's your smart guide:

Group	Daily Functional Dose
Adult Men	11–15 mg
Adult Women	8–12 mg
Pregnant/Lactating	11–13 mg
Athletes / Stressed	Up to 20 mg (short-term)

⚠ Stay under 40 mg/day unless under medical advice. Balance matters.

◯ Best Food Sources of Zinc

Before you grab a supplement, look at your plate. Food-based zinc is more absorbable, and it usually comes with supportive nutrients like protein and healthy fat.

Food Item	Zinc per serving
Oysters (3 oz)	74 mg (super high)
Beef (3 oz)	5.5 mg
Pumpkin seeds (1 oz)	2.2 mg
Chickpeas (½ cup)	1.3 mg
Cashews (1 oz)	1.6 mg
Eggs (2 large)	1.3 mg
Greek yogurt (¾ cup)	1.2 mg

✅ Tip: Plant sources contain **phytates**, which block some zinc. Soak beans/seeds to improve absorption.

🔄 What Helps or Blocks Zinc Absorption?
Your body loves zinc — but it doesn't hold on to it for long. Here's what supports better uptake, and what competes with it.

Boosters	Blockers
Protein-rich meals	High-phytate grains (unsoaked)
Vitamin A and selenium	Calcium supplements (if timed poorly)
Zinc from animal sources	Alcohol, sweat, and stress loss

Pro tip: If supplementing, **take zinc on an empty stomach** (unless it causes nausea) and **away from iron or calcium.**

💀 Long-Term Deficiency Risks
Zinc is involved in **growth, immunity, hormones, and healing** — so long-term deficiency hits deep.
- Reduced fertility or low testosterone
- Chronic skin issues (eczema, acne, psoriasis)
- Hair loss or bald patches
- Frequent illness and poor wound repair
- Mental health dips: low resilience, more stress reactivity

Zinc is especially critical during pregnancy, adolescence, and recovery periods — when your body's rebuilding or growing.

📊 Weekly Zinc Food Tracker

Let's keep it practical. You don't have to overthink — just rotate through a few zinc-rich foods during the week and you'll stay covered.

Day	Beef	Yogurt	Pumpkin Seeds	Cashews	Eggs	Chickpeas	Estimated Zinc
Monday	✓	✓	✓			✓	~14 mg
Tuesday		✓	✓	✓	✓		~12 mg
Wednesday	✓			✓		✓	~13 mg
Thursday	✓	✓	✓	✓			~15 mg
Friday		✓	✓	✓	✓	✓	~13 mg
Saturday	✓	✓	✓		✓		~14 mg
Sunday	✓	✓	✓	✓	✓	✓	~17 mg

🎯 Aim for 10–15 mg/day consistently from food. Go higher only short-term if healing, training, or under stress.

🍬 Selenium — The Cell Protector

"Why do I feel sluggish, cold, or prone to getting sick?"

You're doing everything right — but you're tired, your hair's not growing the way it used to, and your thyroid meds don't seem to be kicking in. Or maybe you just seem to catch every virus going around.

This might not be about food quantity. It's about **micronutrient protection.**

Selenium is your body's **internal antioxidant manager** — defending DNA, activating thyroid hormones, and supporting immune precision.

💪 What Selenium Actually Does
Though it's needed in tiny amounts, selenium does big jobs:
- Converts inactive thyroid hormone (T4) into active T3
- Strengthens immune response, especially antiviral
- Protects cells from oxidative stress (like rust control)
- Boosts fertility and sperm function
- Supports skin health and slows aging

Think of selenium as your **microscopic guardian** — it fights quietly, but powerfully.

⚠ Signs You Might Be Low on Selenium
These symptoms often overlap with other issues — but when they stack up, it's a red flag for selenium deficiency.

Physical Signs	Mental/Emotional Signs
Hair thinning or brittle nails	Brain fog or mental fatigue
Frequent colds or infections	Low mood or motivation
Dry, flaky skin	Irritability or restlessness
Cold sensitivity / slow metabolism	Lack of resilience under stress
Sluggish thyroid labs	Feeling tired for no reason

Selenium is soil-dependent — so if your food comes from low-selenium soil regions (many U.S. and European zones), your diet might fall short.

How Much Selenium Do You Really Need?
You don't need much — but you do need **enough, consistently.** Oversupplementing isn't better — balance is key.

Group	Functional Daily Dose
Adults	55–100 mcg
Pregnant/Lactating	60–70 mcg
Thyroid support use	100–200 mcg (temporary)

⚠ Over 400 mcg/day long-term can be toxic — don't overdo Brazil nuts.

🥜 Best Food Sources of Selenium
Most selenium-rich foods are protein-based — especially seafood and nuts. Here's where to focus:

Food Item	Selenium per serving
Brazil nuts (1 nut)	~95 mcg (extremely high)
Tuna (3 oz)	~92 mcg
Eggs (2 large)	~35 mcg
Chicken breast (3 oz)	~22 mcg
Sunflower seeds (1 oz)	~18 mcg

Food Item	Selenium per serving
Brown rice (1 cup cooked)	~19 mcg

✅ Just 1 Brazil nut per day can meet your needs — more isn't better.

🔄 What Boosts or Blocks Selenium?

Your selenium intake is only part of the picture — let's see what helps your body actually **use and conserve** it.

Boosters	Blockers
Vitamin E (synergistic)	Heavy metals like mercury (from fish)
Zinc + selenium combo	Alcohol or processed foods
Protein-rich meals	Soil depletion in industrial farms

💡 If you're taking selenium for thyroid support, combine it with **iodine, zinc, and magnesium** for optimal conversion.

💀 Long-Term Deficiency Risks

Selenium is small but mighty. When it's low, serious health issues build up silently.

- Hypothyroidism (especially Hashimoto's)
- Poor immunity and frequent infections
- Infertility in men and women
- DNA damage and increased aging
- Higher risk of chronic disease or heart issues

Inflammation, poor detox, and sluggish metabolism often stem from **zinc + selenium + magnesium** being too low.

📊 Weekly Selenium Food Tracker

Rotate your selenium sources. Just a few well-placed meals can restore your levels without overdosing.

Day	Brazil Nut	Tuna	Eggs	Chicken	Seeds	Rice	Est. Selenium
Monday	✓	✓		✓			~140 mcg
Tuesday	✓		✓	✓		✓	~135 mcg
Wednesday	✓	✓		✓	✓		~180 mcg
Thursday	✓	✓	✓			✓	~190 mcg
Friday	✓		✓	✓	✓		~170 mcg
Saturday	✓	✓	✓	✓	✓	✓	~200 mcg
Sunday	✓	✓	✓	✓	✓	✓	~210 mcg

🎯 Daily goal: 55–100 mcg. 1–2 Brazil nuts, a few eggs, and some clean fish — that's your selenium strategy.

🔄 Chromium — The Blood Sugar Balancer
"Why do I crash after meals or crave sugar so often?"
You eat, then crash. You crave sweets even when you're full. Your energy feels like a roller coaster. This may not be willpower — it might be **chromium**.

Chromium enhances insulin sensitivity, helping your body **stabilize blood sugar** and burn fuel efficiently.

💪 What Chromium Does
Here's how chromium keeps your energy steady, your appetite honest, and your metabolism more responsive:
- Improves **insulin sensitivity**
- Reduces sugar cravings and crashes
- Supports **lean muscle preservation**
- May reduce cholesterol and fat buildup
- Helps brain fuel usage and energy metabolism

⚠️ Signs You Might Be Low on Chromium
If you're caught in a cycle of cravings and crashes — especially after carbs — these signs could be pointing to low chromium.

Physical Signs	Mental/Emotional Signs
Sugar cravings	Anxiety or irritability
Blood sugar crashes	Trouble focusing
Weight gain around belly	Mood swings after meals
Fatigue post meals	Emotional eating urges

How Much Chromium Do You Need?

You don't need much — but missing even a few micrograms can send your blood sugar on a roller coaster.

Group	Daily Dose
Adult Men	35 mcg
Adult Women	25 mcg
Insulin-resistant	Up to 200 mcg (supervised)

Best Food Sources of Chromium

These aren't exotic — just simple whole foods that support better glucose control and fewer cravings.

Food Item	Chromium per serving
Broccoli (1 cup)	22 mcg
Grape juice (1 cup)	8 mcg
Turkey breast (3 oz)	2.5 mcg
Whole wheat bread (1 slice)	1.4 mcg
Green beans (1 cup)	2.2 mcg
Apples (1 medium)	1 mcg

Boosters & Blockers

Let's look at what helps chromium work better — and what disrupts blood sugar even if you're eating "healthy."

Boosters	Blockers
Vitamin C-rich foods	Refined sugar
Chromium + magnesium combo	High iron or antacids
Balanced protein meals	Chronic stress

💀 Long-Term Deficiency Risks

Chromium has a direct effect on how your body handles food — especially carbohydrates. Low chromium = chaotic blood sugar.

- Blood sugar instability
- Weight gain and insulin resistance
- Mood imbalance and sugar dependence
- Fatigue and brain fog
- Prediabetes or type 2 diabetes progression

📊 Weekly Chromium Food Tracker

Use this tracker to rotate chromium-rich foods into daily meals — it's a subtle shift with big blood sugar benefits.

Day	Broccoli	Grape Juice	Turkey	Green Beans	Apples	Bread	Est. Chromium
Monday	✓	✓	✓	✓			~35 mcg
Tuesday	✓	✓	✓		✓	✓	~38 mcg
Wednesday	✓		✓	✓	✓	✓	~34 mcg
Thursday	✓	✓	✓	✓	✓		~40 mcg

Day	Broccoli	Grape Juice	Turkey	Green Beans	Apples	Bread	Est. Chromium
Friday	✓	✓	✓	✓	✓	✓	~43 mcg
Saturday	✓		✓	✓	✓	✓	~36 mcg
Sunday	✓	✓	✓	✓	✓	✓	~45 mcg

🔬 Copper — The Forgotten Spark

"Why does my energy feel flat, or my skin dull, even with good nutrition?"

You might be eating well, getting your iron and B12 — but something's still off. You feel tired, your skin isn't glowing, and maybe you're short of breath even with light activity.

It's easy to overlook **copper**, but without it, your iron doesn't work, your skin doesn't glow, and your body stops making energy effectively.

💪 What Copper Actually Does

Copper plays a quiet but crucial role in keeping your metabolism, circulation, and skin in top shape:

- Helps your body **absorb and use iron**
- Supports **collagen and elastin** production (skin, joints)
- Boosts **energy metabolism** in mitochondria
- Protects against oxidative stress (antioxidant role)
- Aids **brain development** and nerve function

Without copper, your iron supplements won't work — they'll just sit there.

⚠ Signs You Might Be Low on Copper

These symptoms mimic iron deficiency — but if iron therapy isn't working, copper might be missing from the equation.

Physical Signs	Mental/Emotional Signs
Fatigue or breathlessness	Brain fog or poor memory
Pale or dull skin	Low mood or apathy
Premature graying	Slow thinking or low motivation
Weak or thinning hair	Nervous system imbalance
Frequent infections	Feeling flat or unproductive

▨ How Much Copper Do You Need?

Copper needs are small — but essential. Too little and your iron can't activate; too much and it competes with zinc.

Group	Daily Dose
Adults (all genders)	900 mcg (0.9 mg)
Pregnant/Lactating	1–1.3 mg

⚠ High-dose zinc supplementation over time can **deplete copper**.

▨ Best Food Sources of Copper

Copper hides in foods rich in color and nutrients — especially nuts, seeds, legumes, and shellfish.

Food Item	Copper per serving
Oysters (3 oz)	0.4–0.6 mg
Cashews (1 oz)	0.6 mg
Chickpeas (½ cup)	0.4 mg
Lentils (½ cup, cooked)	0.25 mg
Dark chocolate (1 oz)	0.5 mg
Sunflower seeds (1 oz)	0.5 mg
Shiitake mushrooms (½ cup)	0.9 mg

What Helps or Blocks Copper?

Copper is influenced by mineral ratios — especially **zinc and iron.** Here's how to support balance:

Boosters	Blockers
Moderate zinc intake	High-dose zinc (>25 mg/day)
Vitamin C-rich foods	Chronic antacids or PPI use
Fermented or sprouted grains	Processed cereals

Long-Term Deficiency Risks
- Anemia that doesn't improve with iron
- Weak bones or connective tissue problems

- Brain fog, mood disorders, low motivation
- Weak immunity and viral susceptibility
- Early aging of hair, skin, and nerves

If you're taking iron or zinc, make sure copper is **on the team**.

📊 Weekly Copper Food Tracker

Copper is easy to miss — but easy to restore with a smart mix of snacks and whole foods.

Day	Cashews	Lentils	Seeds	Chocolate	Chickpeas	Mushrooms	Est. Copper
Monday	✓	✓	✓	✓			~1.4 mg
Tuesday	✓		✓	✓	✓		~1.3 mg
Wednesday		✓	✓		✓	✓	~1.2 mg
Thursday	✓	✓	✓	✓	✓		~1.5 mg
Friday		✓	✓	✓	✓	✓	~1.6 mg
Saturday	✓		✓	✓		✓	~1.3 mg
Sunday	✓	✓	✓	✓	✓	✓	~1.8 mg

🧠 Iodine — The Thyroid's Fuel

"Why do I feel slow, cold, or puffy even when I'm eating clean?"

You're sleeping enough, eating well, and exercising a little — but your body feels slower, colder, and puffier. You can't explain the weight gain, or the fatigue that hits like a fog.

That's exactly how an **iodine deficiency** feels. Iodine powers your thyroid, and your thyroid controls metabolism, temperature, and cellular energy. When iodine is low, everything slows down — from your digestion to your thinking.

💪 What Iodine Does

Before we look at numbers, let's get clear on what this unsung mineral actually powers:

- Produces **thyroid hormones** (T3 and T4)
- Regulates **body temperature** and energy output
- Supports **fetal brain development** during pregnancy
- Aids in **detoxification** of heavy metals and halides
- Boosts **mental clarity** and focus

Think of iodine as the **spark plug** for your metabolism.

⚠️ Signs You Might Be Low on Iodine

If your thyroid isn't getting what it needs, these symptoms will show up slowly — and usually get blamed on aging or stress.

Physical Signs	Mental/Emotional Signs
Fatigue and weight gain	Brain fog and slow thinking
Cold hands and feet	Low mood or depression
Puffy face or body	Anxiety or poor stress response
Constipation	Trouble focusing

Physical Signs	Mental/Emotional Signs
Dry skin or thinning hair	Lack of motivation

Iodine deficiencies are **extremely common** in people avoiding salt, seafood, or dairy.

🪨 How Much Iodine Do You Need?

Before reaching for supplements, know what your body actually needs. Iodine is potent — and more is not always better.

Group	Daily Dose
Adults (Men & Women)	150 mcg
Pregnant Women	220 mcg
Breastfeeding Mothers	290 mcg

⚠ Consistent small doses are better than large spikes. Never megadose without medical guidance.

🌿 Best Food Sources of Iodine

Here's where to find iodine naturally — even if you're avoiding dairy or salt. It hides in ocean foods and a few land-based surprises.

Food Item	Iodine per serving
Seaweed (1 sheet nori)	40–90 mcg
Cod (3 oz)	~99 mcg
Greek yogurt (3/4 cup)	~75 mcg

Food Item	Iodine per serving
Eggs (2 large)	~48 mcg
Iodized salt (1/4 tsp)	~75 mcg
Shrimp (3 oz)	~35 mcg

✅ Tip: Many "natural" salts (like pink or sea salt) contain **zero iodine** unless fortified.

🧠 Boosters & Blockers

These factors can help you absorb iodine — or shut down its use, even if your intake looks good.

Boosters	Blockers
Selenium (activates thyroid)	Fluoride and chlorine (in tap water)
Protein-rich meals	Raw cruciferous veggies (excess)
Adequate iron and zinc	Soy and millet (in high amounts)

Iodine doesn't work alone. It needs **selenium + tyrosine** to make thyroid hormones.

⚠️ Long-Term Deficiency Risks

Chronic iodine deficiency doesn't just affect energy. It reshapes hormones, metabolism, and long-term brain function.

- **Goiter** (enlarged thyroid)
- Hypothyroidism or Hashimoto's
- Poor fetal brain development during pregnancy

- Weight gain, hair loss, and dry skin
- Depression and cognitive decline

In the West, low-iodine diets are increasingly common due to low-salt trends.

📊 Weekly Iodine Food Tracker

Here's a gentle weekly approach to keeping your thyroid fueled. A little seaweed here, a little cod there — and you're covered.

Day	Seaweed	Yogurt	Cod	Eggs	Salt	Shrimp	Est. Iodine
Monday	✅	✅		✅	✅		~160 mcg
Tuesday		✅	✅		✅	✅	~180 mcg
Wednesday	✅		✅	✅		✅	~200 mcg
Thursday	✅	✅		✅	✅		~190 mcg
Friday		✅	✅		✅	✅	~180 mcg
Saturday	✅	✅		✅	✅		~190 mcg
Sunday	✅	✅	✅	✅		✅	~220 mcg

💥 Aim for 150–200 mcg/day — through food first, then support with supplements if needed.

🌼 Manganese — The Joint Supporter & Brain Helper
"Why are my joints stiff, or my thoughts sluggish?"
Your joints feel older than you are. Your mood's a bit off, and your focus fades faster than before. These aren't always signs of stress or aging — sometimes, they point to **manganese**. It's one of those trace minerals no one talks about — yet it helps your brain stay sharp and your joints stay mobile.

💪 What Manganese Actually Does
Before we get into the numbers, here's what manganese is actually doing every day without credit:
- Supports cartilage and **connective tissue repair**
- Helps create antioxidants that reduce **brain aging**
- Aids in **blood sugar balance**
- Supports wound healing and enzyme activity
- Assists bone formation and nutrient metabolism

Manganese works best with magnesium, zinc, and copper — it's part of the **trace mineral dream team**.

⚠️ Signs You Might Be Low on Manganese
These warning signs are easy to ignore or blame on stress, but they often trace back to low manganese — especially in refined, modern diets.

Physical Signs	Mental/Emotional Signs
Joint stiffness or cracking	Low mood or irritability
Muscle tightness or soreness	Poor focus or brain fog
Brittle hair or slow healing	Low stress tolerance

Physical Signs	Mental/Emotional Signs
Blood sugar crashes	Fatigue during recovery

▦ How Much Manganese Do You Need?

Most people have never tracked manganese — but a small, consistent dose daily can prevent inflammation and stiffness from creeping in.

Group	Daily Dose
Adult Men	2.3 mg
Adult Women	1.8 mg
Pregnancy/Lactation	2 mg

⚠ Avoid excess from supplements — high doses may impair iron absorption.

⬤ Best Food Sources of Manganese

These are the foods that quietly fill your manganese tank — not flashy, but essential for keeping your joints and mind functioning smoothly.

Food Item	Manganese per serving
Brown rice (1 cup)	1.8 mg
Pineapple (1 cup)	1.5 mg

Food Item	Manganese per serving
Oats (1 cup cooked)	1.4 mg
Spinach (1 cup cooked)	1.7 mg
Pecans (1 oz)	1.1 mg
Black tea (1 cup)	0.5 mg
Tofu (½ cup)	1 mg

🔄 Boosters & Blockers

Let's talk about what helps you **absorb** manganese — and what works against it. Think of this like your mineral matchmaking chart.

Boosters	Blockers
High-fiber, plant foods	Excess calcium or iron (competes)
Magnesium-rich meals	Refined sugar and alcohol
Moderate tea consumption	Antacids or low stomach acid

💀 Long-Term Deficiency Risks

Manganese doesn't make headlines — but when it's low, wear and tear builds up fast.
- Osteoarthritis or joint degeneration
- Sluggish antioxidant defenses
- Mood imbalance and irritability
- Slower wound and tissue healing
- Blood sugar dysregulation

📊 Weekly Manganese Food Tracker

Here's your simple strategy — sprinkle in a few of these daily, and your joints, brain, and blood sugar will thank you.

Day	Brown Rice	Pineapple	Oats	Pecans	Spinach	Tea	Est. Manganese
Monday	✓	✓		✓		✓	~3.8 mg
Tuesday	✓		✓	✓	✓		~4 mg
Wednesday	✓	✓			✓	✓	~3.5 mg
Thursday	✓	✓	✓	✓	✓		~5 mg
Friday		✓	✓	✓		✓	~3.2 mg
Saturday	✓	✓		✓	✓	✓	~4.6 mg
Sunday	✓	✓	✓	✓	✓	✓	~5.4 mg

🤍 Vitamin A — Vision, Immunity, and Glow

"Why is my skin so dry, my eyes irritated, or my immunity so weak?"

If your skin feels dull, your eyes strain easily, or you're constantly getting sick — it may not be a surface issue. It might be **Vitamin A**.

Vitamin A supports your **first line of defense** — from your eyes to your gut lining. It keeps your vision sharp, your skin resilient, and your immunity strong.

💪 What Vitamin A Does
Let's look at what this powerhouse nutrient supports day to day:
- Promotes healthy **vision and night vision**
- Protects the lining of the **gut, lungs, eyes, and skin**
- Boosts **immune defenses** against viruses and pathogens
- Supports **skin healing** and glow
- Helps with hormone production and growth

⚠️ Signs You Might Be Low on Vitamin A
These symptoms often get misattributed to allergies or bad skincare — but the root could be a lack of Vitamin A.

Physical Signs	Mental/Emotional Signs
Dry eyes or poor night vision	Low immunity or frequent colds
Dry, rough skin or acne	Fatigue and poor recovery
Brittle nails	Feeling "fragile" or depleted
Frequent infections	Low stress tolerance

📊 How Much Vitamin A Do You Need?
Here's what your daily goal should look like — whether from food or supplements:

Group	Daily Dose
Adult Men	900 mcg RAE (3,000 IU)
Adult Women	700 mcg RAE (2,300 IU)

Group	Daily Dose
Pregnancy/Lactation	770–1,300 mcg RAE

⚠ Excess preformed Vitamin A (from liver/supplements) can be toxic — focus on food first.

🥕 Best Food Sources of Vitamin A

Now let's look at where to find it — both from **preformed A (retinol)** and **pro-vitamin A (beta carotene)** sources.

Food Item	Vitamin A (RAE)
Beef liver (3 oz)	6,600 mcg (super high)
Sweet potato (1 medium)	1,096 mcg
Carrots (1 cup, cooked)	1,200 mcg
Kale (1 cup, cooked)	885 mcg
Eggs (2 large)	300 mcg
Whole milk (1 cup)	149 mcg

🥬 Beta-carotene from veggies must convert to usable A — so you need healthy fat to absorb it well.

🔄 Boosters & Blockers

Absorption of Vitamin A can vary depending on your gut health and food pairings. Here's how to help it work better:

Boosters	Blockers
Healthy fats (avocado, olive oil)	Low-fat diets
Zinc and iron (cofactors)	Poor liver or gallbladder function
Cooked carotenoid veggies	Gut inflammation or leaky gut

☠ Long-Term Deficiency Risks

Vitamin A deficiency often builds up slowly — but when it shows, it hits immunity, hormones, and vision first.

- Night blindness and eye degeneration
- Dry skin, eczema, and acne
- Weak immunity, frequent respiratory infections
- Fertility and hormone imbalances
- Increased oxidative stress in tissues

📊 Weekly Vitamin A Food Tracker

Here's a smart way to rotate preformed and plant-based sources so you never run low — and don't risk overdosing.

Day	Liver	Carrots	Kale	Eggs	Milk	Sweet Potato	Est. A (RAE)
Monday		✓	✓	✓		✓	~1,900 mcg
Tuesday	✓	✓		✓			~3,400 mcg
Wednesday		✓	✓	✓		✓	~1,600 mcg

Day	Liver	Carrots	Kale	Eggs	Milk	Sweet Potato	Est. A (RAE)
Thursday	✓		✓	✓		✓	~3,200 mcg
Friday		✓	✓	✓	✓	✓	~2,100 mcg
Saturday	✓	✓		✓	✓		~3,300 mcg
Sunday	✓	✓	✓	✓	✓	✓	~4,000 mcg

✺ Vitamin D3 — The Sunshine Hormone

"Why am I tired, moody, or achy — even after rest?"

If you're getting decent sleep but still feel worn down, unmotivated, or achy — it could be **Vitamin D3**.

D3 acts more like a hormone than a vitamin. It helps regulate your immune system, bones, mood, and even your weight. And in modern life? Most people are running low.

💪 What Vitamin D3 Does

Let's unpack how this "sunshine vitamin" powers you:

- Regulates calcium and **bone strength**
- Enhances **immune defense** and lowers inflammation
- Boosts mood and supports **dopamine and serotonin**
- Helps maintain **muscle strength and recovery**
- Improves insulin sensitivity and metabolism

⚠ Signs You Might Be Low on Vitamin D3

Vitamin D3 is often missing for years before symptoms show up — but your body is always trying to tell you.

Physical Signs	Mental/Emotional Signs
Frequent illness or colds	Low mood or mild depression
Bone pain or weakness	Brain fog and poor focus
Fatigue despite rest	Low motivation or drive
Muscle soreness or twitching	Sleep disruption

How Much Vitamin D3 Do You Need?

Depending on sun exposure and skin tone, your needs may vary — but here's a smart general range:

Group	Daily Dose
Adults (maintenance)	1,000–2,000 IU
Deficient levels	4,000–5,000 IU (short term)
Pregnant/Lactating	2,000–4,000 IU

✅ Always take with **fat** for better absorption. Get your levels tested for accurate dosing.

Best Food Sources of Vitamin D3

Not many foods contain natural D3 — which is why food + sunlight + smart supplements matter.

Food Item	Vitamin D3 (IU)
Salmon (3 oz)	~570 IU

Food Item	Vitamin D3 (IU)
Cod liver oil (1 tsp)	~450 IU
Eggs (2 large)	~80 IU
Fortified milk (1 cup)	~100 IU
Mushrooms (UV-exposed)	~400 IU per cup

☼ 15–30 mins of midday sun on skin (no sunscreen) can make up to 10,000 IU!

🔄 Boosters & Blockers

To actually use Vitamin D3, your body needs some backup — and needs to avoid common absorption mistakes.

Boosters	Blockers
Healthy fats (with meals)	Low-fat or fasted state
Magnesium and Vitamin K2	Gut inflammation or leaky gut
Sun exposure on bare skin	Sunscreen or covered clothing

😷 Long-Term Deficiency Risks

Low Vitamin D doesn't just affect bones and mood — it has deep implications for your **heart, arteries, and overall survival**.

- **Arterial calcification** — calcium deposits in arteries instead of bones
- **Cardiac arrest risk** — due to poor calcium handling and silent inflammation

- Osteoporosis and brittle bones
- Autoimmune conditions (MS, RA, Hashimoto's)
- Depression, anxiety, and poor sleep
- Muscle loss and poor recovery after exercise

⚠ Important Note:
Vitamin D helps your body absorb calcium — but **without enough Vitamin K2**, that calcium can settle in your arteries and soft tissues instead of your bones. Over time, this may contribute to **arterial calcification and heart blockages.** That's why **Vitamin D3 should always be paired with K2 MK7** for safe and effective calcium use.

Low D3 = High inflammation + mismanaged calcium = higher heart risk. Keep levels optimal.

📊 Weekly Vitamin D3 Tracker
Here's how you can meet your D3 goals through a combo of food, sun, and supplements.

Day	Salmon	Eggs	Milk	Mushrooms	Cod Liver Oil	Sunlight	Est. D3 (IU)
Monday	✓	✓	✓			✓	~1,900 IU
Tuesday		✓	✓	✓	✓	✓	~2,000 IU
Wednesday	✓		✓		✓	✓	~2,100 IU

Day	Salmon	Eggs	Milk	Mushrooms	Cod Liver Oil	Sunlight	Est. D3 (IU)
Thursday	✓	✓	✓			✓	~1,800 IU
Friday	✓	✓	✓			✓	~2,200 IU
Saturday	✓	✓	✓	✓		✓	~2,500 IU
Sunday	✓	✓	✓	✓	✓	✓	~3,000 IU

🎯 Target: 2,000–4,000 IU/day total — combine sun, food, and supplements with **K2 for safety**.

🌿 Vitamin E — The Antioxidant Shield
"Why does my skin age fast, or why do I bruise and tire so easily?"

Your skin feels dry and dull. You bruise easily. You feel tired even though your diet seems "fine." These aren't just surface issues — they may point to **Vitamin E deficiency**.

Vitamin E protects your cells from oxidative damage. It's like your internal rust protector — helping your skin stay youthful, your heart strong, and your immune system calm.

💪 What Vitamin E Does

Here's what Vitamin E is quietly doing to keep your body resilient:

- Neutralizes free radicals and protects cells

- Improves skin texture, elasticity, and glow
- Supports **immune balance** and inflammation control
- Enhances blood flow and prevents **clotting issues**
- Helps repair damaged tissues and reduce scars

⚠ Signs You Might Be Low on Vitamin E

These signs can sneak up over time — especially if your diet lacks whole fats or plant oils.

Physical Signs	Mental/Emotional Signs
Dry or thinning skin	Fatigue or low stamina
Poor wound healing	Brain fog or poor memory
Easy bruising or bleeding	Mood dips or restlessness
Vision issues (light sensitivity)	Poor stress tolerance

🏷 How Much Vitamin E Do You Need?

Let's talk dosage — not too little, not too much. Most people fall short because they avoid fats or processed oils.

Group	Daily Dose
Adults (Men/Women)	15 mg (22.5 IU)
Pregnancy	15–19 mg
Active/Lipid support	Up to 200 IU (short term)

✅ Always choose **mixed tocopherols** (natural) over synthetic "dl-alpha" versions.

🌰 Best Food Sources of Vitamin E

Whole plant foods and healthy fats are your best friends here. Here's where Vitamin E naturally shows up:

Food Item	Vitamin E per serving
Sunflower seeds (1 oz)	7.4 mg
Almonds (1 oz)	7.3 mg
Avocado (1 medium)	2.7 mg
Spinach (1 cup, cooked)	3.7 mg
Olive oil (1 tbsp)	1.9 mg
Peanut butter (2 tbsp)	2.9 mg

💡 Pair these with healthy fat to boost absorption — think olive oil on spinach, or avocado with seeds.

🔄 Boosters & Blockers

Vitamin E relies heavily on your fat digestion and antioxidant system. Here's what can help or hinder it:

Boosters	Blockers
Healthy fats (omega-3s)	Low-fat or no-fat diets
Selenium and Vitamin C	Excess iron or oxidized seed oils
Antioxidant-rich meals	Smoking, pollution, and fried foods

☠ Long-Term Deficiency Risks

Vitamin E isn't just about beauty — it plays a protective role in major systems.
- Accelerated aging and oxidative damage
- Poor immune response and chronic inflammation
- Increased risk of blood clots
- Nerve damage or poor coordination
- Memory decline and brain aging

🛡 Your antioxidant defense depends on E — don't leave your cells unprotected.

📊 Weekly Vitamin E Food Tracker

This tracker helps you rotate Vitamin E-rich foods without relying on supplements:

Day	Almonds	Avocado	Spinach	Olive Oil	Seeds	Peanut Butter	Est. Vit E
Monday	✓	✓	✓	✓			~15 mg
Tuesday	✓		✓	✓	✓		~16 mg
Wednesday	✓	✓		✓	✓		~14 mg
Thursday	✓		✓	✓		✓	~17 mg
Friday	✓	✓	✓	✓		✓	~18 mg

Day	Almonds	Avocado	Spinach	Olive Oil	Seeds	Peanut Butter	Est. Vit E
Saturday	✓		✓	✓	✓	✓	~19 mg
Sunday	✓	✓	✓	✓	✓	✓	~21 mg

🦴 Vitamin K2 MK7 — The Calcium Director
"Why are my joints stiff or arteries stiff — even when I'm taking calcium?"

You take your calcium. You get your D3. But your joints are creaky and your blood pressure is high. That's a red flag for **Vitamin K2 MK7** deficiency.

K2 tells your body **where to put calcium** — into bones, not arteries. Without it, calcium may harden the wrong places.

💪 What Vitamin K2 Does
This lesser-known nutrient is quietly life-changing:
- Directs calcium into **bones and teeth**
- Prevents **arterial calcification and stiff vessels**
- Boosts bone density and reduces fracture risk
- Improves insulin sensitivity and mitochondrial health
- Activates proteins that prevent **vascular damage**

⚠️ Signs You Might Be Low on K2
You likely won't see K2 deficiency on blood tests — you feel it over time through stiffness and slow healing.

Physical Signs	Subtle Systemic Signs
Joint stiffness or cracking	High blood pressure
Plaque buildup in teeth	Early signs of heart strain
Weak bones or fractures	Poor postural alignment
Artery calcification	Poor circulation

⚠ If you take D3 and calcium, but skip K2 — calcium may harden your arteries instead of your bones.

How Much Vitamin K2 Do You Need?

Let's dial in the dosage — especially if you're already supplementing with Vitamin D.

Group	Daily Dose (MK7 form)
Adults	90–200 mcg
On D3 or calcium	180–320 mcg
Bone/joint support	200–300 mcg (ongoing)

✅ K2 MK7 has longer half-life and better bioavailability than K1 or MK4.

Best Food Sources of Vitamin K2

Western diets often miss K2 — unless you eat fermented foods and organ meats.

Food Item	Vitamin K2 (MK7/MK4)
Natto (1 tbsp)	1,000+ mcg (very high MK7)
Hard cheeses (1 oz)	75–100 mcg (MK4)
Egg yolks (2)	40–50 mcg
Grass-fed butter (1 tbsp)	15–30 mcg
Chicken thighs (3 oz)	60 mcg
Sauerkraut (½ cup)	5–10 mcg

🫘 Natto is the highest source — but even cheese, eggs, and butter can do wonders when eaten regularly.

🔄 Boosters & Blockers

K2 works best when supported by the right nutrient stack — and suffers when gut health is compromised.

Boosters	Blockers
Vitamin D3 and magnesium	Long-term antibiotics or gut issues
Fermented foods	Highly processed diets
Healthy fat in meals	Low-fat or anti-fat mindsets

💀 Long-Term Deficiency Risks

Skipping K2 — especially if you take D3 or calcium — can backfire. Here's how:

- **Arterial calcification** and hardened blood vessels

- **Increased cardiac arrest risk**
- Osteoporosis or brittle bones
- Joint and tendon stiffness
- Calcium buildup in soft tissues and kidneys

📊 Weekly Vitamin K2 Food Tracker

Add these foods weekly to keep calcium flowing into your bones, not your arteries:

Day	Cheese	Eggs	Chicken	Sauerkraut	Butter	Natto	Est. K2
Monday	✓	✓	✓	✓	✓		~180 mcg
Tuesday	✓	✓		✓	✓		~150 mcg
Wednesday	✓	✓	✓		✓	✓	~300 mcg
Thursday	✓	✓	✓	✓	✓		~220 mcg
Friday	✓	✓	✓	✓	✓	✓	~320 mcg
Saturday	✓	✓	✓		✓	✓	~280 mcg
Sunday	✓	✓	✓	✓	✓	✓	~350 mcg

🍊 Vitamin C — The Repair Vitamin

"Why do I bruise easily, feel rundown, or heal slowly?"

You eat well enough. You try to sleep right. Yet your gums bleed when brushing, your cuts heal slowly, and your skin looks a little less vibrant than it used to. Sound familiar?

That might not be aging — it might be **Vitamin C deficiency**.
We often associate Vitamin C with "immunity" or cold prevention. But that's just the tip of the iceberg. This nutrient is your **internal glue** — holding together everything from skin and bones to blood vessels and brain chemicals.
Without it, you literally begin to break down.

💪 What Vitamin C Actually Does
Think of Vitamin C as a **cellular handyman and antioxidant firefighter**. Here's what it's quietly doing in the background every day:

- Creates **collagen**, which holds your skin, tendons, gums, and arteries together
- Accelerates **wound healing**, tissue repair, and scar remodeling
- Strengthens the **immune system** against infections and toxins
- Helps your body **absorb iron** from plant-based foods
- Neutralizes **free radicals**, reducing aging, inflammation, and cell damage
- Assists in the **production of neurotransmitters** like dopamine and serotonin

Without enough Vitamin C, even small problems like dry skin or fatigue can snowball into chronic illness.

⚠ Signs You Might Be Low on Vitamin C
These aren't just cosmetic issues — they're early signs of **structural weakness** in your body.

Physical Signs	Mental/Emotional Signs
Bleeding gums or mouth sores	Low energy, sluggish thinking
Easy bruising or slow healing	Brain fog or low emotional resilience
Dry, cracked skin or brittle hair	Mild depression or poor mood
Frequent infections or sinus issues	Anxiety or irritability
Red bumpy skin (like keratosis pilaris)	Feelings of being easily overwhelmed

⚫ Many people with "mystery fatigue" or "skin issues" are simply low on Vitamin C.

▨ How Much Vitamin C Do You Really Need?

Official recommendations are low — just enough to avoid **scurvy**, not enough for **optimal repair** and **resilience**. Here's a more functional breakdown:

Group	Daily Functional Dose
Healthy Adults	75–90 mg (minimum)
Smokers or Drinkers	100–150 mg
Under stress / Illness	200–1,000 mg (short-term)

Group	Daily Functional Dose
Wound healing / Recovery	500–1,500 mg (temporary use)

🧪 Vitamin C is **water-soluble**, so your body excretes the excess. You need a steady daily supply, not big weekly bursts.

🥝 Best Food Sources of Vitamin C

Fresh, raw, and colorful is your best approach. Cooking destroys Vitamin C — so you need to eat **some raw** foods daily to stay topped up.

Food Item	Vitamin C per serving
Bell pepper (½ cup, raw)	95 mg
Kiwi (1 medium)	71 mg
Strawberries (1 cup)	89 mg
Oranges (1 medium)	70 mg
Broccoli (½ cup, cooked)	51 mg
Brussels sprouts (½ cup)	48 mg
Pineapple (½ cup)	39 mg
Papaya (½ cup)	43 mg

🥔 Vitamin C starts degrading minutes after chopping. Eat fresh, raw, and quickly.

🔄 Boosters & Blockers of Vitamin C

Your body can't make Vitamin C on its own — and several things drain it fast. Let's look at what helps, and what hinders.

Boosters	Blockers / Depleters
Zinc and bioflavonoids	Smoking, alcohol
Eating fruits with skin/seeds	Chronic stress, intense workouts
Vitamin E and glutathione	Cooking, boiling, or long storage
Fermented foods + veggies	Certain medications (like aspirin, birth control)

😟 Every stressful moment, puff of smoke, or polluted breath **uses up** your Vitamin C stores.

💀 Long-Term Deficiency Risks

Over time, low Vitamin C becomes serious — not just inconvenient.

- **Scurvy:** tissue breakdown, bleeding gums, weak joints
- **Iron-deficiency anemia:** especially in women or vegetarians
- **Connective tissue breakdown:** sagging skin, gum recession, poor posture
- **Poor brain chemistry:** fatigue, low mood, slow memory
- **Inflammatory buildup:** premature aging and chronic disease risk

Many signs of "aging" — like wrinkles or easy bruising — are actually signs of slow Vitamin C loss.

📊 Weekly Vitamin C Food Tracker

You don't need supplements to meet your Vitamin C goals — you just need color, rawness, and consistency.

Day	Oranges	Kiwi	Berries	Bell Pepper	Broccoli	Sprouts	Est. Vit C
Monday	✓		✓	✓	✓		~270 mg
Tuesday	✓	✓		✓	✓	✓	~310 mg
Wednesday		✓	✓	✓	✓		~280 mg
Thursday	✓	✓		✓	✓	✓	~320 mg
Friday	✓	✓	✓	✓	✓		~340 mg
Saturday	✓		✓	✓	✓	✓	~330 mg
Sunday	✓	✓	✓	✓	✓	✓	~360 mg

🍊 A glass of orange juice helps — but **real, raw foods** offer fiber, enzymes, and synergistic nutrients too.

⚡ Vitamin B1 (Thiamine) — The Spark of Energy

"Why do I feel exhausted, anxious, or foggy — even after a full night's sleep?"

Your sleep tracker says you slept fine. You're eating meals. You even drank coffee. Yet your brain is foggy, your body feels drained, and you're anxious without any reason.

That's how **Vitamin B1 deficiency** can feel — like your mind and muscles are low-voltage.

Thiamine is the **first B vitamin** because it's the **first step in creating energy**. It turns food into fuel — and fuels your nervous system, heart, and focus.

💪 What Vitamin B1 Does

Thiamine doesn't get much attention — but without it, you'd feel like your battery was drained 24/7.

Here's what it supports:

- Converts carbs and food into usable **ATP energy**
- Powers your **nervous system** and keeps brain firing smoothly
- Supports a steady **heartbeat and heart strength**
- Improves mood, memory, and **mental clarity**
- Helps maintain **digestion and appetite regulation**

B1 is like your cellular ignition switch. Without it, you stall.

⚠ Signs You Might Be Low on B1

These symptoms often masquerade as "stress" or "burnout" — but are clear signs of B1 deficiency:

Physical Signs	Mental/Neurological Signs
Fatigue and low endurance	Brain fog, poor memory

Physical Signs	Mental/Neurological Signs
Muscle weakness or heaviness	Anxiety or sudden mood shifts
Numbness or tingling (hands/feet)	Difficulty concentrating
Poor digestion or appetite loss	Sensitivity to noise or light
Irregular heartbeat	Panic or unexplained fear

⚠ Chronic low B1 can lead to **beriberi** or **Wernicke's encephalopathy** — serious neurological disorders.

🏛 How Much Thiamine Do You Need?

Thiamine needs increase with carb intake, stress, alcohol, or exercise. Let's break it down:

Group	Daily Dose
Healthy Adults	1.1–1.2 mg
Pregnant / Lactating	1.4 mg
High-carb diet / Athlete	1.5–3 mg
Alcohol / Stress support	5–100 mg (therapeutic)

✅ Thiamine is **water-soluble** and not stored — you need it **daily**, especially under stress or poor digestion.

Best Food Sources of Vitamin B1

Thiamine is fragile — it's easily lost in processing, cooking, and poor gut absorption. Here's where to find it naturally.

Food Item	B1 per serving (mg)
Pork chops (3 oz)	~0.8 mg
Sunflower seeds (1 oz)	~0.4 mg
Navy beans (½ cup, cooked)	~0.2 mg
Green peas (½ cup, cooked)	~0.2 mg
Brown rice (1 cup, cooked)	~0.2 mg
Asparagus (½ cup)	~0.1 mg
Eggs (2 large)	~0.1 mg

⬤ White rice, white flour, and sugar **strip away B1** — and increase your need for it. Go whole.

Boosters & Blockers

Let's look at what supports thiamine levels — and what rapidly depletes or blocks its absorption.

Boosters	Blockers / Depleters
Whole grains, nuts, seeds	Refined carbs and white sugar
High-quality protein (like pork)	Alcohol, caffeine, and chronic stress

Boosters

B-complex synergy (especially B2, B6)

Blockers / Depleters

Antibiotics, diuretics, acid blockers

⚠ Alcohol is a major B1 depleter — heavy drinkers often have severe hidden deficiencies.

💀 Long-Term Deficiency Risks
When thiamine runs low for too long, **energy, nerves, and heart function** break down — slowly but seriously.
- **Beriberi** — nerve and heart degeneration
- Loss of memory, balance, and cognition
- Weak digestion and nutrient absorption
- Irritability, anxiety, and sleep disturbances
- Heart enlargement or palpitations
- In extreme cases: brain swelling (Wernicke's)

🧠 B1 is *critical* for brain protection — especially under chronic stress, alcohol, or sugar overload.

📊 Weekly Vitamin B1 Food Tracker
Here's a realistic plan to rotate B1-rich foods through your week — helping you stay energized and mentally sharp.

Day	Pork	Rice	Peas	Eggs	Beans	Seeds	Est. B1
Monday	✓	✓	✓			✓	~1.7 mg
Tuesday	✓	✓		✓	✓		~1.5 mg

Day	Pork	Rice	Peas	Eggs	Beans	Seeds	Est. B1
Wednesday	✓	✓	✓	✓	✓		~1.6 mg
Thursday	✓	✓	✓		✓	✓	~1.8 mg
Friday	✓	✓	✓			✓	~1.9 mg
Saturday	✓		✓	✓	✓	✓	~1.8 mg
Sunday	✓	✓	✓	✓	✓	✓	~2.0 mg

⚡ Keep it whole. Keep it varied. A few servings a day = a strong, steady brain and heart.

🦋 Vitamin B2 (Riboflavin) — The Cell Brightener
"Why do my eyes feel sensitive, my skin look dull, or my mouth feel sore?"

You're eating enough. Maybe even taking a multivitamin. But your lips crack easily, your eyes feel tired or dry, and your skin seems lifeless no matter how much you hydrate.

That's classic **riboflavin deficiency** — a nutrient that powers energy, skin glow, and even your eyesight.

Vitamin B2 is like **sunlight inside your cells** — lighting up your metabolism, protecting your tissues, and activating other B vitamins like B6 and folate

💪 What Vitamin B2 Does
Riboflavin is needed in nearly every cell — but especially your eyes, skin, nerves, and energy systems.

Here's what it helps your body do:
- Converts carbs, proteins, and fats into usable **ATP energy**
- Protects skin, eyes, lips, and mucous membranes from oxidative stress
- Regenerates **glutathione**, your master antioxidant
- Helps produce **B3, B6, and folate** (cofactor role)
- Supports healthy **iron use** and red blood cell production
- Enhances **vision and eye repair** (especially UV damage)

Riboflavin is like a cellular co-pilot — activating and protecting nearly everything else.

⚠ Signs You Might Be Low on Riboflavin

Most signs show up in soft tissues first — the parts that renew fast and need constant energy.

Physical Signs	Neurological / Emotional Signs
Cracks at mouth corners	Fatigue or low mental stamina
Red or itchy eyes	Brain fog or forgetfulness
Sore, swollen tongue	Low mood or irritability
Dry lips or peeling skin	Light sensitivity or blurry vision
Frequent mouth ulcers	Tension headaches

🪨 Many of these are mistaken for "dehydration" or allergies — but B2 might be the real issue.

▪ How Much Vitamin B2 Do You Need?

Riboflavin requirements increase with physical activity, stress, illness, and pregnancy.

Here's what your body typically needs:

Group	Daily Dose (Riboflavin)
Healthy Adults (M/F)	1.1–1.3 mg
Pregnant / Lactating	1.4–1.6 mg
High exercise/stress	2–3 mg

✅ Riboflavin is water-soluble and not stored — your tissues need it replenished daily.

🏠 Best Food Sources of Vitamin B2

Riboflavin gets its name from "flavin," meaning yellow. Many rich sources — like eggs or liver — have a golden hue.

Here's where to find it in everyday foods:

Food Item	Riboflavin per serving
Beef liver (3 oz)	2.9 mg
Eggs (2 large)	0.5 mg
Greek yogurt (¾ cup)	0.6 mg
Almonds (1 oz)	0.3 mg
Spinach (½ cup cooked)	0.2 mg

Food Item	Riboflavin per serving
Mushrooms (½ cup cooked)	0.2 mg
Fortified cereals (1 cup)	1.1–1.5 mg

✺ Pro tip: Riboflavin is destroyed by light. Don't store milk or yogurt in clear glass under fluorescent lighting.

↻ Boosters & Blockers

Let's protect this vitamin and make sure your body absorbs every milligram.

Boosters	Blockers / Depleters
High-quality protein	Alcohol and poor liver function
Whole foods with B-complex synergy	UV light (destroys riboflavin)
Gut-friendly bacteria	Acid blockers or long-term antibiotics

⚠ Acid reflux drugs may interfere with riboflavin — especially in older adults.

☠ Long-Term Deficiency Risks

Riboflavin deficiency affects everything from your **skin to your cells** — and usually flies under the radar.

- Chronic fatigue or low stamina
- Recurrent eye strain, infections, or inflammation
- Cracks in lips or mouth sores

- Burning tongue or red eyes
- Poor iron absorption or mild anemia
- Hormonal issues from B6 or folate dysfunction

Riboflavin deficiency is common in vegans, heavy drinkers, and those under chronic stress.

📊 Weekly Vitamin B2 Food Tracker

Mix and match these simple foods daily to keep your riboflavin tank full — and your energy + skin glowing.

Day	Eggs	Yogurt	Liver	Spinach	Almonds	Mushrooms	Est. B2
Monday	✓	✓		✓	✓		~1.7 mg
Tuesday	✓	✓	✓		✓	✓	~2.8 mg
Wednesday	✓		✓	✓		✓	~2.7 mg
Thursday	✓	✓		✓	✓	✓	~2.0 mg
Friday	✓	✓	✓		✓	✓	~2.9 mg
Saturday	✓	✓		✓	✓	✓	~2.2 mg
Sunday	✓	✓	✓	✓	✓	✓	~3.1 mg

✨ Just one egg and a cup of yogurt daily can easily cover 70–80% of your needs.

🥚 Vitamin B3 (Niacin) — The Metabolic Multitasker
"Why do I feel tired, foggy, or inflamed — even when I eat well?"

You eat okay. Maybe you even take supplements. But you still feel tired after meals, your skin flushes oddly, your mood feels dull, and your focus is… just not sharp.

Welcome to the hidden world of **niacin deficiency** — a B vitamin that your cells depend on to **create energy, repair DNA, and regulate inflammation.**

Vitamin B3 (niacin) is like the **currency of metabolism**. Without it, your body simply can't "spend" the food you eat for energy. You burn out — physically, mentally, emotionally.

💪 What Vitamin B3 Does
Niacin doesn't just support metabolism — it's involved in **over 400 enzymatic reactions**, making it one of the most essential and versatile vitamins.

Here's what it fuels:
- Converts food into **ATP energy** in every cell
- Supports the creation of **NAD+**, a coenzyme tied to longevity and DNA repair
- Maintains healthy **nervous system and brain function**
- Improves **cholesterol balance** (raises HDL, lowers LDL)
- Supports skin, digestive tract, and joint health
- Helps regulate **inflammation and blood sugar**

Niacin is a cornerstone of **resilience** — your brain, cells, and mood can't function well without it.

⚠ Signs You Might Be Low on Vitamin B3

Niacin deficiency shows up in tissues with high energy needs — especially your skin, nerves, and brain.

Physical Signs	Mental/Emotional Signs
Fatigue, low stamina	Brain fog or low alertness
Cracking, red skin (especially sun-exposed areas)	Depression or anxiety
Digestive discomfort, nausea	Low motivation or drive
Sensitivity to sunlight	Mood swings, restlessness
Muscle aches or tingling	Poor memory or mental fatigue

⚠ Severe deficiency leads to **pellagra** — a triad of dermatitis, diarrhea, and dementia.

🔢 How Much Vitamin B3 Do You Need?

Needs vary based on your stress level, diet, and alcohol or sugar intake. Let's break it down:

Group	Daily Dose (Niacin Equivalents)
Healthy Men	16 mg NE
Healthy Women	14 mg NE
Pregnancy / Lactation	17–18 mg NE

Group	Daily Dose (Niacin Equivalents)
Cholesterol therapy	500–2,000 mg (medical supervision)

NE = "niacin equivalents," including tryptophan-derived niacin from protein-rich foods.

🍗 Best Food Sources of Vitamin B3

Niacin is found abundantly in **protein-rich** foods — both plant and animal — and can be made from tryptophan (an amino acid).

Food Item	Niacin per serving
Chicken breast (3 oz)	~10 mg
Tuna (3 oz)	~11 mg
Turkey (3 oz)	~10 mg
Beef liver (3 oz)	~14 mg
Peanuts (1 oz)	~3.8 mg
Brown rice (1 cup cooked)	~2.6 mg
Mushrooms (1 cup cooked)	~2.5 mg

🫘 Tryptophan from eggs, dairy, and turkey can also convert into niacin — **if B2 and B6 are present.**

🔄 Boosters & Blockers

Let's look at what helps your body absorb and make niacin — and what silently drains or blocks it.

Boosters	Blockers / Depleters
Protein-rich meals (with tryptophan)	Alcohol and smoking
B2 and B6 (for conversion)	Birth control pills
Fermented foods (better gut)	Stress and excess sugar

✏️ Niacinamide (a form of B3) does **not** cause flushing, while plain niacin may.

💀 Long-Term Deficiency Risks
Because niacin is so critical for energy, repair, and immunity — its absence can affect everything from skin to memory.
- Skin cracking, rashes, and sun sensitivity
- Poor memory and concentration
- Digestive issues or appetite loss
- Depression, low mood, or irritability
- Weak circulation and cholesterol imbalance
- Increased inflammation and oxidative stress
- Severe: Pellagra (dermatitis, diarrhea, dementia, death)

⚠️ B3 deficiency is more common in **alcoholics, diabetics, and high-sugar diets** than we realize.

📊 Weekly Vitamin B3 Food Tracker
Rotate these foods throughout your week to keep your niacin levels strong — and energy/metabolism running smooth.

Day	Chicken	Tuna	Liver	Peanuts	Rice	Mushrooms	Est. B3
Monday	✓		✓	✓	✓	✓	~22 mg

Day	Chicken	Tuna	Liver	Peanuts	Rice	Mushrooms	Est. B3
Tuesday	✓	✓		✓	✓		~20 mg
Wednesday		✓	✓	✓	✓	✓	~24 mg
Thursday	✓		✓	✓	✓	✓	~23 mg
Friday	✓	✓		✓	✓	✓	~22 mg
Saturday	✓	✓	✓	✓	✓	✓	~28 mg
Sunday	✓	✓	✓	✓	✓	✓	~30 mg

🧬 Niacin isn't just a nutrient — it's the backbone of your cell's ability to breathe, move, and repair.

🧩 Vitamin B5 (Pantothenic Acid) — The Stress Buster & Repair Tool

"Why do I feel burned out, achy, or slow to heal?"

You're not under dramatic stress — but you're tired, foggy, and your body takes longer to bounce back. Your skin doesn't heal like it used to, and mentally, you're running on fumes.

You may be low on **Vitamin B5**, the **"anti-stress vitamin"** that helps your body **respond to pressure, heal damage, and generate energy** — right down to your cells' engine room: the mitochondria.

Pantothenic acid is the **backbone of coenzyme A**, a molecule required in nearly every metabolic process. Without it, energy production, hormone balance, and detox all suffer.

💪 What Vitamin B5 Does

B5 may not be trendy — but it's foundational. Your body uses it constantly to adapt, repair, and manage stress.

Here's what it supports:
- Produces **coenzyme A (CoA)**, vital for energy metabolism
- Helps build **adrenal hormones** like cortisol and sex hormones
- Supports **skin repair**, healing, and oil balance (especially acne-prone skin)
- Aids in **wound recovery, scar formation, and tissue building**
- Helps synthesize fats, cholesterol, and neurotransmitters (especially acetylcholine)

B5 is a **recovery vitamin** — for your skin, your stress, and your stamina.

⚠ Signs You Might Be Low on Vitamin B5

Though rare in extreme form, subclinical B5 deficiency is common — especially if you're under stress, eating poorly, or recovering from illness.

Physical Signs	Mental/Emotional Signs
Burning feet or tingling	Chronic stress sensitivity
Fatigue and low stamina	Brain fog or poor memory
Slow wound healing	Mild depression or apathy
Greasy or acne-prone skin	Anxiety or panic episodes

Physical Signs	Mental/Emotional Signs
Muscle cramps or weakness	Sleep disruption

🌑 Many people with chronic fatigue or post-COVID exhaustion are functionally low on B5.

📊 How Much Vitamin B5 Do You Need?

Pantothenic acid needs are modest — but **increase significantly** with stress, illness, or poor diet.

Group	Daily Dose (Adequate Intake)
Adults (Men/Women)	5 mg
Pregnancy	6 mg
Lactation	7 mg
Therapeutic use (stress/adrenals)	10–500 mg (under care)

✅ B5 is often found in **B-complex** formulas. It's water-soluble and very safe even at high doses.

🌑 Best Food Sources of Vitamin B5

"Pantothen" means "from everywhere" — and sure enough, B5 is in nearly all foods. But heat, freezing, and processing reduce its potency.

Here are the richest and most usable sources:

Food Item	B5 per serving (mg)
Beef liver (3 oz)	~6.8 mg
Avocado (1 medium)	~2 mg
Chicken breast (3 oz)	~1.5 mg
Eggs (2 large)	~1.4 mg
Mushrooms (1 cup cooked)	~1.5 mg
Sunflower seeds (1 oz)	~2 mg
Sweet potatoes (1 medium)	~1 mg

🔥 Cooking losses can be 20–40% — so include **some raw or lightly cooked sources** in your weekly plan.

🔄 Boosters & Blockers

Let's help your body absorb more B5 — and protect it from hidden drains.

Boosters	Blockers / Depleters
Whole, unprocessed foods	Caffeine, alcohol, processed carbs
Probiotics + good gut flora	Chronic stress or infection
Balanced B-complex (with B1–B6)	Antibiotics, birth control pills

🧬 Your **gut bacteria also help produce B5** — but only if your microbiome is healthy.

💀 Long-Term Deficiency Risks
Chronic low B5 can lead to adrenal fatigue, weak immune response, and poor skin barrier function.
- **Burning feet syndrome** (nerve sensitivity)
- Hormone imbalances (low cortisol, estrogen, testosterone)
- Poor scar formation or healing delays
- Fatigue and reduced stress tolerance
- Acne, seborrheic dermatitis, or oily scalp
- Weakened immune defense during recovery

⚠️ Low B5 is common after surgery, illness, trauma, or long-term stress — when your body's rebuilding mode is on.

📊 Weekly Vitamin B5 Food Tracker
Let's rotate foods that naturally keep your B5 levels strong — no need for megadoses unless advised.

Day	Liver	Chicken	Eggs	Avocado	Mushrooms	Seeds	Est. B5
Monday	✓	✓	✓	✓	✓		~9.5 mg
Tuesday	✓	✓	✓		✓	✓	~10 mg
Wednesday		✓	✓	✓	✓	✓	~7.5 mg
Thursday	✓		✓	✓	✓	✓	~8.5 mg
Friday	✓	✓	✓	✓	✓	✓	~10 mg

Day	Liver	Chicken	Eggs	Avocado	Mushrooms	Seeds	Est. B5
Saturday	✓	✓	✓	✓	✓	✓	~11 mg
Sunday	✓	✓	✓	✓	✓	✓	~11 mg

🛠 If you're healing, recovering, or stressed — increase intake temporarily with food or B-complex support.

🧠 Vitamin B6 (Pyridoxine) — The Mood & Mind Regulator
"Why do I feel anxious, PMS-y, or have nerve tingling — even when everything seems normal?"

You're eating fine. Maybe even taking a supplement. But your hands or feet feel a little tingly. You're more anxious or irritable than usual. PMS hits harder. And your sleep? Restless.
That's how **Vitamin B6 deficiency** can show up.
It's the **emotional and neurological support vitamin** — quietly helping your brain produce feel-good chemicals, balance hormones, and calm your nervous system.

💪 What Vitamin B6 Does
Vitamin B6 isn't just another B — it plays a **direct role in how you feel, think, and function** every day.
Here's what it powers:
- Produces key neurotransmitters: **serotonin, dopamine, GABA**
- Helps regulate **PMS, mood swings, and estrogen balance**
- Builds and repairs **nerves and red blood cells**
- Converts food into energy (especially protein)

- Assists in **homocysteine regulation** — protecting your heart and brain
- Supports healthy **immune function**

B6 is the **emotional stabilizer** in your nutrient toolbox.

⚠ Signs You Might Be Low on Vitamin B6

These signs are often blamed on hormones or mood disorders — but B6 might be the missing piece.

Physical Signs	Neurological/Mood Signs
Tingling in hands or feet	Anxiety or panic without reason
Dry skin or cracking lips	Irritability or quick frustration
Muscle twitches or cramps	PMS or heavy cycles
Low immune response	Trouble sleeping or vivid dreams
Fatigue or weakness	Brain fog or low resilience

💭 If you're low on serotonin or dopamine, **you're probably low on B6** too.

📋 How Much Vitamin B6 Do You Need?

Your B6 needs increase if you're stressed, pregnant, on birth control, or eating a high-protein diet.

Group	Daily Dose (Pyridoxine)
Adults (Men/Women)	1.3–1.7 mg
Pregnancy/Lactation	1.9–2.0 mg

Group	Daily Dose (Pyridoxine)
PMS/Anxiety Support	25–100 mg (short-term)
High-protein intake	~1.5x base requirement

⚠ Too much supplemental B6 (>200 mg/day for long periods) may cause nerve issues. Food-based intake is safest.

◯ Best Food Sources of Vitamin B6

B6 is found in a variety of animal and plant foods — but heat and storage can reduce its potency. Aim for some lightly cooked or raw options.

Food Item	B6 per serving
Salmon (3 oz)	~0.6 mg
Turkey (3 oz)	~0.7 mg
Bananas (1 medium)	~0.4 mg
Chickpeas (½ cup, cooked)	~0.6 mg
Potatoes (1 medium, baked)	~0.4 mg
Eggs (2 large)	~0.3 mg
Spinach (1 cup, cooked)	~0.4 mg

🥦 B6 is one of the most **easily lost B vitamins** during cooking, freezing, or storage. Eat fresh when possible.

🔄 Boosters & Blockers

Let's talk about what enhances your B6 — and what quietly depletes it, even if your diet looks good on paper.

Boosters	Blockers / Depleters
High-quality protein (animal or plant)	Alcohol, smoking
Magnesium and B2 synergy	Birth control pills
Gut health and probiotics	Processed food, chronic stress

B6 works **with magnesium** — for sleep, mood, and nerve support. They're a dream team.

💀 Long-Term Deficiency Risks

B6 is essential for your **emotional stability and nerve health**. When it's missing, your systems slowly unravel.

- Hormonal imbalance (especially estrogen dominance or PMS)
- Mood issues: anxiety, depression, irritability
- Tingling or numbness in limbs (neuropathy)
- Poor protein digestion or muscle weakness
- Weakened immunity or chronic infections
- Elevated homocysteine → higher heart and brain risk

Low B6 is a **common root** behind emotional burnout and PMS that no one talks about.

📊 Weekly Vitamin B6 Food Tracker

Rotate these B6-rich foods across your week — and feel your mood, nerves, and hormones shift into balance.

Day	Salmon	Turkey	Banana	Chickpeas	Eggs	Spinach	Est. B6
Monday	✓		✓	✓	✓	✓	~2.4 mg
Tuesday	✓	✓		✓		✓	~2.3 mg
Wednesday	✓	✓	✓		✓	✓	~2.6 mg
Thursday	✓	✓	✓	✓	✓		~2.8 mg
Friday	✓	✓	✓	✓	✓	✓	~3.0 mg
Saturday	✓	✓	✓	✓	✓	✓	~3.2 mg
Sunday	✓	✓	✓	✓	✓	✓	~3.3 mg

🎯 Bonus tip: Add **magnesium-rich foods** (like pumpkin seeds, dark chocolate, or almonds) for better B6 activation.

🌿 Vitamin B7 (Biotin) — The Beauty & Stability Nutrient
"Why is my hair thinning, my nails weak, or my skin breaking out?"

You're eating fine. You've tried shampoos, creams, and even collagen — but your hair still sheds more than it should. Your nails split or crack. Your skin feels dry, irritated, or inflamed. That's the world of **biotin deficiency**.

Often marketed for beauty, Biotin is actually far deeper — it helps your **body break down fats and proteins**, repair tissues, stabilize blood sugar, and fuel growth from the inside out.

💪 What Biotin Does

While it's best known for hair and skin, Biotin is **a coenzyme for essential metabolic reactions** — especially those involving **amino acids and fats**.

Here's what it really supports:
- Promotes healthy **hair, skin, and nail growth**
- Converts fat, carbs, and protein into **usable energy**
- Supports **thyroid function and metabolic rate**
- Helps stabilize **blood sugar** and insulin sensitivity
- Plays a role in DNA repair and gene expression
- Supports **fetal development** and cellular growth

Biotin gives structure — not just to your hair and nails, but to your body's repair system.

⚠️ Signs You Might Be Low on Biotin

Biotin deficiency may be mild and still cause **visible, frustrating symptoms**, especially in fast-growing tissues.

Physical Signs	Neurological/Mood Signs
Thinning hair or hair loss	Fatigue or sluggish thinking
Brittle or splitting nails	Mild depression or low mood
Scaly or dry red skin	Numbness, tingling in limbs
Adult acne or cradle cap	Poor concentration or irritability
Slow skin healing	Anxiety or restlessness

🧠 In severe cases (often from antibiotics or genetics), deficiency can lead to seizures or hallucinations — showing just how essential it is for **brain stability.**

📸 How Much Biotin Do You Need?
Though no official RDA is set, here's what's considered **adequate** for most — and how needs change with stress, pregnancy, or antibiotics.

Group	Daily Dose (Adequate Intake)
Adults (Men/Women)	30 mcg
Pregnancy	30–35 mcg
Hair/nail repair support	2,500–5,000 mcg (under guidance)

⚠️ Many hair gummies provide **megadoses** (5,000–10,000 mcg), which are safe short-term but not always necessary.

🥚 Best Food Sources of Biotin
Biotin is found in **small amounts in many whole foods**, especially **egg yolks,** seeds, and organ meats.

Food Item	Biotin per serving
Egg yolks (2 large)	~20–25 mcg
Liver (3 oz, cooked)	~30 mcg
Almonds (1 oz)	~1.5 mcg

Food Item	Biotin per serving
Sunflower seeds (1 oz)	~2.6 mcg
Salmon (3 oz)	~5 mcg
Sweet potatoes (½ cup)	~2.4 mcg
Avocados (½ medium)	~1.8 mcg

✖ Raw egg whites contain **avidin**, a compound that binds and blocks biotin — another reason to skip raw eggs.

🔄 Boosters & Blockers

Biotin absorption can be influenced by both gut health and specific food compounds. Here's what to watch:

Boosters	Blockers / Depleters
Gut-friendly probiotics	Raw egg whites (avidin blocks B7)
B-complex synergy (B2, B6, B5)	Long-term antibiotics
Fermented foods and fiber-rich diet	Alcohol, sugar, and poor microbiome

🥚 Your gut bacteria can **synthesize biotin** — if they're supported with good fiber and minimal antibiotics.

☠ Long-Term Deficiency Risks

While rare in developed countries, biotin deficiency can cause **significant issues** with appearance, nerve health, and even fetal development.

- **Hair loss or alopecia** (especially at the crown)
- Seborrheic dermatitis or dry, flaky skin
- Brittle, thin, or slow-growing nails
- Increased insulin resistance or blood sugar swings
- Birth defects (cleft palate, limb abnormalities) if low during pregnancy
- Neurological: hallucinations, unsteady gait, seizures (in severe cases)

⚠ Biotin deficiency is often triggered by **antibiotic use, genetic mutations (biotinidase deficiency), or chronic gut damage.**

📊 Weekly Biotin Food Tracker

You don't need megadoses to see beauty and mood benefits — just consistency. This weekly tracker keeps your growth nutrients in check.

Day	Eggs	Liver	Almonds	Seeds	Avocado	Salmon	Est. Biotin
Monday	✓	✓	✓	✓	✓	✓	~65 mcg
Tuesday	✓		✓	✓	✓	✓	~50 mcg
Wednesday	✓	✓		✓	✓	✓	~60 mcg
Thursday	✓	✓	✓	✓	✓		~55 mcg
Friday	✓	✓	✓	✓	✓	✓	~65 mcg

Day	Eggs	Liver	Almonds	Seeds	Avocado	Salmon	Est. Biotin
Saturday	✓	✓	✓	✓	✓	✓	~70 mcg
Sunday	✓	✓	✓	✓	✓	✓	~75 mcg

✏️ Your nails and hair grow **slowly** — so it may take 4–8 weeks of consistent intake to see a visible change.

🌱 Vitamin B9 (Folate) — The Builder of Life

"Why do I feel tired, foggy, or emotionally fragile — even with a healthy diet?"

You're not skipping meals. You eat your greens. Yet you feel mentally off, physically drained, and your emotions swing more than they used to.

This isn't just stress — it might be **low folate**, the vitamin your body uses to **build cells, protect your heart and brain, and carry oxygen** through your blood.

Folate (Vitamin B9) is the **foundation of DNA synthesis and methylation** — two behind-the-scenes processes that affect everything from fetal development to mood regulation and cancer risk.

💪 What Folate Does

Folate is often known as "the pregnancy vitamin," but its benefits span all ages and systems — not just the womb. Here's how it keeps your body running:

- Helps form **DNA and RNA** — the blueprint for all cells
- Produces **red blood cells** and prevents anemia
- Supports **fetal development** — especially neural tube formation

- Lowers **homocysteine** — protecting the brain and heart
- Plays a major role in **mood, memory, and methylation**
- Helps with **cell repair, detox, and inflammation control**

Folate is the **architect of your health** — building, repairing, and balancing from deep inside.

⚠ **Signs You Might Be Low on Folate**

These signs can mimic other issues — like stress, B12 deficiency, or low iron — but folate might be the key player behind them.

Physical Signs	**Mental/Emotional Signs**
Fatigue or pale skin	Low mood, irritability, or apathy
Shortness of breath	Memory issues or brain fog
Sore tongue or mouth sores	Trouble focusing or learning
Digestive discomfort	Anxiety, especially during PMS
Slow wound healing	Emotional fragility or overwhelm

⚠ Folate deficiency is more likely if you drink alcohol, take birth control, or have gut absorption issues.

🪻 How Much Folate Do You Need?

The key here is **active folate (L-5-MTHF)** — the form your body actually uses. Many people cannot convert synthetic folic acid properly.

Group	Daily Dose (Dietary Folate Equivalents)
Healthy Adults	400 mcg DFE
Pregnancy	600 mcg DFE
Lactation	500 mcg DFE
MTHFR gene mutation / mood support	600–800 mcg (in methylfolate form)

✅ Choose **methylated folate** (L-5-MTHF) over synthetic folic acid if possible — especially if you have the MTHFR gene variation.

🌿 Best Food Sources of Folate

Folate gets its name from "foliage" — leafy greens are its natural home. But legumes and whole foods also pack a powerful punch.

Food Item	Folate per serving (mcg DFE)
Spinach (½ cup cooked)	~130 mcg
Lentils (½ cup cooked)	~180 mcg
Asparagus (½ cup cooked)	~130 mcg
Avocados (½ medium)	~80 mcg
Black beans (½ cup)	~110 mcg
Broccoli (½ cup cooked)	~90 mcg

Food Item	Folate per serving (mcg DFE)
Orange (1 medium)	~50 mcg

🧠 Lightly cooking greens **preserves folate** better than boiling — and steaming is ideal.

🔄 Boosters & Blockers
Folate depends on your gut health, liver, and genes. Let's see what helps you absorb it — and what works against it.

Boosters	Blockers / Depleters
B12, B2, and B6 synergy	Alcohol, smoking
Healthy gut flora	Birth control pills, antacids
Methylated folate (L-5-MTHF)	Genetic issues (MTHFR mutation)

Folate and B12 are **deeply connected** — always make sure you're getting both to prevent imbalance.

😵 Long-Term Deficiency Risks
Folate deficiency builds up slowly — but the effects are widespread and deeply damaging.
- **Megaloblastic anemia** (large, weak red blood cells)
- Birth defects (neural tube, cleft palate)
- Depression, anxiety, or memory decline
- Elevated homocysteine → cardiovascular risk
- Poor cell repair = cancer risk and aging

- Hormonal mood imbalances, especially in women

🧂 Folate is one of the **most critical nutrients during pregnancy** — but also for anyone repairing, growing, or under stress.

📊 Weekly Folate Food Tracker

Use this folate-powered meal planner to keep your cell-building systems supported and your mood balanced.

Day	Spinach	Lentils	Avocado	Beans	Broccoli	Orange	Est. Folate (mcg DFE)
Monday	✓	✓	✓	✓	✓	✓	~640 mcg
Tuesday	✓	✓	✓	✓	✓		~600 mcg
Wednesday	✓	✓	✓	✓	✓	✓	~650 mcg
Thursday	✓	✓	✓	✓	✓	✓	~660 mcg
Friday	✓	✓	✓	✓	✓	✓	~680 mcg
Saturday	✓	✓	✓	✓	✓	✓	~700 mcg
Sunday	✓	✓	✓	✓	✓	✓	~700 mcg

🌱 Even one cup of cooked greens and half a cup of legumes daily gets you well on your way to folate success.

🧬 Vitamin B12 (Cobalamin) — The Nerve Protector
"Why do I feel exhausted, dizzy, or mentally off — even with good food and rest?"

You've tried eating better. You're getting some sleep. But you still feel drained, foggy, or like your body isn't responding the way it used to. Maybe your hands feel tingly. Or your balance feels... off.

That's a warning sign from your **nervous system** — and one of the first nutrients it needs is **Vitamin B12**.

B12 is not just for "energy." It's essential for building red blood cells, protecting your brain and spinal cord, and regulating the very DNA that defines you.

💪 What Vitamin B12 Does

Vitamin B12 is like a **guardian of your nervous system and blood supply**. It's also a key player in long-term energy and cognitive protection.

Here's what B12 supports:
- Forms **red blood cells** to carry oxygen throughout the body
- Protects and repairs **nerves and brain tissue**
- Produces neurotransmitters like dopamine, serotonin, and norepinephrine
- Regulates **DNA synthesis, methylation**, and detox
- Lowers **homocysteine** (cardiovascular risk marker)
- Supports mood, focus, memory, and **mental clarity**

B12 is like your **cellular electrician** — wiring energy and function throughout your brain and body.

⚠ Signs You Might Be Low on Vitamin B12

B12 deficiency can be subtle at first — and often goes undiagnosed for years. But the signs build slowly and can become serious.

Physical Signs	Neurological / Cognitive Signs
Fatigue or shortness of breath	Brain fog or forgetfulness
Pale skin or dizziness	Tingling/numbness in hands or feet
Weakness or poor endurance	Trouble with balance or coordination
Sore tongue or mouth ulcers	Mood swings, irritability, apathy
Rapid heartbeat or palpitations	Depression or anxiety

⚠ Long-term deficiency can cause **irreversible nerve damage** — even in people who eat well.

▦ How Much Vitamin B12 Do You Need?

While daily needs are modest, absorption is complex — especially if your digestion or stomach acid is weak.

Group	Daily Dose (Cobalamin)
Healthy Adults	2.4 mcg

Group	Daily Dose (Cobalamin)
Pregnancy/Lactation	2.6–2.8 mcg
Older adults (50+)	100–500 mcg (low absorption)
Deficiency treatment	1,000–5,000 mcg (oral or injections)

✅ B12 is stored in the liver — but if you stop absorbing it, your reserves deplete silently over months or years.

🥩 Best Food Sources of B12

Unlike most vitamins, B12 is **found only in animal-based foods**. Vegans and vegetarians must supplement.

Food Item	Vitamin B12 per serving
Beef liver (3 oz)	~70 mcg
Clams (3 oz)	~84 mcg
Salmon (3 oz)	~4.8 mcg
Sardines (3 oz)	~7.6 mcg
Eggs (2 large)	~1.2 mcg
Fortified plant milk (1 cup)	~2.5 mcg
Greek yogurt (¾ cup)	~1.1 mcg

🌱 Fortified plant milks are vital for vegans — but **methylcobalamin** (active B12) supplements are even better.

🔄 Boosters & Blockers
B12 is hard to absorb — and multiple digestive steps must function well. Here's what helps or hurts:

Boosters	Blockers / Depleters
Intrinsic factor (from stomach)	Antacids, PPIs, metformin
Gut flora and enzymes	Alcohol, smoking, chronic inflammation
Methylated B12 supplements	Parasites, autoimmune gut conditions

🏷️ Sublingual or injectable B12 **bypasses gut issues** — ideal for low stomach acid or absorption problems.

💀 Long-Term Deficiency Risks
B12 deficiency is **serious and progressive** — especially for the nervous system and mental health.
- Megaloblastic anemia (large, ineffective red cells)
- Nerve demyelination (irreversible nerve damage)
- Memory loss, cognitive decline, or early dementia
- Depression, paranoia, or hallucinations
- Poor balance, coordination, and muscle weakness
- Increased risk of miscarriage, infertility, and neural tube defects

🔘 B12 is your **brain's safety net** — once damaged, it's difficult to restore. Prevention is key.

📊 Weekly Vitamin B12 Food Tracker

This planner includes animal and fortified sources to keep your brain and blood running strong all week.

Day	Liver	Eggs	Yogurt	Salmon	Sardines	Fortified Milk	Est. B12
Monday	✓	✓	✓	✓	✓		~90 mcg
Tuesday		✓	✓	✓		✓	~10 mcg
Wednesday	✓	✓		✓	✓		~85 mcg
Thursday	✓	✓	✓	✓	✓	✓	~95 mcg
Friday	✓	✓	✓	✓	✓	✓	~100 mcg
Saturday	✓	✓	✓	✓	✓	✓	~105 mcg
Sunday	✓	✓	✓	✓	✓	✓	~110 mcg

🛡 Even small daily doses (2.4 mcg) are enough — but if your gut isn't absorbing, **go higher or switch to sublingual/injections.**

🛡 Glutathione — The Master Detoxifier

"Why do I feel heavy, foggy, or sensitive to everything — even healthy things?"

Your labs look "normal." You eat clean. But you're tired after eating, sensitive to smells or chemicals, and your skin breaks out under stress. Maybe your sleep feels unrefreshing. Or your hangovers hit harder than they used to.

That's a sign your body's detox systems are **overloaded** — and your **glutathione levels** may be low.

Glutathione is your body's **frontline defense against toxins, inflammation, and aging**. It's made in your liver, works in every cell, and protects you from oxidative stress — the hidden cause of many chronic issues.

💪 What Glutathione Does

Think of glutathione as your **internal security team**, cleaning up damage, neutralizing toxins, and protecting your cells.

Here's what it does every day behind the scenes:

- Neutralizes **free radicals and heavy metals**
- Regenerates other antioxidants (Vitamin C, E, CoQ10)
- Supports **liver detoxification** (especially Phase II)
- Protects brain and nerve tissue from inflammation
- Reduces skin damage, pigmentation, and oxidative aging
- Helps regulate immune responses and autoimmunity

Without glutathione, your body becomes **defenseless** — even healthy habits can trigger fatigue or inflammation.

⚠ Signs You Might Be Low on Glutathione

Low levels don't show up on basic bloodwork — but your body whispers through symptoms of **poor recovery, heightened sensitivity, and premature aging**.

Physical Signs	Cognitive/Immune Signs
Fatigue after eating	Brain fog or poor memory
Frequent headaches or congestion	Low immunity or frequent colds

Physical Signs	Cognitive/Immune Signs
Skin pigmentation or dullness	Autoimmune flares or inflammation
Poor tolerance to alcohol, meds, or supplements	Anxiety, sleep disruption
Slow healing or bruising	Joint stiffness or flare-ups

⚠ Glutathione is depleted by toxins, stress, infections, sugar, and even too much exercise.

How Much Glutathione Do You Need?

Glutathione is made **inside your body** — but depends on precursors, cofactors, and your overall lifestyle.

Group	Daily Need / Target
Healthy adults	Support via diet & precursors
High oxidative stress	NAC: 600–1,200 mg / Glutathione: 250–500 mg (liposomal)
Chronic illness/recovery	500–1,000 mg liposomal or IV-based
Maintenance (oral forms)	Whey, sulfur-rich foods, NAC, ALA

✏ Most glutathione supplements are poorly absorbed unless they're **liposomal, acetylated**, or IV-based.

🥦 Best Food Sources That Boost Glutathione

You don't "eat" glutathione directly — you eat the **building blocks** that help your body produce more of it.

Food Item	How It Helps
Broccoli, kale, cauliflower	Sulfur compounds (sulforaphane) boost production
Garlic and onions	Rich in sulfur — key for synthesis
Avocados	Contain glutathione + healthy fats
Whey protein (undamaged)	Provides cysteine, a building block
Brazil nuts	Selenium — a cofactor for glutathione recycling
Asparagus, spinach	Contain glutathione and its precursors

🧠 You can't just "pop a pill" — your **liver needs raw materials** to make and recycle glutathione effectively.

🔄 Boosters & Blockers

Let's look at what increases your body's glutathione production — and what quietly destroys it.

Boosters	Blockers / Depleters
NAC (N-acetyl cysteine)	Sugar, alcohol, and smoking

Boosters	Blockers / Depleters
Alpha-lipoic acid (ALA)	Chronic infections
Selenium, B2, and B6	Excess acetaminophen (Tylenol)
Intermittent fasting & exercise	Overtraining, sleep deprivation

⚠ Glutathione isn't just about what you take — it's about how well you **sleep, recover, and manage stress.**

🧠 Long-Term Deficiency Risks
Chronic glutathione depletion leads to **cellular damage, accelerated aging, and disease vulnerability**.
- Brain inflammation, memory loss, and early cognitive decline
- Autoimmune disorders (RA, MS, Hashimoto's)
- Fatty liver or liver toxicity
- Premature aging, pigmentation, and skin dullness
- Chronic fatigue, fibromyalgia, or post-viral syndrome
- Increased risk of diabetes, Parkinson's, and cancer

💡 Glutathione is often **low in people with chronic, unexplained conditions** — it's the missing piece.

📊 Weekly Glutathione Builder Tracker
You don't need direct supplements daily. Use this schedule to support **natural production** through food, movement, and smart stacking.

Day	Garlic/Onion	Broccoli/Kale	Avocado	Brazil Nuts	Whey Protein	NAC / ALA	Glutathione Support
Monday	✓	✓	✓	✓		✓	High
Tuesday	✓	✓		✓	✓		Moderate
Wednesday	✓	✓	✓		✓	✓	High
Thursday	✓	✓		✓	✓	✓	High
Friday	✓	✓	✓	✓		✓	High
Saturday	✓	✓	✓	✓	✓		High
Sunday	✓	✓	✓	✓	✓	✓	Very High

🍬 If you're recovering from illness, consider **NAC + liposomal glutathione** until your energy returns.

📖 CoQ10 (Coenzyme Q10) — The Heart's Energy Generator
"Why do I feel drained, short of breath, or older than I am — even with good habits?"

You eat well. You try to exercise. But even simple activities feel tiring. You get winded easily. Your heart seems more sensitive. And your recovery — physical and mental — takes longer than before.

That's a classic sign of **CoQ10 deficiency**.

Coenzyme Q10 is the **spark plug** in your body's energy engine. It fuels every cell — especially high-energy organs like the heart, brain, and muscles.

Without enough CoQ10, your body can't make enough ATP — the energy that powers literally everything.

💪 What CoQ10 Does

CoQ10 isn't just another antioxidant — it's a **core piece of your mitochondrial energy system** and your first line of defense against oxidative stress.

Here's what it powers:
- Generates **ATP (energy)** inside mitochondria — especially in heart, liver, and brain cells
- Neutralizes free radicals and reduces **oxidative stress**
- Improves **blood flow and oxygen delivery**
- Supports **healthy blood pressure and cardiovascular function**
- Enhances physical performance and post-exercise recovery
- Slows signs of **aging** at the cellular level

CoQ10 = cellular voltage. Low CoQ10 = dim lights, low power, fast fatigue.

⚠ Signs You Might Be Low on CoQ10

CoQ10 deficiency can look like just "getting older" — but it's actually your **cellular batteries struggling to charge**.

Physical Signs	Cognitive / Emotional Signs
Fatigue or low stamina	Brain fog or poor focus
Shortness of breath	Low mood or mild depression
Muscle weakness or soreness	Anxiety or low resilience

Physical Signs	Cognitive / Emotional Signs
Chest discomfort under exertion	Poor memory or slow recall
Early signs of gum disease	Sleep disruption

⚠ Statin drugs (for cholesterol) **drastically lower CoQ10**, leading to many of these side effects.

📋 How Much CoQ10 Do You Need?

Your body makes some CoQ10, but **production declines with age, stress, and medication**.

Group	Daily Dose (Ubiquinone / Ubiquinol)
Healthy adults under 40	100 mg (maintenance)
Over 40 or low energy	100–200 mg daily
Statin users / Heart patients	200–300 mg (split dose, with fat)
Mitochondrial support	300–600 mg (medical guidance)

✅ **Ubiquinol** is the active form — more absorbable, especially in people over 40.

🍖 Best Food Sources of CoQ10

You can't rely on food alone for therapeutic CoQ10, but here's where it's naturally found in modest amounts:

Food Item	CoQ10 per serving
Beef heart (3 oz)	~11–12 mg
Chicken thighs (3 oz)	~2–3 mg
Sardines (3 oz)	~2–5 mg
Mackerel (3 oz)	~3–5 mg
Spinach (1 cup, cooked)	~2 mg
Broccoli (½ cup)	~1 mg
Pistachios (1 oz)	~0.6 mg

🌑 Even though food has small amounts, a diet rich in **organ meats + fish + greens** supports natural CoQ10 function.

🔄 Boosters & Blockers

Here's what enhances CoQ10 use — and what might be silently depleting it, especially in aging or medicated bodies.

Boosters	Blockers / Depleters
Healthy fats (for absorption)	Statins, beta-blockers, and some antidepressants
Ubiquinol form (active CoQ10)	Age over 40 (natural decline)
Mitochondrial nutrients (B2, B3, Mg, ALA)	Excess stress, poor sleep

🍬 CoQ10 works best **in synergy** with magnesium, B vitamins, and lipoic acid.

☠️ Long-Term Deficiency Risks
Low CoQ10 has been linked to several chronic diseases — especially those involving **low energy, inflammation, and poor circulation**.

- Cardiomyopathy (heart weakness)
- Hypertension and arterial stiffness
- Chronic fatigue syndrome or fibromyalgia
- Parkinson's disease or cognitive decline
- Infertility (especially sperm motility)
- Muscle pain or weakness from statins
- Gum disease, oral inflammation

🩺 If you're on statins and feel drained, ask your doctor about **CoQ10 support immediately**.

📊 Weekly CoQ10 Food & Supplement Tracker
Use this practical plan to combine **food sources and supplements** — keeping your cells charged and inflammation low.

Day	Organ Meat	Fatty Fish	Leafy Greens	CoQ10 Supplement	Healthy Fats	Support Level
Monday	✓	✓	✓	100 mg	✓	High
Tuesday	✓	✓	✓		✓	Moderate
Wednesday	✓	✓	✓	200 mg	✓	Very High
Thursday	✓	✓	✓	100 mg	✓	High

Day	Organ Meat	Fatty Fish	Leafy Greens	CoQ10 Supplement	Healthy Fats	Support Level
Friday	✓	✓	✓		✓	Moderate
Saturday	✓	✓	✓	200 mg	✓	Very High
Sunday	✓	✓	✓	100 mg	✓	High

⚡ CoQ10 builds up in tissues — so consistency is key. You'll feel results in energy, focus, and stamina within 2–3 weeks.

🪨 Alpha Lipoic Acid (ALA) — The Energy Recycler
"Why do I crash after meals, feel nerve pain, or age faster — even with supplements?"

You've reduced sugar. You're watching carbs. Yet your energy dips after meals. You feel that weird tingling in your feet or fingers. Your skin seems duller, and inflammation flares easily. This might not be food — it might be your **mitochondria running out of fuel**.

Enter **Alpha Lipoic Acid (ALA)** — your body's **universal antioxidant** and **energy recycler**.

ALA helps recharge other antioxidants like Vitamin C and E, supports blood sugar control, and even **reverses nerve damage** over time. It's one of the most unique compounds your body can make — and supplement.

💪 What Alpha Lipoic Acid Does

ALA is both **fat-soluble and water-soluble**, meaning it works in nearly every cell and tissue — making it one of the most versatile healing agents in your body.

Here's what it supports:

- Recycles and restores **Vitamin C, E, and Glutathione**
- Improves **insulin sensitivity and blood sugar regulation**
- Enhances **mitochondrial energy production**
- Helps relieve **nerve pain and diabetic neuropathy**
- Reduces **inflammation and oxidative stress**
- Supports **skin clarity, liver detox, and brain protection**

ALA isn't just an antioxidant — it's your body's internal **clean-up crew and battery booster.**

⚠ Signs You Might Be Low on ALA

Although your body produces small amounts, you may feel the effects of low ALA during illness, stress, aging, or blood sugar swings.

Physical Signs	Metabolic / Neurological Signs
Low energy or sluggish metabolism	Numbness, tingling, or burning in limbs
Dull skin, pigmentation	Blood sugar crashes or carb cravings
Poor recovery post-exercise	Brain fog or forgetfulness
Inflammation or joint stiffness	Poor liver detox / sensitivity to toxins
Premature aging signs	Mood instability or fatigue after meals

⬤ ALA is one of the few antioxidants that can **cross the blood-brain barrier** — making it crucial for neurological repair.

How Much Alpha Lipoic Acid Do You Need?

ALA is produced in tiny amounts by your body — but therapeutic benefits come from **higher doses** taken as supplements.

Group	Daily Dose (ALA)
Healthy adults	100–200 mg (antioxidant support)
Blood sugar/nerve support	300–600 mg (split dose)
Neuropathy/PCOS/metabolic repair	600–1,200 mg (doctor-guided)

✅ Always take ALA **on an empty stomach** or with a small amount of healthy fat for best absorption.

Best Food Sources of Alpha Lipoic Acid

ALA in food is very low — but eating these regularly supports your natural synthesis and antioxidant bank.

Food Item	ALA per serving (approx.)
Spinach (1 cup cooked)	Very small (~0.3 mg)
Broccoli (1 cup cooked)	Very small (~0.1 mg)
Organ meats (kidney, heart)	Trace amounts (~1 mg)
Brussels sprouts	Trace (~0.1 mg)
Tomatoes (1 cup cooked)	Trace (~0.05 mg)

🔬 You'll need **supplemental ALA** for therapeutic effect — especially in cases of nerve pain or insulin resistance.

🔄 Boosters & Blockers
To optimize ALA's power, you'll need to support key minerals and avoid blood sugar-spiking habits.

Boosters	Blockers / Depleters
Magnesium, B1, and Biotin	High sugar or refined carbs
Chromium and Zinc (blood sugar helpers)	Chronic stress and inflammation
Omega-3s and healthy fats	Smoking, toxins, heavy alcohol use

⚠️ Biotin should be taken with high-dose ALA — they **share pathways** and balance each other out.

☠️ Long-Term Deficiency Risks
Low or suboptimal ALA leaves you vulnerable to **metabolic damage, inflammation, and premature aging**.
- Diabetic or age-related **nerve pain**
- Insulin resistance or erratic blood sugar
- Inflammation-driven skin conditions
- Accelerated mitochondrial aging
- Sluggish liver detox and toxin buildup
- Increased oxidative stress in the brain

🍬 ALA is being studied in **Parkinson's, Alzheimer's, MS, and PCOS** for its anti-inflammatory and metabolic repair roles.

📊 Weekly ALA Support Tracker

You don't get much ALA from food — so use this to **track supplements and ALA-supportive meals**.

Day	Spinach	Broccoli	Liver	Omega-3s	ALA Supplement	Biotin	Support Level
Monday	✓	✓	✓	✓	300 mg	✓	High
Tuesday	✓	✓		✓	600 mg	✓	Very High
Wednesday	✓	✓	✓	✓	300 mg	✓	High
Thursday	✓	✓	✓	✓	600 mg	✓	Very High
Friday	✓	✓	✓	✓	300 mg	✓	High
Saturday	✓	✓	✓	✓	600 mg	✓	Very High
Sunday	✓	✓	✓	✓	300 mg	✓	High

⚡ ALA may take 2–4 weeks to improve nerve symptoms, but cellular repair starts immediately.

👁 Lutein — The Vision Protector

"Why do my eyes feel tired, strained, or dry — even when I'm not overusing screens?"

Your vision blurs by evening. Your eyes burn or feel dry in air conditioning. Reading under bright lights strains your focus. Or maybe the sun feels a little harsher on your eyes than it used to.

That's your body asking for **Lutein** — a pigment that protects the most fragile part of your visual system: the **retina**.

Lutein is your eyes' internal **sunglasses and shield** — filtering harmful blue light, preventing oxidative damage, and supporting long-term visual sharpness and clarity.

💪 What Lutein Does

Lutein isn't just about "eye care." It's a **macular antioxidant** that also benefits your skin, brain, and even aging markers. Here's how it supports you:

- Filters **high-energy blue light** from screens and sunlight
- Protects the retina from **oxidative and UV damage**
- Helps prevent **age-related macular degeneration (AMD)**
- Reduces glare sensitivity and improves night vision
- Supports **skin hydration, elasticity, and tone**
- Enhances **cognitive speed and visual processing**

Lutein lives in your eyes, skin, and brain — and defends them all from daily stress and screen time.

⚠ Signs You Might Be Low on Lutein

These signs creep in gradually — and are often dismissed as "normal aging" or screen fatigue.

Eye Symptoms	Skin/Brain Symptoms
Eye strain or dry eyes	Dull or thinning skin
Blurry vision at night	Poor memory or slowed cognition

Eye Symptoms	Skin/Brain Symptoms
Poor contrast or color detection	Sensitivity to light
Fatigue when reading	Increased skin damage or sun spots

🔍 If you stare at screens all day or avoid leafy greens, your Lutein tank is probably running low.

📋 How Much Lutein Do You Need?

There's no official RDA, but research shows **daily intake matters** — especially for long-term vision and skin health.

Group	Daily Recommended Intake
Healthy Adults	6–10 mg (eye/skin support)
Eye strain / AMD support	10–20 mg
Long-term screen exposure	12–20 mg

☑ Lutein is fat-soluble — take it with healthy fats like avocado or olive oil for better absorption.

💊 Best Food Sources of Lutein

Lutein gives many plants their green/yellow hue — the deeper the color, the better the source.

133

Food Item	Lutein per serving (mg)
Kale (1 cup, cooked)	~23.8 mg
Spinach (1 cup, cooked)	~20.4 mg
Egg yolks (2 large)	~0.5–1.3 mg
Corn (½ cup, cooked)	~1.4 mg
Zucchini (½ cup, cooked)	~2.6 mg
Yellow peppers (½ cup)	~1.1 mg
Avocados (½ medium)	~0.3 mg

🧠 Egg yolks, though lower in Lutein, **increase its bioavailability** more than most plant sources.

🔄 Boosters & Blockers

Your ability to absorb Lutein depends on your diet, digestion, and fat intake.

Boosters	Blockers / Depleters
Healthy fats (eggs, olive oil)	Low-fat or fat-free meals
Good bile flow (liver/gallbladder)	Gut inflammation, IBS, leaky gut
Antioxidant synergy (Vitamin C, E, Zinc)	Smoking, blue light overload

💡 Think of Lutein like **sunscreen for your eyes** — but it works from the inside out.

💀 Long-Term Deficiency Risks
Without Lutein, your eyes and skin age faster — and you're more prone to **chronic visual degeneration**.
- Dry, irritated, or inflamed eyes
- Vision loss (especially AMD)
- Increased sensitivity to sunlight
- Fine lines and skin sagging
- Slower visual reaction time or mental fatigue
- Higher risk of cataracts in later life

👁 Lutein doesn't reverse eye damage — it **protects what's still healthy**. Start early.

📊 Weekly Lutein Food Tracker
Here's how to stack Lutein-rich meals with good fats to keep your eyes, skin, and brain protected year-round.

Day	Spinach	Kale	Corn	Zucchini	Eggs	Avocado	Est. Lutein (mg)
Monday	✓	✓	✓	✓	✓	✓	~28 mg
Tuesday	✓	✓		✓	✓		~25 mg
Wednesday	✓	✓	✓	✓	✓	✓	~28 mg
Thursday	✓	✓	✓	✓	✓	✓	~30 mg
Friday	✓	✓	✓	✓	✓	✓	~30 mg
Saturday	✓	✓	✓	✓	✓	✓	~30 mg
Sunday	✓	✓	✓	✓	✓	✓	~30 mg

👀 You may not "feel" Lutein immediately — but after 3–4 weeks, your **eye strain, glare sensitivity, and skin tone** often improve.

👀 Zeaxanthin — The Macular Defender
"Why do bright lights hurt my eyes, or colors seem duller — even though my vision test is normal?"

Your eye exam says everything is fine — but **you don't feel fine**. Sunlight feels harsh. Your vision fades under LED lights. Colors don't pop like they used to. Your eyes fatigue by afternoon, and night driving feels unsafe.

That's where **Zeaxanthin** steps in — a powerful antioxidant **stored in the very center of your retina** to protect it from damage, strain, and degeneration.

Paired with Lutein, Zeaxanthin is part of your **macular pigment shield** — defending your sight, your clarity, and your quality of life.

👍 What Zeaxanthin Does

Zeaxanthin specifically protects the **macula**, the central part of your retina responsible for **sharp, detailed, and color-rich vision**.

Here's what it supports:

- Filters **blue light** to reduce visual strain and oxidative stress
- Enhances **color vision, contrast, and detail perception**
- Prevents or slows **age-related macular degeneration (AMD)**

- Supports **night vision and glare recovery**
- Defends eye tissue from **UV and LED damage**
- May support **skin tone, brain function, and cognitive clarity**

Zeaxanthin isn't just for eyesight — it helps you **experience the world more vividly and clearly**.

⚠ Signs You Might Be Low on Zeaxanthin

The deficiency doesn't cause blindness overnight — it builds slowly through **subtle eye discomfort and sensory dullness**.

Visual Signs	Sensory / Functional Signs
Blurry or faded color vision	Poor contrast in low light
Sunlight feels painfully bright	Eye strain under blue/LED light
Slower focus adjustment	Struggle with night driving
Dry, itchy, or fatigued eyes	Reduced depth or clarity perception

🔑 You're more at risk if you're indoors a lot, stare at screens, or avoid leafy greens and yellow/orange veggies.

🏷 How Much Zeaxanthin Do You Need?

Like Lutein, Zeaxanthin has no RDA — but clinical studies show **benefits start around 2 mg daily**, and up to 10 mg for therapeutic use.

Group	Daily Recommended Intake
Healthy Adults	2–4 mg
AMD prevention / visual support	6–10 mg
High screen use / night driving	6–8 mg

✅ Zeaxanthin is fat-soluble — always consume with healthy fats for proper absorption.

🥕 Best Food Sources of Zeaxanthin

Zeaxanthin tends to show up in **yellow-orange fruits and dark leafy greens**, but the quantity is far smaller than Lutein — so intake must be consistent.

Food Item	Zeaxanthin per serving (mg)
Goji berries (¼ cup dried)	~1.8–2.5 mg
Corn (½ cup, cooked)	~0.3–0.5 mg
Egg yolks (2 large)	~0.3–0.4 mg
Orange bell peppers (½ cup)	~1.5 mg
Kale (1 cup, cooked)	~0.2–0.3 mg
Spinach (1 cup, cooked)	~0.1–0.3 mg

🟤 Goji berries are **the richest natural source** — just a small handful gives you a solid daily dose.

🔄 Boosters & Blockers

Let's make sure your body **absorbs and utilizes** the Zeaxanthin you consume.

Boosters	Blockers / Depleters
Healthy fats (eggs, avocado)	Low-fat or processed meals
Lutein synergy	Excessive screen time
Zinc and Vitamin A (for retina health)	Smoking, alcohol, inflammation

🍬 Zinc helps shuttle both Zeaxanthin and Lutein to the retina — they work best as a **team**.

💀 Long-Term Deficiency Risks

Your eye tissues are fragile and constantly exposed to light. Without Zeaxanthin, damage accumulates silently.
- Age-related macular degeneration (AMD)
- Fading color vision and detail perception
- Difficulty reading or focusing in dim light
- Early onset of cataracts or eye dryness
- Slower visual processing and coordination
- Higher sensitivity to sunlight or blue light

👁 Zeaxanthin is **one of the few nutrients proven to improve macular pigment** and preserve lifelong vision.

📊 Weekly Zeaxanthin Food Tracker

This plan combines yellow/orange vegetables, leafy greens, and eggs — with consistent small doses of Goji berries or supplements.

Day	Goji Berries	Corn	Peppers	Kale/Spinach	Eggs	Healthy Fat	Est. Zeaxanthin (mg)
Monday	✓	✓	✓	✓	✓	✓	~5.5 mg
Tuesday	✓	✓	✓	✓	✓	✓	~6 mg
Wednesday	✓	✓	✓	✓	✓	✓	~6.2 mg
Thursday	✓	✓	✓	✓	✓	✓	~6.4 mg
Friday	✓	✓	✓	✓	✓	✓	~6.5 mg
Saturday	✓	✓	✓	✓	✓	✓	~6.5 mg
Sunday	✓	✓	✓	✓	✓	✓	~6.5 mg

🔦 Zeaxanthin + Lutein = your **macular insurance policy** — especially for long-term screen users and aging eyes.

🍷 Resveratrol — The Longevity Molecule
"Why do I feel older, inflamed, or sluggish — even when I live a clean lifestyle?"

You avoid junk food. You stay active. But your body still feels inflamed, your recovery is slow, your energy isn't what it used to be. Maybe your skin has lost its glow. Or your metabolism feels sluggish for no clear reason.

That's when **Resveratrol** comes in — a rare plant compound found in grapes and berries that mimics the benefits of fasting, supports **cellular renewal**, and may even **slow down biological aging**.

Resveratrol activates survival pathways inside your cells — switching on longevity genes, reducing chronic inflammation, and helping your body repair faster.

💪 What Resveratrol Does

Resveratrol isn't a vitamin — it's a **polyphenol**, a plant-based antioxidant that activates your body's most powerful repair systems.

Here's what it supports:
- Activates **SIRT1 "longevity genes"** — linked to aging control
- Mimics effects of **calorie restriction and intermittent fasting**
- Reduces chronic **inflammation and oxidative stress**
- Improves **blood vessel flexibility and circulation**
- Protects the brain, heart, and skin from age-related decline
- Helps reduce **insulin resistance and metabolic slowdowns**

Resveratrol is like a **cellular switch** — it tells your body to pause aging and begin self-repair.

⚠ Signs You Might Be Low on Polyphenols Like Resveratrol

There's no test for "resveratrol deficiency," but the symptoms of low polyphenol intake are very real — especially if your diet lacks colorful fruits, red wine, or plant pigments.

Signs of Low Polyphenol Intake	Related Symptoms
Dull, sagging skin	Accelerated signs of aging

Signs of Low Polyphenol Intake	Related Symptoms
Slow recovery after workouts	Fatigue or poor circulation
Mild insulin resistance	Weight gain around belly
Poor blood vessel flexibility	Cold hands/feet or varicose veins
Low resilience to stress or toxins	Brain fog, poor memory, low libido

🪨 A lack of plant-based antioxidants speeds up **cell damage, inflammation, and biological aging.**

🧱 How Much Resveratrol Do You Need?

There's no RDA — but therapeutic doses start **far above** what you'd get from a glass of wine.

Group	Daily Resveratrol Intake
General antioxidant support	50–100 mg (diet + supplement)
Longevity / SIRT1 activation	150–250 mg (with healthy fat)
Metabolic or cognitive support	250–500 mg (split dose, medically guided)

⚪ Resveratrol works best in **trans-resveratrol form** — and is **synergistic with Quercetin, Curcumin, and NMN.**

🍇 Best Food Sources of Resveratrol

Resveratrol is produced in plants as a defense compound. The richest sources tend to be deeply colored fruits and fermented plant products.

Food Item	Resveratrol per serving (mg)
Red grapes (1 cup)	~0.2–0.5 mg
Red wine (5 oz glass)	~0.5–1.5 mg
Blueberries (½ cup)	~0.3–0.6 mg
Cranberries (½ cup)	~0.2 mg
Dark chocolate (70%, 1 oz)	~0.1–0.2 mg
Peanuts (1 oz)	~0.15 mg
Japanese knotweed (root)	~50–100 mg (used in supplements)

🍷 You'd have to drink over 40 glasses of wine daily to hit therapeutic doses — **food supports, but supplements matter.**

🔄 Boosters & Blockers

Let's make sure your body uses Resveratrol effectively — and isn't blocked from absorbing or activating it.

Boosters	Blockers / Depleters
Black pepper (piperine)	High blood sugar or insulin spikes

Boosters	Blockers / Depleters
Quercetin + healthy fat (olive oil)	Poor gut health or chronic alcohol
Intermittent fasting (synergy)	Processed foods, low fruit intake

⚡ Take Resveratrol **with food + fat** — or with black pepper extract for up to 2,000% better absorption.

💀 Long-Term Deficiency Risks
If your diet is low in antioxidants like Resveratrol, you may experience **faster aging**, poorer circulation, and slower cellular recovery.

- Inflammation-related fatigue or pain
- Increased heart disease or insulin resistance
- Faster wrinkle development and skin dullness
- Weaker brain recovery after stress or toxins
- Poor mitochondrial function and low stamina
- Reduced nitric oxide = low libido, cold extremities

🛡 Think of Resveratrol as a **fire extinguisher** for low-grade inflammation that silently accelerates aging.

📊 Weekly Resveratrol Intake Tracker
Use this tracker to rotate food-based polyphenols and **stack your supplements** for optimal longevity support.

Day	Grapes	Berries	Red Wine	Chocolate	Supplement (mg)	Healthy Fat	Est. Resveratrol
Monday	✓	✓	✓	✓	100 mg	✓	~105 mg
Tuesday	✓	✓		✓	250 mg	✓	~255 mg
Wednesday	✓	✓	✓	✓	150 mg	✓	~155 mg
Thursday	✓	✓	✓	✓	250 mg	✓	~260 mg
Friday	✓	✓	✓	✓	250 mg	✓	~260 mg
Saturday	✓	✓	✓	✓	250 mg	✓	~260 mg
Sunday	✓	✓	✓	✓	250 mg	✓	~260 mg

⌛ Most people feel the **skin, brain, and recovery benefits** of Resveratrol after 3–6 weeks of consistent use.

🌿 Curcumin — The Inflammation Fighter

"Why do I feel sore, stiff, or inflamed — even without an injury?"

You haven't had any trauma. Yet your joints feel stiff in the morning. You get bloated after eating. Your energy crashes after stress. And your mood? Off.

These are all signs of **chronic, low-grade inflammation** — the hidden root behind fatigue, brain fog, and even serious diseases.

And one of nature's most powerful answers? **Curcumin** — the bright yellow compound in turmeric.

Curcumin is a **natural anti-inflammatory molecule** that targets pain, swelling, oxidative damage, and even the mood-brain-gut connection.

💪 What Curcumin Does
Curcumin isn't just a trendy spice — it's a **multi-target healing agent** that modulates inflammation at the cellular level.
Here's how it works in your body:
- Suppresses **NF-kB**, a key inflammation switch linked to aging and disease
- Reduces joint pain, muscle soreness, and tissue swelling
- Enhances **gut lining repair** and reduces bloating or leaky gut
- Supports brain function and lifts mood (especially when paired with Omega-3s)
- Neutralizes free radicals and oxidative damage
- May help fight cancer cell formation (early-stage studies)

Think of curcumin as your **body's inflammation dial** — turning down the heat when things go out of control.

⚠ Signs You Might Be Inflamed (and Could Benefit from Curcumin)
Chronic inflammation often flies under the radar — but your body gives you plenty of signals.

Inflammation Symptoms	Emotional/Metabolic Signs
Joint stiffness or pain	Mood swings or depression
Puffy face or swollen hands	Insulin resistance / belly fat

Inflammation Symptoms	Emotional/Metabolic Signs
Gut bloating or food sensitivity	Fatigue after eating
Skin redness, acne, or psoriasis	Brain fog or memory issues
Sore muscles after light activity	Trouble sleeping

⚠ Inflammation is the **root of most chronic conditions** — and curcumin helps calm it without side effects.

How Much Curcumin Do You Need?

Turmeric alone contains very little curcumin. Therapeutic doses require **concentrated, bioavailable extracts**.

Use Case	Curcumin (standardized extract)
General antioxidant support	300–500 mg/day
Joint pain, inflammation	500–1,000 mg/day
Gut, skin, or mood support	750–1,500 mg/day
Severe inflammation or injury	1,500–3,000 mg/day (doctor-guided)

✅ Choose curcumin with **black pepper extract (piperine)** or **liposomal delivery** for 2,000% better absorption.

🥕 Best Food Sources (and Why They're Not Enough Alone)

Turmeric root is where curcumin comes from — but it contains only **2–6% curcumin** by weight. Still, it's a helpful base.

Food Item	Curcumin content (approx.)
Turmeric powder (1 tsp)	~200 mg curcumin
Fresh turmeric root (1 tbsp)	~300 mg
Golden milk (8 oz, w/ fat)	~150 mg (varies)
Curcumin capsule (standardized)	500–1,000 mg (bioavailable)

🥣 Golden milk and turmeric teas are soothing — but **don't expect therapeutic results without a high-potency extract.**

🔄 Boosters & Blockers

To absorb and use curcumin properly, pair it with **fat and piperine** — and watch out for digestive blockers.

Boosters	Blockers / Depleters
Black pepper extract (piperine)	Poor fat absorption / low bile
Omega-3s (EPA/DHA)	Ultra-processed food and sugar
Olive oil, ghee, or coconut milk	Low stomach acid / gut inflammation

148

🍃 Curcumin + piperine is one of the most **well-studied combos** for reducing inflammation and improving joint mobility.

💀 Long-Term Deficiency / Inflammatory Risks
When inflammation stays high and curcumin is low, long-term wear and tear speeds up across all systems.
- **Arthritis and chronic joint pain**
- Brain fog, depression, and slow recovery
- Autoimmune flare-ups and skin conditions
- Gut inflammation → food sensitivities, IBS
- Slow wound healing and soreness
- Higher risk of heart disease and metabolic dysfunction

💡 Curcumin may not cure disease — but it reduces the **fire that feeds it.**

📊 Weekly Curcumin Support Tracker
Here's how to stack curcumin through food, lifestyle, and supplements — to stay cool, sharp, and pain-free.

Day	Turmeric Root	Golden Milk	Curcumin Supplement	Omega-3	Black Pepper	Support Level
Monday	✓	✓	500 mg	✓	✓	High
Tuesday	✓		1,000 mg	✓	✓	Very High
Wednesday	✓	✓	500 mg	✓	✓	High
Thursday	✓	✓	750 mg	✓	✓	Very High

Day	Turmeric Root	Golden Milk	Curcumin Supplement	Omega-3	Black Pepper	Support Level
Friday	✓		1,000 mg	✓	✓	Very High
Saturday	✓	✓	500 mg	✓	✓	High
Sunday	✓	✓	750 mg	✓	✓	Very High

🌿 Many users report **better digestion, calmer mood, and reduced joint pain** within 2–3 weeks of consistent curcumin use.

🧅 Quercetin — The Natural Antihistamine
"Why do I react to dust, foods, or stress so quickly — even when I'm not 'allergic'?"

Your allergies aren't severe. But you often feel puffy, itchy, or inflamed. Your sinuses clog in the morning. You're sensitive to foods, weather changes, or even strong smells. You may also bruise easily or feel wiped out after exposure to pollution.

These are signs your body is struggling to **regulate histamine, inflammation, and immune overactivity** — and **Quercetin** could be your missing link.

Quercetin is a plant pigment (flavonoid) found in apples, onions, and berries. It's one of nature's most powerful **mast cell stabilizers and anti-inflammatories**, helping your body calm down allergic reactions, regulate immunity, and recover from oxidative stress.

💪 What Quercetin Does

Quercetin isn't just an "antioxidant" — it's a **bioflavonoid with antihistamine, antiviral, and anti-inflammatory** effects across multiple systems.

Here's what it supports:

- **Stabilizes mast cells**, reducing histamine release and allergic symptoms
- Eases **sinus congestion, rashes, and food sensitivities**
- Protects lungs from inflammation and environmental toxins
- Reduces bruising, swelling, and oxidative damage in blood vessels
- Supports **immune resilience and recovery from infection**
- Works synergistically with Vitamin C and Zinc to fight viruses

Think of Quercetin as your **body's natural antihistamine** — without drowsiness or side effects.

⚠️ Signs You Might Be Low on Bioflavonoids Like Quercetin

These symptoms often mimic food sensitivities, "dust allergies," or chronic low-grade inflammation — but the root issue may be a **lack of flavonoid protection**.

Physical Signs	Immune / Allergic Signs
Easy bruising or fragile capillaries	Sinus congestion or runny nose
Puffy eyes or swelling	Itchy skin or mild hives

Physical Signs	Immune / Allergic Signs
Sore throat after eating	Histamine headaches (wine, cheese)
Fatigue after air pollution	Chronic sneezing or watery eyes
Frequent food intolerance	Mold, pollen, or dust sensitivity

🪙 Many people who react to "healthy" foods (like tomatoes, spinach, or avocados) may benefit from Quercetin for **histamine support**.

📊 How Much Quercetin Do You Need?

Quercetin from food is helpful, but supplements are often needed for **antihistamine or immune effects**.

Use Case	Daily Quercetin (Supplemental)
General antioxidant support	250–500 mg
Allergies, hay fever, or histamine issues	500–1,000 mg/day
Post-viral fatigue or immune support	1,000–1,500 mg (short term)

✅ Pair with **Vitamin C** and **Bromelain** for better absorption and synergy.

🫐 Best Food Sources of Quercetin

The deeper the color, the richer in flavonoids. Quercetin loves **red, purple, and bitter** plant foods.

Food Item	Quercetin per serving (approx.)
Red onions (½ cup, raw)	~45 mg
Apples (1 medium, skin on)	~10–15 mg
Blueberries (½ cup)	~8 mg
Kale (1 cup cooked)	~8 mg
Capers (1 tbsp)	~18 mg
Cranberries (½ cup)	~7 mg
Grapes (1 cup)	~5 mg

🌙 Capers are **the most concentrated food source** — but eating onions and apples daily provides a strong base.

🔄 Boosters & Blockers

Quercetin absorption is tricky — but there are ways to **amplify its bioavailability** significantly.

Boosters	Blockers / Depleters
Vitamin C (500–1,000 mg)	Chronic stress and gut inflammation

Boosters	Blockers / Depleters
Bromelain (from pineapple core)	Poor bile flow / fat malabsorption
Black pepper (piperine)	High sugar or ultra-processed food

🍍 A supplement with **Quercetin + C + Bromelain** is the gold standard for **allergy and immune relief.**

😷 Long-Term Deficiency or Low Intake Risks
Without enough Quercetin, your body may struggle to **recover from inflammation or control histamine properly**, leading to:
- Chronic nasal congestion or sinus pressure
- Frequent allergic responses or itchy skin
- Asthma flares, lung irritation, or coughing
- Poor circulation, bruising, or swelling
- Weakened immune response to viruses or toxins
- Persistent post-viral fatigue or malaise

🛡️ Quercetin is your **immune and allergy "brake pedal"** — especially in a world full of irritants and triggers.

📊 Weekly Quercetin Support Tracker
This tracker combines food sources, synergistic nutrients, and supplement options to manage inflammation and histamine overload.

Day	Onion	Apple	Berries	Kale	Supplement	Vitamin C	Support Level
Monday	✅	✅	✅	✅	500 mg	✅	High

Day	Onion	Apple	Berries	Kale	Supplement	Vitamin C	Support Level
Tuesday	✓	✓	✓	✓	1,000 mg	✓	Very High
Wednesday	✓	✓	✓	✓	500 mg	✓	High
Thursday	✓	✓	✓	✓	1,000 mg	✓	Very High
Friday	✓	✓	✓	✓	500 mg	✓	High
Saturday	✓	✓	✓	✓	1,000 mg	✓	Very High
Sunday	✓	✓	✓	✓	1,000 mg	✓	Very High

🫁 Within 1–2 weeks, most people report **lighter sinuses, fewer reactions, and clearer skin.**

🔴 Lycopene — The Red Shield
"Why is my skin dull, my heart under strain, or my digestion sluggish — even though I eat well?"

You eat your veggies. You try to stay active. Yet your skin looks tired, you feel more sensitive to the sun, and your digestion or prostate health isn't what it used to be.

This isn't just aging — your body may be low on **Lycopene**, a red carotenoid pigment that protects your **heart, skin, and internal organs** from oxidative stress and chronic inflammation.

Unlike beta-carotene, Lycopene doesn't convert into Vitamin A — instead, it acts as a **cellular bodyguard**, defending against UV rays, environmental toxins, and degenerative damage.

💪 What Lycopene Does

Lycopene is a powerful **antioxidant and anti-inflammatory compound** that accumulates in the **skin, eyes, prostate, and blood vessels** — acting as your body's defense against long-term stress and aging.

Here's what it supports:

- Protects skin from **UV damage and pigmentation**
- Reduces **oxidative stress in the heart and arteries**
- Improves **blood pressure and LDL cholesterol balance**
- Supports **prostate health** and reduces risk of BPH
- Helps detoxify the liver and support immune function
- May reduce risk of **cancer (especially prostate, skin, and stomach)**

Lycopene is like your body's **internal sunscreen and vascular cleaner** — quietly defending your most vulnerable tissues.

⚠️ Signs You Might Be Low on Lycopene

These signs are subtle but cumulative — often showing up in appearance, inflammation, or male health markers.

Physical / Skin Signs	Metabolic / Hormonal Signs
Dull or uneven skin tone	Elevated cholesterol or BP
Increased sun sensitivity	Early signs of prostate enlargement
Pigmentation or age spots	Poor circulation / cold hands/feet
Acne or slow healing	Low sperm motility / sexual stamina
Digestive sluggishness	Oxidative stress or fatigue

🧑‍🦲 ♂ Lycopene plays a major role in **men's health**, but women benefit just as much — especially for skin and heart protection.

🟫 How Much Lycopene Do You Need?

Lycopene needs vary based on sun exposure, age, oxidative stress, and gender (men typically need more).

Use Case	Daily Lycopene Intake
General antioxidant support	6–10 mg/day
Prostate / skin health support	10–20 mg/day
Cardiovascular / cancer prevention	15–30 mg/day (long-term)

✅ Lycopene is **better absorbed from cooked or processed tomatoes** — yes, pizza sauce wins here.

🍅 Best Food Sources of Lycopene

Lycopene loves heat — cooking tomatoes **in oil** makes it up to **4x more bioavailable** than raw sources.

Food Item	Lycopene per serving (mg)
Tomato paste (2 tbsp)	~13.5 mg
Cooked tomatoes (½ cup)	~15 mg
Watermelon (1 cup)	~6.9 mg
Pink grapefruit (½ fruit)	~1.8 mg
Red bell pepper (½ cup, cooked)	~0.5 mg

Food Item	Lycopene per serving (mg)
Guava (1 medium)	~5.2 mg

▶ Your tomato-based meals aren't guilty pleasures — they're **Lycopene powerhouses**, especially with olive oil.

🔄 Boosters & Blockers

To maximize Lycopene's benefits, pair it with **healthy fats** and avoid high-sugar, low-antioxidant diets.

Boosters	Blockers / Depleters
Olive oil, ghee, or coconut oil	Low-fat / fat-free meals
Cooked tomato (vs raw)	Excess alcohol and smoking
Beta-carotene and lutein synergy	UV overexposure, pollution

🫒 Lycopene works best in **tomato-based sauces, soups, and stews** — add olive oil for peak absorption.

⚠️ Long-Term Deficiency Risks

Without Lycopene, tissues exposed to sun, toxins, and oxidation become **vulnerable to damage and disease**.

- Increased risk of prostate problems and BPH
- Poor skin tone, sun damage, or aging spots
- Sluggish circulation or early vascular aging
- High LDL cholesterol and blood pressure
- Inflammation in the stomach or gut lining
- Slower immune defense and detox function

🛡 Lycopene is especially protective against **"invisible aging"** — the kind that happens deep in your arteries and organs.

📊 Weekly Lycopene Food Tracker

This meal plan gives you a rich mix of **cooked tomato dishes**, fruits, and absorption enhancers like healthy fats.

Day	Cooked Tomato	Watermelon	Grapefruit	Guava	Olive Oil	Est. Lycopene (mg)
Monday	✅	✅	✅		✅	~20 mg
Tuesday	✅	✅		✅	✅	~21 mg
Wednesday	✅	✅	✅		✅	~22 mg
Thursday	✅	✅	✅	✅	✅	~24 mg
Friday	✅	✅	✅	✅	✅	~25 mg
Saturday	✅	✅	✅	✅	✅	~25 mg
Sunday	✅	✅	✅	✅	✅	~26 mg

🍅 Just ½ cup of cooked tomatoes + olive oil daily = Lycopene protection for **skin, heart, and prostate**.

💚 Astaxanthin — The King of Antioxidants

"Why do I look tired, feel sore, or burn in the sun — even with a healthy lifestyle?"

You exercise. You eat clean. You take your supplements. But your muscles stay sore longer than they used to. Your skin feels older, less elastic. You sunburn easily. And your eyes tire faster than expected.

Your body might be **oxidizing faster than it's recovering** — and **Astaxanthin** could be your missing shield.

Astaxanthin is a **deep red carotenoid**, found in wild salmon, krill, and algae. It's often called the **most powerful antioxidant on Earth**, with studies showing it can **outperform Vitamin C, E, and CoQ10** in protecting your cells.

💪 What Astaxanthin Does

Astaxanthin acts like a **forcefield inside your cells**, spanning both water- and fat-soluble membranes. It can cross the blood-brain barrier, protect your mitochondria, and support **whole-body resilience**.

Here's what it supports:

- Reduces **oxidative stress by 6,000x more than** Vitamin C
- Improves **skin elasticity, hydration, and UV resistance**
- Enhances **muscle endurance and recovery**
- Protects the eyes from **blue light and macular stress**
- Lowers inflammation and supports heart health
- Boosts **immune response and mitochondrial health**

Astaxanthin isn't just another antioxidant — it's **cellular armor** that works where others can't.

⚠️ Signs You Might Be Low on Antioxidants Like Astaxanthin

This is especially true if you're athletic, sun-exposed, stressed, or aging faster than you'd like.

Skin & Appearance Signs	Internal / Functional Signs
Sun sensitivity or easy burning	Muscle soreness after mild exertion

Skin & Appearance Signs	Internal / Functional Signs
Wrinkles, dry or sagging skin	Eye fatigue or screen sensitivity
Loss of skin elasticity or glow	Brain fog or recovery fatigue
Uneven skin tone or red patches	Slow recovery after workouts or stress

🔘 If you're feeling "worn out" from life, workouts, or the environment — Astaxanthin is the **cellular anti-friction agent**.

🔲 How Much Astaxanthin Do You Need?

Food sources offer tiny amounts — so for full-body benefits, **supplements are required**.

Use Case	Daily Astaxanthin Dose
Skin, eye, and antioxidant support	4–6 mg
Athletic recovery or joint support	8–12 mg
Advanced cellular protection	12–16 mg

✅ Astaxanthin is **fat-soluble** — always take it with healthy fats or a meal for proper absorption.

🍤 Best Food Sources of Astaxanthin

Astaxanthin gives wild salmon and crustaceans their red-orange glow. But the amounts in food are **very small**.

Food Item	Astaxanthin per serving
Wild salmon (3 oz)	~1–3 mg
Krill (3 oz)	~1–2 mg
Red trout (3 oz)	~1–2 mg
Lobster, shrimp, crab (3 oz)	~0.5–1 mg
Haematococcus algae (used in supplements)	~4–12 mg (high quality)

🧬 Most supplement-grade Astaxanthin comes from **algae** — the same one wild salmon eat to build their endurance.

🔄 Boosters & Blockers

Maximize Astaxanthin absorption by pairing it with fat and **taking it with other carotenoids** for synergy.

Boosters	Blockers / Depleters
Omega-3s, olive oil, or avocado	Low-fat or fasting without fat intake
Vitamin E, CoQ10, Lutein synergy	UV radiation, air pollution

Boosters	Blockers / Depleters
Antioxidant-rich whole foods	High sugar and seed oils (pro-oxidant)

🫐 Astaxanthin shines brightest in **a healthy fat-rich, antioxidant-rich diet** — especially alongside Omega-3s.

💀 Long-Term Deficiency Risks
Without strong antioxidants like Astaxanthin, oxidative stress **accelerates tissue aging**, especially in skin, brain, and muscle.

- Skin damage, sunburn, and wrinkles
- Slow recovery after workouts
- Inflammation-driven joint pain
- Eye strain, cataracts, or AMD risk
- Weak immune defense and poor healing
- Faster brain aging or fatigue after stress

🛡️ Astaxanthin is a **deep-tissue defender** — from your retina to your heart to your mitochondria.

📊 Weekly Astaxanthin Tracker
Here's how to consistently protect your body through **smart supplementation and supportive meals**.

Day	Salmon	Shrimp/Crab	Omega-3s	Astaxanthin Supplement	Healthy Fat	Support Level
Monday	✅	✅	✅	4 mg	✅	High

Day	Salmon	Shrimp/Crab	Omega-3s	Astaxanthin Supplement	Healthy Fat	Support Level
Tuesday	✓	✓	✓	8 mg	✓	Very High
Wednesday	✓	✓	✓	4 mg	✓	High
Thursday	✓	✓	✓	8 mg	✓	Very High
Friday	✓	✓	✓	4 mg	✓	High
Saturday	✓	✓	✓	12 mg	✓	Max Support
Sunday	✓	✓	✓	8 mg	✓	Very High

💚 Most people notice **glowing skin, faster recovery, and less fatigue** within 2–3 weeks.

🔄 **Amino Acids Summary: Your Body's Repair Team**
"You don't just rebuild muscle with protein — you rebuild everything."

Amino acids are more than just gym fuel. They're your body's **repair crew, neurotransmitter makers, hormone helpers, gut guardians, and mental motivators**. Without the right balance, your mood dips, your focus fades, and your recovery stalls. This section gave you the most important amino acids to support **modern life, performance, and healing**.

❀ Essential Amino Acids — The 9 You Must Get from Food

Amino Acid	Core Functions	Best For
Leucine	Muscle growth, fat burning, anabolic signal	Building muscle, preventing age-related loss
Isoleucine	Energy, blood sugar balance, muscle endurance	Exercise recovery, stamina, glucose control
Valine	Mental focus, muscle repair, brain fuel	Fatigue, brain fog, exercise resilience
Lysine	Collagen formation, immune defense, antiviral support	Cold sores, wound healing, joint health
Methionine	Detox, methylation, antioxidant (glutathione) production	Liver health, aging, stress recovery
Phenylalanine	Mood, focus, dopamine synthesis	Motivation, ADHD, thyroid support
Threonine	Gut lining, skin, immune function	Digestion, recovery, tissue repair
Tryptophan	Serotonin, melatonin, emotional regulation	Sleep, mood, anxiety, PMS
Histidine	Immunity, nerve protection, histamine balance	Skin health, allergic reactions, fatigue

🧪 **Special Nutrients Covered in This Section**

Compound	Category	Function
Choline	Vitamin-like nutrient	Brain signals, liver fat metabolism, memory
(Coming up?)	(e.g. Carnitine, Glycine, Glutamine, Tyrosine)	Optional additions for advanced readers

🪨 Together, these amino acids help you **recover faster, think clearer, feel calmer**, and **age slower**.

📝 **Tips for Optimizing Amino Acid Intake**
- Don't chase just protein grams — focus on **quality and diversity** of protein sources
- **Animal proteins** (eggs, meat, fish) are complete — but **vegans** must combine legumes, tofu, seeds, and grains wisely
- Support amino acid usage with **B-complex vitamins, zinc, magnesium, and healthy fats**
- If under stress, healing, or aging — consider **targeted amino acid supplements** like Leucine, Tryptophan, or Glycine

---

🪨 **Memory Trick:**
"**LIVe TALL-MTPH**" — A mnemonic for the essential amino acids:
- **L**eucine
- **I**soleucine
- **V**aline
- **T**hreonine

166

- **A**rginine *(conditionally essential in kids)*
- **L**ysine
- **M**ethionine
- **T**ryptophan
- **P**henylalanine
- **H**istidine

✅ Adults mainly need the bolded 9, but growing kids and healing bodies benefit from **all 10**.

💪 Leucine — The Muscle Builder
"Why do I lose muscle so fast, feel weaker, or recover slower — even when I eat enough?"

You've been eating well. Maybe exercising. Yet your muscles feel sore for days. You're not getting stronger. Or worse — your arms, legs, or jawline feel softer with time, not tighter.

That's often a sign your body is low in **Leucine** — the most powerful **muscle-preserving, tissue-repairing amino acid** your body depends on.

Leucine isn't just for bodybuilders. It's for anyone who wants to maintain **strength, resilience, and recovery** — from aging adults to active teens.

💪 What Leucine Does
Leucine is one of the **branched-chain amino acids (BCAAs)** and is the most anabolic (growth-promoting) of them all. It signals your body to **build muscle, repair tissue**, and resist breakdown — even during illness or stress.

Here's what it supports:
- Triggers **muscle protein synthesis (MPS)**

- Helps **preserve lean mass** during dieting, aging, or illness
- Supports **wound healing and physical recovery**
- Prevents **muscle loss (sarcopenia)** in older adults
- Regulates **blood sugar** and reduces post-meal glucose spikes
- Helps produce energy during exercise and fasting

Leucine is like your body's **anabolic switch** — telling your muscles to grow, stay strong, and repair.

⚠ Signs You Might Be Low on Leucine

These symptoms often show up in aging adults, vegans/vegetarians, or anyone recovering from stress, illness, or injury.

Physical Signs	Recovery / Performance Signs
Muscle loss or weakness	Soreness after light activity
Slow wound or injury healing	Poor stamina or endurance
Low body strength or tone	Craving protein or salty foods
Flabby arms, thighs, or midsection	Weight loss but no strength gain
More fat gain than lean mass	Blood sugar crashes or fatigue

🔘 Leucine is **especially important over age 40**, when muscle loss accelerates naturally.

How Much Leucine Do You Need?

Leucine needs increase with activity, stress, illness, or age. Athletes and aging individuals need **more per meal** than the general population.

Group	Daily Leucine (Min Target)
Healthy adults	2.5–3 g/day
Muscle maintenance (40+ yrs)	3–4 g/day
Active / strength training	4–6 g/day
Muscle recovery / illness	5–7 g/day (spread across meals)

✅ For best muscle response, aim for **2.5+ grams of leucine per meal** — especially in meals with >20g protein.

Best Food Sources of Leucine

Leucine is most abundant in **animal proteins**, but some plant foods also contribute. Quality matters — not just quantity.

Food Item	Leucine per serving (approx.)
Chicken breast (3 oz)	~2.8 g
Eggs (2 large)	~1.0 g
Whey protein (1 scoop, 25g)	~2.5 g
Tuna (3 oz)	~2.0 g
Lentils (1 cup, cooked)	~1.3 g

Food Item	Leucine per serving (approx.)
Tofu (½ block, firm)	~1.1 g
Pumpkin seeds (1 oz)	~0.7 g

🥩 Animal proteins are more **"leucine dense"** and better absorbed — but you can build plant-based meals to hit your target with planning.

🔄 Boosters & Blockers

To maximize Leucine's impact, support it with the full spectrum of essential amino acids — and don't skip carbs or healthy fats.

Boosters	Blockers / Depleters
Resistance training	Crash diets / fasting without protein
B12, Zinc, and Vitamin D	Chronic stress or inflammation
Full-spectrum protein (not just BCAAs)	Low total protein intake

⚠️ Leucine doesn't work in isolation — your body still needs **the other EAAs** to actually build tissue.

☠ Long-Term Deficiency Risks

Leucine deficiency often leads to **weakness, aging-related frailty**, and poor recovery — especially if you're under-eating protein.

- **Sarcopenia** (age-related muscle loss)
- Increased fat gain despite exercise
- Slower recovery after illness or injury
- Frail bones and increased fall risk
- Poor glucose tolerance or insulin resistance
- Lower mood, stamina, and metabolic rate

✖ The lower your leucine… the **faster your body breaks down muscle** to fuel recovery and energy.

📊 Weekly Leucine Meal Tracker

This plan helps you **reach 2.5–3g per main meal**, especially post-workout or with aging muscle concerns.

Day	Chicken	Eggs	Whey	Tofu	Lentils	Tuna	Est. Leucine
Monday	✓	✓	✓				~5.8 g
Tuesday	✓		✓	✓	✓		~5.5 g
Wednesday	✓	✓			✓	✓	~6.1 g
Thursday	✓		✓		✓	✓	~6.0 g
Friday	✓	✓	✓				~5.8 g
Saturday	✓	✓	✓	✓		✓	~6.8 g
Sunday	✓	✓	✓		✓	✓	~7.0 g

🥤 **Post-workout whey protein + eggs** = the fastest way to get your daily leucine in and trigger muscle repair.

💪 Isoleucine — The Muscle Stabilizer
"Why do I feel weak, shaky, or exhausted during workouts — even with good food?"

You eat your meals. You hydrate. But during workouts, your strength fades faster than expected. You may feel lightheaded, sore, or like your muscles aren't keeping up with your energy level.

That's when your body might be lacking **Isoleucine** — a branched-chain amino acid (BCAA) that helps maintain **energy, blood sugar, and stamina** during physical and mental effort. While Leucine triggers growth, **Isoleucine sustains** it. It helps you **last longer, recover better**, and stay balanced when life gets intense.

💪 What Isoleucine Does
Isoleucine is part of the BCAA trio (with Leucine and Valine), but it plays a unique role in **fuel regulation, immune resilience**, and tissue balance.

Here's what it supports:

- Helps regulate **blood sugar** and energy during workouts or fasting
- Supports **muscle repair and lean mass preservation**
- Boosts **endurance and stamina** by feeding muscle tissue directly
- Improves **immune response** during stress or illness
- Enhances **glucose uptake into muscles** — crucial for recovery
- Aids in **hemoglobin production** for oxygen delivery

Think of Isoleucine as your **muscle stabilizer and stamina guard** — keeping you fueled, even when glucose runs low.

⚠ Signs You Might Be Low on Isoleucine

Isoleucine issues often show up during stress, illness, intense activity, or in low-protein diets.

Physical Signs	Metabolic / Performance Signs
Low muscle tone or loss	Fatigue during light exercise
Feeling shaky when hungry	Poor blood sugar stability
Weak immune response	Slow wound healing
Headaches or lightheadedness	Reduced stamina or early burnout
Skin irritation or rashes	Poor recovery post-exertion

🍪 Many of these mimic blood sugar crashes — because **Isoleucine helps buffer glucose dips.**

▓ How Much Isoleucine Do You Need?

Needs increase during exercise, calorie restriction, infection, or post-surgery recovery.

Group	Daily Isoleucine Intake
Healthy adults	1–2 g

173

Group	Daily Isoleucine Intake
Endurance / strength athletes	2–4 g/day
Illness recovery / 40+ age group	2.5–4.5 g/day (divided meals)

✅ You rarely need to supplement it alone — instead, focus on **complete proteins or BCAA-balanced meals.**

🔍 Best Food Sources of Isoleucine

Isoleucine appears in many of the same foods as Leucine, though in slightly smaller amounts. Consistency across meals is key.

Food Item	Isoleucine per serving
Chicken breast (3 oz)	~1.2 g
Eggs (2 large)	~0.9 g
Whey protein (1 scoop, 25g)	~1.4 g
Soybeans / Tofu (½ block)	~1.0 g
Lentils (1 cup, cooked)	~0.9 g
Beef (3 oz)	~1.3 g
Quinoa (1 cup, cooked)	~0.6 g

◯ Plant-based meals can meet your Isoleucine target — just make sure the **total protein** is high enough.

🔄 Boosters & Blockers

Your body needs more Isoleucine during stress, fasted training, or immune challenge. Here's how to enhance it:

Boosters	Blockers / Depleters
B-complex vitamins (especially B6)	Overtraining without recovery
Complete protein sources	Crash dieting / low-carb starvation
Zinc and magnesium (for uptake)	Gut inflammation / IBS

💡 Isoleucine is **more about blood sugar and stamina** than growth — but it's vital for keeping strength over time.

💀 Long-Term Deficiency Risks

Without enough Isoleucine, you may experience fatigue, poor glucose control, and reduced immune recovery.
- Blood sugar spikes and crashes
- Weakness or dizziness during exercise
- Poor muscle density with age
- Skin problems and slower healing
- Increased fatigue after meals
- Greater muscle breakdown during illness or stress

💡 Isoleucine helps your body **manage stress, exercise, and hunger without crashing.**

📊 Weekly Isoleucine Meal Tracker

Plan meals to meet your daily goal and stack with Leucine for balanced muscle, energy, and glucose support.

Day	Chicken	Eggs	Lentils	Whey	Tofu	Quinoa	Est. Isoleucine (g)
Monday	✓	✓	✓	✓			~4.4 g
Tuesday	✓		✓	✓	✓	✓	~4.2 g
Wednesday	✓	✓	✓	✓	✓		~4.8 g
Thursday	✓	✓	✓		✓	✓	~4.5 g
Friday	✓	✓	✓	✓	✓		~4.6 g
Saturday	✓	✓	✓	✓	✓	✓	~5.0 g
Sunday	✓	✓	✓	✓	✓	✓	~5.0 g

🧊 Add BCAAs or a scoop of **complete protein powder** to reach your daily muscle-fuel goals more easily.

🔵 Valine — The Recovery & Focus Amino

"Why do I feel mentally foggy, physically drained, or sore longer — even when I'm not overtraining?"

You're not doing extreme workouts. You're not sleep-deprived. But your mind feels slow. Your muscles ache longer. And you recover from physical or mental stress **slower than expected**.

These are signs your body may be running low on **Valine** — the third **Branched-Chain Amino Acid (BCAA)** that supports **endurance, muscle repair**, and even **neurotransmitter balance**.

Valine isn't just a physical recovery tool — it helps maintain **mental clarity and coordination** during stress, fatigue, or intense focus.

💪 What Valine Does

Valine plays a crucial role in **balancing the central nervous system**, fueling muscles, and rebuilding tissues during stress. Here's how it supports your body:

- Fuels **muscle tissue directly** during exercise
- Aids in **muscle recovery** and repair
- Prevents **muscle breakdown** during illness or calorie restriction
- Supports **focus, alertness, and neurotransmitter balance**
- Regulates **nitrogen balance** — essential for muscle and organ function
- Helps rebuild **immune cells** and promote wound healing

Valine is like your body's **resilience switch** — powering both your muscles and your mind under pressure.

⚠ Signs You Might Be Low on Valine

Valine deficiencies often go unnoticed — but they show up as poor **mental and physical endurance**, especially when you're under strain.

Physical Signs	Cognitive / Neurological Signs
Muscle soreness or fatigue	Brain fog or mental slowness
Slower recovery from workouts	Trouble focusing or staying alert
Poor skin healing or dullness	Irritability or low motivation
Loss of lean body tone	Shaky hands when stressed or hungry
Immune weakness	Trouble with coordination or memory

⬤ Valine helps buffer brain chemicals like **serotonin and dopamine** — critical for mood, focus, and movement.

▓ How Much Valine Do You Need?

Valine needs increase with physical exertion, immune stress, injury, and aging.

Group	Daily Valine Intake
General adult population	1.5–2 g
Active or strength training	3–4 g
Immune support or tissue repair	3.5–5 g (divided doses)

✅ Like the other BCAAs, Valine works best when **consumed with Leucine and Isoleucine** — ideally in a complete protein.

🥚 Best Food Sources of Valine

Valine-rich foods tend to be high-protein and well-rounded in all BCAAs. Diversity helps hit your daily goal.

Food Item	Valine per serving
Eggs (2 large)	~0.9 g
Chicken breast (3 oz)	~1.2 g
Tuna (3 oz)	~1.4 g
Whey protein (1 scoop, 25g)	~1.6 g
Lentils (1 cup, cooked)	~0.9 g
Tofu (½ block)	~0.9 g
Greek yogurt (¾ cup)	~1.0 g

🔍 Eggs and whey offer **all three BCAAs** in great proportions — they're your best friends for muscle + mind support.

🔄 Boosters & Blockers

To activate Valine effectively, combine it with other amino acids and avoid habits that drain neurotransmitter balance.

Boosters	Blockers / Depleters
B-complex (especially B1, B6)	Chronic stress and burnout
Complete protein intake (20–30g/meal)	Poor liver detox / inflammation

Boosters	Blockers / Depleters
Magnesium and Tyrosine synergy	Over-reliance on caffeine or sugar

⚠ Valine is highly sensitive to **mental fatigue** — it helps maintain **alertness during stress or fasting.**

☠ Long-Term Deficiency Risks
Without Valine, you risk faster muscle breakdown, slower nervous system responses, and weaker recovery from stress.
- Muscle loss or tone reduction
- Slower mental processing and decision-making
- Poor coordination or physical control
- Compromised immune response
- Weaker memory and resilience under pressure
- Sluggish recovery from exercise, illness, or trauma

🍬 Valine is about more than muscles — it's about **maintaining performance when your body or mind is tired.**

📊 Weekly Valine Meal Tracker
This tracker ensures you're rotating Valine-rich foods for full recovery, balance, and endurance.

Day	Eggs	Tuna	Chicken	Whey	Lentils	Yogurt	Est. Valine (g)
Monday	☑	☑	☑	☑		☑	~5.1 g
Tuesday	☑	☑	☑	☑	☑	☑	~5.8 g
Wednesday	☑	☑	☑	☑	☑	☑	~6.0 g

Day	Eggs	Tuna	Chicken	Whey	Lentils	Yogurt	Est. Valine (g)
Thursday	✓	✓	✓	✓	✓	✓	~6.0 g
Friday	✓	✓	✓	✓	✓	✓	~6.0 g
Saturday	✓	✓	✓	✓	✓	✓	~6.0 g
Sunday	✓	✓	✓	✓	✓	✓	~6.0 g

💡 Pair Valine-rich meals with B6 + magnesium to enhance neurotransmitter support and mental clarity.

🔗 Lysine — The Immunity & Tissue Builder

"Why do I keep catching colds, feel achy, or notice slower healing — even with good nutrition?"

You're eating protein. You're supplementing. But your lips still get cold sores. Your joints feel stiff. You bruise easily or heal slowly from cuts and workouts. Maybe your hair and skin aren't bouncing back the way they used to.

Your body might be running low on **Lysine** — the essential amino acid responsible for **tissue repair, collagen production**, and **immune defense**.

Lysine is especially critical for **recovery, beauty, and viral resistance**. Without enough, your body can't rebuild strong tissues or fight off lingering stressors.

💪 What Lysine Does

Lysine isn't just for muscles — it's deeply involved in **connective tissue strength, calcium absorption**, and immunity.

Here's how it supports your body:
- Helps form **collagen and elastin** — key for skin, joints, and blood vessels
- Promotes **bone density** by improving calcium retention
- Supports **antibody production and immune strength**
- Inhibits **herpes virus replication** (cold sores, shingles)
- Accelerates **wound healing, tissue repair, and iron absorption**
- Supports **hair growth, skin health, and hormonal balance**

Lysine is the **mortar that holds your body's bricks together** — without it, tissues weaken and recovery slows.

⚠ Signs You Might Be Low on Lysine

These symptoms are especially common in athletes, vegetarians/vegans, and anyone recovering from illness or surgery.

Physical Signs	Immune / Structural Signs
Frequent cold sores or mouth ulcers	Poor healing after cuts or bruises
Hair thinning or brittle nails	Easy bruising or poor skin tone
Anxiety or irritability	Joint stiffness or cracking
Craving salty foods or red meat	Frequent colds or infections
Poor bone density	Slow recovery from workouts

🅾 Lysine deficiency can trigger **latent viruses**, fatigue, or skin issues — even in people who eat "clean."

How Much Lysine Do You Need?

Lysine requirements increase during illness, injury, viral outbreaks, or physical training.

Group	Daily Lysine Requirement
Healthy adults	2–3 g/day
Immune support or tissue repair	3–4.5 g/day
Herpes prevention / recovery	3,000 mg (in divided doses)

✅ Lysine competes with **arginine** — so in viral infections (cold sores, shingles), reduce arginine-rich foods like nuts, seeds, and chocolate temporarily.

Best Food Sources of Lysine

Lysine is plentiful in **animal-based proteins**, and can be obtained from select plant foods with careful planning.

Food Item	Lysine per serving (approx.)
Chicken breast (3 oz)	~2.7 g
Eggs (2 large)	~0.9 g
Lentils (1 cup, cooked)	~1.3 g
Tofu (½ block, firm)	~1.2 g
Greek yogurt (¾ cup)	~1.2 g
Fish (3 oz)	~2.3 g

Food Item	Lysine per serving (approx.)
Parmesan cheese (1 oz)	~0.8 g

🧀 Dairy, fish, and lean meats are lysine-rich — but **vegans must combine legumes and quinoa or soy** to meet requirements.

🔄 Boosters & Blockers

To absorb and utilize Lysine fully, your body needs a good gut environment, key cofactors, and sufficient total protein.

Boosters	Blockers / Depleters
Vitamin C and Zinc	High-arginine foods (for viral balance)
Bone broth and collagen synergy	Chronic stress / elevated cortisol
Magnesium and Iron synergy	Frequent alcohol or gut inflammation

🍬 Lysine + Vitamin C = **collagen production**. You can't build healthy skin or joints without both.

😷 Long-Term Deficiency Risks

Low Lysine impacts tissue repair, viral resistance, and appearance — even if protein intake seems "okay."

- Frequent colds, herpes outbreaks, or viral illness
- Sagging skin, wrinkles, poor hair/nail growth

- Poor calcium retention or bone density loss
- Bruising, poor capillary strength
- Mood instability and lower serotonin production
- Weak wound healing or chronic joint tightness

🌀 Lysine is essential for **structure, beauty, and immunity** — it's more than just a protein.

📊 Weekly Lysine Meal Tracker

Plan meals to consistently hit your **3–4g daily goal**, especially during stress, cold sore outbreaks, or healing periods.

Day	Chicken	Eggs	Yogurt	Lentils	Fish	Tofu	Est. Lysine (g)
Monday	✓	✓	✓	✓	✓		~6.3 g
Tuesday	✓	✓		✓		✓	~6.0 g
Wednesday	✓	✓	✓	✓	✓		~6.5 g
Thursday	✓	✓	✓	✓	✓	✓	~6.8 g
Friday	✓	✓	✓	✓	✓		~6.5 g
Saturday	✓	✓	✓	✓	✓		~6.5 g
Sunday	✓	✓	✓	✓	✓	✓	~7.0 g

🧊 For cold sore prevention: aim for **3,000 mg of lysine daily** and **limit high-arginine foods** during flare-ups.

🌿 Methionine — The Detox & Longevity Spark

"Why do I feel heavy, slow to recover, or inflamed — even when I'm eating clean?"

You eat well. You stay active. But you still feel puffy, foggy, or inflamed. Maybe your joints crack more. Your skin isn't healing well. You're sensitive to smells, meds, or stress. These are signs that your body's **detox and repair systems aren't running at full speed**.

That's where **Methionine** comes in — an essential amino acid and **methyl group donor**, meaning it plays a major role in **detoxification, liver health, tissue repair, and antioxidant creation**.

Without Methionine, your body can't build **glutathione**, remove toxins, or maintain sharp focus and a calm nervous system.

💪 What Methionine Does

Methionine is a building block for several powerful compounds in the body — including **SAMe, cysteine**, and ultimately **glutathione**, your master antioxidant.

Here's how Methionine supports your body:

- Provides **sulfur** for joint and tissue repair
- Converts into **SAMe** — vital for mood, methylation, and detox
- Supports **liver function and fat metabolism**
- Helps make **glutathione**, the body's master antioxidant
- Strengthens **skin, nails, and hair** through keratin synthesis
- Assists in breaking down **histamine, hormones, and toxins**

Methionine is your body's **cellular reset button** — especially for your liver, mood, and longevity.

⚠ Signs You Might Be Low on Methionine

Methionine deficiency shows up subtly — through poor detox, weak tissue, and mood changes.

Physical Signs	Metabolic / Mood Signs
Brittle nails or hair loss	Fatigue, especially after meals
Slower healing or cracked skin	Mood swings or mild depression
Poor tolerance to alcohol	Poor detox or skin breakouts
Joint stiffness or cracking	Brain fog or slow focus
Histamine sensitivity	Bad breath, body odor

💡 Many people who feel "foggy" after eating or bloated from protein may lack **sufficient methylation support** — Methionine is the first step.

▦ How Much Methionine Do You Need?

Methionine needs vary with protein intake, liver load, stress, and how well your methylation pathways work.

Group	Daily Methionine Requirement
Healthy adults	~1–2 g/day

Group	Daily Methionine Requirement
Methylation support / detox phase	2–3 g/day
Liver support / post-illness	Up to 3 g (with cofactors)

☑ Methionine is converted into **SAMe**, which supports mental health, mood, and liver resilience — especially in high-stress lifestyles.

🔍 Best Food Sources of Methionine

Methionine is most abundant in **animal-based proteins**, but some nuts and seeds also provide good support.

Food Item	Methionine per serving
Eggs (2 large)	~0.7 g
Chicken breast (3 oz)	~0.8 g
Tuna (3 oz)	~0.9 g
Brazil nuts (1 oz)	~0.4 g
Sesame seeds (1 oz)	~0.3 g
Beef (3 oz)	~0.9 g
Cottage cheese (½ cup)	~0.3 g

◯ Eggs and fish offer a perfect **balance of Methionine + cofactors (B12, choline)** for complete support.

🔄 Boosters & Blockers
Methionine metabolism relies on methylation cofactors — without them, it can become toxic rather than helpful.

Boosters	Blockers / Risks
Vitamin B12, Folate, B6, Zinc	High Methionine + Low B-vitamins = buildup of homocysteine
Choline and betaine (methyl donors)	Alcohol, gut dysbiosis, processed meats
Adequate magnesium and sleep	Heavy metal toxicity or low liver function

⚠ Always balance Methionine intake with **B-complex vitamins and antioxidants** to keep detox safe and smooth.

💀 Long-Term Deficiency Risks
Without Methionine, your body can't **methylate, detox, or rebuild** efficiently — putting you at risk for chronic issues.
- Sluggish liver and toxin overload
- Mood instability or depressive symptoms
- Low glutathione = high oxidative stress
- Weak nails, slow-growing hair, and joint pain
- Increased homocysteine if not methylated properly
- Slower wound healing and poor collagen maintenance

🛡 Methionine builds the foundation for **clean blood, sharp brain, and resilient tissues** — don't ignore it.

📊 Weekly Methionine Meal Tracker

Use this tracker to pair **Methionine-rich meals with B-vitamin cofactors**, ensuring clean detox and clear energy.

Day	Eggs	Tuna	Chicken	Beef	Nuts/Seeds	B12 / Folate	Est. Methionine (g)
Monday	✓	✓	✓		✓	✓	~2.7 g
Tuesday	✓	✓	✓	✓	✓	✓	~3.0 g
Wednesday	✓	✓		✓	✓	✓	~2.9 g
Thursday	✓	✓	✓	✓	✓	✓	~3.1 g
Friday	✓	✓	✓		✓	✓	~2.6 g
Saturday	✓	✓	✓	✓	✓	✓	~3.2 g
Sunday	✓	✓	✓	✓	✓	✓	~3.2 g

💥 Combine Methionine with leafy greens, eggs, and beets to **fuel methylation and detox with precision**.

🎯 Phenylalanine — The Focus & Mood Engine

"Why do I feel mentally tired, unmotivated, or emotionally flat — even when life's okay?"

You're not depressed. But you're also not driven. Focus slips. Motivation dips. Joy feels muted. You're not crashing — just coasting. And no matter how many to-do lists you write, it's hard to *start*.

This could be low **Phenylalanine** — the amino acid that fuels your **dopamine system,** supports **alertness,** and lifts your **emotional tone.**

Phenylalanine is your brain's **first raw material** for making dopamine, norepinephrine, and even thyroid hormones. Without it, energy and motivation fade from the inside out.

💪 What Phenylalanine Does

Phenylalanine is a **precursor amino acid** — meaning it converts into **tyrosine,** which becomes key neurotransmitters. Here's how it supports you:

- Converts into **Tyrosine → Dopamine → Norepinephrine** (focus, drive, mood)
- Enhances **alertness, motivation, and memory recall**
- Supports **thyroid hormone production** (T3/T4 via tyrosine)
- Reduces **pain sensitivity** and improves emotional resilience
- Helps treat **ADHD, depression, and low energy** in research studies
- Supports **melanin** formation (pigment for skin, eyes, brain protection)

Phenylalanine is your brain's **starter fluid** — without it, your drive runs dry.

⚠ Signs You Might Be Low on Phenylalanine

Deficiency can show up subtly — through low mood, foggy brain, or trouble finishing what you start.

Cognitive / Mood Signs	Physical Signs
Low drive, dull mood	Reduced energy or muscle tone

Cognitive / Mood Signs	Physical Signs
Poor focus or motivation	Cold hands, low thyroid function
Brain fog or sluggish recall	Fatigue that worsens with stress
Mood swings or apathy	Light sensitivity or poor pigment
Mild depression or anxiety	Less enjoyment from usual activities

⬤ Phenylalanine is often **low in people with burnout, dopamine deficiency**, or underactive thyroid.

▦ How Much Phenylalanine Do You Need?

Your body can't make this amino acid, but it can **convert it to Tyrosine** as needed.

Group	Daily Phenylalanine Requirement
Healthy adults	~1,000–1,500 mg
Mental clarity / mood support	1,500–2,500 mg (divided doses)
Cognitive recovery / burnout	2,500–5,000 mg (doctor guided)

⚠ People with **PKU (phenylketonuria)** should avoid Phenylalanine — always check medical background.

🔍 Best Food Sources of Phenylalanine

High-protein foods are the best sources. Phenylalanine is found in **all complete proteins**, with a concentration in meats, dairy, and soy.

Food Item	Phenylalanine per serving
Eggs (2 large)	~0.9 g
Chicken breast (3 oz)	~1.2 g
Salmon (3 oz)	~1.1 g
Tofu (½ block, firm)	~0.9 g
Greek yogurt (¾ cup)	~0.8 g
Lentils (1 cup, cooked)	~0.9 g
Almonds (1 oz)	~0.4 g

◯ Tyrosine can be consumed directly, but Phenylalanine provides **broader benefits**, including emotional support and thyroid synthesis.

🔄 Boosters & Blockers

Phenylalanine must be **converted properly** — meaning your body needs cofactors like iron, copper, and B6.

Boosters	Blockers / Depleters
Vitamin B6, Iron, Copper	Chronic stress / cortisol excess

Boosters	Blockers / Depleters
Magnesium and Vitamin C	Antidepressants (can affect uptake)
Adequate sleep and sunlight	Ultra-processed, high-sugar diets

💡 Pair with Tyrosine-rich meals for a **strong dopamine foundation** — especially if under mental fatigue.

🧠 Long-Term Deficiency Risks

Long-term low Phenylalanine can lead to mental and emotional depletion — even in people who appear physically healthy.

- Dopamine deficiency → low motivation or drive
- Mood flattening, emotional dullness
- Brain fog, memory issues, or mental fatigue
- Cold hands/feet from thyroid hormone imbalance
- Loss of resilience during stress
- Decreased skin or eye pigmentation over time

⚫ Phenylalanine keeps your **inner spark alive** — for focus, energy, and motivation.

📊 Weekly Phenylalanine Meal Tracker

Use this tracker to hit your **1,500–2,500 mg/day target**, especially during stress, focus work, or low-mood phases.

Day	Eggs	Chicken	Fish	Yogurt	Tofu	Lentils	Est. Phenylalanine (g)
Monday	✓	✓		✓	✓		~4.0 g

Day	Eggs	Chicken	Fish	Yogurt	Tofu	Lentils	Est. Phenylalanine (g)
Tuesday	✓	✓	✓	✓	✓		~4.5 g
Wednesday	✓	✓	✓	✓		✓	~4.6 g
Thursday	✓	✓	✓	✓	✓	✓	~5.0 g
Friday	✓	✓	✓	✓		✓	~4.5 g
Saturday	✓	✓	✓	✓	✓	✓	~5.2 g
Sunday	✓	✓	✓	✓	✓	✓	~5.2 g

🍬 For burnout or low drive, combine Phenylalanine + Tyrosine + B-complex — your **natural productivity stack**.

🍬 Threonine — The Tissue & Immunity Stabilizer

"Why does my skin feel dry, digestion stay off, or recovery drag — even with supplements?"

You're getting protein. You're active. But your skin looks dull, wounds heal slowly, digestion stays iffy, and your muscles feel stiff or puffy even with rest. You might feel run-down — not sick, just *off*.

These are signs your body may be low in **Threonine** — an amino acid that supports **collagen formation, gut lining health, and immune system balance**.

Threonine doesn't get much hype. But it's one of the few nutrients that strengthens **every soft tissue in your body** — from your skin to your intestines to your immune defenses.

💪 What Threonine Does

Threonine helps your body **maintain structure, protect barriers**, and modulate immune response. It's essential for **collagen, elastin, mucus membranes**, and white blood cell function.

Here's what it supports:
- Builds **collagen and elastin** — vital for joints, skin, and blood vessels
- Supports the **intestinal lining and gut mucus layer**
- Aids in **fat metabolism and liver function**
- Helps synthesize **tooth enamel and skin integrity**
- Regulates **immune response** and inflammation
- Plays a role in **serine and glycine production** — key for detox and tissue repair

Threonine is your **structural insurance policy** — it keeps your skin, gut, joints, and immunity solid and supported.

⚠️ Signs You Might Be Low on Threonine

Threonine deficiency can sneak up, especially in those with chronic gut issues, skin conditions, or poor recovery.

Skin & Tissue Signs	Gut & Immune Signs
Dry, thin, or sagging skin	Leaky gut, bloating, or IBS-like issues
Slow healing wounds or bruises	Weak immunity or frequent infections
Joint stiffness or poor flexibility	Food sensitivities or poor barrier function

Skin & Tissue Signs

Cracked lips, fragile nails

Muscle stiffness or loss of tone

Gut & Immune Signs

Chronic fatigue, especially post-viral

Trouble absorbing other nutrients

🪨 If your skin is dry, your digestion is sensitive, and your body feels brittle — it could be a **Threonine problem.**

How Much Threonine Do You Need?

Threonine needs are highest during growth, tissue damage, digestion issues, and immune stress.

Group	Daily Threonine Requirement
Healthy adults	~500–1,000 mg/day
Gut repair or injury recovery	1,000–1,500 mg/day
Skin, immune, or aging support	1,500–2,000 mg/day (divided)

✅ Threonine is best absorbed through **balanced meals with complete protein** — especially when paired with Vitamin C and zinc.

◯ **Best Food Sources of Threonine**

It's widely present in animal proteins, but also available in select legumes and seeds. Here's where to find it:

Food Item	Threonine per serving
Eggs (2 large)	~0.5 g
Chicken breast (3 oz)	~1.1 g
Cottage cheese (½ cup)	~0.5 g
Lentils (1 cup, cooked)	~0.6 g
Tofu (½ block)	~0.6 g
Beef (3 oz)	~1.0 g
Pumpkin seeds (1 oz)	~0.3 g

👉 Animal proteins are more bioavailable, but **plant combinations** like lentils + seeds can work for vegetarians.

🔄 Boosters & Blockers

To fully use Threonine for collagen and gut repair, your body needs **Vitamin C, zinc**, and low inflammation.

Boosters	Blockers / Depleters
Vitamin C and Zinc	Gut inflammation, leaky gut
B-complex (esp. B6)	High stress or chronic illness
Collagen and glycine synergy	Alcohol, poor digestion

🖊 Threonine + glycine + Vitamin C = your **collagen building trio** — critical for beauty and resilience.

💀 Long-Term Deficiency Risks
Chronic low Threonine weakens your **barrier systems** — from your gut lining to your skin to your immune shield.
- Leaky gut and chronic digestive sensitivity
- Slower skin healing, increased stretch marks
- Weak bones and joints from poor collagen turnover
- Persistent fatigue due to low tissue recovery
- Dry skin, split nails, or frequent infections
- Increased inflammation or food intolerances

🛡 Threonine is a **silent structural hero** — keeping everything sealed, supported, and stable.

📊 Weekly Threonine Meal Tracker
Use this chart to consistently support your **gut, skin, joints, and immune tissues** with rich, absorbable sources.

Day	Eggs	Chicken	Lentils	Cottage Cheese	Beef	Tofu	Est. Threonine (g)
Monday	✓	✓	✓	✓			~2.7 g
Tuesday	✓	✓	✓	✓	✓		~3.5 g
Wednesday	✓	✓	✓	✓	✓	✓	~3.8 g
Thursday	✓	✓	✓	✓	✓	✓	~3.8 g
Friday	✓	✓	✓	✓	✓	✓	~3.8 g

Day	Eggs	Chicken	Lentils	Cottage Cheese	Beef	Tofu	Est. Threonine (g)
Saturday	✓	✓	✓	✓	✓	✓	~3.8 g
Sunday	✓	✓	✓	✓	✓	✓	~3.8 g

💡 For gut healing: pair Threonine-rich meals with **collagen powder, bone broth, or glutamine** to seal and repair the digestive lining.

🌙 Tryptophan — The Sleep & Serotonin Builder
"Why do I feel anxious, restless, or struggle to sleep — even when I'm exhausted?"

You lie in bed, tired but wired. Your thoughts race. You feel down for no reason. Or maybe you're craving sugar, snapping at small things, and struggling to feel emotionally stable.

This is your nervous system asking for more **Tryptophan** — an essential amino acid that helps your brain **make serotonin and melatonin**, the two key regulators of **mood, relaxation, and sleep**.

Without enough tryptophan, even healthy people can feel disconnected, emotionally flat, or sleepless.

💪 What Tryptophan Does

Tryptophan plays a foundational role in your **mental and emotional health** by enabling your body to produce **serotonin (for mood)** and **melatonin (for sleep)**.

Here's how it supports you:
- Converts into **serotonin** — helps regulate mood, anxiety, and digestion

- Converts into **melatonin** — helps you fall asleep and stay asleep
- Helps regulate **appetite, body temperature, and stress hormones**
- Improves **pain tolerance** and emotional resilience
- Supports **gut-brain axis** and reduces IBS symptoms
- May reduce **PMS symptoms, anxiety, and seasonal depression**

🔘 Tryptophan is your body's **peacekeeper** — calming both the gut and the mind.

⚠ Signs You Might Be Low on Tryptophan

Tryptophan deficiency is common in people under high stress, poor gut health, or on low-protein diets.

Emotional / Sleep Signs	Physical Signs
Anxiety or irritability	Sugar cravings, especially at night
Low mood or mild depression	Light or broken sleep
Insomnia or trouble falling asleep	Digestive issues (IBS-like symptoms)
PMS or mood swings	Feeling "wired but tired"
Stress sensitivity or weepiness	Jaw tension or grinding teeth

🔘 If your **mood feels fragile** or your **sleep feels shallow**, low tryptophan might be the root cause.

🧱 How Much Tryptophan Do You Need?

Even though you only need milligrams, tryptophan can dramatically change your **emotional stability and circadian rhythm** when taken consistently.

Group	Daily Tryptophan Needs
General maintenance	250–400 mg
Mood, PMS, or anxiety support	500–1,000 mg (divided doses)
Insomnia / sleep optimization	1,000–2,000 mg (short term use)

✅ Tryptophan works best when taken with **B6, magnesium, and complex carbs** — they help shuttle it into the brain.

🥚 Best Food Sources of Tryptophan

Tryptophan is found in most proteins, but absorption into the brain depends on what **other amino acids** are present — making **smart food pairing** essential.

Food Item	Tryptophan per serving (mg)
Turkey breast (3 oz)	~250 mg
Chicken (3 oz)	~240 mg
Eggs (2 large)	~200 mg
Pumpkin seeds (1 oz)	~110 mg

Food Item	Tryptophan per serving (mg)
Tofu (½ block)	~180 mg
Cheese (1 oz)	~90 mg
Oats (½ cup cooked)	~50 mg

🥣 **Best combo for absorption**: tryptophan food + **healthy carb (like oats)** + **magnesium-rich food** = better mood and sleep within days.

🔄 Boosters & Blockers

Tryptophan needs cofactors to convert into serotonin/melatonin — and can easily get blocked by stress or sugar.

Boosters	Blockers / Depleters
Vitamin B6 and Magnesium	High sugar and processed foods
Complex carbs (brown rice, oats)	Chronic stress / cortisol overload
Omega-3s and Zinc (mood synergy)	Alcohol, caffeine, late-night screen time

🌑 For sleep: take tryptophan foods or supplements **1–2 hours before bed** with calming carbs and magnesium.

💀 Long-Term Deficiency Risks

Without tryptophan, your brain can't make serotonin or melatonin — which affects everything from mood to hormones to immune health.

- Depression, anxiety, or chronic irritability
- Insomnia or inconsistent sleep cycles
- Cravings for sugar, carbs, or late-night snacks
- Low emotional resilience or burnout
- PMS and hormonal instability
- Gut-brain issues like IBS or nervous digestion

🛏 Tryptophan = your **emotional buffer** and **biological dimmer switch** — critical in modern overstimulated life.

📊 Weekly Tryptophan Support Tracker

Use this tracker to support your serotonin and sleep cycles through **targeted meals** and **smart supplementation**.

Day	Turkey	Eggs	Pumpkin Seeds	Oats	Cheese	B6/Zinc Added	Est. Tryptophan (mg)
Monday	✓	✓	✓	✓		✓	~600 mg
Tuesday	✓	✓	✓	✓	✓	✓	~750 mg
Wednesday	✓	✓	✓	✓	✓	✓	~750 mg
Thursday	✓	✓	✓	✓	✓	✓	~800 mg
Friday	✓	✓	✓	✓	✓	✓	~800 mg
Saturday	✓	✓	✓	✓	✓	✓	~800 mg
Sunday	✓	✓	✓	✓	✓	✓	~800 mg

💤 Many people notice **better sleep, fewer cravings, and calmer emotions** within 5–7 days of steady tryptophan intake.

🛡 Histidine — The Immunity & Repair Agent

"Why do I feel inflamed, foggy, or easily irritated — even when I'm resting?"

You're not under heavy stress. But you feel puffy or itchy. You get weird skin reactions or sinus issues. Your focus isn't sharp. Maybe your joints crack more. You recover slowly, even after minor stress.

This could be a sign your body is low in **Histidine** — an amino acid crucial for making **histamine (yes, the immune one)**, regulating inflammation, protecting nerves, and repairing damaged tissue.

Histidine also supports **wound healing, antioxidant production, and neurotransmitter balance** — making it a critical player in both physical and emotional recovery.

💪 What Histidine Does

Histidine plays a unique role in managing **immune activation, tissue growth**, and **nerve protection**.

Here's how it helps your body:
- Converts into **histamine** — key for immunity, inflammation, and gut health
- Builds **myelin sheath** — insulating nerves for better focus and protection
- Supports **wound healing, tissue growth**, and blood pH balance
- Boosts production of **hemoglobin** for oxygen delivery
- Acts as an **antioxidant** by supporting zinc and copper balance
- May reduce **mental fatigue, allergy reactivity**, and immune overactivity

Histidine is like your body's **sensor and stabilizer** — helping you respond to threats, then calm down and rebuild.

⚠ Signs You Might Be Low on Histidine

Histidine depletion often shows up during long-term illness, overtraining, gut inflammation, or low-protein diets.

Immune / Physical Signs	Mental / Metabolic Signs
Skin irritation, rashes, or hives	Brain fog or low mental stamina
Slower wound healing	Sensitivity to smells or allergens
Dry or inflamed eyes	Numbness or tingling in hands/feet
Frequent sinus issues	Cracking joints or cartilage issues
Poor temperature regulation	Chronic fatigue or blood pH imbalance

🧠 Histidine is also crucial in early development — and supports **neuroprotection at all ages**.

🎞 How Much Histidine Do You Need?

Histidine needs vary with growth, illness, injury, and immune load. It's especially important in **children, athletes, and post-illness recovery**.

Group	Daily Histidine Requirement
Healthy adults	700–1,000 mg/day
Immune or skin recovery support	1,000–1,500 mg/day
Chronic inflammation or gut repair	1,500–2,000 mg/day (divided)

✅ Balanced intake of **zinc + B-complex** is crucial to properly metabolize Histidine and regulate histamine levels.

🥩 Best Food Sources of Histidine

Histidine is present in most complete proteins, with especially rich sources in meats, soy, and legumes.

Food Item	Histidine per serving
Chicken breast (3 oz)	~1.0 g
Eggs (2 large)	~0.5 g
Tofu (½ block, firm)	~0.7 g
Lentils (1 cup, cooked)	~0.7 g
Salmon (3 oz)	~0.9 g
Yogurt (¾ cup)	~0.6 g
Pumpkin seeds (1 oz)	~0.4 g

🫒 Histidine works well when combined with **anti-inflammatory fats** (like olive oil or omega-3s) to calm the immune system.

🔄 Boosters & Blockers

To absorb and utilize Histidine properly, your body needs **zinc, copper, and B-vitamins** — while avoiding immune stress overload.

Boosters	Blockers / Depleters
Zinc and Vitamin B6	Histamine overload (from allergies)
Balanced copper intake	Gut dysbiosis or leaky gut
Omega-3s and glutamine synergy	Overuse of antihistamines or steroids

⚠️ Long-term low Histidine may **reduce tolerance to allergens** — making reactions feel more extreme.

💀 Long-Term Deficiency Risks

Histidine isn't just for building tissue — it's essential for **nerve function, immune regulation, and emotional recovery**.

- Chronic skin rashes or sinus inflammation
- Poor nerve protection (numbness, tingling)
- Brain fog, memory decline, or anxiety
- Weak tissue repair or slower wound healing
- Histamine imbalance → overreactive immunity
- Weak cartilage and joint stiffness

🛡 Think of Histidine as your **post-stress repair crew** — essential for nervous system, immunity, and skin resilience.

📊 **Weekly Histidine Meal Tracker**
Ensure you're reaching **1,000–1,500 mg daily** for stable immunity, skin repair, and nerve support.

Day	Chicken	Eggs	Tofu	Lentils	Salmon	Seeds	Est. Histidine (g)
Monday	✓	✓	✓	✓	✓	✓	~3.2 g
Tuesday	✓		✓	✓	✓		~2.8 g
Wednesday	✓	✓	✓	✓	✓	✓	~3.2 g
Thursday	✓	✓	✓	✓	✓	✓	~3.2 g
Friday	✓	✓	✓	✓	✓	✓	~3.2 g
Saturday	✓	✓	✓	✓	✓	✓	~3.2 g
Sunday	✓	✓	✓	✓	✓	✓	~3.2 g

🍬 Want better healing, calmer reactions, and stronger nerves? Keep Histidine steady — especially during stress or inflammation

Bonus Amino

🥩 Carnitine — The Fat-Transporting Powerhouse

What it does:
Carnitine helps **shuttle fat into your mitochondria** so it can be burned for energy — making it essential for **endurance, heart health, and fat metabolism.**

✅ Best For	❌ Signs of Low Carnitine
Energy during workouts or fasting	Fatigue, poor endurance
Heart health and mitochondrial repair	Muscle weakness, brain fog
Male fertility and sperm health	Poor fat metabolism or weight gain

Top Sources: Red meat, lamb, poultry, dairy
Support Nutrients: B12, Vitamin C, Iron
Suggested dose: 500–2,000 mg/day (L-Carnitine or Acetyl-L-Carnitine)

💡 Acetyl-L-Carnitine crosses the blood-brain barrier and supports **mental clarity + fat loss.**

🌿 Glutamine — The Gut & Muscle Healer

What it does: Glutamine fuels your **intestinal lining and immune cells**, while also reducing **muscle breakdown** during illness or stress.

✅ Best For	❌ Signs of Low Glutamine
Leaky gut and IBS	Bloating, food sensitivities
Immune recovery (post-illness)	Slow healing, frequent infections
Muscle preservation	Muscle soreness, sugar cravings

Top Sources: Beef, chicken, eggs, cabbage, bone broth
Suggested dose: 5–10 g/day (especially post-workout or during gut repair)

🌿 Often used during **gut-healing protocols** to seal and restore the digestive barrier.

🌙 Glycine — The Sleep & Collagen Supporter
What it does:
Glycine supports **collagen production, sleep quality**, and nervous system calm. It also helps **detoxify** and stabilize blood sugar.

✅ Best For	❌ Signs of Low Glycine
Sleep, calmness, and relaxation	Restlessness, poor sleep quality
Skin, joint, and connective tissue	Sagging skin, weak joints, brittle nails
Blood sugar balance	Sweet cravings, anxiety, hot flashes

Top Sources: Bone broth, collagen powder, meat, gelatin
Suggested dose: 1–3 g before bed (or in collagen-rich meals)

🧠 Combine with magnesium and Tryptophan for **deep, restorative sleep.**

⚡ Tyrosine — The Brain's Dopamine Driver
What it does:
Tyrosine is made from **Phenylalanine** and helps produce **dopamine, norepinephrine, and thyroid hormones** — making it key for **motivation, mood, and mental sharpness.**

✅ Best For	❌ Signs of Low Tyrosine
Focus and mental performance	Lack of motivation, low drive
Stress resilience / burnout	Trouble concentrating under pressure
Thyroid hormone production	Brain fog, low body temperature

Top Sources: Chicken, eggs, dairy, soy, turkey
Suggested dose: 500–1,000 mg on an empty stomach (short term)

🧠 Use during **stressful or high-output days** to stay focused and avoid crashing.

🧠 Choline — The Memory Molecule

"Why do I forget small things, feel foggy, or gain fat around the belly — even on a clean diet?"

You're eating well. You're sleeping enough. But names slip your mind. Words get stuck. You feel mentally foggy, emotionally dull, or physically soft — especially around the waist.

This could be a sign your body is low in **Choline** — a vitamin-like nutrient critical for **memory, liver detox, fat metabolism, and nervous system balance**.

Your brain, liver, and hormones all depend on Choline — and most diets, especially plant-based ones, don't provide enough.

💪 What Choline Does

Choline is essential for your **cell membranes, brain signals**, and liver's ability to metabolize fat. It's also a key player in **methylation**, detox, and hormone regulation.

Here's how it supports your body:

- Converts into **acetylcholine** — your brain's memory and learning neurotransmitter
- Helps the liver **export fat** and prevent fatty liver disease
- Supports **methylation** — like B12, Folate, and Methionine
- Essential for **fetal brain development** and lifelong cognition
- Supports **hormone balance and estrogen clearance**
- Maintains **nervous system stability and coordination**

Choline is like the **Wi-Fi signal for your brain and liver** — when it's weak, everything slows down.

⚠ Signs You Might Be Low on Choline

Choline deficiency is **extremely common** — especially among vegans, vegetarians, pregnant women, and those under stress.

Cognitive Signs	Physical / Metabolic Signs
Brain fog or forgetfulness	Fatty liver or belly weight gain
Struggle to find the right words	Muscle fatigue or poor coordination
Mood swings or emotional dullness	PMS or estrogen dominance
Anxiety or low stress tolerance	High homocysteine (low methylation)
Poor memory under pressure	Trouble digesting fat or bloating

⬤ Choline is especially critical in **pregnancy, menopause, and high-performance lifestyles.**

▦ How Much Choline Do You Need?

Choline needs vary widely by age, sex, stress load, and liver function. Most people don't get even the **minimum** required.

Group	Daily Choline Requirement
Adult women	425–550 mg/day
Adult men	550–650 mg/day
Pregnant or breastfeeding women	450–930 mg/day

Group	Daily Choline Requirement
High-performance / detox support	650–1,000 mg/day (with cofactors)

☑ Up to **90% of people** fall short of optimal Choline intake — especially if avoiding eggs or meat.

🥚 Best Food Sources of Choline

Choline is found in both animal and plant foods, but **eggs are the richest and most absorbable** source.

Food Item	Choline per serving (mg)
Egg yolks (2 large)	~275 mg
Beef liver (3 oz)	~350 mg
Chicken breast (3 oz)	~75 mg
Salmon (3 oz)	~60 mg
Tofu (½ block)	~70 mg
Brussels sprouts (½ cup)	~30 mg
Quinoa (1 cup, cooked)	~45 mg

🥚 Just **2 egg yolks per day** can meet half the requirement — but many people avoid yolks, and that's where the trouble begins.

🔄 Boosters & Blockers
Choline requires proper **fat digestion and methylation cofactors** (like B12 and Folate) to do its job.

Boosters	Blockers / Depleters
B12, Folate, B6, and Zinc	Alcohol and poor liver function
Betaine (from beets or spinach)	High estrogen or fatty liver
Healthy fats (to improve absorption)	Gallbladder issues or low bile

🧬 Choline + B12 + Folate = your **methylation support trio** — critical for DNA, detox, and emotional regulation.

💀 Long-Term Deficiency Risks
Choline deficiency is now linked to many chronic conditions — especially those related to the **brain, liver, and metabolism**.
- Non-alcoholic fatty liver disease (NAFLD)
- Depression, memory loss, or early dementia
- Hormonal imbalances, estrogen dominance
- Slow metabolism or fat storage in belly/liver
- Poor fetal brain development (during pregnancy)
- Muscle loss or poor performance under stress

🛡️ Without Choline, your body loses its ability to **signal, detox, and repair itself.**

📊 Weekly Choline Support Tracker

This tracker helps ensure you meet your **minimum daily needs**, especially during stress, pregnancy, or hormone challenges.

Day	Eggs	Liver	Tofu	Quinoa	Greens	B12 + Folate Added	Est. Choline (mg)
Monday	✓		✓	✓	✓	✓	~600 mg
Tuesday	✓	✓		✓	✓	✓	~750 mg
Wednesday	✓		✓	✓	✓	✓	~600 mg
Thursday	✓	✓	✓	✓	✓	✓	~800 mg
Friday	✓		✓	✓	✓	✓	~600 mg
Saturday	✓	✓	✓	✓	✓	✓	~800 mg
Sunday	✓	✓	✓	✓	✓	✓	~800 mg

🎯 If you skip eggs or animal foods, consider a **Choline supplement (e.g., Alpha-GPC or CDP-Choline)** — especially for brain or liver support.

🖊 Antioxidant Power: Your Body's Silent Defense Squad

"You don't just age from time — you age from oxidation, inflammation, and neglect."

We're exposed to toxins, stress, blue light, and pollution every single day. And most of the damage it causes? You can't see it — not immediately.

But deep inside, your cells are rusting, your nerves are fraying, and your mitochondria are gasping for air. That's where **antioxidants** come in — not to slow time, but to **slow damage**. They are the unsung heroes of modern health — fighting oxidative stress, inflammation, and age-related degeneration **before symptoms even begin**.

This section gave you **9 powerhouse compounds**, each with a specialty — and all stronger together.

🧪 The Big 9: Antioxidants Covered

Antioxidant	Primary Benefits	Best For
Glutathione	Detox, immunity, oxidative damage repair	Chronic illness, fatigue, toxin buildup
CoQ10	Cellular energy, heart health, circulation	Fatigue, statin users, heart support
ALA	Blood sugar, nerve pain, mitochondrial support	Neuropathy, diabetes, metabolic repair
Lutein	Blue light protection, eye health, skin tone	Screen fatigue, aging eyes, clearer skin
Zeaxanthin	Macular protection, night vision, color clarity	AMD prevention, visual sharpness

Antioxidant	Primary Benefits	Best For
Resveratrol	Longevity gene activation, heart and brain resilience	Aging, brain fog, slow metabolism
Curcumin	Inflammation relief, joint, gut, and mood support	Arthritis, IBS, PMS, leaky gut, brain health
Quercetin	Natural antihistamine, immune modulation, mast cell control	Allergies, sinus, food sensitivities
Lycopene	Skin UV defense, prostate, heart, and circulatory protection	Men's health, cardiovascular aging, skin glow
Astaxanthin	Master antioxidant, UV defense, muscle recovery	Sun exposure, athletes, aging skin and eyes

🜚 Key Takeaways from the Antioxidant Section

- **You don't need all 9 every day** — but rotating them keeps your cells strong and adaptable.
- **Pair fat-soluble antioxidants** (like CoQ10, Curcumin, Lycopene, Astaxanthin) with healthy fats for best absorption.
- Use **Vitamin C, E, B-complex, Zinc, and Magnesium** to **synergize and recycle** many of these compounds.
- Most benefits come from **consistent, moderate use over time** — not megadoses.
- Antioxidants **don't "fix" damage — they stop it from happening.** Prevention is where they shine.

🪶 Pro Tip: Build a Weekly "Antioxidant Stack"

Each week, aim for:
- **1–2 eye and skin protectors** → Lutein, Zeaxanthin, Astaxanthin
- **1–2 inflammation fighters** → Curcumin, Quercetin
- **1 detox + 1 mitochondria booster** → Glutathione, CoQ10, ALA
- **1 longevity enhancer** → Resveratrol or Lycopene
- Rotate based on your needs (energy, immunity, recovery, aging)

🦋 Final Word

Antioxidants aren't trendy.

They're timeless.

And when used wisely, they can make the difference between simply living longer — and **living better**.

Protect your cells today... and they'll protect you tomorrow.

🚀 What to Do Next
"Because knowledge isn't power — action is."
You now know what most people don't.
You've unlocked the truth behind everyday symptoms, food-based healing, and the nutrients your body has been quietly craving.
Now it's time to use it.

⚫ Step 1: Know Your Symptoms, Then Match Your Nutrients
Feeling anxious? → Check Tryptophan, Magnesium, B6
Waking up tired? → Could be Iron, B12, or Potassium
Bloated or inflamed? → Consider Zinc, Curcumin, Glutamine
Craving sugar at night? → You might need Glycine or Chromium
Use the symptom tables to **decode your body's signals**. You don't need every nutrient — just the ones that fit your puzzle.

🍽 Step 2: Choose Food First, Then Fill Gaps with Supplements
1. **Print the Weekly Nutrient Tracker** from this book
2. Circle the nutrients you know you're missing
3. Add 1–2 new foods per week that support those gaps
4. Use supplements **only when food isn't enough** (gut issues, aging, healing, etc.)

📝 **Tip:** Start with **eggs, leafy greens, oily fish, yogurt, pumpkin seeds, lentils, and bone broth** — they cover most gaps.

🕐 Step 3: Build a Daily Nutrient Rhythm
- Morning → B12, D3, Magnesium, CoQ10, Tyrosine
- Afternoon → Balanced lunch, Omega-3s, Zinc

- Evening → Magnesium Glycinate, Tryptophan-rich snack, Glycine
- Weekly → Collagen, Liver support, Antioxidants (Curcumin, Astaxanthin)

Don't chase perfection. Chase consistency.
A few good habits daily will do more than a full shelf of pills you forget.

📅 Step 4: Give it 30 Days
Start small. Track symptoms once a week. Adjust based on what works. Most people see real results — better energy, sleep, mood, digestion — in just **3–4 weeks** of consistent care.

💡 Final Thought
Your body wasn't broken —
It was just missing the raw materials to **heal, energize, and thrive.**
Now you have the map.
Let your food be your language of healing.

"You did it. You gave your body a second chance — and it's going to thank you every day from here."

✅ You Did It. This Is Just the Beginning.

"Healing doesn't start in the doctor's office. It starts in your kitchen."

If you made it here — page by page, symptom by symptom — then you've already done what most people never do:

You **listened to your body**.

You followed the clues.

You re-learned how to nourish yourself from the inside out.

Whether you're tired of feeling tired, recovering from burnout, or just want to age with energy — you now have a map.

Not a diet. Not a theory. A **nutrient-first strategy** backed by food, function, and common sense.

🌟 What This Book Gave You:

✅ A deep understanding of **why symptoms show up** and which nutrients fix them

✅ The full spectrum of **vitamins, minerals, amino acids, and antioxidants**

✅ Clear food sources, meal trackers, and easy-to-follow routines

✅ The ability to **decode fatigue, cravings, mood dips, bloating, pain, poor sleep**, and more

🧠 **Now You Know:**
- **Bloating** might be low Zinc or low stomach acid
- **Anxiety** may point to low Magnesium or Tryptophan
- **Brain fog** could come from Choline, Iron, or low amino acids
- **Fat gain or fatigue** might be a signal — not a failure

You're no longer guessing. You're solving.

🔧 **Keep This Book as a Tool, Not a Trophy.**
Refer to it when symptoms come back.
Highlight the parts that spoke to you.
Share it with someone who's still in the fog.
And remember — **you don't need to be perfect to get results.**
You just need to start.
Even small improvements, repeated daily, create massive change over time.

💬 **Final Words**
Your body is always talking to you.
Now you know how to listen — and how to respond.
This isn't a health trend.
This is your new normal.

🏷️ **Welcome to nutrient-driven living. Welcome to clarity. Welcome to you.**

About the Author

Sachin Gothwal is a wellness researcher, product innovator, and passionate educator with a background in design, systems thinking, and health entrepreneurship. With over 20 years of experience in project leadership and real-world product development, Sachin brings a fresh, practical perspective to nutrition — rooted in science, not trends.

Tired of vague advice and generic wellness books, he created *Everyday Nutrients* to help people decode everyday symptoms and fix them with food-first solutions. He believes healing begins with understanding — and that when you learn to listen to your body, you change your life.

✏️ Why I Wrote This Book

I didn't write *Everyday Nutrients* because I'm a doctor.
I wrote it because I've been the patient.
The one who felt tired, foggy, achy, or anxious — and was told, "Everything looks normal."
But nothing felt normal.
Like many people, I tried diets, supplements, and hacks.
But the real change didn't come from a new pill or plan.
It came when I began to understand **nutrient function** — not just food.
What magnesium *really* does.
Why low zinc *feels* like constant bloating or brain fog.
How amino acids shape not just your muscles — but your mood.
This book is the guide I wish I had 10 years ago.
Not technical. Not overwhelming. Just clear, helpful, and practical.
If you've ever felt off... but didn't know what was missing — this book is for you.
You don't need to memorize science.
You just need to listen to your body.
It speaks the language of nutrients.
Let this book be your translator.
— Sachin

Printed in Dunstable, United Kingdom